COLLISION COURSE!

The interior hull of the *Skate*'s control room echoed with the pinging of Mead's sonar as he followed the unseen ship's path.

"Captain," Mead called out. "Target turning. Collision course! Collision course!"

Burkhart turned toward the sonarman. "Dammit, are you sure?"

"Range less than one hundred yards and closing, sir. Speed twelve knots!"

"Close and dog all watertight doors," Burkhart ordered. "Sound collision alarm!"

"Target crossing our stern—"

A violent shudder of steel fighting steel passed through the *Skate* and every man in her. The submarine began to roll on her beam, fighting the momentum of the unknown ship running her down. The grinding grew louder as the intruder's engines pounded a death knell throughout the *Skate*.

THE FINAL VOYAGE OF THE
S.S.N. SKATE

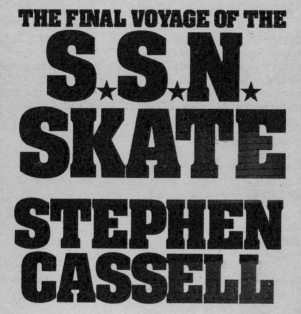

STEPHEN CASSELL

PINNACLE BOOKS
WINDSOR PUBLISHING CORP.

PINNACLE BOOKS

are published by

Windsor Publishing Corp.
475 Park Avenue South
New York, NY 10016

First printing: January, 1989

Printed in the United States of America

For Bonnie Isa, who always believed, and for my companions Dani, Betty Ann, Gramp, Bob, and Mollie, who will always be with me.

"Think the unthinkable. Act unpredictably."
—Winston Churchill

"The ship, a fragment detached from the earth, went on lonely and swift like a small planet."
—Joseph Conrad

1

THE GULF OF FINLAND

The mournful echoes erupting from the seal rookery at Gogland Island punched easily through the fog and low clouds shrouding the Bay of Suurkyla, midway between Leningrad and Helsinki. Intermittently, tides of fog swept over the leeward bay, dropping visibility to less than five hundred yards.

It wasn't the snow-white fog that lulled seamen on cold northern runs, Jake Niven thought, but a horrid oil stained gas sludge. Nothing was clean anymore. Even the light bouncing off his face was diffused and obsessive. A sort of Venusian twilight, although it was only two in the afternoon.

Impulsively, Niven focused on the low horizon. He could feel Vasili Lykov's presence. He was close, lurking out there as a damn ghost in that black ocean, waiting for just the right moment to show himself. Niven sucked in a breath of dirty ice air and allowed the feeling to squeeze his stomach. So it was finally beginning.

"*Generah'l-Mayo'r* Lykov, you're a complete bastard," he said softly and shivered inside the warmth of his bulky arctic parka. Again, he studied the empty ocean, his concentration unyielding, as he sorted through the yelping bark of seals and the squawking gulls circling above. The racket was amplified into a roar by the echoes of a freezing Buran wind, fanning south from the Barents Sea. Gogland Island was a soulless place of unforgiving rock cliffs and desolation, painted in blacks and grays, that canceled out any of nature's softness.

Niven knew that looking would help his hearing as he listened for the delicate, far-off clatter of oncoming diesels. The difficulty was compounded by the wave action against the sun-shrunken, worm-rotted hull of the anchored *Johann Mansson*. The run-down smack, built for Dogger Bank fishing, flying the yellow-and-blue Swedish flag, was rigged for salmon found in the Gulf of Bothnia.

Niven smiled and raised a fist skyward. "Welcome home, Vasili. The most careful man alive. I've been waiting." He turned and opened the weather-stained door of the radio hut, and stepped into the warmth of the small compartment crowded with shortwave sideband radios and a dark radar scope. "He's hovering out there in the bloody haze, but I can hear those damn *werkspoor* diesels twenty miles away."

An older, grizzled man was sitting at the transmitter table eating cold ravioli out of a half-open can. "Our goddamn British friends at Six ought to have their hands cut off for the way they maintain their electronics." He pointed to the radar scope. "The spare circuit board was also defective."

"You hear me, Sorrell? He's out there."

John "Brahma" Sorrell, retired Navy Chief Petty Officer, raised a massive hand and pointed at the mute telegraph key. "So what? We're here and all that matters is that telegraph key when it comes alive." He leaned back in the chair and rubbed a hand over his bald head, offset by a heavy salt-and-pepper beard and mustache that neatly wrapped itself around his forty-seven-year-old face. "Maybe he stopped for borscht and brown bread. Glasnost has done weird things to these people.

The damn dirty air stinks of a setup, Jake."

"This will work," Niven said. "It's a trade, not a butchering. Our Russian general needs this exchange. I'm betting our lives on it. He has as much at stake as I do."

Sorrell raised his massive body from the chair and towered almost a foot above Niven. "Maybe he lost count of what he owes you. Saving his life in Kabul's *Shorbazaar* may no longer count.

Lykov is still a big goon who specializes in lead pipes. He's got the ethics of running water. Could be, he suckered us into this shithole, just for us. We'd be one hella'va prize in Moscow."

Niven shrugged and opened the rotting door to survey the cove.

"He's got a sick belly, Jake." Sorrell zipped up his parka and stood in the doorway with his pipe. "That might have something to do with it."

Out of the corner of his eye Niven watched the deck crew looking at him for some sort of signal. Now they all could hear the faint rumble of the Russian diesels out in the Gulf of Finland. Then suddenly the rumble deepened.

"Sorrell, he's getting ready to come in! He's powering up. When Lykov's gunboat reaches that hundred-meter buoy, he'll answer an ALL STOP bell and look us over. If we look decent, that key of yours will come alive with his half of the go code. He'll only send it once."

Off in the distance the Soviet gunboat drew closer as she probed through the fog, occasionally showing her sleek bows to the *Johaan Mansson*.

11

"Don't do anything stupid like taking on that boat with a machine pistol."

Silently, Niven shoved two pear-shaped grenades into Sorrell's stomach. "English thirty-sixes. Best fragmentation grenade around."

Sorrell's eyes widened. "Fusing?"

"Seven seconds. If we have to kill that gunboat, this is the way it will be. Her bunkers are loaded with oil and she'll burn for a week." Niven's breath was puffing into the cold like a steam engine as he followed Lykov's gunboat running toward them.

"Set up a field of fire behind the radio shack." Do it now—"

Niven's voice was cut down by the loud buzzing of the telegraph key. Sorrell whirled and dove through the door, knocking an empty can of ravioli to the deck as he reached for a pencil.

"Well, we're in it now, Brahma!"

"Come on, Lykov, send your signal. You've kept this nightmare alive too long, you bastard."

Suddenly, the shrill blipping of the telegraph key filled the tiny radio hut.

K-H-A-H-B-R-E-E L-E-E K-A-H-Z-A-H K-E-E

"Are the Cossacks brave? That it, Jake?"

"Yeah, that's his half of the go." Niven stared at the *461*, her deadly form idling some sixty meters out.

"For Chrissakes, Jake! Give!"

"WE CALL A PERSON BRAVE WHO DOESN'T FEAR ANYTHING. As fast as Niven spoke the words, Sorrell translated them into Russian.

CHEH-LOV-YEH-KAH KOH-TOH-REE NEE-CHEE VOH N' YEH BOH-EET SAH MEE NAH ZEE-VAH-YWM KHRAHB-REEM.

Sorrell's fingers moved with a special grace as he tapped out the electronic message, then it was strangely quiet.

12

"Why the damn hesitation?" Sorrell rose and pushed past Niven. "You're just a burned out—"

"I've had enough left to save your butt, more times than I care to remember. You just make certain the deck and that vodka boat are covered and our prisoner is up to traveling."

Then Sorrell was gone and Jake was alone with his fear and the hollow belly spasm that never got any better. He expelled a breath and wondered if General Lykov was even aboard that gunboat. A shrieking horn brought him back.

The *461* had grown into an art form of steel and aluminum as a rising tide of Russian voices spread over the narrowing gulf.

"Lykov's on the bow!" Sorrell shouted.

Niven was on him with the glasses as the Soviet gunboat idled closer.

"He's set up a field of fire, Jake."

"Just stay at the ready." Niven could now clearly see Lykov with his heavy Russian face, scowling across the water.

"Lykov looks like he just put his dirty hands all over a nun," Sorrell mumbled into steam.

"Go below and get Koslov."

Cautiously, Sorrell moved away, then turned and stopped. "Watch it. Lykov's got eyes in the back of his head and a soul to match. *Panimayiti?*"

"I understand."

Niven turned and watched the gunboat's crew dropping large Day-Glow orange fenders over her port side. A moment later the Soviet warship and the *Johaan Mansson* bumped with a jar, just as a Great Brown Skua with pencil-thin wings swooped low over the strange union, searching for food.

2

Niven moved cautiously, his body a light flush in the stinging cold. Quickly the deck party of the *Mansson* secured mooring lines to the Soviet gunboat with a smooth orderly precision, as if nothing was wrong. Then it was quiet except for the birds and the popping of the giant green-and-white ensign on the stern of the *461*. In the dark corners of the gunboat, Niven saw the dull glint of automatic weapons.

"Stand by to be boarded!" a voice in Russian shouted.

Where the hell is he? Lykov screamed across the deck. Typical Lykov protocol Niven thought as he watched the Russian force himself across the wooden brow to the deck of the *Mansson*.

"Your time schedule and choreography stink, Vasili," Niven shouted, his Russian thickly accented with a Polish drawl. "Where the hell is the painting?"

"Your Russian is still shit." Suddenly Lykov thought that funny and laughed. "English, Jacob. I don't want you to feel cheated, Ashbal." The Oxford inflection was out of place with Lykov's Russian face and sad eyes.

Up close Lykov looked horrible. He had lost his

edge. His thumping aggressiveness was less intense, dulled by an invisible pain. Somehow his belly pain had defied gravity and arced upward into the soft vulnerable flesh surrounding his still brilliant blue eyes. Niven was shocked that Lykov had slipped so quickly. Someday, it would be his own body reeling and giving in to the pressure, looking into another man's eyes, hoping for a tiny, unspoken shred of pity. In the three weeks since their last meeting in their Roman furniture studio in Via Margutta, Vasili's impressive face had been reduced to a caricature. A prune, carved from yellowing paraffin.

"Where is he, Jacob?"

Niven looked down at the shorter, beefier man; their eyes locked. "He's below. We're bringing Colonel Koslov up now. He's almost yours."

"But not quite." Lykov nodded grudgingly.

"I've brought you a care package from Rome."

"What package? What the hell are you talking about?"

"I know about your stomach. I—I took the liberty of bringing the medication specially ordered for you."

"You expect something for this?"

"Nothing. I just brought your medicine. I'm sure the pain is incredible." He stared into Lykov's blue eyes. "I'm also sure Moscow and the General Staff don't know. It would be that way for me. It seems you and I are an embarrassment, except when they want something."

"They'd eat us, if they sensed weakness." Niven tried to smile, but the gesture spread into a frown.

"Only we know what all this is, eh, Jacob?"

"I also included five cartons of Camels. I can't stand the smell of those goddamned Papirosis. They stink like goat shit. Camels cost favors in Moscow."

"They cost favors here also, Ashbal."

15

Cautiously, Lykov allowed Niven to guide him toward the radio shack." We have five minutes, Jacob. I will conclude the exchange in five minutes."

Niven leaned into the open radio shack door and pulled a small package off the radio table.

Lykov's heavy-lidded eyes narrowed as they regarded the package. The next moment he had ripped off the paper. The cartons of cigarettes tumbled over his outstretched hands. A clear plastic capsule bottle bounced at Jake's feet. He bent down and picked it up.

"The pills will help the pain, Vasili." Niven said, and watched the distrust dissolve in Lykov's eyes.

"Pills and cigarettes are one thing, but they have very little to do with us. Someday maybe we will exchange on the dark side of the moon. We are running out of places." Carelessly, Lykov, tossed the cigarettes over to the deck of the *461* and pocketed the medication in his greatcoat.

"So, you know about my belly? At your age there is energy to follow up on details like that." He smiled awkwardly. "It's a hella'va world. Maybe we should stop doing this shit and let this garbage choke them all to death. That—"

A stretcher basket appeared through the main cabin hatch.

"How long, Vasili? It's been a lot of years since you've seen Colonel Yuri Koslov of the KGB's elite First Directorate."

Lykov's eyes had grown large with excitement, then he saw the head dangling over the edge of the basket. "Is he dead? Is he dead, you bastard?"

"He should be, but he's only sedated."

Lykov suddenly wheeled on Niven and grabbed at his parka, pulling him close. His foul breath made Jake sick. General Vasili Lykov, senior section chief of the

16

Glavnoye Razedyvatelnoye Upvaeleniye, the GRU, the clandestine appendage of the Soviet General Staff, was dying. Jake could see it in his face.

"I want him alive, Jacob. I need him alive." Lykov ran a chunky hand through his thick white hair. Its color added ten years to his sixty-eight year-old face. "Is it a trick, Jacob? Did you kill him?"

"Of course not, you paranoid bastard."

"Paranoid?" Lykov smiled. "And what the hell was going through your mind when I was rumbling around in that fucking fog, an hour behind your timetable?" A Papirosi appeared from his wool greatcoat and a moment later Lykov inhaled deeply, allowing the yellow smoke to tickle the hairs of his nose.

"Without Yuri Koslov, that asshole Viktor Chebrikov and his KGB pimps, sitting in sterile little computer cubicles on Moscow Ring Road, would string my balls from Saint Basils. He's just looking for any excuse he can find to kill the whole damn lot of us at the GRU and remove his competition."

Niven shook his head. "Your face is a goddamn Rosetta stone of trouble. How the hell does your family live with you?"

"There was only one son—" Lykov shrugged.

"Here he is." Jake pulled back the blanket covering part of Colonel Yuri Koslov's head and slapped the man's face with an angry crack. "Satisfied?"

Koslov opened his eyes and looked up at Vasili Lykov. He was horror-stricken. His pale lips began to protest with fish-mouth movements.

"You look like shit, Yuri," Lykov said and for a moment floated free of his sick stomach. "After all these years, your face has turned to soft caviar, you fucking *stukachi*. We have a date at Serbsky Prison where we can talk about all that information you supplied about Allende in Chile." Lykov rubbed viciously at his liver-spotted hands. "You killed eighteen of my elite Rezidenturas with the information you supplied the Israelis about the Iraqi reactor at El-Tuwaitha. You turned into a fucking cannibal. What a damn life." The light reflecting off the water only accentuated the dark creases of pain in his fleshy face. "Now all I need is a new stomach and a prostrate gland of a twenty-five-year-old."

Jake's eyes followed the rise of Lykov's chest and the movement in his throat. "A quick knife in his stomach wouldn't do, Vasili. Do it at Mount Elbrus in the Caucasus. That's one of your favorite haunts. Just not here on this boat."

"Relax, Jacob, I'm not going to kill him here. But this is still my duck pond, isn't it?" Lykov turned and motioned over three sailors from the gunboat. "I must be certain. My team will check his dental charts and fingerprints to make certain Yuri Koslov is hiding in that broken-down body." Lykov smiled. "When I know, I'll bring the painting across to this Halloween barge."

Five minutes later Lykov crossed to the *Mansson* holding a two-foot-square packing case. "It is Koslov, Ashbal! You are still my Arabic lion cub." His voice and body movements were taut. "What happened to his right leg? Is it recent?"

Jake nodded. "Complications from diabetes. A circulatory problem." He fingered the packing case.

"The real "Madonna Litta," Vasili? It seems light."

"Light? You idiot! You don't buy Da Vinci by the pound, like *bif-shteks*." Lykov's eyes widened. "This is no ordinary *spetsnaz*. It's a goddamn crucible!" He grabbed at Jake's parka again. "You know that Yuri Koslov is my only ticket for survival. Maybe I'm only buying time. But I'm not a fool. A damn Mediterranean street thief? Our shop in Rome must stay open. It is a vital link for me. It doesn't matter if we trade at the Glienicker Bridge in Berlin or Manzhouli Pass in Mongolia. Even this frozen armpit!" Lykov swept his arm toward the fog-shrouded island. "You should never doubt my word, Ashbal. The Da Vinci for Colonel Yuri Koslov is a fair trade. There are fourteen Da Vincis in the world, but only one Yuri Koslov."

Niven laughed for the first time and looked down at the flat case. "This would only be a forgery, if you thought you could get away with it." He looked into Vasili's eyes and felt himself go soft for a moment. "But we know where to find each other, don't we."

Vasili searched Jake's open face. "I wouldn't fuck you, Ashbal."

"You'd fuck anyone to get Koslov back." Jake was tired and cold and suddenly wanted the exchange to be over.

"See you in Rome, Ashbal. We've both done well today."

Niven turned away and scanned the obscured horizon. "Your bullshit time schedule has done its work. Who's waiting for us beyond the cove?"

Lykov's face grew dark. "The circle tightens for us both, Jacob. I can only hope it is clear."

"Until Rome, Vasili," Niven said and then mumbled half aloud. "Watch your backside." Lykov nodded, then disappeared into an open hatch.

Sorrell stood close to Jake as the *461* rang up FULL AHEAD. Slowly at first, then with authority, after clearing the *Johaan Mansson,* the *461* stood smartly out of the small, protected cove. Jake was hardly breathing as he watched the squared fantail of the Russian gunboat grow smaller, then finally clear the rock-guarded entrance to Suurkyla Bay.

He turned slowly and watched the relief grow on

19

Sorrell's face. It was over for Brahma. Jake exhaled a long, steamy breath into the late-afternoon cold and tried to fine-tune his concentration. Carefully, he pulled a small black transmitter from his left pocket, then toggled the ON switch. His hands were rock steady. It was no larger than a pack of cigarettes. Slowly he extended its aerial. Sorrell turned his face toward Jake. The hawk-nose fierceness was beginning to lighten.

"What's that for?" His voice was laughing. Then he noticed the terror in Niven's eyes and his own eyes bulged in disbelief.

3

Dr. Martina Kalya, the young physician assigned to Vasili Lykov's GRU staff, moved with great skill as she carefully and gently began her extensive examination of Yuri Ivanovich Koslov. After a few minutes she stepped back clumsily on the rocking deck and removed the stethoscope from her neck. She spoke quietly, but frustration nibbled at the edges of her voice. The futility of her mission—an examination before the execution.

"Koslov's vital signs are stable. Considering the diabetes and his age, he seems in fairly good health. His blood pressure is elevated, but that is understandable."

Lykov saw the protest grow in Kalya's eyes as he stared at her. He hated her remedies and her youth. If he had been younger and his belly quiet, he would have taken her on that bucking deck, and been done with it. Now all he could do was think about it. In another hour he would be physically sick and he could justify being an old man.

"I'll have a blood workup within the hour. It will tell me exactly what his insulin needs are."

"The leg, Doctor? What about Koslov's leg?" Ly-

21

kov forced her to make eye contact. His need to know overwhelmed and frightened her.

"Does it really matter about his leg or his well-being? You're just going to torture and kill him." She tried to keep her voice away from the now-conscious Koslov.

Carefully, Dr. Kalya swabbed her hands with alcohol and backtracked to Koslov's bunk. Lykov watched her every movement, with an indelible scowl on his face. Then he pushed her aside and leaned over the bunk. Koslov was staring up at him wide-eyed, his face a mask of disbelief.

"Welcome home, old friend." Lykov leaned over as far as he could, to be close to Koslov's face. "It seems age and turmoil have ravaged you. But it's not enough. Your chin has grown weak and puffy, to match your character, you bastard."

He patted Koslov's shoulder. "They sent you back, you fool. Just when you thought you were out of reach. Jacob Niven and his Spook Shack traded you back to me for a goddamn painting. I hope this all frightens you, Yuri." Vasili's voice was edging on warmth, his face free of expression. He was doing what he had practiced for forty years.

"I want you to be frightened. The last face you ever see, before you die, will be mine."

"General! This man is still my patient."

Vasili turned to Dr. Kalya. "He's not even human. He's garbage. You'll save no lives or souls in this compartment with your childish ethics. Now the leg, Doctor."

Dr. Kalya shivered and leaned over Koslov's bunk. Tenderly she smiled at Koslov and pulled down the blanket covering him. "I'm just going to examine your artificial leg, Colonel. There won't be any pain."

"Too damn bad." Vasili laughed.

22

Kalya shook her head and regarded the artificial limb, which was attached to a covered stump just beneath the right knee. Carefully, she untied a thick leather thigh lace attaching the limb above the knee. Next she unsnapped a cuff suspensions strap that gave additional support to the leg. With a noticeable tremor in her hands, the doctor pulled the seven-pound limb away from the leg stump.

"I'll be as gentle as possible," she mumbled as she began to peel down the woolen stump sock.

"What is it?" Vasili was staring over her shoulder.

"Nothing."

"Why did you stop, then?"

"Well, the incision," she said, pointing at the raw and puffy tip of Koslov's stump, "is very recent. It all makes little sense. There are two small drains still attached to the area of the incision to help in the removal of excess cellular material."

"What the hell are you telling me?" Vasili's mood was growing foul.

"The surgical procedure is far too recent for this man to have been properly fitted with a prosthetic device. There still is a great amount of swelling. It would be impossible for him to put any weight on it." She paused and looked at Vasili over her shoulder. For the first time she looked unsure and puzzled.

For no particular reason she reached down and ran her right hand over the surface of the artificial leg, as she thought the problem through. Suddenly, Kalya frowned.

"The material is soft." She squeezed it gently as if it were alive. "It is not rubber or foam. It is like putty." She turned again to Vasili, but the siren had already gone off. Without hesitation he savagely sent her tumbling to the deck. Gingerly he touched the artificial leg, then smelled it with his nose only an inch

23

from its surface. The siren was now a death scream, but his body was moving sluggishly. He wasn't prepared for this. Not with Ashbal. He looked down at the doctor who was staring at him in fright. His pulse was in his mouth.

"Explosives! Plastique!" he shouted, as he collected his wits. There was no time to hate. That was for later. He must live. Koslov must live. Vasili had come too far to be denied by his own carelessness. With a pained expression on his face, Vasili ran his old hands under the detached limb. Koslov was breathing heavily in short panic spurts, while Vasili dared not breathe at all. He was afraid to think. He could only react to try and save their worthless lives. He worked mechanically as he marked the porthole and how far he would have to go. Carefully he picked up the limb and cleared himself from the bunk.

"Unbolt the port window, Doctor. For shit's sake, hurry!" Now there was just a wisp of panic in his voice. It was only eight meters, but it seemed a kilometer. If only he could freeze and throw away the nightmare. Koslov's death limb was waist-high as he approached the port. Vasili Lykov, Hero of the Soviet Union was about to lift the device and shove it through the open port, when his world seared red. It was the most intense red he had ever seen. For a millisecond he glanced down at the leg-bomb, but it was gone. So were his hands. He began screaming to erase the most hideous nightmare of his life, but the ripping blast of six pounds of C-4 plastique explosive set into the limb as a concussion tube overtook Vasili's voice and life. A delicate bone and blood confetti choked the cabin, searing deckplates as the power of the concussion spread and took on its own horrid meaning.

The explosion now gathered a more intense force, tearing at the vitals of the Soviet gunboat. Cabin bulkheads and frames were blown out over the entire aft section of the vessel. Quickly, the explosion ripped through the sleek hull and keel of the *461*, swallowing her in a life-shattering fireball. Secondary explosions ignited the massive fuel bunkers as one last dull roar tore at the whitehot wreckage, sending the boat and her crew to their deaths in the Gulf of Finland.

Jake Niven convulsively squeezed the small transmitter as he watched the explosive fireball grow and feed off the sea as a fast, angry cancer. Then his face winced in visible pain and his entire body sagged. Slowly, he began to retreat toward the radio hut, but Brahma Sorrell was on him, stunned and crazy.

"You killed him! My God, you killed him! I should'a picked it up in Stockholm, the way you were acting."

"You didn't pick anything up in Stockholm or anyplace else." Niven was trembling visibly. "It was planned from the beginning." Jake was giving way to gravity as a shock rippled through his brown eyes.

"Why, dammit?" Sorrell's face was twisted by the shock.

"I'll tell you why, you big dumb bastard." Niven's voice was barely audible. "Because Vasili Lykov was a talented, smart son of a bitch who would have found out where the painting was going."

Sorrell shook his head. "But I thought you and Lykov—"

"Me and Lykov, what?" Jake pushed a fist into Sorrell's broad chest. "Admiral Brandon Langor and the assholes at the Spook Shack wanted this from the start. So did Langley and Fort Meade. For all I know the White House wanted it this way! I just did what I was told, for Chrissakes! Vasili was tired and hurting. He lost just enough of an edge and couldn't read the setup.

The Soviet General staff gave him a blank check, because they desperately wanted Koslov back."

Niven threw the small transmitter into the colorless water and reached into his jacket pocket. "Pardon me for not checking with you, first, Sorrell!" He pulled out a crumbled slip of paper and shoved it into Brahma's face.

"Here's your code and frequency for transmission." Jake hung onto the railing to keep from shaking apart. "MOSES IS ALIVE. Got it?"

"Then what?"

"You're just full of goddamn questions today." Niven rubbed his numb face. "There's a pickup arranged on the Finnish coast at Kotka. Now move it, or they'll bury us with that lousy painting!"

4

Jake Niven was disoriented and moving in a dark twilight with a white fireball streaking toward him. His brown, unseeing eyes blinked open with the instinct and speed of a professional killer stalking a prey, but his mind was trapped in a thick cotton webbing of heavy dreams in the seam between troubled sleep and consciousness. From deep within, Jake felt his lean body shake and quiver from the hammer blows of his pumping heart and jabbing pulse. He was some sort of involuntary instrument of terrible emotion. Oh, Christ, he was doing it all again.

The dark-red mud death maze of the Vietnamese Delta. The stink of tepid water and moist decayed roots along the Mekong River banks. The whole collage, shimmering in oppressive heat from the white sun and three white phosphorus grenades, lobbed from nowhere onto his anchored Swift Boat by invisible slopes. The distant moans of his men gasping breaths of thin, searing heat echoed off the unforgiving jungle foliage that went on forever.

Death and hanging black flesh in the white sun. Friendly hands pulling the few survivors ashore. The dust off to an aid station. A blurred morphined flight to Yokota Air Force Base, Japan, then another chopper flight to Zama Army Hospital. No flags or noise or mud. Wham. Just the sweet burn smell of dying apple blossoms in the burn ward. A strange bed, his own metal arched Stryker Frame. The debriding torture of pulling off the dead and dying skin on one square foot of his upper leg in the whirlpool. All those liters of pain tears streaming down his flushed cheeks onto the floating wooden board. God how he hated that unyielding board. What a damn horrid joke. In the burn ward at Zama they never let anyone see a mirror.

Jake felt his voice screaming and fighting at the pain. Finally, a successful graft of pig skin to cover muscle fibers deep within his oozing hole. A thousand rubdowns with Sulfamyalon cream to fight off the killing infections. The inhalation of cool, fresh sea air. No more air of sweet-smelling burn death. No more enemy rucksacks filled with grenades. He looked into the shimmering water of the whirlpool and there was Vasili's pained Russian face and questioning blue eyes shouting his name.

He was shaking uncontrollably. No, there was a hand shaking him. A soft warm comforting hand. From somewhere he smelled a sweet fragrance that wasn't apple blossoms.

The early dawn was real enough and so was the sound of the distant crashing surf. He could feel a steady metronome beating in his ear. A warm firm body was holding his head as he tried to shake off the old frayed images. His blinking brown eyes slowly came alive and focused. The roaring fright subsided, leaving only glistening snail tracks of sweat on his smooth face and heaving chest.

"Jake, you were screaming in your sleep again." Elena Mallori was gently rocking him with her arms cradling his head against her breasts. "It's over now.

It's all over." Her voice was a gentle stream of love and caring. She held tighter, trying to choke the trembling from his body.

"What time is it, Ellie?" He was throwing off the thick cotton clogging his throat as he pulled free of her grasp.

"About five-thirty."

Through the faint natural light in the bedroom Jake could make out the concern and even fright masking her dark, incredibly beautiful face. He swallowed painfully and moved to the bay window of his small two-bedroom home, filled with redwood and stained glass, in the coastal hills overlooking La Jolla Cove, on Inverness Drive. The rising sun was just beginning to splash the western sky pink, casting a bizarre glow over the Pacific. Jake unconsciously rubbed a hand over the burn patch on his leg.

"Bothering you?" Ellie followed him to the window and was holding him from behind with her arms wrapped around his naked midsection.

"Hm?"

"The leg?"

"No, it's not the leg." He drew a long breath of sweet air. He turned and drew his hands gently to her face. Her large brown cow eyes, more visible in the growing light, had taken on an unusual helpless cast, which only heightened her sensuality. The soft crescent sweep of her full breasts and flat hard belly offset the outward reach of her hips. Slowly she reached up on her toes and gently brushed her lips against his. Jake was a head taller as his chin came to rest on the top of her head. He closed his eyes as Ellie coiled her body around him, still trying to ward off his demons. They were quiet for a very long time.

"You must have been dreaming in Russian last night." She pulled back and examined him, shaking her short black hair in his face. As the dim pink light grew more intense, Ellie could make out Jake's boyish face. He looked drawn, which only accentuated the circles under his eyes. "You haven't slept well since you've been home. I haven't pressed it but it must have been very difficult for you." A cautious note crept into her tone as she walked to the closet and wrapped herself in Jake's blue terry robe to ward off the chill.

Jake exhaled a long deep breath and turned his face from Ellie to the window. "When I was married, my wife didn't give a damn about what I did or how I felt. I can't remember her ever asking." Jake idly watched two wet suit-clad scuba divers slide over the side of their rubber boat in the cove below.

Carefully Ellie retreated and sat on the edge of the bed, wanting him to talk. It was one of those frail moments and she was experienced enough to allow it to ripen without tearing at it. She had waited a long time for him.

"I care, Jake." There was morning softness in her voice.

"I know," he nodded, then he grew distant still facing the window. "My former wife was preoccupied with appearances and a ritzy lifestyle to distract her boredom. According to my daughter, it hasn't changed much in all these years."

Ellie swallowed and held herself back. They had been together six months and this marked the first time Jake had ever opened himself to her. Their lovemaking had always been passionate until Jake reached his wall, then he would quickly back away, closing off his past, his hurts, protecting his scars. Carefully she studied the back of his head and neck. His boyish strength was still evident.

"When I'd come home from sea duty or an assignment, I was great for a one-night stand. I was just a

30

toy." He turned to face Ellie, his voice a whisper, his eyes glassy. No matter what the pain or difficulty, he had to find the right words to tell her. He thought about it and shivered. Now he was keeping a promise he had made to himself, waiting for Lykov in the Gulf of Finland. A sob reached up into his throat.

"Jake!"

"I'm all right, dammit. I have to get it said." He wiped his eyes with a hand. "Jesus, look at me. I haven't cried since I was—" He still wouldn't look at her. "I was talking about my former wife. My past. I was a toy, then I became an interruption from her social schedule. I played a lousy net game. Life on the Sound. Tennis, bridge, the right people and sport fucking in that order. White wine by the pool and German cars in the U-shaped driveway. God, I just never fit into that old line Newport parade. I never was a summer aristocrat."

Niven turned to face her. This woman of light, passion, and caring. "She was the coldest bitch I ever knew and I married her." He tossed a hand into the air. "It took me so long to accept what she was and wasn't."

They were quiet for a long time. Finally Ellie spoke. "There's Danielle. At least the marriage produced a beautiful child. Besides, she looks just like you." She was determined to shatter that psychic glass wall that he had built to protect himself. "You're always showing her pictures."

"Yes, you're right, Ellie." The room was now in the full glow of sunrise. He smiled softly, still hiding himself.

"When is she coming out from Rhode Island?"

Niven searched Ellie's face. He wasn't sure what to say. There was only the urge to be with her. To watch her move and listen to her talk. She made it all so easy.

31

"I'm supposed to get Dani for Christmas vacation. I know a little hideaway in Switzerland where the skiing is quiet and virgin."

"Where, Jake?"

"A place called Murren. A little village in the shadow of the Alps, tucked away on a plateau in the Bernese Oberland, halfway up to the top of Schilthorn Peak. It faces the Eiger." He paused. "It's two hours by train and tram from Bern. Only way to get there." He drew a deep breath and turned back to the small boat in the cove below. A faint trace of bubbles marked the surface near the empty boat. A sudden vision of Vasili Lykov's face spread across those bubbles and Jake shivered.

"What is it, Jake? Please. Please let me in."

He rubbed his burned leg. *"Skushno."*

"I don't understand." She touched his face.

"I know. In Russian it means a vague, empty feeling that's overwhelming. It also means a great sense of loss. There's no word in English that conveys the same feeling."

Let it all go, he thought. For once throw it up. Let it all drop on her and see what she does with it. No, that wasn't it. He simply had to face her now, if there was anything of value between them.

"Ellie, I just killed a man very important in my life. I set him up and then took him when his back was turned." Jake moved away and waited for the words to crush her. He was naked in the morning chill, but his face and neck were bathed in hot sweat. "I've killed before, when my survival was at stake, but it never brought me down like this did."

The woman bit her lip and scrutinized Jake's nakedness as she silently assembled her answer. "If the situation was reversed, would he have killed you?"

Jake shook his head and squinted. "Yes, but—"

Ellie was next to him, with a finger drawn to his lips. "But nothing. You just answered the cogent question. As a criminal lawyer, I've seen your behavior often, on the stand."

"Seen what?" His voice wanted to drop the subject.

"That guilt obscures the facts. It always does." She scanned his face for reaction and saw he was growing distant again. "Jake, I'm not your ex-wife. I won't use what you tell me against you." She bit her lip and her voice dissolved into a shrill. "Let me in, Jake. I'll never judge you. Promise."

Cautiously Jake eyed the woman standing before him. She was giving Jake a future and that frightened him. The conversation had gone further than he wanted. He couldn't ever remember talking about his work, yet here he was listening to his own voice vibrating against his jaw bone, forming the words.

"Was this man's death necessary?" Her hands were softly stroking his face.

Jake barely nodded without answering, like a rusted tin man. He was growing afraid that his own voice would betray him.

"Death is all around us, Jake. I see it all the time in the courts and penal system. Maybe I've grown hard about it or maybe I just understand, by forcing myself to look at it."

Jake turned his head away and gazed out the window searching for the divers in the cove. His eyes came up empty except for the bubble tracks as he thought about Ellie. She seemed to understand and even anticipate him and that was frightening. He felt her gentle hands turning his head back to face her.

"It's over and done. Get rid of it, now!" Her voice was stern, which caught Jake off guard. "Often all my plea bargaining ever buys my rapist or wife-beater client is a sharp knife in the gut in the shower at Soledad or San Quentin for not bending over at the right time. I know from the start how it's going to end. It's my job and I leave it where it is, otherwise I'd be certifiable.''

At least she was trying to understand. Yet there was an impossible quality to it. There was no way Ellie could ever understand what had gone on between the two men for the past eight years. Garbage men shoveling garbage. The significance of their maneuvering and hostile closeness defied all rational understanding. Niven stroked her hair.

"Let my words in, Jake, for our sake."

"It's just that you live in a rational world. I don't." He paused and thought about it. "Each time I come back, it becomes more difficult. Maybe it's night fatigue. Occupational hazards." He shook his head.

"Don't bury yourself with that man." Her facial features softened again. Ellie nestled her head against his warm chest as the silence gathered in around them. "We have to matter and so does your daughter," she finally said. "There's so little that has meaning." A lovely smile opened her lips revealing white, moist teeth.

She could almost talk the terror away. What had happened in the Gulf of Finland and what was to come in the North Pacific. She had filled his void with caring and there was something important and primordial in this woman that he needed. That need frightened him.

"You scare the hell out of me."

She cocked her head. "Don't let me. I think you're frightened of anything or anyone demanding commitment. I only want what every other woman wants. I just want it in a little different way." She searched his face for a response.

"If you're alive and not happy, what the hell's the point? Can't you understand that?" She paused

34

searching for the right words. "So bright, so dumb." She shrugged and padded to the window, looking out at the marching lines of swells, waiting to take their turn on the beach.

"You're sunshine and grief. A real shadow man."

Niven looked at her sharply, then pushed his face into a grin. "I understand now. I did when I was a kid. My brother and I would spend every vacation at our summer place on the Miramichi River in New Brunswick, way up there in Canada. We had a small cabin near a place called New Castle and my parents owned a pool on the river where my older brother, Bobby, taught me to fish for Atlantic salmon and hand-tie Jock Scott flies made from speckled bustard feathers. I haven't been there since I left Brown." Jake stepped back and looked into Ellie's rich Italian face. It possessed the best of both the old and new worlds. Her tanned skin had blushed slightly from her anger and compassion. The mixture was astounding. Ellie's soul was painted to her face as her eyes watched him talk.

"I was the happiest kid in the world then." He laughed for the first time that morning and glanced down at her. "Sometimes I was so up I'd feel like I was going to bust out of my skin. The nights before we'd hit the pool I'd lay awake all night trying to keep my eyes closed but I was so expectant I was just a mass of charged energy with a thousand fingers tickling me all over." Jake shrugged his naked shoulders.

"Somewhere I lost that simple, unquestioning happiness." There was resignation in his tone. "But, Christ, I've felt it, Ellie."

Ellie slowly shook her head and her brown eyes turned to liquid. "In my thirty-six years, I've seen very few men worth wanting for more than a one-night stand. With law school and building a practice, my personal needs took a backseat. Quality doesn't come along that often, so I'm just not going to let go without a struggle."

Jake tasted the salt as tears streamed down her face. She was an incredible woman.

"Return my love, Jake. I haven't offered it very often—not completely." Slowly she placed his hand on her ample breast. With great tender care she curled her tongue and began nibbling at his chest and stomach. She was determined to bring him back from wherever he had been.

"I do love you, Ellie," Jake groaned as she kneeled and worked her way down past his waist. After a few moments she pulled her feathery mouth free of him and rose to her feet. "What time do you have to leave?"

"Don't rush me. I don't have to be at Point Loma until tomorrow morning." Out of the corner of his eye he saw her smiling.

"Who ever heard of someone going to work at a submarine base? Hm? Most people work in offices." Ellie was teasing him with her hands. "A damn shadow man of questionable background and deed."

"You said you wanted something different." Niven's voice was barely audible.

"I'm so wet, Jake, hurry!"

Suddenly they were on the bed, the time for foreplay long since past. Softly, their yielding motion and energy dissolved into a blur of instinct and love.

5

The stuttering hum of the generators draped the control center of the *Skate,* SSN 578, as she tracked her prey two hundred ten feet down in the San Clemente Trench, a submarine canyon eight miles off shore of La Jolla, California.

"Log it, Quartermaster. 0935, Blue Watch, Seventeen May, entering final phase antiship drill at Pacific Undersea Test and Evaluation Center." Commander Charles Burkhart looked up from the large black-faced bulkhead clock and rubbed a burly hand over his face.

"Logging that information now, Captain."

"Very well."

"Captain, DIMUS tracking in the green." It was the tissue-thin voice of Lieutenant Virgil "Spike" Mead, senior electronics and sonar officer aboard *Skate.*

The telephone talker next to Mead spoke in a muted hush. "Lieutenant, did you ever figure up yet how much we got left in the boat's rec fund?"

"Enough." He smiled easily at the young sailor, eagerly shaking his head. "But there's a real problem."

"Sir, what's that?" The youngster was crestfallen. Any problem, no matter how small, in *Skate* could be monumental, and the seaman knew it.

Spike Mead looked out of the corner of his eye and his mouth twitched with concern. "There's still eight guys aboard with the clap from the last lady who paid us a visit."

"That all, sir? No sweat. Ben Eisner in Radio knows this lady who's really hot. But she's clean, sir. Guaranteed. Know what I mean, sir?" The sailor was pleading with a whisper.

"Certainly I know, but—"

"Target, Mead! Give me the damned information!"

"Aye, aye, Captain." Mead winked at the telephone talker. "Sonar approach." His voice was a musical burlesque of George Burns. "Target making forty-five beats per minute. Solid echo return. No scattering effect," Mead pronounced sternly from a set of metal consoles five feet behind the periscope stand.

"Cut the crap, Mead! Just give me range and target data." Commander Burkhart's voice was a sharp razor, cutting across the tiny control center of the nuclear attack submarine *Skate,* the oldest, noisiest and least proficient nuclear sub on the line.

Burkhart was disgusted. If it wasn't a problem with the boat, it was some foul ball in the crew like Mead, an officer no less. Well, screw Mead, he mumbled as his eyes slowly scrutinized his control center from the elevated periscope stand.

The boat was old and cramped all right, Burkhart thought. There wasn't a longitudinal corridor more than three feet wide or a ceiling over seven feet high. Technological litter was strewn all about the compartment. Banks of large and small, round and square meters, gauges, glowing translucent plastic squares, unforgiving steel tables, various-sized green-and-gray computer display screens and delicate styluses were all cramped into every conceivable space, with the sterility and life-giving function of a hospital emergency room.

Yet it all had the look of inefficiency with scopes dropping dangerously low from the overhead, while black metal boxes jutted out just waiting to snag a brittle elbow or hip.

If you weren't conditioned to *Skate*, no matter what your submarine experience, your windpipe would constrict when the boat nosed under in a dive and the faded green-and-white linoleum deck became a steep slope under foot. The edge of panic was always close. You were sure you were being sucked down into a black swamp for the last time with no strength left to resist. Then there was always that final insult, as your nose would protest the constant acrid smell, like a smoldering short inside an old television.

At least that was Burkhart's first impression of *Skate* and it had always stayed with him. Somehow a select number of crewmen managed to forge through the control room litter to keep the submarine functioning. The same men never talked of the fear, it just showed in their eager faces. Christ, she still had her original Westinghouse nuclear propulsion system, always subject to unpredictable breakdowns. She was just rundown, with an overused look about her.

Burkhart turned back to face the dive station before him, but it was difficult to refocus his attention. He had run through it all a thousand times during the year and a half he had served in her as her captain. It just always came up the same. *Skate* was a shabby circus.

In 1970, during an extensive refit at Mare Island Shipyard, two rebuilt Fairbanks-Morse diesels had been dusted off and installed for what *BuShips* called "surface emergencies." Burkhart's persistent nightmare was that *Skate* would never make the surface.

He laughed coldly to himself, momentarily resting his bulk against the periscope stand railing. *Skate* belongs in a maritime museum, Burkhart thought. He pushed out a long breath. From a distance he heard Mead's grating voice. As usual Burkhart's razor had worked.

"Aye, Captain. Range, three zero one zero yards. She bears right one seven two." Mead's voice was still without dignity. She's running steady on that bearing. Speed eighteen knots."

Burkhart grunted as he squashed his entire face into the rubber eye piece of the small starboard attack scope that narrowed into a tiny tracing feather on the rolling surface two hundred ten feet above. For a moment he stepped back and wiped his large right forearm over his capless head and wrinkled his face. He looked slovenly with sweat staining the entire back and armpit areas of his short-sleeved khaki shirt. But there was poetry beneath his surface.

After a moment he dug in and moved in on the periscope. His large six-foot-two-inch body was wrapped in familiar python coils around the shiny steel periscope barrel, with each arm dangling over the handles on either side of the scope face. Suddenly he postured to full height, taking the scope up with him. His hands seized the scope handles, as he pirouetted, pulling the stainless steel barrel around on a full three hundred sixty degrees on its quadrant as he searched the surface for anything Mead might have missed.

Even at full extension his thick neck was creased into alligator skin. The forty-two-year-old man was working his craft with every ounce of his strength and mental capacity. Although it was only an antiship torpedo drill, for Charles Burkhart, Naval Academy Class of Sixty Seven, the target ship was his sworn enemy.

Apparently satisfied, Burkhart grunted, "Down scope," to the Quartermaster of the Watch standing next to him. Burkhart then flipped the steel handles upward.

"Aye, sir. Scope going down." The quartermaster was pulling hard on the periscope "pickle" to pull the scope eye tip, in lizard tongue movements, down from the surface, down through the boat's massive sail into the open well housing two decks below.

As usual the scope was responding slowly. "Goddammit! Another glitch for the discrepency list. Doesn't anything on the damned boat ever work?" His face and voice were blazing. Burkhart caught a heavy whiff of the quartermaster's foul-smelling armpits and it only increased his rancor.

"She's tired, sir." it was the sympathic voice of Quartermaster Bobby Kay, Petty Officer Second Class. "*Skate*'s a lame old lady. She needs a long rest on the beach, sir."

"I know that, Kay, but I love this damn boat." He looked around the control room. "We all want out, but the old girl sure has gotten under my skin. She's living history."

He'd read about her when he was still a student at the Academy. How *Skate* had become the first nuclear sub production model, when her keel was laid in 1955, and was now finally worn out after a generation of pioneering the tough runs. In the late 1950's, under direction of Hyman Rickover, *Skate* had done it all. Her log read like the Old Testament. She was the first submarine to cross the Atlantic submerged and the first submarine to surface at the north Pole.

Burkhart laughed to himself. No attention had been given to creature comforts within the awkward guppy-shaped steel hull and she was pushed along by two old steam turbines that were less than reliable. The new attack boats were twice *Skate*'s size and could cruise at freeway speeds in the depths, virtually undetectable. She was in a time warp, her species extinct. Once she had been the promise of America, now *Skate* was struggling to stay afloat.

Burkhart knew *Skate* should have been pulled from the line ten years before, but Submarine Deck at *BuShips* still needed her to help counter the growing Russian fleet roaming the Pacific.

Skate's performance was questionable, and that lack of proficiency forced Burkhart to push himself and his crew all the harder. Burkhart was never sure of *Skate*. She was alive with a bizarre personality all her own. To her crew she was the Siberia of active submarine duty. Often, in frustration, many of the ninety-five enlisted men and nine officers pushed back at *Skate* or Burkhart.

To many, Burkhart was *Skate*.

6

At last the periscope was properly secured in its well. Without apparent motion, Burkhart leaned over the scope stand's chrome railing. His thick freckled face tightened into sourdough. Quickly he caught sight of his prey, Mead, and motioned him over. Burkhart's face was flushed but his voice was still soft.

"Look, clown face, as usual you're highly visible and it stinks." The softness in his voice vaporized. Mead's eyes widened in surprise. The captain had never taken him apart in the presence of the crew.

"I'm fed up with your cheap comedy. You're just a goddamned blemish come to life. A bad flu." Mead felt a large stabbing finger thumping painfully into his bony chest. "Listen up, mister. You square your act right now. I don't even want to hear your footsteps until this drill is in the bag. If I do, I'll jam one of your basketballs up your ass." Burkhart drew a deep breath and evened out his anger. "Let's have a small chat in my cabin when this is over, and I promise that by the time I'm done with you, you'll at last be qualified to wear those gold dolphins pinned on your chest. No smart ass is gonna screw up my boat, got it?"

Spike Mead tried a limp smile for effect. "Aye, aye,

sir." He nodded his lean, angular head in appease-ment. The gesture apparently satisfied Burkhart, who turned away from his junior officer, moving quickly to the opening of the scope stand.

When he was sure it was reasonably safe, Mead looked up and moved his lips just above a whisper. "Iron in the soul. Stiff upper lip and all that shit. Eat it, Steamboat Willy."

The close-quartered telephone talker let go with a pig squeal of laughter, acknowledging Mead's private war with Burkhart.

Burkhart had once again removed himself from ev-erything but the target. Leaning over the forward stand rail he sighted the digital depth gauge on the bulkhead of the Operational Control Center, called the Diving Panel. Before the bulkhead was the helmsman, seated in a bright blue vinyl pilot seat. He controlled the di-rection and depth of the boat. The diving officer sat behind him, feeding orders to the helmsman as they were received from the conning officer. The helmsman sat holding a pilot's steering wheel supported by a con-trol column. The "joystick" controlled the huge diving planes rigged forward in the bows of the *Skate* and aft in the rear of the hull, just forward of the deep rudder and twin propellers that drove *Skate*.

"Make your depth one hundred twenty feet," Burk-hart commanded. "Helm, steady up on course zero six zero."

"Aye, sir," answered the dive officer. "Ten degrees up bubble. Heading up to one two zero feet. Course holding steady on two nine five."

On command the helmsman began to slowly ease back on his control stick. No tanks were emptied to raise the boat. She was being driven up by her two steam tur-bines which powered two massive drive shafts, in turn pushing the two large propellers abaft the rudder.

44

Taking up slack from the canted deck, Burkhart unlocked his knees as the boat skied toward one hundred twenty feet. He intently watched the depth gauge as the numbers clicked off. As the depth and sea pressure fell away the weight of the boat decreased. Within three minutes of Burkhart's order, the two hundred sixty-seven-foot steel boat had been driven up to its final attack depth.

Burkhart's ears had come subconsciously alive to the entire hunt. He was listening to the steady minuet-like rhythmic pings of the active sonar sending out probing electronic fingers every two seconds searching for the target. A shrill angry eruption from the returning echo told him the *Skate* was locked tightly to her target.

Burkhart's tense moves began to spill over to the other crewmen and officers in the control room. It was always that way. Most had begun to believe his lie. The men worked their consoles and battle stations with pumped energy. It was Burkhart on the final turn stretching for everything during that last furlong. Burkhart wanting the final bearing for shoot.

"Up scope!" His voice was hoarse and dry. As the barrel rose up again through its well, Burkhart snagged the steel handles just above his knees. Burkhart's "crotch run" had begun in earnest.

"Open muzzle doors one and four." He was smiling. Closing in on his little pretend war. Sweat was pouring from his face and forearms. "Depth ten feet."

The telephone talker standing just beneath the periscope platform spoke rapidly into his breast plate microphone. "Open outer doors one and four. Make torpedo depth ten feet."

While awaiting a reply from the forward torpedo room, the young seaman talker searched his captain's face. The blazing eyes and intense bulging of his cheeks frightened him. Burkhart looked reptilian.

45

"Muzzle doors one and four open and in the green, Captain. Tubes one and four loaded. Torpedoes set for ten feet, sir."

Burkhart wrapped his arm coils around the scope handles and once more swept the surface. He wanted a perfect run to compensate for an imperfect crew and an imperfect boat. Easily he found his target clawing along at twelve knots, and carefully studied her lines. Even a squatty auxiliary target like the *Mizar* was worthy, with her bows rolling into the morning swell.

With deliberate care Burkhart turned the right scope handle until he felt the light tumbler lock on the next setting of higher magnification. He swiveled the quadrant three degrees to starboard and found what he was seeking. The aft bridge of the *Mizar*. Another click of the steel handle and the scope magnified once again to reveal with remarkable clarity the entire bridge and wing structure of the target.

Mizar was still over fifteen hundred yards away, but Burkhart found the captain, dressed in foul weather jacket and blue baseball cap. A tiny stick pipe was stuck into the middle of the distant face.

"Plotting and firing parties, this will be a manual approach and firing sequence." His voice was clear and demanding.

"Aye, sir" came the response from Lieutenant Commander Neil Brennen, officer of the plot and the boat's Executive Officer. "DIMUS and all automatic systems disengaged. You have complete control of the boat, sir."

Good old Irish, Burkhart thought. The only mustang aboard and the most dependable man around. Limited but dependable. Not like that asshole, Mead.

From nowhere a screaming claw of noise shot through Burkhart. He was momentarily knocked off balance. Whoop. Whoop. Whoop. Whoop. The lights

46

flickered in the control room. Then everything went pitch-black one hundred twenty feet below the Pacific Ocean. Whoop. Whoop. Whoop.

"Shut that fucking horn off, Irish! Shut it off, on the double!"

Burkhart felt his boat nose slightly down. She was growing heavy. His mind was running down the possibilities.

Finally there was reasonable silence. "Russotto. Find Russotto! Kick in aux—"

Comforting bright lights quickly flooded the control room of *Skate*.

Burkhart moved like a man possessed, with pure, highly trained motion. He picked up the ship intercom phone positioned on a bulkhead next to the attack scope and spoke to every compartment on the boat.

"Now hear this. This is the captain. Chief Russotto, phone the control room on the double. All compartments and watches report damage to division heads." The boat was canting down even more noticeably.

"Shut down active sonar, Mead. Damage control party to the forward torpedo room on the double." He then looked up and swept his practiced eyes around the control room. Frightened young faces and tight white lips greeted his stare. There was nothing to say. His actions would calm them all.

But all eyes were on the depth gauge positioned above the Dive Panel. It was blinking off the feet with its orange light. 130. 135. 140. 150.

The diving officer broke the oppressive silence by calling off the depth. "155. 160. 163. 165. 170."

The buzz of the intercom phone interrupted the cadence.

"Captain, this is Russotto. I'm in the forward torpedo room. Looks like number four torpedo tube wouldn't take full impulse pressure. Three bolts gave

47

way on her breech door. The compartment is shipping some water. We got a real mess here. Two light casualties."

"Chief, can you close and secure that breech door?"

"Yes, sir, can do. Should have her watertight in another five or six minutes, but the water has to be pumped out. We're carry'n too much weight forward."

Burkhart's face sagged. He picked up the boat's loudspeaker. "Now hear this. This is the captain. This firing exercise is canceled. We've had an accident in the forward torpedo room. A DC party is securing the problem. Possible casualties. I want Corpsman Ginepra to lay up to the forward torpedo room on the double. Stand at General Quarters until further notice. Division commanders report to the wardroom in thirty minutes."

Dropping the phone back on its cradle, Burkhart momentarily sagged against the bulkhead wall. Then quickly he turned to his XO, Neil "Irish" Brennen. "Get her up fast! Emergency surface. I want a stop trim, then blow negative and safety to the mark. That should do it with plenty to spare." Burkhart leaned heavily into the scope stand railing, his head bowed in defeat. Lady *Skate* had cursed him again.

"Emergency surface! Emergency surface!" It was Brennen shouting orders to the Officer of the Dive, three feet away.

AH OO GAH. AH OO GAH. The klaxon horn pierced every deck of the boat as her crew prepared to take her up.

"Officer of the Dive. Hard rise on the planes." Burkhart's voice was rock hard and steady. "Make surface turns for sixteen knots."

"Aye, sir." The Maneuvering Officer flipped the annunciator indicator that in turn signaled the Propulsion Officer one deck below and thirty frames aft. "Sir, answering bells for sixteen knots."

Slowly *Skate* decreased her downward arc, leveled off, and then began clawing toward the surface.

"Helm, come right to three one zero." Burkhart was keeping his men busy.

"Aye, sir. Fifteen degrees right rudder. The new course is three one zero. Rudder amidships."

"When decks are awash, rig in the bow planes."

"Sir."

Burkhart wheeled around to see a young frightened yeoman standing beneath the periscope stand railing.

"Yes son?"

"Action-dispatch from COMSUBGRU FIVE, via underwater radio telephone from Dipper Sierra." He handed the clipboard to Burkhart and waited for him to sign for the dispatch.

Burkhart quickly scanned the message typed on tissue thin yellow paper. A puzzled frown rippled his large open face.

U.S. NAVAL ACTION DISPATCH

TO: COMM BURKHART:	SKATE
CLASSIFICATION	PRECEDENCE
TOP SECRET	OP-IMMED

FROM: COMSUBGRU FIVE

ACTION: BREAK OFF ANTI SHIP EXER-
CISES IMMEDIATELY.

INFO: RETURN SAN DIEGO CONTROL
FLANK SPEED. REPORT TO REAR
ADMIRAL BRANDON LANGOR
AT NAVSEGRUPAC BALLAST
POINT 0630 HOURS 18 MAY.

Slowly he folded the message in half, his eyes staring vacantly at the backs of the men at the diving and helm station in front of him. After a few moments he turned to Brennen.

"Irish, when we surface, belay the order for emergency repairs. It'll have to wait."

Brennen wrinkled his fleshy nose at Burkhart. "That's a hella'va strain to put on propulsion, Charley."

"Can't be helped." Burkhart was looking down at the folded flimsy. "I've gotta date with NAVSEGRU-PAC and an Admiral Langor." Both men exchanged vague glances as the activity in the control room moved around them.

Brennen reached up and tapped the message. "What the hell does Naval Security Group, Pacific, want with you? High level people. The highest. Maybe they're going to lift Skate's security clearance." He laughed.

Burkhart shrugged his shoulders. "The hell with it. Admiral Langor ring a bell with you, Irish? Brandon Langor?"

"Nothing, Skipper."

Burkhart drew in a long breath. "Have plot lay in a track for Point Loma, all ahead two-thirds." Let 'em wait, Burkhart thought. He wasn't coming in flank ahead and do more damage to the old lady, not with all that weight forward.

7

Vice Admiral Brandon W. Langor widened his eyes and steadied his glare on Jake Niven as both men sat facing each other in a small nondescript office overlooking Ballast Point Submarine Base.

"Are you ready to work? Finland is now behind us, Jake." Admiral Langor, feudal baron of Task Force 157, in a naval uniform, came forward to the last inch of the borrowed oak-ribbed chair, rubbing his hands together."

"Us? I like the ring of that, Admiral."

"Figure of speech, Niven." Although Langor was three thousand miles away from his home base at Norfolk, Virginia, the strange chair couldn't diminish his control or his energy. "The tweed sports jacket and eggwhite turtleneck make you look half civilized. I like the effect that lady lawyer has had on you. Indeed I do. A certain light in the eyes."

Jake regarded him carefully before fueling the conversation. "The instinct to survive is the only light in my eyes." Langor was setting him up. "Pressure without pain, Admiral?" The verbal fencing would end momentarily.

"Had word from London last night, Jake."

First names mean trouble, Niven thought.

Langor inhaled deeply and directed his faded hazel eyes down toward the manila folder lying under his right hand. "It was before my time. I mean, the real beginnings of you and Vasili Lykov. I read the file on him last night. Interesting that at one point Lykov served as a terrorist instructor at the GRU's Sanprobal Military Academy in the Crimea and held the same position at the Higher Infantry School in Odessa. It was part of his overall function as chief of the Second Directorate." Langor popped his right thumb against the flat file, like he was shooting his favorite cat's-eye marble into the circle.

"He's dead, Admiral."

Slowly Langor opened the file and then flashed his best fatherly smile.

"London is very concerned and wants to see you. It's obvious that it is all too important to be left to a courier. Besides, he wants you and I'm not one to trample on his best impulses."

"Go on, I assume there's a connection with Lykov." Niven slouched back in the hard chair for support.

"In time, Jake."

"You realize, Admiral, that my life isn't worth a nickel in Europe since the Lykov matter." He shivered inside. "What the hell is London so damned concerned about?"

Langor hooked a stubby finger in midair. "About the destination of the DaVinci and of course Mister Belous. You remember, Jake. The infamous Viktor Belous." He laughed sarcastically, then his face turned sour. "When Belous is the topic of conversation, you go listen. I don't give a damn if it's in the center of the Soviet Embassy in London or the lobby of the Rossiya Hotel in Moscow with the entire KGB sniffing your ass. Captain Viktor Belous of the Soviet Navy and that little painting, are HAWKSCREECH. You remember HAWKSCREECH. Langor's words flowed in thick cold spurts of buttermilk.

There was more. "Go on, Admiral." Niven's voice had grown bleak.

"After Finland, we really kept our ear to the railroad track. The computer boys at Langley really helped out.

"Let the computer go to London."

Langor smiled again." I believe your lady has made you cautious."

Niven stared at Langor through his silence, beginning to grow angry. Langor was an easy man not to like. The professional user. The results man. Every company needed one. Langor, the spook, would tell him soon enough where this nonsense was leading.

"We don't know if HAWKSCREECH has been compromised."

Niven sat up, watching Langor smile with bad news.

"When Lykov returned to Moscow with Koslov, they were going to take him to house number 3A in Energyiske Ulitsa. Know the place?"

Langor was really in heat with the smooth curved lips always smiling while the even, white, star-quality teeth talked. Langor made eye contact with the mouth as he carefully watched Jake's twisted expression grow.

"It's Lefortovo Prison." Jake looked devastated. "The KGB's little funhouse."

Langor nodded his head. "Exactly. Seems we did Vasili a favor by killing him quickly. Very few people ever leave Lefortovo alive, especially high-ranking party members."

Jake turned away and stared out the dirty window, swallowing into his dry throat. The bastard. He wanted to choke Langor for saying it. Vasili Lykov had been squeezed from both sides, with no way out.

"Get to the point, Admiral."

"Indeed. The Kremlin wanted Lykov to tie his one loose end—Koslov. Obviously there were certain promises made but the hierarchy on Moscow Ring Road couldn't bring the GRU under its control without killing the old Stalinist, Lykov. He refused to become their pawn, so he simply outlived his usefulness." Langor paused and looked out the window, down at the submarines gathered in neat rows of three.

"And our proposal played right into the KGB's hands."

Jake was interrupted by a long, slow, moaning blast, echoing below from the ancient garbage barge *Shoshone,* signaling early-morning duty rounds of the black steeled submarines, cattled into hemp-tied stalls along the long concrete pier. The entire scene was dominated by the massive sub tender, *Dixon.*

"Indeed, Jake. The Kremlin simply moved Lykov, who had grown sloppy, into the KGB's camp for the purpose of helping him steal the Da Vinci painting from the Hermitage."

Niven shook his head.

"We just don't know, Jake, how much Lykov and the KGB found out about where the painting was going. Indeed, they wanted Lykov's hide. That's why no radio contact was allowed. The perfect sting. You have to go to London and find out how far the Russian ream job really went."

"Lykov didn't know," Niven protested.

Langor turned purple. "An order, Niven. A goddamn order, not a request for room service. This operation is too big. It's not like the old days of you and Lykov playing trenchcoat and pistols on the Glienicker Bridge, dividing Berlin. No more bodies dropped into Lake Wannsee. The November cold of Berlin was very romantic, but—" His voice trailed away.

Niven raised his eyes and searched Langor's face.

He was loving it. Cut from the same cloth as that dead cop, Andropov, only the uniform and address were different.

"You're not like the old Niven." Langor shook his head. "Indeed, that woman has really slowed you down. A year ago, London wouldn't have frightened you, but now . . ." He tossed his head to one side.

"It's called living, Admiral. I'm beginning to enjoy the experience."

"And the experience of being distracted can blow the whole mission sky high." Langor's small head was a giant organic marble, swept clean of hair, radiating with delicately hued textures of purple and rose. A cheap replica of Rance Belgian marble, Niven decided, that commanded complete attention. Langor was a physical shock.

"You may have soft hands today, Admiral, but you're still a street assassin in your heart. I've lived with the prospects of this mission for the past year. I know exactly what I have to do to make it all work."

Langor flashed a quick smile. "I have your best interests at heart, Jake. Remember that Vasili Lykov lost his edge and now he's fish food. I don't want that for you."

Slowly, Niven rose and leaned over Langor's desk. Langor knew just where to stick the hot poker. "I'll keep my edge, count on it, Admiral." His voice was hushed. God knows I'll need it so you can slowly walk with great pride into the Oval Office if we get back and report the boldest theft in the history of warfare. Admiral Brandon Langor, the architect of modern strategy. Then maybe a CIA directorship or a Cabinet appointment, accompanied by the proper media hype. Just spare me the crap, Admiral, sir." Jake sat down heavily as Langor pushed the comments aside without effort.

"I want you in London within the next two days. You know the program."

"The Soviets will smell me coming. Their British operation will know about it before my wheels touch down."

"Don't feed me that red herring noise about my organization being compromised. We're tight, dammit!"

"So you say, from a warm chair."

"I say, get to London and confirm the Bering program." Langor sat back. "London only trusts you. Jake, I need you to read the winds, for Chrissakes." Langor was almost whining.

"How flattering."

"I need your assurances, your experience, your eyes and gut, to tell me if it's possible without starting World War Three."

He paused and played with his gold lighter. "Jake, we have to know if Captain Belous is being strung out. If he's changed his mind. Besides, London is crying like a damn baby for his pay voucher from DeBeers. He thinks I'll keep his diamonds out of reach until the mission is over."

Jake turned and stared out the window at the fog.

"You know what we need, Jake. What we've been waiting for. His assurance that his people at the Plesetsk assembly and launch facility in northern Russia, will do their ream job on that Cosmos sky spy, scheduled to go up the last week in July."

"I know, I know."

"You bastard! Don't give me that sullen 'I know.' A dead Cosmos ocean sky spy is the only damn chance we have for our blind spot. By the time they put up another orbiter, we'll be long gone. No blind spot in that narrow sector of their North Pacific network and

HAWKSCREECH is down the tubes." Langor's head flushed.

"Get me those assurances, Niven, and when this business is completed, there'll be a big, fat bonus in it for you. After all, you're thinking for two these days."

"Iron-clad assurances are only for cancer patients." Jake looked at Langor's delicate features. "How much?"

"A hundred thou."

"Not big and not fat, Admiral. Make it five hundred thou, tax free. Not a great deal with inflation and all—"

Admiral Langor thought about it for a few moments, then he nodded. "If you pull this off, it'll be worth every damn penny."

Brandon Langor stood and pulled down on his blue uniform coat, clean of campaign ribbons. He looked better sitting down, Jake decided. Sitting masked his squat five-foot-five-inch frame. Powerful people shouldn't be squat. Casually Langor reached into an inside breast pocket and extracted a pack of cigarettes. He pushed the pack to his mouth and pulled a cigarette out with his lips. A small gold lighter appeared and Langor inhaled deeply. I should have switched them with a pack of Vasili's Papirosi cigarettes, Jake thought, never taking his eyes from Langor's face. The price of impunity. He would have choked to death right in this little gray shoebox of an office.

"Everything is set up on this end, Jake. The floating dry dock is ready to accept *Skate*, and the special tarp just arrived last night from Florida. The work crews are standing by for round-the-clock shifts. The entire area has been sealed off."

"What if Burkhart says no." Jake couldn't help grinning. "Timing is critical now."

Langor wasn't amused. "He won't refuse me."

57

"One lie is a lie, and two lies are Langor's politics." Jake laughed in his face.

"Why the hell do you always push me?"

"Because I always do your bidding on the important ones. I suppose that gives me a few extra privileges." This time Jake didn't grin. "I happen to like Burkhart. He's a hard-working line officer."

"You ready now for Burkhart?" Langor smiled again.

8

Langor leaned over his desk and pressed down on an intercom switch. Almost instantly a sailor opened the door, allowing Commander Charles Burkhart to enter. He was dressed in winter blues, his thick sunburned neck chafing in a stiff white collar. His service ribbons and gold dolphins, tarnished green, were all neatly in place.

Burkhart came to attention and saluted smartly before Langor who was again seated behind the desk.

"Sit down and relax, Commander." Langor pointed to another wood-ribbed chair in front of the desk.

"Thank you, sir." His voice was a vague puzzle. Burkhart then turned and looked over at Jake, his face instantly breaking into a shocked grin. Langor, watching both men's eyes, timed his entry perfectly.

"I believe you are acquainted with Jake Niven."

"Yes, sir." Burkhart reached over and squeezed Jake's extended hand. "Jake, how ya doing? Long time, old buddy." The tension in Burkhart's voice eased but the question was bulging in his eyes.

"Sure has been a while, Charley." Langor's smile, with a character all its own, was moving back and forth across the room.

Burkhart looked at Jake, then smiled tentatively.

"I'll tell it, Jake. An old worn-out story might take the edge off. It's like this, Admiral. In the fall of 1967, when Jake was just commissioned a regular ensign out of Brown, he was assigned for SEAL training in Coronado. One night we met and I took him in tow and we ended up at the Ballast Tank Officer's Club, here on the sub base. To make a long story short, we rounded up Lloyd Bucher, Captain of the *Pueblo,* whose crew was here for training before heading to the Korean coast and a date with a prison camp. He joined us at the bar. One thing led to another, and within an hour we had stolen the Ballast Tank's famous reclining nude painting from behind the bar and had stowed it in *Pueblo*'s wardroom. Only a direct threat from the Base Commander forced us to return the nude three days later. We left our package on the doorstep and escaped."

Burkhart folded his face and squinted at Jake. He was waiting for something even more ominous than *Skate* to fall on his head. Where was the punch line? Langor picked up the signal and smiled again.

"Let's get down to it, Commander."

"I'd like that, sir." Burkhart stiffened in his chair and planted his spit-shined black shoes to the floor, expecting the worst.

"Have you ever heard of the Spook Shack?"

Burkhart nodded his head slightly before he answered.

Langor picked at Burkhart's dilemma. "Don't worry. Just tell us what you know, off the record."

Burkhart again shifted uncomfortably in his seat. He was used to grilling, not being grilled himself. "Ah, yes, I've heard of the Shack. Every line officer in the sub service has heard stories."

"What kind of stories, Charley?"

Burkhart threw a puzzled sideways glance at Jake. "Last year over at the Ballast Tank I had a conversation with an officer who said his boat had once penetrated Vladivostok Harbor. I think that—"

Jake squeezed Burkhart's massive shoulder. His voice was cold. "It was *Drum,* Charley. She lay on the bottom of Vladivostok for a week in 1986. Our unit aboard *Drum* photographed the entire installation and took sound signature recordings of every warship and sub leaving and entering the harbor. We then did the same thing at Petropavlovsk. I commanded that civilian unit aboard *Drum.* The program was HOLY-STONE."

Burkhart's mouth dropped as he turned to meet Jake's eyes. The last he had heard, Jake had resigned his commission. Langor was leaning back in his oak chair enjoying the show.

"Charley, the Russians never knew we were there. We entered and exited both harbors undetected. It was a very clean operation." The excitement rose in Jake's voice.

Burkhart held up a pink hand in defense. His head was turned away from Langor. The admiral was giving nothing away. Maybe for the sake of past friendship Jake would give him a clue. At least he was doing most of the talking.

"I don't see where I fit into this, Jake." The steel was back in Burkhart's voice. "This is all highly—"

A series of three sharp raps on the door interrupted Burkhart.

"Come." Langor jumped from his chair as Langor's aide, a young lieutenant, entered the office carrying a yellow sheet. His young blond face was free of character and expression.

"Sir, I have a NODIS from Norfolk, via satellite from Misawa, Japan."

61

Burkhart watched as Langor signed for the message and exchanged a knowing glance with Jake. Burkhart wouldn't get a thing out of Jake, until they were alone. Admiral Langor was the beacon and now with a god-damned super secret cable he had lost Jake completely, at least for this meeting. He watched Langor's face wrinkle with concern.

Langor read the message silently, then leaned over the small desk and handed the cable to Jake.

Niven studied the message for a long time before he handed the cable back. Another moaning blast from the barge *Shoshone* pressed at the heavy silence. Burkhart looked from one to the other and realized he had to stab at that silence to reestablish his presence.

"Admiral Langor, why am I here?"

Langor folded the message neatly and put it into his inside breast pocket. His voice was strangely excited. "We are planning a very special project and we need your help."

Burkhart shifted his gaze uncomfortably from Langor to Jake, then laughed at the apparent moment of humor. "My help?"

"Something funny, Commander?" It was Langor. His clean bald head twitched.

"Yeah, funny, sir. But let me clarify something." He rubbed a thick hand over the back of his neck. "Do you want me or my boat?" His large rugged face lightened for the first time since he had entered the office.

Admiral Langor came forward in his chair pulling his entire upper body weight onto the small desk. His face hardened as he thrust out his shoulders.

"We want you and *Skate*."

Burkhart glanced from Langor to Jake. Their faces were stone. For a moment Burkhart was knocked off balance.

"Christ, sir, with all due respect to your rank and

the Spook Shack, I think a terrible error in judgment has been committed within your group." He set his jaw waiting for Langor to pounce, but there was only a vacuous silence and Langor's dazzling smile. Burkhart suddenly grew tired of the light sparring.

"I'm going to speak freely. *Skate* is worn out, gentlemen." He swept his eyes from Langor to Jake Niven and back again. "She's ready for the scrapper's torch. My crew is willing but—inexprienced. At best she should be struck from the line. She's over thirty years old and her systems are old and unreliable. Our daily discrepancy glitch sheet is a weekly shopping list. It would cost more to modernize her than it cost to build her."

From under Lykov's file, Langor slowly pulled open the service jacket sitting on the desk. Jake could see the slight smile at the corners of Langor's mouth.

"Commander, during the past year and seven months you have served in *Skate* as her skipper, you have requested a transfer of command no less than five times." Langor gently closed the folder and looked up at Burkhart. "Are these facts from the Submarine Desk at BuPers correct?"

Burkhart let out a long, audible sigh. "Yes, sir. Those facts are correct. But I don't really see—"

Langor was holding up a hand. "Do you want command of a newer class attack boat?"

"Jesus, yes, sir. I do. That's obvious." Burkhart's eyes had grown very large and his voice quiet. Then his face clouded over. "A nice dangling carrot, but what's the hook, sir?" He turned and looked squarely at Jake.

Langor glanced at Jake and nodded.

"The carrot is HAWKSCREECH, Charley."

Burkhart stared at Jake, but his face remained passive. Slowly he turned the term over with his tongue.

63

"HAWKSCREECH. Doesn't mean a thing to me. Should it?"

"We hope to hell not, Charley." Jake was deadly serious. "Based on the need to know concept we'll tell you just enough for you to make a decision."

"Do I have a choice, gentlemen?"

"There are always choices, Commander." Langor's tone had grown dark. Burkhart knew that if he refused, his career would definitely grind to a halt and he would end up on the Island of Yap counting blankets. It had happened to a thousand other guys.

"I understand, sir."

"No you don't, Burkhart. Not yet anyway, but you soon will. You couldn't guess in your wildest fantasy." Langor turned to Jake. "Is the showing set up?"

"Yes, Admiral. We're expected aboard *Dixon.*" Jake turned his head to a puzzled Burkhart.

9

An eerie silence dominated the walk down the hill through the huge submarine facility. Finally the three men arrived at the brow of the massive tender *Dixon,* painted traditional dull Navy gray. The entire area was a beehive of activity with *Dixon* as the focus. She was moored Mediterranean fashion with her broad fantail backed in alongside the long concrete pier. Bow and stern mooring lines, as large as a man's fist, held the tender securely in place.

With Admiral Langor walking between, Burkhart didn't have a chance to exchange questioning glances with Jake Niven. Burkhart looked to the starboard side of *Dixon* and found his *Skate* sandwiched between *Dixon* and *Sculpin,* her repair parties, with Brennen supervising, already at work. Forward of *Skate,* sitting alone, was the black monster attack sub *Los Angeles,* lying low and deadly in the water, her flat back hull a lethal shadow. She was almost a hundred feet longer than *Skate* and every inch of her showed muscle and strength, Burkhart thought. *Skate*'s high-riding guppy shape stood out like an old pregnant cow.

Suddenly they were piped aboard, with credentials carefully checked by a young hard-nosed officer of the deck. Finally they were led down into the bowels of *Dixon*, past a mammoth seven-hundred-man machine shop, various supply facilities, barber shops, and torpedo repair facilities.

Finally, six decks down, they were admitted to a large steel compartment forcing two crisply dressed Marine guards to brace smartly.

The large double-sized steel hatch slammed shut behind them as the three men entered the compartment. There were six rows of thickly padded theater seats, amphitheater style, sloping down to a large white viewing screen. A projection booth dominated the rear of the compartment.

For a moment Langor was distracted by a buzzing telephone signal from a console next to a seat in the front row.

"All right, Jake. What the hell is this?" Burkhart kept his eye on Langor's back and barely moved his lips. "What the hell have you dragged me into?"

"You'll have it all in the next five minutes."

Langor put down the receiver, turned, and smiled. "It won't even take that long, Commander. In case you're wondering, Burkhart, this compartment is completely sealed off from the rest of *Dixon*. We call this our white room. Complete lead shielding on all surfaces, to keep any errant microwave beams from intercepting us. The Russians have made a habit of stealing signals for the past dozen years with satellites. We call it white sound. Nothing in. Nothing out." Langor sat down in his chair forcing Jake and Burkhart to sit, one on either side of him.

Langor turned to Burkhart on his right. "What we are about to explain to you and then show you is higher than secret." Langor's smile was gone. "Members of my Task Force have given their lives for what you are about to hear and see, Commander. Do you understand what I'm saying?''

"Yes, Admiral. I understand, but what about HAWKSCREECH? Let's get to it. I've got a damaged boat waiting for her skipper.'' Burkhart turned his head away and rubbed a hand over his face and set his jaw.

"Commander, have you ever heard of particle beam weapons?'' Langor forced Burkhart to make eye contact.

Burkhart turned and squinted. His knowledge was somewhat vague and general and, besides, he didn't care. He began to grow very uneasy and that only helped to bolster his anger.

"Nothing about beams that I can recall, sir.''

"Not many people have, Commander.'' Langor paused and folded his hands very carefully in his lap. "Very simply, it means a beam of directed energy that is focused on a large target. That target is then destroyed by bombarding it with high energy subatomic particles.''

"Anything yet, Charley?''

"Not much, Jake.'' He shrugged.

"The Soviets have a weapon based on the beam target interaction principle that is on the verge of becoming operational.''

Burkhart tried to sound interested. "Don't we have the Strategic Defense Initiative and layered defenses. I think it's called HIGH TOWER. I attended a lecture once at the War College about the Navy's SDI program. Ah, I think it was called SKYLITE. Isn't there a beam weapon anywhere in those programs?''

"Nowhere, Charley. At least one that works and we're spending about five billion dollars a year on SDI. More importantly, about four years ago, we started hearing rumblings that the Russians had developed a realiable weapons system that was capable of shooting down an incoming ballistic missile warhead with a god-damned beam of neutral high energy particles."

Burkhart's face grew dark as he stared at the deck. Finally he looked up. "So this has to do with that Star Wars business. Star Wars and *Skate* is more like it, I suppose."

"You might say that," Jake added. "The Russians have come up with a canned bolt of lightning that changes the rules of the whole ballgame."

"To be more precise, the Russians are literally ten years ahead of us." Langor forced his way back into the conversation. "Our people tell us the Soviets have been experimenting with beam weapons powered by betatron accelerators for some twenty years. It's been scattered all through their scientific literature about early experiments at Lebedev Institute in Leningrad. We just ignored it until the administration went public with Star Wars."

Burkhart's face darkened with frustration. "Listen—"

"One more minute, Charley, and the whole picture will come together."

"I hope so. I don't think you dragged me here for a bedtime story."

"A year ago, last July to be exact, the Russians consolidated and then moved their entire beam weapon program to an isolated settlement town called Semi-palatinsk, about fifteen hundred miles east of the Caspian Sea in a region called Kazakhstan. A real stinkhole of a place, not far from the Chinese border. Last September the Soviets fired a prototype gun device, shooting a high energy beam of particles at five incoming missile warheads. It was aimed by a powerful radar system. In one swoop the live warheads were destroyed by impulses fired by the accelerator gun."

Admiral Langor lighted a cigarette. "The Russians now have the capability to blanket a field of incoming missiles and blow them into space junk. We know this because during the past six months Soviet rocket forces have conducted eight straight successful test shots against incoming warheads."

"Why the hell are you telling a line submarine officer all this? I'm always the last to know and the first to go." He wasn't smiling.

Niven squatted in front of Burkhart until their eyes were level. "The political and military implications are staggering. With this kind of an advantage we think the Kremlin will take some sort of dramatic military action during the next twelve months."

"You haven't heard the worst yet, Commander." Langor turned in his seat, blowing smoke through his nose. The easy smile had vanished. "Seven months ago we learned the Russians were working to scale down and miniaturize the entire weapon. You can well imagine the energy necessary to shoot a beam of high energy particles into space. Despite our intense efforts, we lost track of this aspect of the program until three months ago, when we observed an ancient Soviet sky spy, suddenly disappear from our tracking scopes."

"Satellites don't suddenly disappear, Admiral."

"Correct, Burkhart. With difficulty we learned the Russians shot down that satellite with the beam weapon. We also learned the beam weapon in question was a scaled-down version, small enough for transport but still massive in size."

Burkhart slumped back in his chair. His face was obsidian black as he forced himself to ask the next question. "Where the hell does *Skate* fit into this beam weapon business?"

Admiral Langor picked up the phone. "We are ready for the film now."

10

As Langor narrated the color film the compartment went black and the screen came instantly alive with an aerial view of buildings in a bleak desert environment.

"This is a long-range sky view of the Soviet particle beam facility at Semipalatinsk. It took us four months of damn hard looking to find this little haystack. The bastards built six dummy facilities in the region to hide their goodies."

The film dissolved into a series of freeze frames quickly moving closer and closer to the building roofs. The growing details, photographed from space, were remarkable, including people moving about the weapons compound.

"This building houses the large storage capacitors or batteries and that circular structure holds the belatron accelerator."

For a moment the screen went black and then came alive again with a series of freeze-frame photographs.

"Commander, watch the large black mass at the upper right of the first frame. It will move diagonally across the frames in sequence. We lost two valuable women operatives to get this verification film."

"What is it, Admiral?" Burkhart turned and squinted at the dim outline of Langor's marble head.

"An incoming warhead, loaded with conventional high explosives, shot from a Soviet missile launch site at Proletarsk directly at Semipalatinsk. That's the type of confidence they have in the beam. They obviously wanted to convince many of their own skeptics."

"Christ Almighty!" Burkhart mumbled.

The frames clicked away as the black mass moved across and down the succeeding frames.

"Watch carefully, Commander. Keep your eye on the dull corner of the mass."

With each continuing frame the dull nick grew larger until the entire warhead was engulfed in a dull flaming light.

"Here's the frame." There was a strange excitement in Langor's voice.

The center section of the frame was engulfed in an explosion.

"The beam set off the high explosives. I have been told by our people at Livermore that thermonuclear warheads do not explode. The molecules are fused together rendering the whole nuclear package inoperative. Then the triggering device of high explosives for the nuke will blow the entire warhead apart when it collides with the high energy beam."

"I can't believe they are that advanced."

"Believe it, Commander."

The screen went black, then brightened with an aerial view of a naval task group plowing through a gray, angry sea. Slowly the camera zoomed down on a large aircraft carrier set off against the sea by her dark green flight deck and narrow clipper bows.

"Commander, this is the Russian attack carrier, *Minsk*. She's big, fast, and carries one hell of a punch. Loaded, she displaces over fifty-thousand tons and carries a squadron of YAK fighters. With a flank speed of thirty-five knots she's tough. *Minsk* was built at Nikolayev Shipyards, Odessa, and joined the Pacific Fleet after her sea trials."

"I know. I've shouldered with her at sea before. Damn tough ship. Excellent sea-keeping qualities."

"We know you're aware of *Minsk,* Commander," Langor said through the dark.

Burkhart drew a long breath, forcing down his impatience and frustration. He tried to relax his shoulders as he sat back in the theater seat. Questioning and pushing admirals wasn't smart. Finally his patience gave out.

"Admiral Langor, how the hell does this fit into my command life? I don't like slow waltzes, sir. I'd just like to know where this briefing is going?" He met Langor's eyes and held his breath.

"In late August, *Minsk,* carrying this weapon, will conduct a series of particle beam tests in the far North Pacific, under cover of fog and ice. The exact location is the Komandorski Islands, off the Asian mainland. *Minsk* will be anchored for nine weeks of testing. We know for a fact *Minsk* has been equipped with a miniaturized particle beam weapon on her hangar deck."

Burkhart looked at both men and rubbed his face. "Christ Almighty! Their carrier forces and battle groups will be able to carry that weapon anywhere in the world."

Langor nodded. "Straight on, Commander." The screen shifted to *Minsk* recovering dark blue YAK fighters. "Here is our dilemma."

Burkhart waited in the dark, watching the jump jets settle slowly to the flight deck.

"Our people at Livermore and Los Alamos have made strides in the last twenty-four months to catch the Russian effort." Langor played with his gold lighter.

"However, our state of the art just cannot cut it at the present time."

"I don't understand what—"

"The Soviets have developed the ability to constrict the beam gun's energy down into a concentrated beam. Last month we attempted to shoot down a jet transport. Even that was a total failure."

"In other words, they caught us with our pants down."

"That's it." Jake was somber. "We just don't have the time to catch up now. The world has changed and so have Soviet priorities, since they developed the key to the beam weapon—something called a six-channeled ring switch, that allows the particle beam to maintain full concentrated power on the target. They call it the Pavlovski Ring Switch, after its inventor."

"So the ring switch thing has upset the entire balance of terror."

"Exactly. With that type of real advantage, the Soviets will eventually make a big move. They will be able to afford the risk of a major move against us." Jake's voice grew faint. "Our intelligence tells us they will make that move—"

The compartment was quiet except for the hum of the air-conditioning system. "We need that damn ring switch gadget to build a similar weapon that will check their advantage. And we have to do it fast, or the whole East–West balance of power will come tumbling down in our faces." Jake felt a chill on his arms and chest.

"That gadget ring switch will—"

A deafening siren flooded over Niven's words and the compartment's harsh theater lights blinked on. Half blinded they waited for the wavering siren to shut down.

"What the hell was that!"

"I'm sorry, Commander," Langor offered. "That's our satellite warning system. We were being scanned by the Russians." Pointedly, Langor looked over at Jake. "That's the third time this morning a Cosmos sky spy has penetrated our air space with their scanners fully operational."

"We do it to them," Burkhart said.

Langor rubbed his eyes. "True, but the Soviets are off schedule. They only scan Ballast Point on a weekly basis. We used to be able to set our clocks by their timetable." Langor stared at Jake. "I wonder what they expected to find? I'm not a believer in coincidence, are you, Commander?"

"Of course not, Admiral."

Langor fixed his gaze on Niven.

"London, Admiral." Niven expelled a long breath, thinking of Vasili's dying face. He hesitated and then shivered, trying to refocus his attention on the moment.

"The ring switch, or gadget, as we call it, will be aboard *Minsk* in August, as the Russians prepare for field tests." He focused on Burkhart, wanting him to understand. "The Shack has been given the job of somehow stealing the gadget intact for our own program." Niven could hear Burkhart breathing in the dark. "This operation has been given the highest national priority and I mean the highest."

The screen shifted from the Russian carrier battle group to a submarine moving on the surface, a large foaming wake boiling behind her.

At least this was something he was familiar with. Burkhart squinted at the sub. "She's an F-Class, Foxtrot diesel-electric boat. Damn fine construction, quiet running, and the Russians turned them out like model T's."

Niven drew a breath. "What else do you know about the Foxtrot, Charley?"

"Her top underwater speed is in the twenty knot range with high energy electric propulsion motors." Burkhart held up a hand, thinking out loud." She's a guppy hull boat with decent sonar and torpedo systems. Carries a crew of seventy to eighty men, I believe." Burkhart turned his eyes back to the screen as the black sub disappeared beneath the choppy sea. "I've played games at sea before with those F-Class boats. They're old but tough."

Langor spoke softy, still staring at the blank screen as the compartment lights came up slowly. "We're planning to refit *Skate* to appear as a Russian Foxtrot sub and then rendezvous with the anchored *Minsk* and her battle group in the Komandorski Islands."

"What?" Slowly Burkhart's mouth dropped open. An expression of utter shock and surprise spread across his face.

"Look, Charley, I know it's a jolt."

"Good Christ! A jolt! You might say that. When I was shaving this morning, it wasn't exactly what I had in mind."

"You're the best damned line skipper around. You've taken *Skate* and brought her back from a mailboat to sub of the line."

He squinted at Niven. "I'm proud of my boat, but she's unreliable. She's worn out, Jake. Skate's a cement mixer. You can hear her coming a hundred miles away. An ocean away, for Chrissakes! What you're asking is to pit her and the lives of a hundred people against the Soviet Navy's finest."

Burkhart paused, thinking about Niven's request. Or was it an order? "Why *Skate*, Jake? There have to be a hundred boats better equipped for your work." He felt his neck go stiff.

"*Skate*'s the last of her kind. Her surface similarities to a Foxtrot are striking and their tonnages are close. Both have guppy-shaped hulls and your auxiliary diesel to match her full diesel power."

"Go on, Jake." Burkhart's eyes narrowed. "Why do you want to rendezvous with *Minsk* and her battle group, if that's even possible to do?"

"Incredible as it seems, we are planning to put a boarding party into *Minsk* to steal that ring switch."

11

"A boarding party! Jesus!" Burkhart stared at them in disbelief as the color drained from his face. "The Spook Shack, Russian satellite warnings, and now a boarding party with *Skate* and a Soviet carrier. I'm glad I don't have a weak heart." He smiled thinly. "You guys don't screw around! You go right for the throat."

"Well, how does it sit with you, Commander?" Langor looked anxiously at Niven.

"Do you really know what you're saying. The impossibility of it all. But Good Christ, a battle star for my old *Skate*. That could warm me on cold nights." He was thinking about it as he talked. "Her first battle star. My first battle star." Then his face turned bleak.

"What the hell am I saying."

Niven and Langor were silent, letting Burkhart bleed his doubts.

"Go on, Charley."

"Look, Jake boy. You can't sit here in a warm, well-lighted compartment and tell me, very matter of factly, that we can dress my old beaten-down *Skate* as a Russian vodka tramp, hoist their ensign, drive north for ten days eluding Soviet sky spies in a major Bering choke point. Then to add insult to injury, you want us to waltz up to *Minsk*, raise the Skull and Crossbones, and jump aboard with cutlesses glinting in the morning sun."

"That is precisely what I am saying, Charley."

"We've know each other for years, Jake. You know that I'm an eternal optimist, if I believe in something. To command *Skate*, I've had to be. Under the right conditions, anything is possible."

"Even this?"

"Show me, for Chrissakes! The Russians will blow us out of the water before we get within fifty miles of their secret test area. Then you want to park alongside and steal their royal jewels. You're a clever bastard, Jake, but no one is that clever, not even you."

"In the past Soviet defenses have proven to be slow to react on the first go-around. I know they'll be damned tough, I'm counting on it. I wouldn't dare minimize what we are facing, but their defenses aren't geared for a hijacking at sea, especially in the cold and fog of the Bering Sea. It took their air defenses eight hours to react to that Korean 747 airliner before they could find it and shoot it down, and it flew right over Petropavlovsk."

"Go on, Jake." Burkhart rubbed the back of his neck.

"In the last two months, I've done nothing but study their naval defensive setups, screens, capabilities, and their reaction times. And, by God, there is an escape window once we get what we've come for."

"Any plan like this breaks down when action starts. I know. Jake, boy, this isn't a shuttle shoot from the Cape, with Howdy Doody as command pilot. This is going to be a dirty business with the gods smiling down on us every step of the way, to make it back alive. We're gonna have to go out there and tickle the dragon's tail, flying by the seat of our pants, dammit!"

Niven glanced over at Langor. "If we don't get that hunk of micro chips out of *Minsk* so our people can build their own mousetrap, we might end up standing in a Russian soup line." The admiral's head flushed pink. "I know it sounds dramatic but—"

"Admiral, this mission is just not passive photo taking, it's an act of war, clear and simple. Yes? Since I am on the verge of being selected, or should I say seduced as your bus driver, I'd like an answer. The glare of klieg lights at a press conference in Moscow with my head and the heads of my crew on the block doesn't sit well in my gut."

Admiral Langor suddenly jumped to his feet. "It doesn't sit well in my gut what their beam weapon will do to our missiles, satellites, and upcoming space stations." He was angry.

Niven rolled his eyes. Langor was about to close him. You didn't get smart-assed with admirals and rate promotion.

"With all due respect, sir, your anger doesn't solve my problem of keeping *Skate* and my crew alive. Our butts are tableside."

Burkhart pushed out a breath and forged ahead. That's what Niven liked about him. Once he was on your team he would never quit. "Why don't you slip someone into the damn place where the, ah, ring switch is manufactured and steal one? It would be a hella'va lot easier."

"We've considered every option, Charley." Jake rubbed his burned leg. "The assembly takes place outside Moscow, at a place called Troitsk, where the Kurchatov Institute of Physics is housed. The place is airtight. The odds are improbable at sea. At the factory, the odds are impossible. If the Russians ever got wind that we wanted that ring switch, we'd never get near it." Jake held up his hands, balancing an unanswerable question. "Anyway, we go. It's a one-shot deal."

"A damn Trojan horse." Burkhart's face sagged. "The carrier *Minsk*, especially with all that secret test equipment aboard, including your beam gun, is way out there someplace on the back forty. Possibly beyond our reach."

"If the Soviets believe it, we're halfway home. Critical situations call for critical methods." Langor reached for a glass of water.

"Maybe this can be pulled off," Burkhart said evenly. Niven saw the shape of Burkhart's eyes change. "Admiral, I have to be certain of something."

Langor gave him his smile and raised a hand.

"Are you telling me that the United States is willing to risk the lives of one hundred men and the sinking, or worse, the capture of *Skate* and her crew, to steal that damned switch?"

Langor's smile was gone. "If you knew, Commander, that your submarine was about to be captured, what would you do?"

Burkhart looked from man to man, filling the silence. Finally he answered. "I'd pull the plug and take her down." His voice was barely audible.

"Of course you would, Commander."

"What about daily fleet recognition codes? Without those, we'd be dead before we started. We can't bullshit our way within a hundred miles of our objective without those codes. No codes and they'd blow our asses right out of the water."

"Commander, Niven will brief you with all the details." His smile was brilliant as he rose and walked to the compartment hatch. The hatch opened, then Langor stopped and turned. "Welcome aboard, Commander. Niven was right. You are the only man for

80

this job." Then he was gone and the hatch slammed shut with a hollow thud.

Burkhart turned to Niven. "I haven't heard from you in years. Then this." He swept a beefy arm around the compartment. "You bastard. I ought to break your damn neck!"

"I know." Jake looked away.

"We were good friends. Friends care, dammit! You just dropped off the earth. I'd heard about the divorce. I can't say I was sorry about that silk fartsack. The bitch with the bucks. The last time I saw you was just after they flew you in from the Mekong Delta to the burn ward at Zama with half your leg torn up."

"I don't remember." Niven was surprised.

"You wouldn't. They had you in a drug stupor. I understand it was pretty rough when Charlie blew your Swift Boat from under you."

"It wasn't too bad." Niven's voice came from a long way away.

"Not what I heard. They don't give the Navy Cross for sitting on your butt. Heard you pulled your crew out of the water before you passed out."

Niven shrugged. "Long time ago. I don't remember much. Just pieces and patches with lots of blur in between."

"How's your daughter, Jake?"

Niven smiled. "Just great. See her twice a year during vacations."

"Anybody in your life worth mentioning?"

"A very neat lady lawyer, Charley. We'll have dinner in the next couple of days. I want you to meet her. She's almost made me into a human again." Niven looked at Burkhart's large face. "Enough about me. Tell me about Betty and the kids. Jesus, I'll bet they're almost grown now."

"Almost. My last assignment before *Skate* was XO

in *Archerfish*. Her home is Fort Lauderdale. We just decided to plant roots there. Keep the kids in one school, friends. A life after I retire." He smiled. "It was really for Betty. After all the years of bouncing around the world, it was time."

"Can we get back to business for a minute?"

"Damn right. Jake the spook. I'll be damned."

"Sorry about the shock of all this, Charley. No other way." Jake shrugged. "For the record, after today *Skate* will no longer exist. She's to be struck from the List. Documented records are being drawn up now that will show her cut up for scrap within the next month."

Burkhart looked bleak. He had formed a strange attachment to *Skate* and one way or the other this cruise into the Bering Sea would be her last.

"Cheer up, Charley. If we make it out of this alive, you'll have your first star within the next ten years and in the meantime, the finest attack boat will be yours." Niven put a hand on his shoulder. "If we pull this off, your career will be clear sailing right to the top of the list."

"If we make it."

Niven slapped the sides of his legs. "We don't have a choice, even with Langor's war hysteria aside."

"I don't follow you."

"The word from upstairs. I mean from way upstairs, from all those good 'ole boys, is 'get that Switch.' "

Niven took a small yellow folded paper from inside his jacket. "Here's a NODIS cable we received less than a hour ago."

"What the hell's a NODIS?"

"The highest priority level message we have. NODIS means no distribution outside the Secretariat. For the eyes of the President, Secretary of Defense,

Chief of Naval Operations, and my beloved Admiral Brandon Langor, to name but a few.''

Burkhart nodded and read the message. ''Who the hell are Dwarfs and Snow White?

''Snow White is code name for *Minsk* and Dwarf is the code for her support ships. The Russians are on their way to set up and secure the test site in the Komandorski Islands.''

Burkhart rubbed his face and handed back the message. ''Seems our little drama has already begun to unfold.''

Niven moved his mouth in what could have passed for a smile and thought about London. He didn't take his eyes from Burkhart, but the old gut-wrenching fear boiled up into his throat as a dry knot.

Ghosts from the past. Not a history or even a dim memory, just goddamn ghosts. Niven turned for a moment, then looked at Charley Burkhart, still digesting his own fear and dismay, and shuddered. He swore Vasili Lykov was staring at him, with that pleading, questioning look in his intense blue eyes. The shock almost knocked Niven off his feet.

The red MG-TD labored up the last hill toward Del Mar Heights Road. The classic roadster turned off and pointed her blunt chrome nose down toward the beach as Niven moved easily through the light gears, down shifting deftly as the grade steepened.

''Jake?'' Ellie Mallori turned her head to avoid the breeze coming over and around the narrow windscreen, but it was impossible.

''Jake, where are you going?'' She stared at his intense face as his feet and right hand worked as an extension of the car, using brakes, clutch, and gears to maneuver through the S curves of the narrow beach road. Actually Jake was quite good at it, Ellie thought. Again she asked the question in a much louder voice to make herself heard above the whine of the engine.

Niven turned and cocked his head in a curious way. For a moment he considered her as he turned back to watch the road. "Who said I was leaving?"

Before she could answer the MG pulled into a very private dirt road that quickly led to a secluded stand of pine trees bordered with brilliant thickets of red, yellow, and purple wildflowers. Silently Niven motioned her from the car and, hand in hand, they wound through the trees. There wasn't a sound except for the late-afternoon breeze rushing through the pines and the distant crash of surf. Suddenly the trees gave way to a small meadow that edged to a sandstone cliff overlooking the Pacific.

Ellie looked about at the trees to her back and the ocean below that gave them complete privacy. The effect was awesome. "Jake, it's magnificent!" She brushed her lips against his warm cheek. "It's the most charming place I've ever seen." She looked at Jake and her eyes were filled with affection and warmth.

"I found it a couple of years ago, when I was very much alone."

Ellie reached down and pulled off her heels and then stripped off her severely tailored navy suit top. Niven watched her stretch in the warmth, pushing hard against her cream-colored silk blouse.

"You never answered my question, Jacob." Her voice became serious.

"What would lawyers do without questions to ask?" Niven shook his head.

"It's called caring. I hope you're not confusing the size of my breasts with my brain. Did I overestimate you?"

"I didn't bring you here to ask questions. Stop directing traffic." He smiled and brushed his hand lightly over her face.

Ellie's flashing dark eyes scanned him. "You bastard," she whispered. "I'm your lover, not your property."

"I've got a quick trip planned for London, early tomorrow. No big deal. Nothing heavy, I promise. Just some official paperwork that has to be cleaned up."

"I've eaten better liars for lunch, shadow man."

Niven turned her head with a strong hand. "Who told you?" His voice grew serious.

"I know you, Jake. I've just learned to know you." Tears filled her eyes.

"Maybe I give off an odor. A travel musk."

"You stupid man. You telegraph everything you do."

Niven pulled back. "How?"

Ellie shrugged. "I love you, Jake. Italian women always take care of their men. It's just an instinct I inherited from my grandmother. The old women could sense danger when their men went to sea. They could see it coming."

"And me?"

"You're always close to trouble." She tried to laugh. "But I accept it." She reached up and buried her tongue in his mouth. "I think it's time for a little afternoon sun on my behind, Jake. How about you?" She moaned from inside her throat. "Let's see how long it takes for me to distract you." She laughed again and moved toward him, trying desperately to hide her own terrible fear.

"Things are simply what they are," Niven whispered.

"I know. I know," she responded, reaching for, and craving, his warmth.

12

The six-year-old Rover swayed like a wounded elephant as Niven rounded a very sharp curve with too much speed. Old English country lanes, especially in Dorset, were built for horse-drawn carts, not cars. The sturdy Rover's tanklike qualities didn't add to its keeping abilities. Luckily the spring weather was holding in southern England as Niven rolled down the window to examine the tiny white direction sign.

WOOL 6 K

Niven nodded with satisfaction. Clear weather and he didn't have to be in London until that evening. With only a hundred forty kilometers to London he had time. Things were working out better than he had hoped. The flight from the States had allowed him a restless sleep, but the Rover had been waiting at the abandoned RAF air station near Moreton. For once there hadn't been a screw up with MI 6. He looked down on the left-hand seat to make certain the Tokarev semiautomatic was in position. He leaned over and pulled the eight shot clip of shells from the butt of the weapon. The brass shells gleamed in the morning light.

The magazine was full so Niven rammed it back into the Tokarev's handle. His left hand moved quickly, jerking back the steel slide stop, forcing a hollow-nosed round into the firing chamber. Niven reached inside his black nylon tanker jacket and pulled a four-inch silencer from his worn shoulder holster.

After the usual administrative squabbling about using a Soviet weapon, special weapons section of the Task Force had finally threaded the inside of the barrel to take the American-made Siconic silencer.

For a moment Niven stared down at the gun. His eyes moved to the engraved Cyrillic initials, just above the steel-ribbed handle. Vasili Lykov's initials. A vague gift from Lykov after the incident in Kabul. A joint venture inside Pul-e-charki Prison, then the ambush with a *mujahidin* rebel in a closed alley of the Shorbazaar. Niven's Browning had jammed, so he killed the rebel with a sharp rock. How many years ago had that been? Five, six years. The sound of a honking car horn behind him woke Niven from his past.

Quickly he placed the gun on the left seat, as carefully as if it were a newborn child, waved out the window, and pulled the Rover off the narrow road into a low hedge. He took the road map off the dash and checked his location. He was heading in a southeasterly direction toward the village of Wool, where he could pick up the main road to Wareham, then turn due south. He checked his watch. Good. The land would begin its rise into the chalk hills of Purbeck, finally giving way to the English Channel at Alban's Head.

Staying off the main roads wherever possible was necessary, to avoid notice and trouble. Niven knew it would come, but why invite it. Tonight, London would be perilous enough. Vasili Lykov's murder had to be answered.

In an hour he had crossed the River Frome, veered

south, and had turned under the main highway, staying to the back roads into the hamlet of Creech. Twenty-five minutes later he drove slowly through the tiny village of Corfe Castle. Niven parked the car off the little road, down in a thickly wooded combe of oak. He holstered the pistol and opened the trunk, carefully removing a tool bag, shovel, and a pair of overalls. In a moment he was walking down the road in the shadow of the ruins of Corfe Castle, squatting on a grassy hill above the slate-roofed houses and cottages. Corfe, built by the Normans and besieged by Cromwell during the Civil War, was now only a rock skeleton.

Niven shifted the tool bag to his left shoulder and made for a narrow dirt path just beyond a mellowed stone cottage with a raised slate porch. Nothing had changed.

"Morning, lad. Which you be do'in here abouts?"

Startled, Niven turned too quickly and almost fell. The old Welshman had materialized out of thin air with his lyrical accent.

"Good day, Guv," Niven tried in his worst London voice. "The bloomin' brass hats 'ave run me a real turn for a damn fortnight."

The old man pointed with his cane to the back of Niven's coveralls. "What would the power blokes want in these damn woods?"

"Dorset Power sees to its own. The dumb twits at the quarry down the road 'ave been drainin' our main transformer for months. We 'ave a main relay box stowed in the muck and I'm to check it." He watched the old Welshman's eyes take him in and slowly nod. Slowly Niven relaxed his fist.

"Well, have a go at it, old chip." Slowly the old man scratched his blotched face and pointed his cane at the cottage. "Just pop it out and do a proper job. Couldn't do without the electrical juice. Nothin' else to do in the bloody place but watch the telly, slurp the cider, and flush the loo."

"I'll 'ave a go at it."

"Well, there you are, then, old son."

Niven took a deep breath and half bowed. The old man limped slowly toward his cottage and Niven continued down the narrow dirt path another hundred yards until it turned into a series of stone steps.

" 'Ere we are, lad," Niven mumbled aloud to himself. "The old Roman monk steps, just like at Kewstoke. And I was worried about someone finding my place." Christ, he thought, half a brain and you're a menace. His mind flashed on Ellie and he smiled.

"Okay, doggie, time to dig up your bone." He laughed grimly and pulled the shovel from his kit bag. Then Niven counted until reaching the fourth step. In a moment he pulled up the loose flat slate stone and began to dig.

"Steps have been here a thousand years, put down here by Roman legions, and you think someone's going to level the place and build a shopping center. Some master of the black arts you are." He laughed again, to burn off his growing tension, just as the point of the shovel struck a solid object. A bit of doing and a black metal case wrapped in thick plastic was pulled from the hole.

Cautiously, he rose and swept his eyes around the dense growth and forestland, searching for any threat, shaking off a lethal feeling in his stomach.

Carefully he flipped the latch and found what he had placed in the hole eighteen months before. Wrapped in plastic and an oil cloth, Niven picked up a little Welrod automatic pistol, developed by British Special Operations at Welwyn Gardens during World War Two for work behind enemy lines. A mean little weapon, with the silencer built right into the barrel. The six-shot clip of 9mm short, acted as the gun handle. His dog hole had served him well.

Niven pulled another plastic packet from the box and unwrapped a roll of masking tape. He then proceeded to tape the automatic to the skin of his right calf. Next came an English passport and driver's license as well as a roll of pound notes and a bag of coins. All that remained in the metal box were two concussion grenades, and those Niven placed in his pocket. He reread the passport and his English name. Anthony Pepper; Hawker-Siddeley Aviation.

"Let the bastards come," Niven grunted. He wished he could have dragged Admiral Langor along to feel that special spinal chill racing down Niven's back at that moment. London needs you. Isn't that what the bastard said. Well, Vasili, maybe you'll get me yet. Then Niven stiffened. Silently he moved back up the path to the Rover, planning his next move as he walked. He would idle his way to London, a hundred miles to the northeast, chewing up most of the afternoon on backcountry roads. He would double-check himself in Winchester, from atop St. Giles Hill, where he could survey the country below and watch for any telltale signs of a shadow. If his stomach was quiet long enough, he would drive through Avington, a small village where the River Itchen fanned into a pond choked with trout. They were always boiling and the sight of a trout taking an insect on the surface of a protected lake brought something warm to his gut.

When night came in London, he would need that extra resource of calm to see him through. From Avington, it was a short run to the M3 and a straight haul into the London night. There was always an ugly dignity about working nights.

*   *   *

Cautiously, Jake emerged from Choy's Chinese Restaurant, into the chilled black evening of London's Soho. Instantly his eyes surveyed the foot and auto traffic on Frith Street as he completed a slow arc. Every shadow or building corner of the major thoroughfare could be trouble. Idly he reached into his jacket to replace his wallet, and his hand came to rest on the worn leather shoulder holster. Jake swallowed, trying to shove down the taste of roast Paul Pang duck and fear as he moved out of the light funneling from Choy's shabby neon sign.

Quickly he stepped into one of the few remaining red phone boxes, unscrewed the ceiling light to make himself less of a blind beacon, and then pulled a small penlight from his jacket pocket. A loud scraping noise forced his body to the sound as the grenades in his jacket banged with a clank into the ledge holding the phone. He reached for a coin and felt his hands shake for the first time. It had started. All for a damned painting, a Russian sea captain, and a bird nest of wires and circuits! He felt weak in his knees.

He dropped a twenty pence coin into the box and dialed the number. A female voice, actually rather pleasant, answered on the first ring.

"Go right ahead," the telephone voice coaxed.

"Mollie for Greenwich." Then Niven gave her the box number and time, then slammed down the receiver. Less than a minute later the phone rang back.

"The parson is tucked in," an old, distant male voice said.

"Good." Niven replaced the receiver breaking the connection. His contact was made. He was a hot target in the midst of Moscow West—London.

Niven stepped from the booth, squinting into the darkened street, with Choy's blinking sign behind him. He was quickly reacquainting himself with the city's

West End. He couldn't stay long in any one spot. He looked down and checked his watch. 7:10 P.M. Quickly he ended a small inner debate and decided to drive instead of taking the Underground east from Tottenham Court to Farringdon Station. He took off at a fast walk, aware of his immediate surroundings, although at night it was damned tough to pick up signs of a tail.

Niven turned right at the corner and found his Rover on Bateman Street, climbed in, and turned over the engine. The time for concentration was now. Staying alive with no wondering thoughts. No flashbacks to Ellie. Just pure energy to heighten every sense.

Niven swung the Rover into light traffic and then, without signaling, turned right into Greek Street, passing the London Casino Cinema, where a crowd was milling about. For the moment he allowed himself to accept the fact he wasn't being followed. At Romilly Street he turned right again into heavy traffic and pulled up to the curb in sight of the Tuscan Hotel. The headlamps were turned off but Niven kept the engine running. Then he waited.

A car slowed and glided past the Rover, the driver seeming to take more than a passing interest. Niven gripped the handle of the Tokarev. In a moment the car was gone, but he felt his whole body quiver. He held out his trembling hands, pushing out a labored breath, as he broke out in a cold sweat. Suddenly his nose was dripping profusely and he could feel the moisture matting his black hair as another vision of Vasili Lykov floated before his closed eyes.

"It's open season on Jake Niven," he croaked aloud, forcing himself to laugh. He swallowed again and the muscles in his belly began to relax. In another moment the fear had passed and Niven wiped the sweat from his nose as he turned on the Rover's headlamps and swung the car south into Dean Street. He used the discomfort of his clammy body to create a razor edge as he pumped himself.

Niven accelerated smoothly, then turned left without signaling into busy Shaftesbury Avenue, pointing the car east toward Smithfield's Central Markets. Somewhere between High Holborn Road and Holborn Viaduct he regained his steely composure with a cold, sardonic smile.

"You're a goddamn neurotic bastard who talks to himself," Niven said aloud. "Who wouldn't talk to himself under these conditions," he mumbled as he slid the Rover left into Farringdon Street, used first as an open marketplace under the Roman occupation two thousand years before. But tonight the street was empty of traffic and people.

He had to have faith. Faith that his London man wouldn't leak their drop point to Lykov's friends. Faith in his own ability to shake any interested shadows and the prayer that Langor's group was airtight. Niven shook his head on that last thought as he crawled on Farringdon, past the western end of Smithfield's Central Markets, scanning the shadows of the domed towers and dimly lighted stone-and-brick structures covering eight acres, as he continued to drive north.

He knew it was coming—he just didn't know when. All his instincts told him that Moscow knew he was in London. His equals on Moscow Ring Road were duty-bound to have a run at him. Well, better here, Niven reasoned, than somewhere in the Bering Sea.

The Central Markets, rebuilt for the last time in 1868, smelled of quick death from the moving Rover, but he still felt obligated by his experience to peer into the black holes enveloping the Tudor and Jacobean buildings, looking for the quick dull glint of a gun barrel, or a sudden movement in the shadows. The task was impossible.

Jake felt his way along the street by instinct and the edge in his belly, as if he were blind. The Rover was his fingertips, feeling the texture and smell of the cold bricks, mortar, and stones as he moved, trying to avoid the terrible consequences that night often held. A thumping staccato of silenced, deadly accurate machine pistol fire, directed from a starscope, could come from any crack in that shabby blackness.

Jake passed Farringdon Station on his right, then wheeled the Rover into an abrupt, tire-squealing, U-turn, and doubled back at speed, as the sedate Rover groaned in protest along the deserted roadway. Almost by feel, and a great knowledge of London, Niven found Snow Hill Court, swung left into a labyrinth of tiny dark alley streets, eventually emerging in front of Saint Bartholomew's Hospital. Then it was just a short turn from Little Britain Road into tiny Cloth Fair Street and the brooding presence of his target, the massive Norman church at Number 10 Cloth Fair.

Jake guided the tanklike Rover into a shadowed alley behind the church and quickly stepped from the car with the Tokarev in his right hand, his forefinger barely brushing the trigger.

13

Widening his sensitive eyes in response to the dim glow, Jake crouched his body down into the back of an ancient brown oak pew and listened to his heart pounding in his neck. He glanced down the cavernous nave and up toward the towering Norman stone chancel wall behind the altar, completed in 1139 during the reign of Henry I. The place smelled musty and heavy with a sweet English mildew. Carefully, his eyes scanned the columns built into the chancel, looking for any sign of shadow movement or the dull glint of steel.

He swallowed and his breathing narrowed down to the undulating hairs in his nose. To the right of the altar, Niven's eyes picked up a vague shadow moving without sound, next to a large stone baptismal font. He tensed his grip on the Tokarev, raising the gun to his chest, gauging the distance at forty feet. A soft cough floated down from the altar.

''Jake! Jake Niven, I know you're down there somewhere in the pews, ready to blow my head off. Put your gun back in your kit.'' The rich Oxford-accented voice laughed nervously. Jake rolled himself into the aisle, pointing the semiautomatic at the voice.

''Holy Christ, Niven, I'm not the GRU!'' The voice

begged. "It's Crabb, for God's sakes." The whine echoed in small, feeble droplets against the damp stone walls. Then the voice turned happy. "Oh really, Jake, this is a most improper time for high drama."

Silently Jake rose to a low crouch and leveled the Tokarev at the center of the noise. Only his hands were rock steady as he duck walked two steps closer. "Step out into the light of the altar so I can see if you're really Crabb. Now move your ass!"

"Please relax, Jacob. Don't you recognize my voice? Ah, the code. The code. Greenwich, you're Mollie!"

"Fuck your voice! Step out or I shoot."

"I'm stepping now." The voice wavered and suddenly there was an old man attached to it forty feet away. A crop of full white hair smiled down at Jake, with improperly fitted false teeth. "I'm too old for this sort of thing. My pumper might stop next time."

Jake talked through the banter. "Hold up the swordstick."

The man held up an old cherry wood walking stick crowned with a large silver crab. Jake then pivoted slowly on his axis, to be as certain they were alone.

"Where's the rector?"

The old man smiled. "He's tucked away in bed like always. A few quid in the box always helps." Former Royal Navy Reserve Commander Lionel Crabb held out a shriveled hand. "My, you do have quite an edge about you." He smiled against Jake. "I truly understand your concerns since the Russians are all about London."

Jake unscrewed the silencer and holstered the Tokarev, waving Crabb into a pew. For the first time he relaxed and expelled a long breath of relief. "You damn bastard. You know I have no desire to be here."

"I can understand it. You're a very hot item in Queen Anne's Gate and Moscow since the Lykov affair." There was fatigue in Crabb's voice. "But business is business, laddy."

"Well, I'm here, dammit! You asked for me. Screamed your head off all the way to San Diego, for Chrissakes!" Niven was angry. Crabb was maneuvering, waiting for Niven to spill some tasty morsel of information. Information was Crabb's prime industry.

"Does Moscow know about my upcoming party?

"Before I answer, Captain Belous wants to know if you have the Da Vinci in your possession?"

Niven felt his hands reaching for Crabb's neck, then he stopped himself. "You wear self-interest like a fucking shield, Crabb."

"I am sorry, Jacob. These are tense times." He smiled at his old friend. "I don't trust any of those bastards but you." His mouth parted in a crooked smile.

Niven nodded and felt his pulse pounding in his neck. "Yes, Crabby, I have the painting."

Crabb waved a hand. "Excellent. Captain Belous is fixated on that damned item. He's flexible on most items, except the painting." He eyed Niven. "You know, his wife and all."

"What about our party?"

"I wish I could give you the straight of it, but I cannot." He drew a deep sickly breath.

"Jesus!"

"Lykov's impending arrest, if he had lived, could have easily involved you, but I just can't be certain. No one can, Jacob."

Niven slumped back in the oak pew as a black wave washed over his face.

"It's not over, Jacob, not at all. "It just makes your journey more of a dice toss. When the KGB was shadowing Lykov, did they stumble across your little operation? Crabb shook his prune-shaped head in the dim church light.

"I don't really have an option, Crabby. The party is a go and—"

"Am I invited?" The cold barrel of a Webley .38 revolver pushed painfully into Niven's temple.

Niven started to turn his body. "Not another inch, you ruddy bastard. I've chased your bloody ass all over the countryside."

The voice. Jesus, it was so familiar. "Do I know you?"

"No, but I know you. You're very famous in certain Eastern circles, you bloody fool."

Bloody. Bloody! That was it. The old man from this morning, poking around his Monk Steps dog hole. Damn! Why didn't I see it. He just came out of nowhere.

"What the hell do you want?"

"Want? I want your last heartbeat, you murdering bastard. Now, hand over the gun in your shoulder holster. Ah, do it with your left hand, very easy and slow."

Niven awkwardly reached over his left breast with his left hand and pulled out the Tokarev. The voice dropped the gun barrel into his right ear.

"Ah, do it slowly. No little problems here."

"Let the old man go."

"Let Lionel Crabb go! By the Queen's justice, my friends in Moscow will pay me a ransom for this double elimination. Now you listen to me, you bastard. You think I'm ruddy daft?"

Niven could barely think. All he could do was smell the gun oil. The white phosphorus grenade in 'Nam blowing his boat out of the water. Ellie!

"What's all the noise out there?" It was the church rector, awakened by the voices. The gun barrel dropped slightly at the unexpected noise and Niven

98

tumbled from the pew, reaching behind him for the barrel. He missed and the loud crack of a shot exploded almost in his face as he lay on the stone floor. A stabbing pain bolted through his face and then he felt something warm and sticky running into his mouth.

Niven rolled under the pew in front and another shot cracked into the thick oak just above his head. Struggling, he reached under his pant cuff, straining to reach the little automatic taped to his leg. He rolled again under another pew.

"Give it up, you bastard," the voice echoed off the Norman walls. "Give it up and we'll make a bargain."

Niven rolled like a drunk tied in a potato sack, struggling for leverage. Slowly his hand found the band of tape on his leg and he ripped the Welrod free.

"I'm going to stand, don't shoot," Niven yelled out.

"That's a good, smart lad."

In the dim light, the killer would have to shoot at a dark outline, nothing more. Niven crouched, his heart pounding in the back of his mouth. He pulled a grenade from his pocket with his left hand.

"Here's a present for your future." With cat quickness Niven rolled the grenade under the pews toward the killer. "A little grenade for your trouble. Just perfect to blow off your balls."

The old man screamed and rose into the dim light. It was all Niven needed as he fired, hitting the man in the right side, spinning him around. Niven fired again at the groaning, gurgling sound. This time the 9 mm bullet smashed into his back, severing his spine. He was dead before his body fell over the pew and hit the floor with a thud.

"You okay, Crabby? Crabby?" Niven tasted the damp fear.

"I am alive, but just barely."

Niven was on his feet and quickly at Crabb's side.

"Try to relax. I never pulled the pull on the grenade. I had—"

"You said it was a very proper meeting."

Jesus! The rector. The man who'd saved their lives.

"I'll take care of it, Jacob." With difficulty Lionel Crabb met the rector before he could approach. In a moment he staggered back. "Scared the man to death. Babbling about shooting off fireworks in a house of God. I promised him another generous donation for his poor box."

"What about the body?" Niven looked in the direction of the chancel opening, but the rector had retired back to bed.

"I'll call my people straight on. Then we'll notify Home Office. It will have to be done most quickly. I don't want the Yard or the local London types involved. It would get rather sticky for us all." Crabb sank to his knees in a nearby pew.

"God, I thought when I heard that grenade bounce toward me, it was over. Something about those sticky bombs."

Niven had been going through the dead man's pockets while Crabb talked. "Nothing here, Crabb. Not a goddamn thing. The bastard must have been on to me the minute I landed."

"Really?" Crabb sounded very surprised.

"He fingered me at a little stopoff that I made in Dorset this morning. What a perfect cover. A damn senile old man drinking his rotten cider in the woods."

"You may be slowing down a bit, Jacob, but your shooting was spot on. Now, let's hurry."

"First, find out where this bastard came from."

"Local talent. Nothing more. The KGB didn't want to dirty their hands. Sending an old man, just like me, to do the work of a lad. Looks to me like someone wanted you dead, but had mixed feelings about it."

He stared into Niven's eyes in the dim light. "They'll try again, make no mistake about it."

"Just find out who he is and where he came from." Niven wiped his head. He was sweating profusely. By accident, he touched his cheek and winced.

"Nasty little cut there, Jacob."

"Piece of stone from his first shot. Now let's get on with the agenda, you old dried-out frogman. I'm jumpy as hell."

Crabb looked down at the crumpled form lying next to them. "You've good reason to be jumpy, lad. I wonder how far this all goes?"

"When I put my feet aboard that Russian carrier, I'll find out. Now get on with it." His voice dissolved into a snarl. "What about that blind spot? What about that Cosmos in August?"

"I told Langor on the scrambler two days ago it was done. Sealed tightly with my people at Plesetsk."

"Tell me, so I can watch your eyes."

Crabb waved a bony, pencil thin arm inside a loose-fitting green knit sweater. A nervous tic dominated his gaunt face.

"You have your blind spot. My employees are very reliable. Cosmos 2118 is scheduled to go into orbit the second week in July and to be routinely brought down on 21 August, to be replaced the same day by the next number in the Cosmos series. Each of these Cosmos carries two fuel cells for their power source. My people will tamper just enough with the fuel cells' cryogenic propellants so that round about 14 August, Cosmos 2118 will experience a power failure and go dead. If that becomes a problem, we'll muck up the film capsule ejector system. It is not an unusual occurrence. It happens often on both sides. Mechanical failure."

"We're paying a damn fortune for this, Crabby." Jake smiled wistfully. "Of course, there's not a thing

I can do about it, if your people fail to kill that Cosmos, is there? I'll be dead or out of reach, compliments of the Soviet General Staff." Niven steadied his gaze on Crabb, then laughed.

"Something funny, laddy?"

"Yeah. I've got to trust you. Trust isn't part of this business."

A bony finger rubbed at Crabb's frail nose. "Just make certain your arse is gone by the time that new Cosmos pops up, or that will be that. And that's the straight of it, lad."

Jake grunted. "The question is, can you really reach that far into the Soviet system and how reliable your employees are at Plesetsk?"

"They've done numerous jobs for me in the past. And yes, I can reach that far." Crabb raised his hands. "I can reach as far as I want. It reads well on paper—" He raised an eyebrow.

"Now, my payment voucher, Jacob?"

Niven reached into his pants pocket and pulled a folded brown envelope. "As per your request, we have purchased one million dollars, American, in industrial diamonds. They are now in your account, or at least will be, when I return to the States." Niven smiled darkly. "Of course, your account is here at DeBeers, under your company name of Belgian Lion."

Crabb tore open the envelope and studied the single sheet with difficulty in the dimness. After a time he nodded approval.

"Not bad for a freelancer with contacts, ah, Crabby?"

"They don't put people like us into old age homes." There was fire in his old eyes as he shoved a delicate finger into Niven's shoulder. "Eventually they just flush us down the loo." His gun-metal gray skin flushed red. "In the meantime there is still life in these old bones, so I do what I can."

Niven sat heavily in a pew. "I understand.

"Don't ever forget. The British have short memories, but the Americans are the worst for taking care of their own. Horrible types. We are nonpeople, Jacob. When the time is ripe and we prove to be embarrassing, it is very easy to get rid of nonpeople. Just make them keep needing you."

"How have you kept it going all these years, Crabby?"

"Art, lad. Pure art. I went under and became a nonhuman while examining the Soviet cruiser *Ordzhonikidze.*"

"When?"

"Back in fifty-six. For a long time my life as a double, especially in Moscow, was fruitful, but after a time both sides wanted to bury me. Eventually everyone falls from the tightrope. Only my constant flow of information to both sides kept me alive." He held up his hands philosophically.

"Well you sure as hell hit it big this time. A real Oscar-winning performance."

"I just became very fortunate on this one, Jake. Viktor Belous, our Russian captain, happened to be a contact I cultivated three years ago at the Soviet Embassy. He paid more attention to me than I ever did to him, then this once in a lifetime opportunity dropped into our laps. This is the first really large amount I have ever made, but I've got to watch out for myself," Crabb said defensively.

"You manage quite well. Now before I get the hell out of London, tell me about this Russian Captain Belous."

"Description, history—"

"Nice try, Crabby. You've the quick skills of a

badger. Aside from our dead friend here, will Belous still be ready for his ride West in August? As ready as he is now?''

Crabb looked at him with understanding and compassion. "Yes now, but in August, who knows. A number of years ago a double operative by the name of Anatoly Filatov, living in Moscow, used to pass me vital information at a dead drop near the Kostomarovsky Embankment on the Yauza River. At his request I made exhaustive arrangements to bring him out and at our last meeting, knowing full well a firing squad was close, he changed his mind and wished to die like a Soviet patriot. But because of your needs, you must take the risk with Kapitan Belous. They're all daft bastards.''

Jake nodded. "Let's just hope his hurt, anger, and loneliness are still strong enough in August.''

"It will be a grand show, regardless. Wish I could ride along. Too damn old.'' Crabb mashed his dentures together in a growl.

Crabb's voice died away and only the dripping of water somewhere in the church punctured the silence. "You are a very fortunate bugger, Jake.'' He leaned back and his tired gray eyes took on a faraway look. His thin, yellowish lips parted three or four times without making a sound.

"If you can really do it!''

"Do what?''

"If you can really board that Russian carrier and escape with your prizes. God, I wish I was young enough to go along.''

He turned to Jake and his eyes lightened a shade and his body became animated. "If you can pull it off, it will be the bloody high of five lifetimes. The last high before technology eats us up.''

"How about the bloody fear?" Niven raised his eyebrows.

"Yes, of course, but you know there is another side to it."

Jake nodded. "I know," The corners of his mouth danced slightly. "It's that special rush during a combat firefight that few people ever admit to."

"Precisely."

Niven grew restless and moved his head around the church nave once again, searching the dark, ancient corners for something alien. "I hate to be abrupt, Crabby, but since there is no real reason for me to be here, except to hold your hand, I want to get the hell out."

Jake turned away from the little old man and buttoned his jacket. A viselike grip seized Jake on the forearm, forcing him to turn back to face Crabb's gaunt face. The old man still had tremendous strength in his bony hands and must have been something in his day.

"I'll find out how our friend here was put onto you, laddy. I promise that much. I'll linger here until our problem is removed, then I'll set an appointment with the Polish Consulate in Weymouth street. For a price, the bastards will sing like the Old Beatles. God's speed, you lucky pirate."

14

The May sunset, tinged with a hint of fog, splashed across the bay window on Inverness Drive. Niven reached up and touched the cut on his cheek, watching the Pacific turn from a deep-blue ocean to a milk-pink lagoon. Slowly he sipped from a glass of beer and watched Ellie, lost with her pencil, scrawling across a yellow legal pad. Even in faded jeans and one of his oversized Oxford shirts, Niven enjoyed watching her, the horn-rimmed reading glasses perched on the end of her nose.

"How's it going, Counselor?"

"Hm?" Ellie looked up, her face caught in the glow of the roaring fire from across the room. She looked so pale, with dark circles under her eyes. So childlike and alone. Yet it was an illusion. She was strong and had mental toughness that Niven admired deeply.

"What, Jake?"

"Nothing vital." He shrugged and bent to the fireplace, idly stoking a log.

"You were thinking about that Russian, weren't you?"

"Yes." His eyes grew distant.

"I was thinking, no, daydreaming, Ellie said pa-

106

tiently, "about a life someday beyond this." She pointed with a pencil to his clothes to distract him. "The plaid shirt and jeans. Robert Frost is in your soul. Maybe Anton Chekhov."

Niven smiled at her. There was such a richness within her that was a spirit beneath the skin. A mixture that other women could only admire and hate.

"I know you're good at what you do, Jake. I guess I am thinking of myself. No, thinking of us." Suddenly she looked drawn and tired. "To want a future is a very vulnerable, human feeling and desire, Jake. To grow old together."

What had Lionel Crabb said. "There are no old age homes for us."

"You're a very private man."

"A man reaching out."

She held his eyes. "Yes," Ellie smiled. How swiftly, how decisively he could move. When he tensed, she could see the animal uncoil just enough beneath the surface to make it visible.

For a long time neither spoke. There was just comfort in their closeness as they watched the sky fade into a deep red-orange.

"If you could ever cage that energy enough to become a small-town college lit teacher in worn and smelly tweeds and I could hang my shingle and settle all the back-fence disputes."

"Where did all this come from?"

"Your love for poetry. Don't look at me like I just stepped off the plane from Mars. For God's sakes, you majored in literature at Brown."

"It was almost twenty years ago and it was Russian literature." He didn't have the energy to protest. He couldn't look that far ahead. He needed to harbor whatever strength he had left. He was growing close to letting everything go. He was staring straight ahead at the Bering Sea.

"I just lost you again, didn't I?" Ellie shook her head.

Niven walked back to the window as darkness swept La Jolla Cove with night. The fire popped and Niven turned with a start, then relaxed, suddenly aware of the tenderness of his right calf, where he had torn off a layer of pink skin to save his life.

"Read some poetry to me. Please." She patted a place next to her on the couch. "It's so soothing when you read to me."

In a moment he was beside her, book in hand. For a moment he thumbed the pages, finally settling on a certain page. "I don't need a great deal of encouragement for poetry. My working partner, John Sorrell, is always putting the rib to me about reading poems in the most obscure places." He looked at her sideways.

"Here's a little euphonious poem by English poet Robert Herrick."

"What's euphonious?"

"Smooth and pleasant sounding. Has to do with the construction of vowels and consonants. Not really important."

"What—"

"Quiet. Let me read:

UPON JULIA'S VOICE
So smooth, so sweet, so silv'ry in thy voice,
As, could they hear, the Damned would make no noise,
But listen to thee walking in thy chamber
Melting melodious words to Lutes of Amber.

Ellie dropped her head to Niven's shoulder. "More Mister Niven."

"What about dinner? I'm hungry."

"Just read for your food. I'll tell you when I've had enough."

"An American poet, Richard Hovey, wrote this. One of my favorites."

"Do I know him?"

"Maybe in the last life. He died in 1900."

THE SEA GYPSY

I am fevered with the sunset,
I am fretful with the bay,
For the wander-thirst is on me
And my soul is in Cathay.

There's a schooner in the offing,
With her topsails shot with fire,
And my heart has gone aboard her
For the Islands of Desire.

I must go forth again to-morrow!
With the sunset I must be
Hull down on the trail of rapture
In the wonder of the sea.

Ellie sat up and looked at Niven, her face very still and very serious.

"That your way of telling me something?" There was a hollowness in her voice.

Niven shook his head.

"You have another job coming up soon, don't you, and the damn poem is a subtle way of telling me?"

"That's the dumbest thing I've ever heard." The lie was in his voice and they both knew it. "Please, don't make something out of this." He kissed the tip of her nose. "Let's make dinner."

She nodded and cupped his hand in hers. "I am just scared. I'm not used to it and I don't like it, dammit!"

She wiped the moisture from her eyes. "I don't even know what I'm scared of." Niven slipped a hand around her waist and could feel her energy and warmth. "We talked about this before. It is what it is."

"I know. I just want you back, to be—"

The telephone interrupted. "I'll get it." She moved away from him, happy to leave the conversation.

She held up the phone. "It's for you. John Sorrell."

Niven went to the phone, never taking his eyes from Ellie. "Yeah, Brahma? It must be important."

"Sorry to break in and bother you at home, Jake. The boss sends greetings."

"What?" Niven stiffened.

"Greenwich is dead. Meeting at nineteen thirty hours aboard Mother." Sorrell hung up and Niven found himself staring at the fire listening to the buzzing phone line.

"Jake, what is it? You look awful!"

"Lionel Crabb is dead."

"Sir, there's a civilian named Niven requesting permission to come aboard and see you. Do you know him, sir?"

Burkhart let out a sigh and puffed out a cloud of stinking brown cigar smoke in his tiny stateroom. His small metal desk was neatly stacked with a pile of repair requisitions, decoded fleet messages, called flimsies, and a growing number of crew disciplinary reports that at some point would require Burkhart to fulfill his time-honored duty of meting out punishment at a captain's mast.

"Sir? There's a—"

"I heard you, Mr. Mead." There was resignation in his voice. Since his meeting with Niven and Admiral

110

Langor, Burkhart had been in a thoughtful funk. Regardless of the outcome of their upcoming mission, this was going to be *Skate*'s swan song. Although he had tried to leave her for a better boat—he would miss her. There was a very special place in his heart for the old beaten-up girl. Maybe in part it was the shock of what HAWKSCREECH would be. His toes tingled with excitement but the idea of taking on the Soviet Navy with the old girl was an ice cube bath.

"Have someone topside escort him below to my stateroom." Burkhart reached back over his bunk and hung up the intercom phone on the bulkhead.

For just a split second he thought about putting on a uniform shirt over his sweat stained T-shirt, then changed his mind. "Screw it," he mumbled with the cigar planted firmly in the corner of his mouth.

A few moments later he heard footsteps in the deserted companionway. It was eight-thirty in the evening and most of the ship's company were on liberty, with only a skeleton crew aboard. It was always a quiet time for Burkhart to catch up on his paperwork and letters to his family. He had called his wife half an hour before, just to hear her voice, and now he really missed her and his two teenage children. Since taking command of *Skate* eighteen months before, Burkhart and his wife had decided to leave the family in Fort Lauderdale. At first Burkhart had rented a small apartment in Point Loma, near the base, but it didn't take long to give it up. He was lonely and the apartment was empty and the taste and smell of his *Skate* drew him back as a live-aboard.

He smiled to himself. His wife Betty Ann had asked what was new. He had diverted her attention but he knew she sensed something. A telephone relationship was part of their marriage. For a moment he tried to imagine her reaction to HAWKSCREECH then laughed.

"What's so damn funny?" Niven poked his head into the open doorway.

"HAWKSCREECH. What the hell do you think." Burkhart looked up at Niven and exhaled a brown cloud of cigar smoke. "Jesus, you look awful. Something you can talk about?"

"No. I was just aboard *Dixon.*" He felt himself sag. Niven looked at him for a moment, then thought better of saying more. "Can I come in?"

"Come." Burkhart waved a beefy arm.

Niven squeezed past Burkhart into the tiny stateroom and sat opposite him on the bunk. We have an appointment with Langor aboard *Dixon* at 0630 tomorrow morning, just about the same time we'd like to move *Skate* into the floating dry dock."

"Jesus, so soon? It seems *Skate*'s finished.

Niven nodded. "We'll need every damn minute we can get for the refit."

"The Russian facelift we talked about? There's lots of holes that need filling in, Jake boy." The hair stood straight up on the back of Burkhart's massive pink neck.

"In the morning." Niven caught his eye with a hard stare. "I promise this won't be another Bucher, like the old *Pueblo,* in North Korean waters. This won't be a sell-out job."

"How the hell do you know that?"

"I'm staking my life on it, Charley." Niven looked away for a moment."

"That's good enough for me, Jake boy."

"A few business details. Orders are now being cut, billeting your crew here on the base. All the details are being handled from Washington. The only member of your crew that will become involved at some point is

112

your executive officer. For obvious reasons, the crew won't be told until after we sail." Niven wiped the sweat and tension from his face.

"Easy, Jake boy."

"I don't want to go home right now and I don't want to be alone right now. How about joining me up on the hill at the Ballast Point? I haven't eaten yet. I thought we could tickle the short hairs on our favorite nude."

"You got it, friend." Burkhart stood and reached into his small closet for a clean shirt. He talked while he dressed. "Something really puzzling me about this little cruise we're going to take. The engines, Jake boy. The engines. Foxtrot boats are diesel. I hope you haven't overlooked that little detail."

"I've saved the best for last, Charley. I promise sound signature won't be a problem. At least I hope." He glanced sideways at Burkhart, who finished adjusting his cap.

"All right, Jake boy. Let's put some meat on those ribs and some unblended Scotch in your gut." He slapped Niven on the back. Just like the old days."

"No. Not like the old days," Jake said quietly. He turned and shivered. Vasili was dead. Now Crabby was gone. So the bastards got their revenge by pulling the string on an old man who had probably served them damned well in Moscow. Moscow had buried a bloodied knife in his front door. A warning. They could reach Niven anytime they wanted.

Niven and Burkhart climbed topside and left *Skate* in the cool sweet evening. Niven reached into his sports jacket to be certain the Tokarev was ready. The message they had sent to him via Crabb was simple. So let the bastards come, he'd take his revenge in August with HAWKSCREECH, or whenever the opportunity presented itself.

15

The morning fog swirled in around the bows of *Dixon* as Jake walked the long concrete pier toward her gangplank. There was a restless urgency to his stride as he passed the black, low-slung submarines of Attack Group Five, gathered in the shadow of the large tender.

"Jacob, wait up." Brahma Sorrell jogged toward him, dressed in tan slacks and brown windbreaker.

"Any more good news for me today?"

"I'm sorry about last night. I know what that did to you." He shook his head. "I had just walked in, when one of Langor's aides ambushed me into calling you. It's damn tough."

"Tell me about it." Jake sounded bleak. "I had a meeting aboard Mother last night with the admiral." He raised his eyes to *Dixon*'s gray hulk.

"We still a go?"

Jake nodded. "From all the evidence we can gather from Europe, our network is still intact." He pushed out a sad breath.

"Meaning?"

"Meaning, that we hope to Christ that Russian spy bird goes dark when it's supposed to." Jake examined

114

Sorrell's big, ugly face. "Enjoy your vacation, Brahma?"

"Boring." Sorrell shrugged. "I'm itchy to get on with this madness. It's all I thought about when I was gone."

He looked down at Jake. "How the hell could I think about anything else? Ever since I came back from Africa, I was hooked by the gills."

Sorrell rubbed his massive hands together as they walked past the huddled submarines. Up ahead, a line of sailors with seabags slung over their shoulders moved slowly off *Skate*. Preparations were being made to move the submarine into the floating drydock.

"When all this is over, I want the bastard that clipped old Crabby. I want it so badly, I can taste it. Will you help?"

Sorrell studied Jake's features. "You really do, don't you? Of course I will. At least you look better than after Finland. That was rough. Damn rough."

"I don't feel any better. The ghosts are all over me."

They stepped aboard *Dixon* and their identifications were carefully checked and verified by a tough-looking officer of the deck and they were escorted below decks into the white compartment.

Admiral Langor introduced Burkhart to Brahma Sorrell and Jake watched his mouth drop slightly as Charley looked over his large size. Sorrell extended a firm, dry hand.

"Gentlemen, the schedule is tight and we're on the home stretch, so let's get down to it."

"I'd like that, Admiral. At least I'll know what I'm facing."

"Commander, HAWKSCREECH is the most sensitive operation this country has undertaken since the Manhattan project." From nowhere Langor produced a pair of wire-framed reading glasses that dangled pre-

115

cariously on the edge of his short nose and opened a metal-jacketed file stamped HIGHER THAN SECRET. "The format will be simple. I will explain the plan, then your questions will fill in the gaps."

"Admiral, may I say something?" Niven rose to his feet.

"Please do."

"Unlike past missions of this type sponsored by the Task Force, you as the boat commander will have direct input into HAWKSCREECH. In the past, other ships involved in an operation were only transportation. Often, in the case of electronic surveillance of an area, a compartment was used with the doors locked and the ship commander had no access or knowledge of what took place."

Burkhart squirmed in his seat, silently drumming his fingers on the arm. Every nerve ending in his body was a tense, waiting sensor.

"Here it is, Commander. On 6 August, *Skate* will depart San Diego control and proceed to the Northwest Pacific on the first leg of your journey, to a point in proximity to the Tenchi Seamount, a distance of some four thousand eight hundred nautical miles. On that first leg you will run submerged on nuclear power, avoiding all contact with commercial and military shipping." Langor paused, reflecting silently on a point in the file, disregarding the question on Burkhart's face.

"Transit time should be approximately nine days and upon arrival at Tenchi Seamount, you will come to periscope depth, raise your satellite scoop, and plug into the Soviet Molniya 3 Communications satellite in stationary orbit."

Burkhart twisted his face. "Water into wine and parting the Red Sea would be easier. How the hell do I do it?"

"We have in our possession a special electronic tape,

containing a series of high speed audio signals, that when transmitted on a precise frequency, triggers a response from that Molniya satellite.''

"Go on, Jake boy." Burkhart's eyes widened in surprise.

"When properly triggered, that Molniya will present *Skate* with the weekly recognition code for all Soviet warships operating in the Pacific Fleet. The cryptographers call it 'bursts of bits and frames.' Meaning that each second that Molniya is triggered, it gives off a high speed burst of code.''

Jake hesitated for a moment. "Every Russian warship carries such a key tape, just like we do. Each Friday, the large ground-based computers in Leningrad feed a new binary code into those Molniyas. For years we've tried to tap into those satellites, but never have succeeded. The codes are randomly selected by the computer, based on millions of possible combinations. Foolproof until now. Advantage *Skate.*''

"The only advantage we're going to have is raw guts.'' Burkhart set his eyes on Langor.

"No doubt.'' Langor glanced at Niven.

Jake smiled to himself. Burkhart was a real pro. Pressing a bit, but who wouldn't in this situation. A real damn meat and potatoes man on the verge of the greatest mission of his life, being talked down to by a manicured admiral. Burkhart knew fear and that was good. He knew when to stand and fight and that was even better.

Langor waited for the moment to pass, then continued. "Once you leave Tenchi Seamount, you will proceed due north on the surface, running with your diesels, during this second leg.''

"Jesus, Admiral!''

Brandon Langor looked up with his stern, unyielding eyes, anticipating Burkhart's protest. "This will be

117

a rough sea voyage, since *Skate* wasn't built to run for long periods on the surface. But Foxtrot subs of the Russian Navy do spend a great deal of time on the surface and you will be commanding a Russian boat.''

"In those latitudes, even with the Bering's false summers, conditions are horrible. The Bering is a real bastard ocean. I don't see how *Skate* can cut it.''

"Yes she can, because we're going to install another diesel propulsion system in *Skate.*''

"What?''

"Put it aside until after the briefing.''

Burkhart sat heavily in his seat.

"Put up slide number one.'' The compartment went black and a satellite photo of two islands appeared. "Welcome to the Komandorski Islands, Commander. Three hundred miles off the Asian coast of the Kamchatka Peninsula. The island on your left is Bering. Your target. The object of all this energy. The smaller island is Medni or Copper Island. Nothing to worry about there.''

"No, of course not,'' Burkhart mumbled.

The second slide appeared, showing an aerial close-up of Bering Island.

"Commander, I direct your eye to the lower left-hand corner of the island. There is a point of land, then a natural bay cut into the land mass. This is your objective, designated POINT LUCK.''

Burkhart strained forward, searching the slide for any detail that would give him something extra. "POINT LUCK. I like your sense of humor, Admiral.''

"We thought you would.'' Langor took a sip of water, clearing his throat. "That *bukhta* is called Lisinskaya Bay. It is a natural deep water anchorage, with no shoaling, that can easily accommodate large, deep draft ships.''

"Like a Soviet carrier named *Minsk?*"

"You've got it, Commander. The actual—"

A sharp buzzing phone cut Langor off.

"Yes?"

"This is the duty officer at North Island. I was told to cut in—"

"Go on!"

"We've scrambled a flight of Tomcats from North Island. We're tracking a formation of three Judys at angels forty, closing the air station."

"What are they, dammit? Where'd they come from?"

"Three Bear Bomber types, sir. Strictly reconn. We've been tracking since they entered southern Mexican airspace from Nicaragua. I was ordered to phone you, if something like this happened."

The young OOD squirmed again. "They're scanning us with full electronic packages. The works. They seem awful curious, sir."

"What's their distance?"

"Just passing one hundred fifty nautical miles. Speed three zero five, at forty thousand feet."

"When will you intercept?"

"Our ETA of their position is eight minutes, unless they break off from their present course."

"Keep me informed." Langor hung up and was silent for a minute. Finally he exhaled a long, pensive breath. "Let the bastards sniff and scan all the Yankee behinds they want—they can't know what we're up to. We're clean," he said, half talking to himself. Langor watched Niven watching him through the darkness of the compartment. "You hear me, Niven, they're just playing games. They flew three thousand miles just for the sights at the San Diego zoo."

Langor caught Burkhart staring at Niven's dark shadow. "I was saying, before the interruption, that the actual importance of the island group is that they are the terminal point for all missile testing from launch pads in the south at Tyuratam and Plesesk in the north.''

The compartment lights came up. "Did you hear me, Niven? It's just part of their overall plan during the past six months. Putting on the squeeze. Indeed, it's a political squeeze.''

"I agree, Admiral. Coastal waters are lousy with Russian spy trawlers," Burkhart said. "During the last few months they've been in our hair during every exercise, just like gnats. Often we've come close to colliding with those little intelligence collectors.''

"Indeed, Jacob." Langor made a fist. "They're just squeezing down, trying to play hardball.''

16

The large Sea Knight utility helicopter strained for altitude in the fog as it cut across the narrow channel from the submarine base to a remote corner of the sprawling North Island Naval Air Station on Coronado.

The angry thumbing growl of the rotors and the terrible vibration worked at Niven's thin calm. The final transformation of *Skate* into a Russian submarine would help them all make the transition. At least he didn't have to worry about Vasili Lykov. Maybe some other bastard from Moscow, but not the haunting presence of the old man. Niven shivered and felt cold fields of sweat form around his mouth. Out of the corner of his eye he saw Brahma Sorrell protectively scanning him.

The wheel shocks bounced heavily against the concrete landing apron, adjacent to a mammoth World War Two domed blimp hangar. Charley Burkhart surveyed both Niven and Langor, his face a growing question mark. Grim-faced Marine guards led the party into the darkened hangar and the steel door slammed shut behind them.

Suddenly the interior was fully lighted with mercury

vapor lamps. "My God!" Burkhart turned to Jake. "I've never seen anything like it. How big—"

Before him stretched two sections of twisted steel wreckage. The third section was perched on a massive steel cradle fifteen feet off the concrete floor. Its shape was vaguely familiar as Burkhart moved closer.

"This whole damn thing must stretch three hundred feet!" For a moment his face froze in disbelief. "It's a goddamn submarine, or what's left of one. Those poor damn bastards." Silently he removed his cap. "How the hell—"

Quickly the small group of men surrounded Burkhart as he stared up at the massive rudder and large bronze propellers attached to drive shafts.

"What an impressively tragic sight."

Niven patted him gently on the back. "It's the booty from the Jennifer Project in 1974."

"Christ Almighty!" Burkhart wiped his face with a hand. "This is that Russian sub?"

Jake nodded. "This is everything we recovered and reconstructed, including a code machine, code books, and sixty-eight bodies with uniforms."

"What class was she?"

An older diesel-electric Golf Class boat. Nineteen-fifties vintage."

"I guess if I live long enough, I'll see it all." Burkhart shook his head and looked about the small circle of men. "My life will never be the same." He touched a cold smooth bronze blade to assure himself it was real.

"Neither will ours," Sorrell offered.

Jake surveyed the huge hangar. "This broom closet is filled with some damn important memories for me."

"I thought the CIA shredded up the sub and buried the recovered crew members at sea?"

"Not on your damned life," Langor said. "This was

one of the most important intelligence recoveries since the Cold War started.''

Jake rubbed his burned leg. ''Why the hell would the United States spend forty million dollars for the ship and barge, and another one hundred ninety million for the entire operation, to dump it all back into the ocean? We waited twenty years for this chance.''

He laughed. ''We've done some damn stupid things, but nothing that stupid. We conducted longterm analyses and study of the way a Soviet submarine spends its operational life and the way its crew actually lives. You just can't do that with a few photos and specie samples. It was one of those rare opportunities to get a look at how a small segment of a massive military machine that we know precious little about operates.''

Burkhart stared skeptically up at the mute remains. ''Jesus! How the hell could we bring up something this massive?''

''The damn grappling platform had a lifting capacity of thirty-two hundred tons stretched on three miles of hydraulic cables.''

''What the hell do I know. I'm just a line skipper. I'd sure hate to have your nightmares at night, Jake.''

''We did the whole damn thing in a three-foot sea with the Russians screaming bloody murder behind closed doors. Thank God for Howard Hughes. He loved it and developed all the technology.''

A phone rang somewhere and a moment later a Marine guard came looking for Admiral Langor who took off at a trot.

Niven watched Burkhart's expression change from shock to awe. It was an impressive sight. A two-thousand-ton twisted carcass in a blimp hangar. A dead submarine once inhabited by dead men on the bottom of a cold ocean. They even brought in Howard Hughes to review the remains. Like everyone else, he shivered and said very little. There was nothing to say.

Slowly Niven guided Burkhart under the propellers and around the stern of the aft section. "We found the forward two sections of the sub, including the radiation contaminated sail and missiles in seventeen thousand feet of water. She exploded and broke up on the surface before sinking, thank God."

"Meaning what?"

"Those first two sections are mashed all to hell. When she sank, she imploded and was mangled by seven thousand pounds of sea water per square inch when she hit bottom. We actually found the remains of Russian submariners. One man had been squashed to the size of a coffee cup. The debris of the dead."

"Those poor, poor people." Burkhart was thinking about his *Skate* and his crew and the admission he had made to Langor to avoid capture.

Burkhart pulled a cigar from his foul weather jacket, slipped off the wrapper and carefully placed it in his mouth.

"You can't light that damn thing in here, Charley. It would foul the entire humidification system."

Burkhart refused to remove the cigar from his mouth. "Screw it. I need something oral." Burkhart pointed up to the rear section. "How come it's not all mashed to hell like the rest of this Russian boat? It looks in decent shape."

"When our trackers found the sub northwest of the Hawaiian Islands, the aft section was perched on the lip of a deep submarine canyon, in only eighteen hundred feet of water. The other two sections, twisted into steel pulp, plunged all the way to the floor of the canyon."

Burkhart shrugged impatiently. "Come on, Jake."

"This aft section contains three large main diesel

engines." Jake shifted his weight. "Those engines sat in deep water for over a year before we raised them."

Burkhart nodded.

"After a careful examination, we think these engines can be reworked. We've never fired them up, but we're very hopeful."

"Why?" Burkhart's eyes narrowed.

"This submarine and Foxtrot subs use the same diesel engines." He paused and watched Burkhart's face. "We're going to install these engines in *Skate*."

"What! You're all crazy." He rubbed his flushed neck. "Christ, I don't know anymore. "My gut tells me no, Jake boy. But, damn, I know you. Brother, do I know you. Look at this. I've seen what you've planned." He swept an arm around the wreckage, thinking about it.

"You brought this boat back from the grave," he said quietly. "I suppose it makes sense. Hell, I'm not sure anything makes sense anymore."

"It was the only way to solve the underwater signature problem. The Russians have damn good sound records. We couldn't get close to *Minsk* without them. It also takes care of the problem of running for long distances in blue water with these Russian brutes."

"So you're gonna rip out *Skate*'s guts." He stared at Niven. "We've only got six weeks to get her ready. It's damn complex, what you want."

Niven circled under the wreckage. "These engines are our only ticket in and out of the screening task force of Soviet warships."

"What about the obvious problems, Jake boy? The engineering problems are monstrous." Burkhart was laboring with the concepts. Trying to digest it all.

"It's all we have, Charley. There are two questions." Niven made a furtive gesture with his hands. "Will the engines run and do we have time to cut open

Skate's hull, install and adapt them and these Russians screws to our needs?''

"We'll get there, you bet your sweet ass, we will," added Sorrell. Slowly he rubbed a massive hand over the hull of the sub. "We are going to ride her back right into their bread basket."

"We won't have hard, definitive word about the engines and propellers until next week." Niven ran a hand around the smooth round tip of one of the bronze screws.

"Rock crushers can be tricky." Burkhart shook his head. "But Russian engines, Jesus." He held up a hand. "What's next week?"

"We're flying in a mechanic who is a whiz with Russian diesels. A certain intelligence organization owes us a very large favor. The man they're sending will stay with our little circus until after we return from the North Pacific."

Burkhart rolled the dry cigar around in his mouth to wet it down. "Our little circus does call for a certain level of optimism, doesn't it?" He removed the cigar from his mouth and inspected its progress.

"What about weight and size? Installing those bastards and oil tanks could really screw up the delicate weight balance and center of gravity in *Skate*."

"Our people tell us it can all be worked out, Charley."

Burkhart stared up at the twisted section of the pressure hull, as if another look would tell him something important. Something Niven's people had missed. He inspected the wet cigar again. "I hope your people are right about all this."

Burkhart slowly walked the entire length of the submarine. He did his best thinking alone. The trained sea wolf stalking a prey. HAWKSCREECH appealed to his nature with his many training years, shadowing

126

fictional enemies. Burkhart circled back to Niven. HAWKSCREECH would be Burkhart's moment of truth. More than likely, his baptism of fire. After all these years, his first test. A tingle welled up in from his feet. By God, he was ready and he'd be damned certain his boat would meet any condition put to her. To be certain, he'd bulldog Niven all the way.

Burkhart watched Niven in silence for a long time, his eyes blinking a sympathetic beat to the air blowers in the hangar. "Are you certain you can get these engines operational?"

"When I was a kid," Niven said, "my family spent summer vacations in New Brunswick and Maine. We were all fishing freaks. One summer vacation we watched a lobster boat sink in about thirty feet of water. Came back the next summer and watched the salvage team raise her with floats, tinker with her diesels for a few hours, then start the bastard up. We couldn't believe it. Salt water and all."

Jake shrugged. "It always stayed with me for some damn reason. Just a worthless bit of information. When I was putting this operation together in my mind, the engine signature problem stopped me cold. One morning it just popped into my head that we could take a crack at these engines sitting right under our noses."

Burkhart put his hand on Niven's shoulder. His voice was very gentle. "Look here, Jake boy, we're not talking about a down east Maine lobsterboat. These engines were on the bottom of the Pacific for over a year, in almost two thousand feet of high pressure salt water. To boot, they haven't been fired up since 1974."

"Under perfect atmospheric conditions since 1974," Niven corrected him.

"Go on." Burkhart shook his head.

"We didn't just stop with a goddamn lobsterboat. It was just a beginning. We then investigated carefully the conditions surrounding the fleet submarine *Squalus*, which went down off the Isle of Shoals, New Hampshire, in 1939, in two hundred forty feet of water. Induction valves were left open and she went down like a rock by the stern, with a flooded engine room. Three months later she was brought to the surface, hauled into drydock, and the official salvage reports found her diesels, despite the imersion, were in perfect condition. *Squalus* was refitted with those same diesels, recommissioned the *Sailfish*, and served in the Pacific throughout World War Two.''

Burkhart examined the now devastated end of the cigar, looked up at Niven and smiled evenly. ''I like it, Jake boy. I goddamn like it.'' Out of the corner of his eye he saw the smooth, demanding face of Admiral Brandon Langor approaching.

''A slight problem, Jacob. A slight problem,'' Langor repeated. Langor's fleshy marble head twitched.

Niven's whole body stiffened.

''Seems the Russians have taken up station five miles off the entrance to San Diego Bay with a very large electronic and intelligence-gathering ship. Looks like the bastards will be camping out here for a while. Not a damn thing we can do, right under our noses.''

Langor studied Niven's face. ''Just like they knew what the hell we were up to.''

17

"How it happened doesn't matter!" Niven shifted the scrambler phone to his other ear and turned his eyes toward the window. Across the expansive concrete and blacktop pier, Niven could see the giant canvas tarp covering *Skate* like a massive circus tent. "It sure as hell is covered now, Admiral."

Niven turned toward Charley Burkhart and shook his head grimly. "Admiral, the yard is moving as quickly as it can. The shifts have gone nonstop. I don't want to get sloppy now." Good-bye, Admiral."

"What the hell happened, Jake boy?"

"Last night there was an alert. A damn Cosmos sky spy blitzed over just before midnight."

"So?"

"So this, dammit! The yard foreman was sloppy and only had the forward section of *Skate* tarped when that Russian photo bird popped over the horizon last night. Of course the yard lights were on."

"Damn!" Burkhart pounded a fist onto his desk." "It's bad enough with those bastards sitting right on our front porch, listening every time we pass gas. Now this. They've been trying to get a peek under that canvas tent ever since we brought *Skate* in. The bastards

129

never give up." Burkhart studied the dark circles under Niven's eyes, the growing tension rising like steam, just beneath the surface of his voice.

"Tell me about it." Niven walked to the window and stared out at the dry dock holding *Skate*. He looked bleak.

"How much time do we have, Jake?"

"Hard to tell. "All their photo people will see is the aft section of an old sub being worked on."

"Enough to keep real tabs on?"

"I sure as hell would, if I was running the photo intelligence section on Moscow Ring Road."

Burkhart held the phone away from his ear and every so often put his mouth to the receiver and uttered a perfunctory "Yes, sir."

At last the agony ended and a red-faced Burkhart hung up the telephone, ready to explode. He was quiet for a long time, calming his nerves by rocking in the old swivel chair in the small trailer office. A land-locked desk was no place for him. Idly he fingered the desk calendar before him, set on Monday, July 21, and finally looked up at a square-bodied man with darting, intelligent hazel eyes. The man facing Burkhart's desk shifted easily in his chair and smiled.

"Another call about me, Commander?"

"You've got it, Mr. Levy. The Base Commander is still livid about your little companion." Burkhart nodded to the UZI machine pistol slung over the back of his chair. "You've apparently broken sixteen Navy regulations about unauthorized personnel carrying firearms on a United States Military Reservation."

The short beefy man with a massive upper torso moved his greasy hands with a small furtive gesture. "Tell him to get fucked. No UZI, no Akivor Levy. No

Levy, no master diesel mechanic." His English was smooth and commanding with just a trace of an Israeli accent. "We've been over this circumstance three times and I'm surprised you haven't worked it all out. Our MOSSAD operates far more functionally," he quipped with growing impatience.

"I know, I know." Burkhart stood and turned to Jake Niven, staring out the small window toward the floating dry dock covered by its enormous canvas roof. He had done his best to stay out of the conversation.

"Jake, what about it?"

"I'll talk to Langor." He stretched his arms indifferently. "But it seems to me you're doing a hella'va job of holding the man off. All we need is another two weeks."

"Bullshit!" Burkhart's neck began to redden.

"Charley, look at the date on your calendar. We've got to have *Skate* finished by this Friday for a go. She still has a large round patch cut out of her pressure hull from frame seventy to frame eighty." Jake's face turned sour and the bags under his eyes, combined with his slightly off-center nose, gave him a crazed look.

"Don't tell me about my goddamned boat!" Burkhart was on his feet pointing a menacing hand at Niven. "I know what she needs and it isn't a bunch of goddamned crazy spooks with UZI machine pistols running around an American submarine base."

Akivor Levy sat back and smiled, his filthy blue coveralls out of character with the UZI slung over his back. "I think both of you are missing the point. I lost my wife and two small children at Maalot."

Through it all his voice remained even and confident. "If I had been carrying this weapon like I should have been I might have saved their lives and salvaged some happiness. Now I carry it as a symbol." His eyes took a faraway look, then instantly he was back. "The

131

point is, my UZI has nothing to do with you, your asshole base commander, or this mission." He smiled coldly.

Burkhart started to speak but Levy cut him off. "I have installed your Russian diesels." Levy wiped his nose with a greasy hand. He stared at Burkhart and Niven with a cold fury. "I promise you my engines will get you wherever you want to go, if you will stop bothering me and let me finish the job I started. Then you can screw the Soviets in the ass." Sweat began pouring from his squat, leathery face.

Russian Katyusha rockets and MIGS still kill Israeli children, so this is the least I can do. A proper mission will be another tiny piece of revenge."

"You have craft without charm." Niven smiled. He liked Levy, his simple honesty and even more simplified logic.

"Let's say my UZI is a reminder that I am always willing to take out a few Soviet foreskins."

All three men erupted into spontaneous laughter and the tension dissolved. Burkhart settled back in his chair and rubbed his tired eyes. "We've been working in round-the-clock shifts in our isolated compound for the past eight weeks and no one on this base knows what the hell we're doing. We've accomplished what I thought was impossible. *Skate* has a Foxtrot-like re-shaped bow and sail facade along with a Russian diesel powerplant." Burkhart looked at Levy.

"You accomplished a major miracle by reworking those engines. I never did ask you where the hell you learned Soviet machinery. I just assumed you'd be a—"

"A Russian?" Levy rubbed a chunky hand over his chin. "My parents were Russian by birth and came to Palestine to work the fields in 1939. I'm a Sabra and grew up in the seat of a tractor, and under its bonnet when it broke down. I was called up to service before the 1967 war and ended up in the motor pool repairing captured Soviet battle tanks, half tracks, and heavy trucks." Levy pulled an oily rag from his back pocket and tried unsuccessfully to wipe the coat of grease from his hands.

"We found engine repair manuals in the vehicles written in Russian and could never figure out what the hell good they would do Egyptian crews. We translated them into Hebrew, and in a period of time we became quite proficient at repairing and rebuilding those diesel and gas power plants."

Levy folded his face into a silent question mark.

"What is it, Mr. Levy?"

"I'm having a few problems with that Kama River diesel."

"What problems?" Niven walked over to him.

"One of its cylinder walls was badly scored, not because of immersion, but because of poor maintenance when it was pushing that sub around the Pacific. I've reground the cylinder walls, but I'm still having trouble reseating the oil drain ring." Levy wiped his face again. "It's damn tricky with this type of machinery."

"What?" Niven tensed. "Oh, Christ, not now!"

"I'll solve the problem. It's just time—"

"We don't have a hella'va lot of it left."

Jake sat and faced Levy. "You said your parents were Russian by birth. "Do you speak the language?"

"Da. Gahvaree'te lee vy pah-roo's kee?"

"Yes," Jake nodded. "I speak it and obviously so do you." The sound of a giant sand blaster, cleaning *Skate*'s hull, overtook them.

"When I grew up, I spoke Russian in our home and Hebrew on the street." Levy smiled. "As a member of MOSSAD, I've had occasion to use my Russian during certain Israeli operations." Levy wiped at his greasy hands again.

"I want you to join me in the boarding party. I like what I see in you." Jake got up and looked out the window. *Minsk* is the question mark of my life. I'm going to need your help."

"Who else will be in your boarding party?" Levy's cold eyes widened.

"John Sorrell, who you've met, and the scientist from Los Alamos, who will actually find the gadget while we ride shotgun."

"What about this scientist?"

"For security, we won't have him aboard until the night we sail. I don't have a clue to him. That's the admiral's province. But, the way it dopes out, we'll do all the talking on *Minsk*. That UZI and your Russian will give me more firepower."

"I'd like to do it. Another small payment." He turned his head.

"Good—" A loud knock on the trailer door interrupted.

"Come," Burkhart called out.

A young woman sailor, with soft green eyes and a patient expression, entered the crowded office, holding a secret file jacket. "Pardon me, sir. I have a message for Jacob Niven from Admiral Langor. A NODIS, sir. The highest priority—"

For a long time Jake thoughtfully studied the cable, then silently handed it to Burkhart. "Take a look. Our friends in Moscow have moved up the heavy artillery. It seems *Minsk* is out of her dinosaur cage and on the way to Point Luck."

111245 ZULU MISAWA 6920TH ELEC-
TRONIC INTELLIGENCE GROUP NODIS.
NODIS. NO DISTRIBUTION OUTSIDE THE
SECRETARIAT.

TO: *UMBRA* REAL ADMIRAL BRANDON LANGOR

TASK FORCE 157

RE: SNOW WHITE REQUEST
MESSAGE AS FOLLOWS:
SNOW WHITE TRANSITED PETROPAV-LOVSK HARBOR INSTALLATION APPROX 0947 ZULU. SNOW WHITE ACCOM-PANIED BY DWARF ADMIRAL ISAKOV. FORMED INTO COLUMN IN PROXIMITY OF CAPE MAYACHNY. NOW PROCEED-ING NORTH NORTHEAST ON HEADING OF 073 MAGNETIC TO POINT LUCK. SPEED 28 KNOTS. SEAS HEAVY. CONDI-TIONS POOR. NO ESTIMATE OF AR-RIVAL TIME.
END TRANSMISSION.

DISTRIBUTION FOR SECRETARIAT:

TASK FORCE 157
THE WHITE HOUSE
SECRETARY OF DEFENSE
CHIEF OF NAVAL OPERATIONS
CHAIRMAN JOINT CHIEFS OF STAFF
DIRECTOR CENTRAL INTELLIGENCE
   AGENCY

"What about our special stores and supplies?"

Niven rubbed his eyes. The pressure of preparing the boat under the pushing and probing eyes of the Soviets had taken its toll. "The Da Vinci is due here Tuesday by special courier. It will be locked in the safe in your stateroom."

"When do we leave, Jake?"

"I'll recommend a final go for Wednesday night."
Slowly, Niven walked to the window facing the yard.
"Now we've got to find a way to slip past that damned
Russkie spy boat sitting offshore without waking the
Kremlin."

18

The late-afternoon sun slid deeper into the water with splashes of color and light. He sipped a cold beer and stared out the window at the sweeping beauty of La Jolla Cove. Somewhere he had forgotten about the light summer air and the Torrey Pines stirring musically in the gentle onshore breeze. There was a sweetness to this place that he would miss—that he always did miss when he was away.

His eyes followed the bleached redwood deck until they found Ellie, her full, dark body glistening in the intense light. Leisurely, she raised a limp hand and followed the curve of her hip. The breeze caught her black hair as she pulled herself up to one elbow on the thick terry blanket. Idly she moved her head about the deck, finally settling on a dark shadow at the sliding window. She smiled and the joy arced toward him.

"Get a good look?"

"I tried. It's been so long, I'd forgotten." He smiled with tired eyes.

"Who's fault is that?" She raised her eyebrows. "I've tried not to miss you, but—" Ellie opened the screen and carefully scrutinized Jake's face.

"You're worn out." Her hand caressed his stubbled

face. Suddenly she was up on her toes and kissed him gently. Ellie pulled back and watched his expression change. She turned her back and shivered, hoping he hadn't seen it. She reached for the terry towel and felt the tight muscles in her belly go soft.

"To all of us!" Niven raised his wineglass and surveyed the dinner table. "May we all do this soon again."

Charley Burkhart, replete in slacks and Hawaiian shirt, Ellie wrapped in a white summer dress offset against her olive complexion, and Brahma Sorrell, looking civilized with his bulk covered by a sports jacket—all raised their glasses.

From another room of the small Italian restaurant in downtown La Jolla the soft strains of a harp drifted above the background noise.

Ellie raised her eye as Jake downed another glass of wine in one swallow. "Damn good Cabernet." He looked at the empty glass.

"What's going on?" Ellie searched the faces at the table.

"Dinner, my love. Dinner."

For a long moment she examined the awkward silence with her knife-edged intellect and intuition. After a long silence, she turned a cold glare on Niven. "You're getting drunk."

"Damn it! So what?" He pulled his voice down below the crowd noise. "Tonight I want to relax. No conditions. No anything." He cocked his head toward her. "Tonight is not open for negotiation." Niven's entire body tensed.

"Easy, Jake boy." Burkhart worked a thick hand over his shoulder. He smiled over at Ellie. "We've all been under a strain. Some of us deal with it better than others.''

Niven slumped in his seat, sipping another glass of red. ''I'm sorry, Ellie. Let's eat.'' Tenderly, he took her hand and met her eyes. ''The artichoke hearts in clam sauce are specialties of the house,'' he offered.

After more wine and menu conversation a flushed glow rose from the table. ''Why do they call you Brahma?'' Ellie asked Sorrell.

Sorrell caught her eye and rolled his mustache with two fingers. His pink face was rose-red. ''Well, Ellie, the only 'they' is Jacob. I was born and raised in Texas.'' He paused and took another drink of wine. ''Not correct. I was raised really in parts of New Mexico and West Texas. Ellie showed interest and Sorrell continued.

''I spent my formative years in places like Tularosa and Mule Peak, New Mexico.''

Burkhart, flushed and glassy-eyed, thought that was very funny. ''Mule Peak. Next to Elephant's Breath?''

Niven tensed. Sorrell was not a man to be toyed with and Burkhart was too drunk to realize what he was doing. ''He doesn't mean anything by it, Brahma.'' Niven smiled and touched the arm of his friend. He had sobered considerably.

Sorrell smiled. At least Niven knew it was a smile. ''I'll tell you, Charley, where Mule Peak is. It's about thirty miles from Tularosa and the most beautiful valley I've ever seen. Gone now.'' He poured another glass of wine. ''Damn ruined now. Sacramento Mountains, too.''

''What happened?'' Ellie probed gently.

''Goddamn government took it all.'' He looked up. ''My valley happened to be next to Alamogordo.''

''I didn't know that.'' Niven seemed mildly surprised.

"Why does he call you Brahma?"

"Eventually settled in Kermit, Texas. Went to high school in Odessa, with all the bulls and cows. I played high school football. My high school coach called me that. I first ran across Niven, while we were both in SEAL training. I always wanted to be a frogman." He laughed again and took another pull from the wine. "When I was a kid. I couldn't have been more than the age of ten, I saw Richard Widmark in this movie about blowing up mines and fighting evil Chinese Communist frogmen during the Korean War."

He caught Ellie's wrist with a hand. "When you grow up in the flats of Texas, with nothing but brown scrub and dust, you dream of the ocean. I swore someday I would be a frogman." He was drunk and rambling. "I told the story of my high school coach to Niven one night, during our training, and the rest is history. Look at me now. Hooked up with a madman."

Ellie waited until the front door closed before exploding. "What's going on?"

"Nothing." He reached for her, but she pulled away with a fury in her eyes that he had never seen before.

"You've shut me out of your life." She picked up one of his poetry books and threw it across the bedroom. "You're a slam-dunk asshole! I've been wide open with you. You've seen every bump and scar I have, because I believed in us, you bastard!" Her voice soared as hot tears streaked her cheeks.

"You don't believe in us anymore?"

"I just don't know." She stared at him across the room. Wanting him. Hating him.

"What the hell is going on, Ellie?"

She raised her swollen eyes. "You tell me, Jacob."

"What?"

"When you're leaving." She held up her hand. "Don't lie to me and dignify this nonsense."

For a long time, Niven was quiet. He paced the bedroom in silence as she watched his every move. Finally he went to her and held her face tightly in his hands. "I have so much to say, so very much." His voice was a whisper. "I love you. You are my life and my reason for being, along with my daughter. That much I know."

Ellie reached for Jake, choking the wind out of him. "How long will you be gone?"

"A long time, Ellie. A very long time." He felt her body sag and then shudder.

She turned away, her arms crossed, holding in the hurt. "Where are you going? What are you going to be doing?"

Niven gently touched the back of her shoulders. "I can't, Ellie. I just can't."

"Why?" She was crying, now. "National secrets and all that damn shit?"

"Something like that, Ellie." She moved across to the bedroom window, staring out into the dark.

"I'm going to—" She stopped herself and shook her head.

"What?"

"Nothing important."

"Tell me, please, Ellie. You're hurt about so many things. You've taught me so very much. How to be open. How to feel." He rubbed her back.

She turned and looked at Niven. His funny nose. The scar on his chin. The open, honest face that she had grown to love and cherish. I've made a lifetime of mistakes, but you're not one of those mistakes." He gently kissed her mouth.

"Don't play with my feelings, please, Jake. I want to know, so I can visualize what you're doing. I think

141

about you so often during the day. Now you're just picking up and walking out of my life, without so much as a clue.''

Ellie was crumbling before him and he couldn't stand it. This proud, independent woman coming apart at the seams. She would hate him before he ever came back. All that way. All that death so close to him and no Ellie when he came back. It was in her eyes.

"All right, Ellie.''

She squeezed his hand, just wanting to be part of him.

"Ah, I'm going to board a Russian aircraft carrier, dressed as a Soviet officer, steal a critical piece of hardware and then kidnap the ship's captain.'' The words slipped quietly from his mouth.

"My God!'' She gasped and closed her eyes, rocking her head. It took her a long time to recover. "I never dreamed, Jake. I—'' She shrugged, her senses numb. "I never—''

"Does it change anything?'' His voice was tender and filled with caring. "Now you have to suffer and I didn't want that. Does it really matter, except to make you unhappy? Turn you inside out.''

"At least I know.'' She held him and tried to smile with her swollen, wet face. "I just want you back.''

"I know, Ellie.'' An image of Vasili Lykov, waiting to take him, danced into Niven's mind and he shivered.

"I've written you a letter, Jake. I don't want you to read it until you're certain you are coming home to me.''

"Christ, Ellie. What kind of nonsense—''

She placed a finger against his lips. "My nonsense. The nonsense that made you tingle all over when you fished those Brunswick rivers as a kid. Don't break faith with me, Jake. Promise me.''

19

"What the hell is going on?" Neil Brennen, *Skate*'s Executive Officer, rubbed his face in frustration. It was Burkhart's boat and he was absolute ruler. A saltwater autocrat and it was Brennen's job to carry out his every wish.

"Where's the goddamn fog the weather boys promised?"

"What's it matter?"

Burkhart smiled thinly. "It sure would help us slip past that damn Russian banana boat out there." Burkhart scanned the control room of *Skate*, watching his crew preparing to get underway in an atmosphere charged with uncertainty. All he knew was that he was glad to be back with a submarine under his feet. He had missed the old girl.

"Skipper, all ship's company present and accounted for, at your command. The watch has been mustered to stations."

"The passengers? They all squared away?"

"We've bumped some people and they've been assigned staterooms."

"Very well, Irish."

"Mechanics with UZIs, hush-hush passengers,

Skate's hull looking like an erector set. All the mystery. I'll bet this is going to be some kinda cruise. And your damn XO doesn't know what the hell is going on."

"You're not supposed to." Burkhart leaned over the navigation plot table, catty-corner to the periscope stand, and studied the large map laid out before him in the bright glow of the overhead light.

"Irish, I want you to lay in a track for coordinates forty-nine north, one sixty-nine five minutes east. Then tell me what our transit time will be."

"Let me get the navigation officer and a plotting party and—"

"I want you to do it, Irish," Burkhart commanded quietly.

Brennen worked quickly on a thin plastic overlay of a navigation chart of the Pacific Basin. After a few minutes he squinted at Burkhart. "The mystery deepens. Tenchi Seamount, approximately seven hundred nautical miles south southeast of the Kamchatka Peninsula. Right smack in the middle of Indian country. That right, Skipper?"

Burkhart nodded. "Arrival time?"

Brennen bent over a pad. "Transit time for 4,968 miles is nine days, based on a daily average of five hundred fifty nautical miles at twenty knots. That's not pushing the old girl too hard, which means we will arrive at Tenchi Seamount on Saturday, 16 August."

"I'll take it, Irish. That is assuming, of course, that our lady behaves." Burkhart caught Brennen's eye. "Go into Radio and call the Coast Guard. Alert them that we'll be clearing Point Loma in half an hour. Use the scrambler. They've already been alerted. If that damned Russian trawler gets wind of us—" His voice dropped away.

"Aye, aye, Skipper."

"Once we're past the Russians, what course do you recommend across the Pacific?"

"A base course of two eight nine degrees. We'll make final course corrections on day eight." Brennen drummed his fingers on the chart, waiting.

Burkhart slapped him lightly on the back. "You'll get the rest of the scoop at the appropriate time. Sorry, Irish."

"Sounds like a Cuban fastball. Must be something crazy when you can't let your XO in on the action." Brennen's eyes were hard, but patient.

"It is, now get that expression off your kisser and tell me how we're doing."

"Whatever you say. Engineering reports the pile is lit, the primary loop is in the green, all heat-up curves are normal, and the screws are clear."

"Very well." Burkhart raised his hands to his face, then looked at his watch. It was 2245. "I'll want a full head of clean steam in fifteen minutes so we can shove off. If we're a secret operation, let's keep it that way. Make sure all wharf lights are extinguished, then have the deck party finish removing the canvas tarps from the bow and sail with flashlights."

"Will do, and the steam is there whenever you want it."

Burkhart smiled at his efficient first officer and shook his head. "I can always depend on you, Irish. Station your maneuvering watch and I'll take the conn. Just as soon as we hit the fifty fathom curve, I want to wet her down. Probing Russian eyes, a full moon, and too damn much light for my liking. The sooner we pull the plug the better."

"Got it, Skipper. By the way, would you say a few words to the crew. They know it's not a routine operation and they're really jumpy. Scuttlebutt has them very nervous." Brennen lowered his voice to a whisper.

"I also recommend a Captain's Mast in the next few days. The list is really growing."

Burkhart exhaled a long, tired breath. This is the part of command that wearied him. "I'll think on it, Irish. I'll think on it."

Brennen shook his head with a scowl. Burkhart took a last look around the control room. Busy crewmen and officers were preparing their stations, but he noted they all had half an eye on him, waiting expectantly for the word. Even Spike Mead was seriously going over his panels and scopes. He wondered how long that would last.

"Well, this is it, Irish. Once the deck party is secured, station your maneuvering watch and single up your lines. I'll be on the bridge in a minute, where I'll be joined by Jake Niven when I take her out." There was finality in Burkhart's tone, so Brennen turned and headed aft toward Radio and the auxiliary machine spaces.

Burkhart picked up a pair of field glasses, walked through the low-level grumbling, and climbed up the sail access ladder through the control room hatch, emerging through the bridge hatch into the small open sail cockpit, fifteen feet above the deck. Old-timers still called it the conning tower. He looked forward over the compass card and ship's intercom squawk box to his deck party dragging the large traps onto the wharf. The moonlight was so intense, they didn't even need flashlights. Burkhart cursed softly to himself, turned his head and silently examined the rear of the reshaped sail sporting a false snorkel and a large bulbous contour fashioned from aluminum to match the Soviet Foxtrot.

The full impact of the changes was brought home to Burkhart with the new paint job, a mixture of flat char-

146

coal and dark brown with a bright red strip marking the water line. Below the water line she was a dark flat gray. All above-deck sonar windows and sound heads were painted a bright white to add to *Skate*'s authenticity. Burkhart moved to the front of the cockpit and looked pensively down at the newly shaped false bow, now heavily rounded.

"Permission to come on the bridge."

Burkhart turned and looked down. Niven, with a Greek fishing hat, popped up through the hatch. "Permission granted."

Niven easily lifted himself up and moved next to Burkhart. "My belly stinks, how's yours?"

"It's a bit tense, Jake boy."

Slowly, Niven surveyed the view from the cockpit. "The damn weather's good enough for a midnight parade."

Burkhart mashed his jaw. "Pray for cold and fog. Where does it say we can get everything we want? We'll just make it all work for us." He stared at Niven in the bright darkness. "You're aboard *Skate* now. She sets the rules, although I don't know who the hell we're going to fool. With her Russian makeup, *Skate*'s a faded woman who looks great at twenty feet, but the illusion falls apart up close in the light." He looked up at the moon.

The intercom in the front of the cockpit squawked metallically. "Bridge, this is Radio."

"Bridge here."

"We've got a patch from NORAD. They're tracking a Cosmos sky spy headed this way. They expect arrival in about twenty minutes."

"Keep me informed, Radio." He turned to Niven. "Dammit! We better get our asses out of here."

Burkhart tripped the lever connecting him with every compartment in the boat. "This is the captain. We've

147

got a hot Russian spy bird that we must avoid at all costs. We expect her in twenty minutes. I want to be the hell out of here by then. Let's move our butts, gentlemen." His voice was calm. He could just see the faces of the crew right now. Large eyes and open mouths, not knowing what the hell to think.

"Bridge, Auxiliary machine room."

"Bridge, aye."

"Permission to shift the internal electrical load to ship's service turbo generators, Captain."

"Permission to shift the load." Burkhart took a breath of sea air, and despite the tension, he was at home. "Cooking on internal power, Jake. The boys are really hauling their tails down below."

Niven stared at Burkhart, then at the bows of *Skate*. HAWKSCREECH was out of his hands now. It was all up to Burkhart and his crew. He exhaled slowly and his mind drifted to Ellie, sitting right this moment in their bedroom staring out into the blackness. He could feel her soul, her energy beside him.

"Bridge, Control." It was Brennen's voice.

"Bridge, aye."

"All deck hatches closed and secured. The brow is secured. *Skate* is standing by to get underway and awaiting your orders, Skipper." They could hear the urgency in Brennen's voice. "The Coast Guard is standing by the moment we clear Zuniga Point."

Niven and Burkhart looked at each other. They were live. There was no turning back. *Skate* strained in her stall, ready to answer bells.

"Thanks, Control. Good quick response time. Ready to get underway. Take in all lines," Burkhart heard himself say. "Maneuvering Room, Bridge. Starboard back one-third, port ahead one-third. Control, this is the Bridge. Right full rudder." Burkhart didn't even wait for responses from below. He wanted *Skate*

148

at sea. Away from probing Soviet eyes that could cost them their lives in the weeks to come.

Burkhart heard the orders repeated into the intercom and turned to Niven, just as distant engines bells sounded from below.

"We'll just swing her stern gently out into the channel and ease out to sea as smoothly as a baby's behind takes powder." Burkhart reached up and rubbed his face and Jake could see a slight nervous tremor. He felt a hard lump in his own belly, but chose not to speak, since Burkhart had his hands full maneuvering the twenty-five-hundred-ton submarine, but still Burkhart did it with confidence and ease.

Niven looked ahead as *Skate* gained momentum and slowly slid to the right. Off in the distance he could easily see the lights of downtown San Diego shimmering in the warm summer night. He looked up into the night sky trying to visualize that Russian Cosmos skidding across space toward them.

"Maneuvering, Bridge."

"Maneuvering here, Bridge."

"Starboard ahead one-third. Port ahead one-third."

The order was repeated over the intercom. "Control, Bridge."

"Control, here."

"Ease your rudder amidships. The course will be one eight zero degrees, inside Sierra Zeus." His voice was rock-steady.

"Aye, Captain. The course is one eight zero. The rudder is amidships and we're well within submarine transit lane Sierra Zeus."

"Control, Bridge."

"Control, here."

"Make turns for ten knots." Burkhart was pushing her.

"Aye, Captain. Making turns for ten knots. Steady on course one eight zero."

Jake sucked in a fresh breath of warm salt air and felt *Skate* begin to surge slightly under his feet. The engine was beginning to put propeller wash across the rudder to give *Skate* steering capability. He looked ahead to the bow and saw a slight phosphorescent bow wave begin to form as his thoughts drifted, trying to visualize the massive form of the Soviet carrier *Minsk*. He swallowed into the hard lump in his stomach.

"Permission to come on the bridge, Skipper."

Both men turned and looked down as a thin, freckled face topped with bright red hair popped up through the hatch. "Permission granted, Winebelly."

Ian "Winebelly" Burns bounced to his feet somehow balancing a metal thermos and two mugs. "Hot coffee, sir." The young face smiled eagerly at his captain.

"Right on schedule, Winebelly." Burkhart reached over and grabbed the mugs, while the young cook poured fresh steaming coffee.

"Got some fresh glazed donuts in the making, sir." He smiled again and left the bridge with the thermos.

"Winebelly?" Jake grinned at Burkhart. "Most cooks are named Cookie or Fats."

"Not on *Skate*. The kid's great at making home-brewed wine. Last Christmas he gave me a special bottle. It knocked my socks off. He's a Scot by birth and came to the States when he was nine. I'm sure before the cruise is over you'll hear him play his crazy bagpipes. Damn fine baker, just like his father who spent years baking on the *Queen Mary* before she was beached. The old man was a piper at one time in the Coldstream Guards.

"I sure could use some of that home brew right about now, Charley."

"Burkhart grunted. "Where the hell is the admiral? I thought His Highness would be here to see us off."

"You thought wrong. Langor is sitting comfortably at home in Norfolk, just awaiting word from one of his men here that we shoved off on schedule."

"It's taken some time for me to understand his brand of poker, but—"

"He never loses, Charley. Never. He has disassociated himself from us until we bring back the bacon. That's always the way it is. He wouldn't dare risk tarnishing the third admiral's star he's bucking for if we screw up or embarrass United States policy." Niven raised his hands thoughtfully.

"If we pull this off, Brandon Langor will be first in line, banging on the door of the Oval Office, with shoulder boards in hand. He wants that third star as badly as you want your wife and kids and I want Ellie."

Burkhart nodded. He was growing tense as he shifted his weight from foot to foot. There was an urgency his crew had communicated to *Skate*, and he felt her surge beneath his feet, pushing for the safety of the open sea.

20

"Bridge, Radar."

"Bridge, aye." Burkhart tensed.

"Our stationary contact is one eight five degrees, range two miles. We have new contacts, bearing zero seven zero. Airborne. Speed one eight zero. Range, one mile."

"How many airborne contacts, Radar?"

"Seven, Captain. Copters from North Island."

Burkhart and Niven swung their glasses to their left. Out of the darkness they could make out the insect silhouettes of the Navy gunships against the moonlight as they raced to the west.

"Bridge, Radar."

"Bridge, aye."

"Two surface targets, dead astern, moving at high speed."

"Aye, Radar. Keep your eyes sharp." Both men swung their glasses aft. Just behind *Skate*, two knife-sharp bows were pushing churning white foam out of their way. As the Coast Guard cutters neared *Skate*, they veered left toward the invisible target.

"That'll give them something to think about." Niven and Burkhart exchanged silent glances. Suddenly the Russian trawler appeared out of the night as a dark mountain against the moonlit night.

"Bastard put himself just beyond the three-mile limit," Burkhart commented. A Navy copter slid past *Skate* with a whining growl, heading for the Soviet ship. A flash of intense light forced Burkhart and Niven to shield their eyes.

"They've got a spot beam on us."

"Control, this is the Bridge. Hard right rudder! Make your new course two three zero. Make emergency turns for twenty-five knots!"

They both tried to see beyond the light but it was impossible as *Skate* heeled under their feet, away from the trawler.

"Oh, Jesus," Niven moaned.

Another Navy gunship swooped past *Skate* toward the Russians. The copter's rotar blades beat a deep vibration into their ears as it flew directly at the beam of light.

A deep plowing motion rose up from *Skate*'s keel as she picked up speed in the coastal swell. The probing shaft of light began to move away from the sail cockpit toward the bow. The light flickered as a small gunship moved into the path of the beam, screening *Skate*. Unable to hold position next to the Soviet trawler's deck, the copter jumped up and away into the dark as the light once again bore down on *Skate*.

One of the cutters, standing five hundred yards off the Russian ship, began to slowly circle. Suddenly her forward gun mount flashed a long tongue of flame. Instantly, the trawler, both cutters, and the hovering copters were bathed in a brilliant, harsh white light without shadow as a star shell burst and descended slowly above the spy ship. Lending following support, the other Coast Guard cutter fired a star shell as *Skate* plowed away from the circle of light. At last, the illumination was behind *Skate*—the operator of the beam blinded by the Coast Guard shells.

Niven turned his glasses on the trawler, bathed in a noon light. Men were scampering about helplessly as the navy gunships moved in, circling the trawler at deck level, creating further distraction. *Skate* silently rounded Point Loma and headed for the open sea.

"What do you think?" Niven sounded bleak.

"I really don't know, Jake boy. They might have gotten a good look and a few camera shots." He shook his head. "I just don't know," he said, staring out toward the bow.

"Bridge. Radio."

"Bridge here."

"Patch from NORAD. That spy bird passed overhead about six minutes ago."

"Thanks, Radio. Keep me informed."

"You can bet to Christ those cameras were blazing away, Charley."

Burkhart nodded silently and turned his eyes back to the black ocean, illuminated by a full yellow moon. "We'll see." He sucked in a breath of warm ocean air.

Niven wiped his sweating palms on his trousers. "Pink elephants at noon." He could barely see the lights of San Diego.

"Dark nights, Jake boy," Burkhart said softly. "Dark nights, fog, and the cover of rotten weather are what we need." He reached over and flipped down the speak lever. "Control, this is the Bridge. Make turns for twenty knots and put us on our base course."

"Aye, Captain. Maneuvering is answering bells for twenty knots and the new course is two six eight degrees true."

"Very well, Control. Make preparations to dive. Just as soon as we hit the fifty-fathom curve, let's wet her down and find out if she's still a submarine."

Niven felt his body begin to uncoil as *Skate*'s easy motion and cadence began to wear at his tension.

The set of black-faced instruments attached to the bulkhead in the cramped wardroom never wavered in their readings. The log indicator displayed a steady twenty knots, the depth gauge registered five hundred feet and the compass repeater read a rock steady two hundred sixty-eight degrees. Yet there wasn't the slightest feeling of movement anywhere in the boat.

Niven turned his gaze back to the table, dressed in a sparkling white tablecloth. Brahma Sorrell picked up Jake's eyes and smiled, expelling a satisfying puff of blue smoke from his curved briar pipe. Sitting next to Sorrell was *Skate*'s Executive Officer Irish Brennen, shifting his body nervously from side to side.

He was a pressurized bomb of adrenaline as he continually screwed his neck disapprovingly to Akivor Levy, who, for the first time Jake could remember, was dressed in clean, grease-free clothes, with his UZI machine pistol draped casually over the back of his chair. It was obvious Levy was taking pleasure in watching Brennen watch him. Levy turned to Dr. David Lathrick, the Los Alamos physicist, who had arrived aboard under armed guard the night *Skate* sailed from San Diego.

Abruptly the door latch clicked and a grim Charley Burkhart stepped into the compartment. He took his place at the head of the table and placed a large brown envelope before him.

"Well, gentlemen, we've been at sea for forty-eight hours and it's time to open and read our orders." He was dressed in clean khaki shirt and pants and felt reasonably relaxed. As reasonably as circumstances permitted. Burkhart reached over and picked up a clean

155

table knife, slit the envelope, and withdrew two sets of sealed orders. He handed one copy to Jake and then read:

SAILING ORDERS HAWKSCREECH
FROM: OPPO-099U TASK FORCE 157/NA-
        VAL SECURITY GROUP PACIFIC
TO: BURKHART, CHARLES B. CMDR
     SKATE SSN 578/NIVEN, JACOB TF
     157.
   COPIES TO:

       THE WHITE HOUSE
       SECRETARY OF DEFENSE
       CHIEF OF NAVAL OPERATIONS
       CHAIRMAN JOINT CHIEFS OF STAFF
       DIRECTOR   CENTRAL   INTELLI-
       GENCE AGENCY
       6920TH ELECTRONIC INTELLIGENCE
       GROUP MISAWA JAPAN

SUBJECT: HAWKSCREECH   PROJECT
          SAIL-ORD NODIS

1. DEPART SAN DIEGO NO LATER
    THAN 6 AUGUST. CHECK OUT ALL
    SYSTEMS THEN PROCEED SUB-
    MERGED ON NUCLEAR POWER, VIA
    NORTHWEST PACIFIC TRANSIT TO
    STATION BONNIE NO LATER THAN
    16 AUGUST. AVOID DETECTION BY
    ALL SOVIET NAVAL UNITS. ONCE
    SURFACE CONTACT IS ESTABLISHED
    YOU WILL PROCEED TO POINT
    LUCK.

2. PROCEED NORTHWEST TO KOMAN-
    DORSKI ISLAND GROUP IN SURFACE

MODE ON DIESEL POWER. YOU WILL ARRIVE POINT LUCK, LISINSKAYA BAY, BERING ISLAND, TUESDAY, 19 AUGUST 0700 ZULU.

3. DESIGNATED PARTY WILL THEN PROCEED TO BOARD MINSK, TAKE POSSESSION OF RING SWITCH AND CAPTAIN VIKTOR BELOUS. ONCE SECURED SKATE WILL TERMINATE OPERATIONS AND DEPART POINT LUCK FOR RENDEZVOUS IN AMERICAN TERRITORIAL WATERS AT STATION MOLLIE. SKATE WILL PROCEED IN SUCH A MANNER SO AS NOT TO ENDANGER ONBOARD PERSONNEL OR EQUIPMENT TAKEN FROM MINSK.

<u>SPECIAL INSTRUCTIONS:</u>

EVEN IN CASES WHERE THREAT TO SURVIVAL IS OBVIOUS FROM SOVIET WARSHIPS, YOU WILL AVOID ANY OFFENSIVE ACTION. THERE ARE NO SPECIAL CIRCUMSTANCES.

Burkhart looked up from the orders and sucked in a breath. He rubbed his puffy face and examined the expressions of the men about the table.

"Mr. Brennen and Dr. Lathrick have only been told about selective segments of HAWKSCREECH, based upon their need to know. Of course, the crew has been in the dark, and as I promised, I'm going to inform them in a general way now."

Burkhart rubbed the back of his thick neck and turned his eyes to Lathrick. "After I make the announcement to the crew, Jake Niven, the mission commander, and I will be happy to fill in any obvious gaps."

Dr. Lathrick nodded his narrow blond head but his expression revealed only thin, motionless features.

Burkhart picked the intercom mike off the bulkhead wall. "Now hear this, this is the captain, may I have your attention. As I promised I have just opened our sealed orders and I can now tell you what the hell this mystery is all about. First of all, *Skate*, former leper of the Pacific Fleet, has been selected for a most sensitive and important mission. Except for a small deck party the majority of you would have no way of knowing that we have been disguised to appear as a Soviet Foxtrot submarine."

Burkhart paused and wiped beads of nervous moisture forming around the corners of his mouth. "Very simply, we're going to drop anchor next to the carrier *Minsk*, and send an armed party aboard her to complete a top secret mission. If any of you ever wanted combat action, this will be your chance. The boarding party will consist of civilians Niven, Sorrell, Dr. Lathrick, and Akivor Levy. I want each of you to extend every possible courtesy on our boat, and assist these people in this most dangerous and difficult task. Your direct involvement will begin on 16 August, when we surface at our first rendezvous point."

He paused and cleared his dry throat. "We're going into the Bering Sea and conditions will be damn tough, so prepare yourselves. *Skate*'s the finest damned fighting boat in the fleet. I'm proud of each of you. That is all." Slowly he replaced the mike.

"Sweet Jesus!" Irish Brennen slumped in his chair. "The diesels, hull work—the whole damn thing." He whistled slowly. "I hope the lepers are up to the task."

"We've all come along way, Irish, in the last year." Burkhart raised his eyes. "Damn good crew now."

"Good point." Dr. David Lathrick rubbed his small hands together and looked up at the bare steel overhead. "I put most of it together with what Admiral Langor told me at Los Alamos." He smiled vaguely at the table. "I'm not surprised by any of it, I must say. I do want to comment about this leper business, however." His voice was clipped.

"Ah, some of your men look a bit sloppy and ragged. Maybe slovenly is a better and more precise description. Captain, do you really think these men are capable of supplying the necessary support? Taking this submarine within a few hundred yards of a Soviet carrier, then boarding that ship takes a great deal of special skill." He raised his eyes and studied the table and the silence.

Burkhart rubbed his mouth with a moist, burly hand. "Let me assure you, Dr. my people can handle any—"

"Listen carefully, Lathass, or whatever your damned name is," Niven interrupted. Admiral Langor had cursed him again.

"Dr. Lathrick, if you don't mind, Mr. Niven." His gaze was steady.

"You don't look so hot yourself, Lathrick. I wonder if you're up to stepping aboard that carrier without your guts turning inside out and your knees dissolving into jelly?"

"Christ, Jake, take it easy."

"You take it easy, Charley! I'm not going to sit here and listen to some high-tech asshole feed on me and this mission. It's you! You and your people who have been whacking off for the past ten years, allowing the Russians to build their advantage with beam weapons, or whatever the hell it is. That's a lot of crust to put us down, because we don't measure up to Madison Avenue ad images, or your vague standards."

"Mr. Niven, I didn't mean any disrespect. I only—"

"The hell you didn't." Jake slammed a fist against the table. "I've stepped over bodies to put all this together. Maybe next time, you puzzle-palace freaks will stay on your toes, so you don't have to depend on a few whores like us, to steal a goddamn ring switch gadget!"

Niven stood and faced Lathrick, his voice turning dark. "I'm going to watch you, Lathrick. I'm going to watch every move you make, because the lives of my boarding party and every man on this boat depend on you not choking. You're the centerpiece at this last supper, Doc. If I were you, I'd worry only about finding that fucking little gadget aboard *Minsk,* and leave the rest of it to us, to protect your soft little ass. Otherwise I won't punch your ticket for roundtrip."

21

The deck vibrated slightly and began to cant down. Burkhart surveyed his control room operation and the men manning *Skate's* vital stations. Finally he looked down at Niven and the massive Sorrell.

"Nothing to worry about, gentlemen. "I'm taking her down another couple hundred feet. We're approaching a deep swell area off the central California coast." He smiled reassuringly. "Just want to keep the Bering Express running smoothly."

Niven looked down at his watch and tapped the faceplate.

"Be right with you, Jake boy. Irish, you take the Conn. I've got a fifteen-minute meeting with Niven and his people."

"Aye, Skipper. I've got the Conn." Brennen stepped up onto the periscope stand, relieving Burkhart.

Niven surveyed the table in the officers' wardroom. "I want to spend a few minutes briefing you on the defensive setup we will encounter as we approach our target at Bering Island."

Sorrell, Lathrick, Levy, and Burkhart looked down at the chart. "This first part is for you, Charley. We will encounter our first real resistance about seventy miles out from *Minsk.*" Niven swept a finger in a large arc on the chart. These will comprise the older but still effective Riga Class frigates, acting as picket boats."

"Where'd the information come from?" Burkhart asked.

"Straight from Viktor Belous, our Russian captain."

"Good enough."

"There will be *Byk* on the north, *Lev* to the east, and *Shakal* to the south. They displace about sixteen hundred tons and carry basic antisubmarine weapons."

Niven went on to describe in detail the guided missile cruiser screen, submarines, and destroyer forces that *Skate* would have to thread in order to reach their objective inside Lisinskaya Bay.

"Remember the majority of ships are there to seek out and pick up what's left of the missile nose cones that are fired from the Soviet mainland during the testing. Let's hope they won't be looking for *Skate* disguised as a Russian sub." Niven swept a hand over the chart in the form of a papal blessing. "There is, however, the chance that the Russians will be alerted to us. We just don't know."

"We have to go on the assumption that we are still secure," Burkhart added.

"Do you mean that the Russians might have the idea of what we are going to do?" David Lathrick looked stricken.

"I'm afraid so, Doctor. But we have to push on." Niven looked at his watch. "I don't mean to be flip about it, Doctor, but there is really nothing we can do at this point." He eyed Lathrick. "We are committed and we go."

"I see," Lathrick said.

"When we pass the missile cruisers, we will be inside the secure area that we've named The Dog Bowl, based on the rounded contour of the land mass in Lisinskaya Bay. Once inside The Dog Bowl, we'll encounter *Komarov*, a large tracking vessel directly related to tracking missile targets for the beam weapon. Close to a thousand yards beyond, we will find our target, *Minsk.*"

"Jake, how the hell am I going to make my entire approach through this screen into Lisinskaya Bay?"

Jake ran his finger on an invisible curved track through the ships to the *Minsk*. "It will be a surface run all the way."

"What is my pretext for being there? Even a Russian sub just doesn't drop in on a task force of eighteen Soviet ships conducting secret tests."

"*Skate* is going in as a wounded duck. Engine problems with one of your surface diesels will force you to reduce speed."

The wardroom was very quiet. There was really nothing to say, just listen.

"What about Captain Belous and the exchange of the painting?" Burkhart asked.

"Let me bring you all up to date on Belous." Idly, Niven tapped the chart, then looked at Lathrick. Obviously, Admiral Langor had painted a very rosy picture and had told this man very little. He had burden written all over his delicate face.

"Our man is Captain First Rank, Kapitan Pervogo Ranga Viktor Belous. Assignments before taking command of *Minsk*, include Naval Attaché at the Soviet Embassy in London, and prior to that he served in *Minsk*'s sister ship *Kiev*, as commanding officer."

Niven detailed Belous's career history as far back as World War Two. "This man is top notch all the way. Not at all short on guts. In 1944, he led his torpedo boat against a German destroyer and an entire surface force in the White Sea. His boat sank that destroyer and he was awarded the Order of Lenin, with two clusters, added during later skirmishes with the Germans."

"When did Belous take command of *Minsk?*" Levy asked.

"Eight months ago. When Belous took over in *Minsk,* she was operating in the Indian Ocean and the Bay of Bengal with her battle group." Niven could feel the tension as he spoke.

"Kapitan Belous comes from a strong Russian family. His late father was Soviet Army Colonel-General E. B. Belous, who fought alongside Lenin during the revolution. Our man was married to the daughter of N. N. Amelko, former deputy commander of the Black Sea Fleet. Communist royalty all the way down the line. Kapitan Belous's marriage never produced children, but according to our source, they had a very strong, loving relationship."

"Go on," Levy said.

"That thirty-year marriage to Anna Belous ended in her death three months after he accepted command of *Minsk.* About five months ago. For years, the Belouses had lived in a very spacious hotel suite apartment in Leningrad and they both shared an obsessive passion for art. With the Hermitage Museum at their doorstep, it was only natural that they both spent a great deal of time at the museum."

"This is all very interesting but—" Levy interrupted.

"The but is that Mrs. Belous contracted cancer of the liver and wrote her husband, begging him to come home. On six separate occasions, Belous asked for leave from Moscow, and all six times permission was denied. In her letters to him, she spared no detail of her agony, pain, and loneliness." Niven thought of Ellie. Of her loneliness. Of the letter he promised to read when he knew he would be coming home. Niven looked into Levy's questioning eyes and understood Viktor Belous's terrible anger.

"I don't really understand this art exchange business. This painting. Why is it so very important?" Levy raised a heavy eyebrow. "Important enough to use as a reason to defect." He shook his head.

"Before Mrs. Belous's final hospitalization, she spent all her waking hours at the Hermitage, in room eleven, sitting before and admiring a painting by Leonardo Da Vinci called 'The Madonna Litta.' It was painted in 1490. The 'Litta' portrayed a beautiful mother nursing her child." Niven watched the distance in Levy's eyes, grow. Now he understood. Remembering his own pain of his own wife and children at Maalot.

"I see what you are saying," Levy said quietly.

"These letters that Anna Belous wrote to her husband were a dying woman's love letters to her husband. In those letters she would analyze that Da Vinci over and over, describing every last detail to her husband." Niven swallowed into a hard lump in his throat. His eyes traveled about the wardroom. Every man understood. "Her last letter to her husband, written from her clinic deathbed, described a dream she had, where she had been visited by Da Vinci's mother and child, as an affirmation of her love for her husband. That was the last time Belous ever heard from his wife. Understandably, these letters just tore the man apart."

Levy raised a hand. "Go on, please, Niven."

"Belous, prior to his wife's death, had made one final appeal to Admiral of the Fleet Vladimir Chernavin to be with his wife when she died. Chernavin turned him down, flat."

"Tough bastards," Burkhart offered.

"It's not quite that simple, Charley. Just after Belous accepted command of *Minsk*, he was told that a particle beam weapon was to be placed aboard his ship. As a gesture of good faith, it was Belous who told us about the weapon." Jake looked sternly at Burkhart. "They've been flying in and hauling by cargo ship all the necessary equipment to *Minsk* at sea, and then building or assembling their major components below the flight deck while *Minsk* carried on her normal routine at sea. This has been going on for months. An incredibly brilliant idea. We could take all the photos of her we wanted from the air or space and it didn't mean a damn thing."

"Admiral Chernavin obviously needed Belous aboard *Minsk*. It was a decision of need and logic opposed to emotion," Burkhart said. "The Naval Ministry was betting that Belous would work through it."

"The Soviet Naval Ministry bet wrong about Belous. Just prior to taking command of *Minsk*, he had been Naval Attaché in London and he really knew his way around." For a moment Niven flashed on Lional Crabb. He rubbed his tired eyes. "Carefully, but in a determined fashion, Belous planned his moves and when *Minsk* put into Bombay he took his first step. He slipped ashore, unobserved, and telephoned our contact in London and asked for help to defect. He told our London contact what he wanted. After a very brief conversation, our London person realized what he had stumbled into. It was just a windfall. Just a damn fortunate turn of the wheel."

"We will see how fortunate in a few days." Levy wiped his face with a clean handkerchief. "Maybe yes, maybe no."

Sometime ago, Mr. Levy, I smuggled myself into Mogadishu." Sorrell fingered the cold pipe like a gun.

Levy's face brightened. "The Somali Republic."

"When *Minsk* visited that African port city, I met with Captain Belous. It was Belous who gave me that Molniya code tape and all the information of Soviet defenses on this chart."

"Still and again, to give up what has to be the most prestigious command in the Soviet Navy . . . Defecting won't bring his wife back," Burkhart said.

"I can only tell you what he told me." Sorrell turned his massive head to face Burkhart. "He said he was very bitter and still deeply in love with his wife. He said that if his country had been at war, he could have accepted his wife dying alone, but not during peacetime. I was skeptical about Belous when all this first came up, but after meeting with him, I am a believer. He wants that painting and will do anything to get it. Just before we met in Somali, Belous was flown home for a briefing on OPERATION FLASHLAMP, *Mah'gneeyevyya Lahm'py*. He said that if he had any doubts, they dissolved when he visited his wife's grave in Leningrad. They had flown him home to discuss the beam weapon, but not to say good-bye to his dying wife."

"Is the Da Vinci we have aboard the original from the Hermitage?" asked David Lathrick.

Niven nodded.

Lathrick's eyes suddenly grew interested. "How the hell did you do that?"

"We have friends everywhere, Doctor." Niven thought of Vasili Lykov and shivered. Dead friends, Lathrick.

"How will Captain Belous know or be certain that the Da Vinci is real?" Levy unconsciously rubbed his hands, although they were clean of grease.

"He's something of an expert." We had a long discussion about it." Sorrell played with his beard. "In 1930, his father, at the request of Stalin, negotiated the sale of Russian art treasures to Western nations, to generate sorely needed foreign currency and foreign exchange credits. The older Belous sold two Rembrandts, 'The Mill' and 'Portrait of an Old Man' to the British. Before the sale, the paintings hung in Belous's Moscow home. The man knows," Sorrell said quietly.

"Let us hope the man knows just where that Ring Switch is located." Levy rose from his chair and faced Niven, who could feel his pores begin to open to the stress of boarding *Minsk*.

Burkhart reached over from his chair and answered the buzzing intercom. "This is the captain."

"Brennen here, Skipper. We've got a problem. In fact, two problems, plus a sonar contact."

"Be right there." Burkhart stood. "That's it for me, gentlemen. Let's just hope the old lady isn't wounded."

"That bad?"

"Any problem in *Skate* can be fatal, Jake boy."

22

"What the hell is it!" The control room was quiet for a few moments, then the deep knocking started again.

Burkhart stepped up on the platform just as Brennen entered the control room. "Something banging around inside that false bow."

"Can we get to it from inside the boat, Irish?"

"Not a chance, Skipper. I've had Chief Russotto looking at the problem." Brennen raised his eyes. "Russotto's kept us going for a very long time with his special know-how."

Burkhart looked up, surprised. Brennen hated the Chief of the Boat's guts. Had almost from day one. Months before, Burkhart had tried to smooth it out, but it was impossible. It was chemistry and all three men knew it and did their best to work around it. This was the first time Burkhart had ever heard his XO pay Russotto a compliment.

"We'll have to take her up, Skipper. The noise is playing hell with Mead's sonar system."

Burkhart stepped off the platform and bent over the plot table, studying the chart. "It's hopefully still safe to surface. We're just eight hundred miles west of the

California coast, just south of San Francisco." He looked over at Brennen. "What's the other problem?"

"We've blown the radar."

"How the hell did that happen?" Burkhart's neck flushed.

"They were warming up the primary and secondary units when something blew. We figured it would be a good time to break the whole system down and repair it before we have to make that surface run into Bering Island." Brennen looked at Burkhart and shrugged. "The entire system checked out before we sailed."

Burkhart mashed his jaw and leaned around the corner of the attack stand and found Spike Mead. "How's our target doing, Sonar."

"About the same, Captain. She still bears one six five degrees true. Speed twelve knots. The range has closed to just under one mile."

"Can you make out what she is?"

"Two screws, light engines. Not a great deal of hull resistance. Maybe four hundred tons." Mead looked up at Burkhart. "Fishing boat?" Mead turned over his hands to form the question.

Burkhart grunted and turned back to find Niven standing next to the navigation table.

"We've got to surface, Jake. There isn't really a choice." Quickly he explained the problem.

"Give me a five-degree up bubble. Let's take her up to periscope depth. Four hundred feet."

The orders were repeated and the planesman pulled back on his control column and *Skate* began her ascent. Burkhart checked the bulkhead clock: 1105. Still the morning sun. Good. That would provide the best resolution for a periscope search.

"We'll use the large scope, Irish. Then—"

"Four hundred feet, Captain," called out the officer of the dive.

"Up scope." Brennen pulled down on the release "pickle," and the scope began rising in telescope fashion out of *Skate*'s bowels. Burkhart flopped down the steel handles and mashed his eyes to the glass before the tip broke free of the ocean.

Silently Burkhart turned the scope on its axis. "Sonar, what's happening?" His voice grew tense.

"That target is close, Captain. The range has closed to six hundred yards, bearing still one six five."

Burkhart swung the scope to one hundred sixty-five degrees. "Can't see a damn thing. We're fogged in. Zero zero visibility on the surface. Waves one to two. It's really socked in."

"Russotto, we need that radar," Brennen called to the back of the control room.

"Sorry, sir, no can do." Russotto stood and faced his Executive Officer. "It's in a thousand pieces and we haven't even found the source of the trouble yet."

Brennen narrowed his eyes. "As fast as you can, Chief."

"Aye, aye, sir."

Burkhart had listened to the conversation and was debating in his mind the best way to deal with traveling blind on the surface with a target somewhere close at hand. Collision was the great fear of all submariners. Collision could mean sudden death and a quick, uncontrolled plunge to the ocean floor.

"Get your repair party ready, Irish." Burkhart had made his decision. "Sonar, give me readings every two minutes. Mead, I want to know where the target is all the time."

"Aye, sir. Bearings every two minutes on the target."

Orders were quietly passed about the control room as each man prepared his station for the surface. AH OO GAH AH OO GAH. The klaxon sounded, giving

171

warning to any crewman who might be off watch, that *Skate* was heading for the surface.

"Surface, surface," Brennen called out. Orders were called out to blow ballast tanks as *Skate's* nose began to slowly climb for the fog-shrouded surface.

"Target, bearing one six five degrees, speed still twelve knots, range three hundred yards."

"Up scope." Burkhart received the rising barrel into his stomach and draped his arms around the handles. He checked the bearing indicator below the scope. "One six five," he said aloud to himself as he aimed the periscope at the invisible electronic echo coming back to *Skate*.

"Anything, Skipper?"

"Nothing, Irish. Not a damn thing but fog." Burkhart pulled the scope around in a slow, cautious circle.

"Passing one hundred twenty feet," the officer of the dive called out.

The interior hull of the control room echoed with the pinging of Mead's sonar as he followed the unseen ship's path.

"Four degrees up bubble." Purposely, *Skate* was not hurrying to reach the surface.

"Captain," Mead called out, "our target is closing us!" There was panic in his voice. "Range is less than two hundred yards. Still bearing one six five." Mead and every man in the control room watched Burkhart, still coiled about the periscope.

"Helm, hard right rudder!"

Instantly, the boat veered to the right forcing everyone to hold tight.

"Passing ninety feet," called out the dive officer.

"Target range now three hundred yards, Captain." The tension was gone from Mead's voice.

"Passing sixty feet."

"Steady up on three five five, Helm."

172

"Aye, sir. The new course is three five five and the rudder is amidships."

"Our target has turned," Mead called out. "He now bears two five zero. Collision course. Collision course!"

"Dammit! Are you sure, Mead?"

"Target range now less than one hundred yards and closing. Speed twelve knots."

"Passing thirty feet. The sail should be breaking the surface anytime, Captain."

Burkhart glanced quickly at Niven and shook his head. The sound of rumbling engines, like a distant freight train, reached Burkhart's ears. That damn ship was close. Close enough to reach out and touch. It was too late to break the ascent. There just wasn't time. By the time *Skate* pushed her twenty-five hundred tons down, she would have already breached. There was nothing to do but pray.

"Move, dammit! Move out of the way!" Burkhart screamed in desperation. "Close and dog all watertight doors! Stand by! Sound collision alarm!"

"Target crossing our stern!" Mead called out frantically.

"Zero bubble, breaking the surface now!"

"Stand by to crack—"

A violent shudder of steel fighting steel passed through *Skate* and every man in her. There was a collective moment when every heart beat and every breath in *Skate* froze. Then *Skate* began to roll on her beam, fighting the momentum of an unknown ship running her down. The grinding grew louder as the intruder's engines pounded a death knell throughout *Skate*.

The control room lights flickered as *Skate* heeled.

"Emergency lights," Burkhart ordered as calmly as he could. "Come on, baby, slide right over the top. We've got important business somewhere else," Burkhart pleaded.

173

A horrid shriek of tearing steel reached the control room. "Get away from my *Skate*, you killing bastard!" shouted Chief Russotto. Then there was silence. A strange silence of waiting for the pain of the injury to reach the proper brain center. Slowly *Skate*'s rolling motion ceased and she began to right herself.

Burkhart, hanging onto his periscope stand reached for the ship's intercom mike. "All compartments report damage. Damage control parties stand by. We've been hit by a ship!"

Finally, the ship's engines began to fade. Niven's heart was in his throat, waiting for *Skate* to begin her downward death plunge.

"Hold on, baby, hold on," Burkhart prayed to himself as *Skate* fought to right herself. "How's the board look?"

"We've still got a straight board, sir." No hatches or valves sprung. She's holding tight."

"Best damn submarine in the fleet," a voice called out from somewhere in the attack center. Cheers broke out all over the compartment. Muted whistles and hollering rose up from other compartments beyond the control room as the main hatch was cracked.

A few moments later charley Burkhart stood in his sail cockpit, bathed in a thick pea soup fog, trying to survey the damage. He cupped his hands and yelled down at Chief Russotto. Even at ten feet, Russotto was just a vague, misty shape.

"How bad, Chief?"

"About thirty feet aft of the sail. Deep grooves in the hull. Just like a damn railroad track. She's still watertight. Can't believe it. Never seen anything like it, Captain."

"What about the rudder and safety track?"

"Rudder looks fine. That ship came close. Played

174

hell with the sonar heads. Looks like we lost about five sound heads."

Burkhart rubbed his leathery face. "What about the safety track?"

"Shot to hell, Captain. Deep grooves right across it. The boys will have to be careful as hell on deck. She won't take a safety harness, that's for sure."

"Permission to come on the bridge."

"Come ahead, Jake boy."

"How bad?" Niven climbed up through the hatch.

"We're still together. God knows how."

Niven surveyed the thick wet fog that held *Skate* in a soundless white glove. It was an eerie sensation as *Skate* plowed ahead in the calm Pacific waters, almost a thousand miles from California. The rolling cadence of the sea and the churning foam were the only tactile signs of movement.

"Sonar, Bridge. Where the hell is that target now?"

"Bridge, aye. "Target still bears two five zero. Range one mile. Speed twelve knots."

"Bastard just kept on going." Burkhart moved to the back of the sail. "Chief, I'm sending you that repair party to clean out whatever the hell is inside the false bow."

"Aye, aye, sir. You'd better reduce your speed. We don't want anyone going overboard in this fog."

"Good thinking, Chief. Control, this is the Bridge. Give me an all-stop bell. Repair party to the deck. Set a sea anchor detail to check our drift."

Slowly *Skate* began to lose way as her bow dropped back into the sea. Quickly crewmen materialized from inside *Skate* as Russotto's command voice took over, directing and cautioning his people at the same time.

"Make it fast, Chief," Burkhart called down to the bow.

"Bridge, sonar."

175

"Go ahead, sonar."

"No new contacts. Our target has extended his range to five miles."

The muted sound of power tools filled the sea air as Russotto's party worked to clear the bow. The sea, almost with human understanding, gentled her swell in sympathy.

"What was that?" Niven looked over at Burkhart.

Burkhart shook his head.

"I head something, Charley."

"What?"

"I don't know. A voice. I'm not sure."

"Not out here. There's not a man alive who's spent time at sea, especially when he's becalmed, who hasn't heard a sound or two."

Niven raised his glasses and searched the gray waters surrounding *Skate*. Visibility had increased to thirty feet. He shivered and saw Vasili Lykov's old fleshy face in the quiet swell.

"Everyone sees a ghost or two, Jake boy." Burkhart's voice was quiet and gentle. "We've all seen our share." He leaned over the cockpit bulwark. "Hurry it up, Chief. What's going on down there?"

"We found the problem, sir. Damn sloppy yard people. They ought to be shot. A goddamn metal lunch box, thermos, and a shitload of tools. We'll have her nose bolted back on in a couple of minutes."

"Well done, Chief."

"Quiet, I just heard it again," Niven said.

Pe-ma-G'I-t'i mn'e. Pe-ma-G'I-t'i mn'e.

Niven swung his glasses to the strange sound. It wasn't a damn ghost from the Gulf of Finland! It was a man in the water! A man speaking Russian. A man calling "Help me. Help me."

"Man in the water," Niven shouted. "Man in the water!"

"Where, dammit?"

Niven pointed.

Burkhart swung his glasses to the spot.

Pe-ma-G'I-t'i mn'e.

"Got it! Chief, man in the water. Man in the water! About eight points off the starboard bow. Fish him out on the double!"

"Jesus Christ, what the hell hit us, Charley? A man in the water, speaking Russian. I don't understand." His eye caught Burkhart in the fog.

"I do, Jake boy. Damn bastards."

Burkhart faced the man in the wardroom with Niven and Sorrell translating. A navy blanket was wrapped around his shoulders. The man, possibly in his early twenties, carried a broad, flat face with light brown hair. He was frightened and cold, standing in an alien world.

"The ship that hit us was a Russian trawler," Niven said. This man is a signalman-quartermaster."

"Kvarteerme'ister signaller," the man repeated.

"What the hell were they doing here?"

"Monitoring missile testing from Vandenberg. They had just come off station and were heading home." Niven turned to the man. "He speaks English, Charley. One of his jobs was monitoring radio traffic. He's not great at it, but he gets by to do his job."

Burkhart squinted at the man. "How the hell did you end up in the water?"

The Russian opened his mouth as if to speak, but nothing came out. He began to shiver as his lips turned blue.

"He's scared shitless, Charley," Sorrell added. "He thinks you've blamed him for his ship hitting us."

Burkhart reached over and touched the young man's

wet shoulder. "How did you fall in the water?" He smiled at the Russian.

"I was standing a deck watch, ah, how you say, ah, to guard against the fog." He made an expressive move with his hands. "My ship turned to left with a great violence, and ah—"

The Russian's lips began to quiver from fright and cold.

"Easy, son." Burkhart touched his shoulder. He turned and flipped down the intercom. "Winebelly, this is the captain. I'm in the wardroom. Bring some fresh coffee and sandwiches up here, on the double."

"Thank you, sir. How do you say, ah—" He turned to Niven and Sorrell. *"Z Dah'Tsa."*

Sorrell shook his large head very slowly. "He wants to surrender."

Burkhart rubbed his neck and examined his problem. Finally he smiled again. "We're not at war with you, son."

Burkhart folded his arms, trying to figure out what to do with the man. "What's your name?"

"Petr Deriabin." For the first time, the Russian smiled.

"Well, Peter, we won't throw you back into the ocean. You say your ship turned and—"

The Russian looked down, embarrassed. "I fell overboard, sir. I fell from my balance."

"What's the name of your ship, Peter?"

"The *Guiroskop,* sir."

"Are you Soviet Navy?" Niven asked.

Petr Deriabin shook his head. "Was before. Not now. Am civilian."

Burkhart followed Niven and Sorrell out of the wardroom. "What are you going to do with him?"

"I can't throw him back, for Chrissakes. I'll just to have him secured somewhere, away from the control

178

room." He raised a hand in the form of a question mark. "I can't let him have the run of the ship. He'll just have to be watched all the time. I'll figure out later what to do with him."

Irish Brennen found the huddle next to the wardroom. "Can I see you in the control room, Skipper."

23

Niven lay on his bunk with his hands behind his head. Sleep was pointless and painful. Slowly he fingered the sealed envelope and thought about opening it. Then he thought of the promise he'd made Ellie. If he opened it and read the letter before knowing what his fate would be, he'd break faith with their future. The reality was subtle but forceful, that his entire life boiled down to the next few days and all that he could do was wait. Of all the people aboard, excluding Sorrell and Burkhart, only Niven really knew how terribly alone *Skate* would be as she bore down on her fate with *Minsk*. So many demons. Lykov, Crabb, Langor, and Ellie, with *Minsk* looming just over the next horizon.

"Jake? Jake, are you sleeping?" Sorrell opened the door and stepped into the small stateroom.

"No." He smiled at Sorrell and sat up on the bunk, swinging his feet to the deck.

"What's up?" He looked at Sorrell with concern. He'd seen that expression countless times and could hear the sense of urgency in his voice.

Sorrell closed the door and sat cross-legged over the small desk chair across from the bunks. "Why didn't you tell me Levy was joining the boarding party?"

"I didn't think it was that important," Jake shrugged. "He's a tough, dependable bastard. We need him."

"With him on board the mission, it fucks it up." Sorrell's voice was even and calm, but his fierce eyes were blazing with anger.

"We don't need him, Jake. He'll just get in the way, and I'm not sure how this guy Levy will act under pressure."

"Levy will act just fine. I've watched him closely for the past two months and he's a tough son of a bitch who's paid his dues with MOSSAD. They're not exactly the Boy Scouts. But I already said that, didn't I?"

"I still don't want him around." Brahma Sorrell shoved the curved briar pipe into his mouth. "It wasn't in the original plan and I know the man will get us nailed. I can sense it in my bones. You and I can handle whatever happens aboard *Minsk.*"

"How the hell do you know we can?" Jake rubbed his hands through his hair in frustration. "HAWK-SCREECH was a crap shoot from the start. Almost nothing in the operation was set in concrete. Akivor Levy just happened and with Lathrick being the question mark he is, Levy can be a great help with his mechanical skills. We only have thirty goddamned minutes aboard that vessel. That just isn't a great deal of time. I'm worried about Lathrick, not Levy."

Sorrell's face turned into a sulk. "I'm worried about the whole thing now. Maybe this guy Levy's a Soviet plant."

For a moment Niven digested the words. "Maybe you're a Soviet plant. Isn't that stupid. You acted the same way in the Gulf of Finland. What the hell is it with you? Have you lost your nerve? What happened to that cold rolled steel attitude of yours?"

181

"You know better than that, Jake," Sorrell replied. "We're a team and—"

Niven reached out and slapped Brahma's knee. "Lighten up. Levy is good and his Russian is as fluent as ours. He never blinks and seems to have ice cubes for a soul. Besides, he knows how to use that UZI." He smiled up at Sorrell's big, menacing face. "He's got a score to settle and I like that."

Sorrell rose from the chair and nodded his head. Slowly he reached for the door and held it open as if he had something else to say when Charley Burkhart popped his head in. Sorrell grunted and pushed past Burkhart in a huff. The light odor of fried chicken from dinner drifted into the cabin as Burkhart stepped in.

"We've developed a major problem I think you should be made aware of."

"What?"

"Reactor Control reports a hairline crack has been found in a brazed joint in the primary heating loop of the reactor envelope."

"What the hell does that mean?"

Burkhart tapped the small exposure badge clipped to Jake's flannel shirt. "It means that if the crack widens or if we find other cracks in the piping we'll have to SCRAM or shut down the reactor. The primary loop holds the radioactive steam." Burkhart held up a hand.

"Look, Jake, the crack could have been there for a long time and it could mean nothing, or it could be a sign of metal fatigue in the entire system. We'll just have to keep a sharp eye on the system. I've already detailed a special watch for just that purpose."

Niven backed up and plopped down on the bunk. "That's just great. I feel like a mule kicked me below the waist."

"There's nothing else to do but watch it for now. I told you people in the beginning that *Skate* was old and run-down. I just plan to maintain revolutions and see what happens."

"Skipper?" Irish Brennen popped his head into the cabin. "We've got another little problem that needs your attention. First, good news. Radar is fixed and operational."

"Good." Burkhart nodded. "What else?"

"It's a personnel matter." Irish looked over at Niven.

"Go ahead, Jake is one of the leper colony in good standing. He ought to own a damn plank in *Skate*."

"It seems that after you told the crew about the mission, your Sonar Officer, Spike Mead, made a crack about your command abilities and it was overheard by Chief Russotto." Brennen dropped his eyes and paused.

"Well, what happened?"

Russotto slugged him in the kisser. Considering the fact that Mead is twice his size, Russotto did one hell of a job on him. Well, Mead put him on report and has a shiner under his right eye."

Burkhart's expression turned sour. "Where'd it happen?"

"In the control room, Skipper."

24

Brennen followed the captain into his tiny compartment and closed the door. Silently, Burkhart unbuttoned his shirt and tossed it on the bunk. Brennen had seen that silence before. It could be awesome. Large dark sweat stains marked Burkhart's T-shirt.

Slowly he rubbed his face and turned to Brennen. "Mead's been a problem since day one, but I kept him because I thought I could straighten him out. Look how he helped out when the radar went down. So bright, so—" Burkhart reached into his desk and pulled out a cigar. Carefully he examined both ends before striking a match. The process relaxed him. "Kid's a paradox."

Brennen leaned against the door and knew it wasn't time to speak, yet. Even tossing the shirt on the bunk was ritual.

"I see part of my job as an instructor to junior officers. How else can we really train them? Mead's great material. If I transferred him out of *Skate*, for the crap he's pulled, his career would be down the tubes." He blew out a large brown cloud of smoke and rolled the cigar in his mouth. Burkhart picked up the form listing Mead's allegations against Chief Russotto.

"Captain, Control."

Burkhart flipped down the intercom switch. "Captain, here."

"Course correction for Station Bonnie in four hours, sir. We are right on schedule and on the course."

"Very well, fine navigating."

Quickly Burkhart finished the form and looked thoughtfully up at Brennen. "What's your recommendation, XO?"

"We don't have a choice. At least I don't see one. It's not even a Captain's Mast offense. Too damn serious. There should be a General Court." He narrowed his eyes at Burkhart.

"You don't like Russotto, Irish. You never have."

"True enough, Skipper. But an enlisted man striking an officer violates the first rule of command. I'd bust him down to boot and give him hard time in the slammer. If it were a hundred years ago, I'd have him keel hauled. Article one twenty-eight—"

"The first rule of command is to carry out your mission, Irish." Burkhart's voice was heavy with disappointment. "We're not operating in a vacuum here."

"I still think—"

"Mead is an immature kid and Russotto has the respect of every enlisted man in this boat. For Chrissakes, Irish, he's my Chief of the Boat! He knows every damn rivet and bolt in her. The enlisted men belong to him. What do you think it would do to the morale of this crew if I busted their chief? What do you think it would do to the mission?"

"Russotto can be replaced."

"You came up through the ranks, Irish." Burkhart shook his head. "You know better than I do. You can't put the whole crew on hack. Russotto stays put."

Burkhart mashed down on the cigar. More than Mead, Brennen's response to the situation would have

185

to go in his next fitness report. He closed his eyes, blotting it out. It would have to wait for another time.

"One other little thing, Skipper. Last night I smelled someone smoking dope in the forward enlisted head."

Burkhart removed the cigar from his mouth. "I'll take care of it, Irish." His voice was barely audible. In his gut he knew that Irish would never have his own boat and he felt sorry for his friend.

"All right, Irish, let's get to it. Find Russotto and send him in here on the double. I can't afford to let this thing fester."

Chief Petty Officer Jerry Russotto, anticipating Burkhart's move, must have been close at hand. Within three minutes he was standing at attention in Burkhart's cramped stateroom.

For a long time Burkhart stared at his desk, then at his fingernails, then he looked up at his chief, still standing rigidly at attention with his open, broad face and squat, tough body.

"Why'd you do it, Chief?"

"Skipper, Mr. Mead's been asking for it for a long time and his comment just pushed me over the edge, sir."

Burkhart worked to keep his temper under control. "What was that comment, Russotto?"

Russotto pointed down at the report on Burkhart's desk. "Ah, sir, it's in the report."

"You tell me, Chief." Burkhart spoke with clenched teeth.

"Well, sir, ah, Mead turned to his telephone talker after you told us more about the mission and said loud enough for the whole control room to hear that 'Steamboat Willy Burkhart couldn't lead *Skate* on a mission to Catalina Island because he's too busy beating off in his stateroom.' "

Burkhart looked down at the report. "Mr. Mead

wrote that all he said was that *Skate* wasn't in shape to make it to Catalina."

"That's a damn lie, sir. There's five guys in control who will back me up, sir." Russotto's face was etched with intense emotional pain and his large fleshy nose had turned bright red.

"I don't care who'll back you up, Goddammit!" Burkhart exploded. "You're my Chief of the Boat. My streetwise overseer of the entire crew. There's just no excuse. There's real cause here for a General Court. I could bust your ass down to seaman apprentice and get you hard time without pay for this. Don't you know that?" Burkhart yelled. "Did you think about those five kids of yours in Seattle and how they'd make out when you put your fist into Mead's face?"

"Ah, no, sir." Russotto cast his eyes downward to the deck. "I was thinking about you, sir, and the dignity of this boat. Mr. Mead's been making cracks about you for as long as I can remember. I even talked to him in private about it a couple of times and he just laughed in my face, sir. I mean, I never seen an officer on a boat talk like that about his skipper. The crew's been jawing about it for months."

"Your timing stinks, you know that, Chief? Of all the bonehead moves." Burkhart sat back in his chair and stared at Russotto, still standing at attention. "Number one, after I'm done talking with him you're gonna march your ass back into that control room and apologize to Mr. Mead. Two, I have to take some action, but for the present I will take the matter under consideration as to what course to follow. Three, you're gonna take this crew in hand and shape them up about this Mead business. Four, if Mr. Mead shoots his mouth off again, you come to me and I'll handle it. Now get your ass out of here and pass the word that I want to see Mead, right now!"

Having temporarily escaped with his life, Russotto exited the stateroom as fast as humanly possible.

Lieutenant Virgil "Spike" Mead came to attention but it was almost comical with the right side of his face already puffed and turning an ugly reddish blue from Russotto's fist.

"Reporting as ordered, sir." A slight smug smile curled at the corners of Mead's well-shaped lips.

"Something funny, Mead?" Burkhart kept his voice even and methodical.

"No, sir."

"Well, it seems you have me just where you want me, Spike." Burkhart smiled up at his sonar officer.

"Yes, sir, it would seem so." He grinned with small white teeth at Burkhart.

"Sit down, Spike." Burkhart waved him to the chair next to his desk with a friendly voice.

"I guess my first question, Spike, is did you in any way provoke this alleged attack?"

"No, sir, I really didn't. It came as a complete surprise. At least the attack did." Mead, feeling more relaxed and in control, sat back in his chair. "Russotto's been a foul ball for some time."

"Oh?" Burkhart cocked his head.

"He's always on the backs of the crew and junior officers about one thing or another. Always trying to show them how to do their jobs. He's even gone over the heads of divisional officers in disciplining the crew."

Burkhart raised his eyes to Mead. "I have a real problem here, Spike, and I need your help." He smiled again.

"Whatever I can do, sir, I will."

"I knew you would, Spike. You see, we've got this

mission. It's pretty important to me that Russotto keeps his rating and serves me as Chief of the Boat."

Mead's face dropped. "Oh, I thought—"

"I know what you thought," Burkhart interrupted. "But let me run it down for you, Mr. Mead, so you and I are really communicating for once. Is that all right with you?"

"Certainly, sir."

"Good. Because here's the way it breaks down for me, as commanding officer of this submarine." His voice was still calm and soft. "You're gonna rewrite that report about Russotto to read that he used vulgar language in the presence of certain crew members. If you don't, and it's certainly your option, Mead, I'll personally bring you up on charges that include dereliction of duty, numerous absences from assigned duties, embezzlement of the boat's recreational funds, endangering the lives of your fellow officers and crewmen on numerous occasions, and finally, but not least, engaging in sexual intercourse with civilian females, illegally brought aboard a commissioned fleet submarine of the United States Navy."

Burkhart took a deep breath to maintain his control, then smiled at Mead, who was sitting stiffly with his back ramrod straight.

"Sir, you can't whitewash what happened to my eye." Mead's voice rose to a nervous shrill.

"Whitewash, Mead? Oh, no." Burkhart's voice turned ice cold. "You slipped and ran into an elbow. It was accidental."

Burkhart rose from his desk and stepped to his bunk. He paused for a moment, then leaned over. Quickly he snapped a rock-stiff elbow into the shiner beneath Mead's right eye. It was perfect and the force of the blow knocked Mead off his chair to the deck.

As Mead thrashed about the small stateroom in pain,

Burkhart picked him up with both hands and planted him firmly back in the chair. Mead had both hands covering his wounded face.

"God, I'm sorry, Mead, they must have waxed the deck and I slipped. Are you all right, son?" Burkhart ripped Mead's hands down and examined his right cheek. It had been a precise shot, catching Mead right on the spot where Russotto's fist had landed. "Shall I call Corpsman Ginepra to have him look at it?"

"No, sir." Mead had trouble talking as a second swelling had begun. Mead, with glassy eyes and chalked lips, looked over at Burkhart who had taken his seat.

"Now listen up, Mead." Burkhart's voice turned sour. "You've fucked up on my boat for the last time. This is no star wagon! We're a rust bucket in the middle of nowhere trying to stay afloat. We're fighting for our lives on this operation and I've got a wife who I love dearly and two wonderful kids, all in Florida, who I plan on seeing again. For that to happen, everyone has to row with the tide. I've taken on the extra burden of turning you into a first-rate line officer and, by God, I'm gonna do it! You're gonna stand straight, follow orders, keep that mouth of yours closed, and for once, become a real member of this crew. When I'm done with you your shit's gonna have muscles! Do you understand me, Mead?"

"Yes, sir." Mead's voice was twisted in pain and the swollen mouse had closed his eye.

"Excellent, Mead. Excellent. I just knew this little chat could resolve all our little problems." Burkhart's voice suddenly grew warm. "This report needs revision. Will you see to it, son?"

Mead took the yellow triplicate form and folded it in half. "Yes, sir, I'll see to it," Mead said as he stood and reached for the door.

"Look after that eye, Mead, because I'm assigning you to double deck watches when we surface at Station Bonnie."

"I'm looking forward to that assignment, sir."

"I just knew you would, Mr. Mead. There is another small favor you could do for me, very unofficially, of course."

Mead squinted with his healthy eye, afraid of the worst. "What, sir?"

"Last night I was making an inspection up forward when I passed by the enlisted head." Burkhart leaned back in his chair and looked at Mead. "Someone was smoking dope in that head, Spike, and I want it stopped. Certain crew members love your ass and I think you can put a stop to smoking that stuff on my submarine. Are we still communicating?"

"Yes, sir. I'll see to it on the double."

"I know I can count on you, son." Burkhart's face turned dark as he blew out a cloud of stinking smoke. "In just a few days, we have a date with the Soviet Navy, then I am really going to find out what you're worth. I am going to find out what we're all worth, as we approach that hornet's nest."

25

You've done an excellent job of setting the defensive screening forces, Captain.''

Viktor Belous swiveled in his command chair, high atop the flight deck of the carrier *Minsk*. His cold brown eyes spent a full minute searching the face of his commanding officer, Rear Admiral Alensandr Veklenko.

''Thank you, Admiral. ''We can handle any problem that may come up.'' Belous rose from his stool and made his way to the other side of the bridge. Carefully he rotated his thickly muscled torso and leaned out an open bridge window. Carefully, he surveyed the flight deck of his ship, the pride of the Soviet Navy.

''May I speak with you in private?'' asked Admiral Veklenko.

Belous stiffened and his eyes darted to his other officers, busy with their own tasks on the bridge. ''Certainly, Admiral. Let's adjourn to my in-port cabin.''

Belous closed the door behind and could feel the fear gripping his throat. It had been years since he had known that particular emotion. In fact, during the past eight months, the only real emotion he had felt was saddness.

''Don't look so concerned, Viktor.'' The admiral sat

in a plush leather reading chair opposite Belous's desk. "We haven't had much of an opportunity to speak about private matters since the operation began." His voice trailed away.

"Yes, Admiral, I understand. At least I believe I do."

"In a few months this phase of the operation will be completed. Successfully, I expect." Veklenko removed his cap and placed it carefully on the thick arm of the chair. Automatically, a cigarette and lighter appeared from inside his navy-blue breast jacket, adorned with five rows of campaign ribbons above the left pocket.

"The Naval Ministry expects great things of you in the years to come, Viktor. These are exciting times for us all. Considering that we started as a small coastal fleet when Gorshkov assumed command in 1956, we've made great strides since then.

Veklenko rubbed his nose, perplexed. "A million years ago. Can you imagine, Viktor, that our real founder, Sergei Gorshkov made rear admiral by the age of thirty-one. I've never recovered from his death last year. I miss him dearly." He arched his eyebrows. "But, Viktor, what a time it was! God, here I am, fifty-nine, and I only have two stars." He looked across the cabin at Belous. "We are the major fleet in the world, Viktor." He smiled with thick lips overhanging yellowing teeth. "Times have really changed."

Belous nodded silently and could feel the heat under his arms. Veklenko hadn't given him the time of day in over a year. Not since his return to sea duty from London.

"First, we have not had a chance to talk of your wife Anna." Veklenko puffed deeply. "I was very sorry to hear of her passing. God, we all were." He stood and walked to Belous's desk. "Your sacrifice has not gone unnoticed in the Kremlin and Naval Ministry in Leningrad. In fact, Viktor, your name is at the top of the list for promotion. Within the next two months, you will have your first star."

Belous felt his body uncoil. "I'm stunned, Admiral. I don't know what to say." Belous felt his face redden. Admiral! Why wasn't Anna alive to see it? To be proud of him. To share what he had worked all his adult life to achieve. His grief was a beacon as he looked up at Veklenko.

"You know, Viktor, that when I flew aboard two days ago, I had orders to bring you back to Petropavlovsk for reassignment."

Belous's heart jumped. "Oh?"

"Yes. Of course the final decision was mine and mine alone. After reviewing all that you have done here, however, I believe that it wouldn't be in our best interests to give you another command at this moment. I am especially pleased with the way you deployed the missile cruisers and missile destroyers. Very clever. Nothing on earth could penetrate that screen. Incidentally, we have additional help for your task force, Viktor."

Belous narrowed his eyes. This was not a time for change. "What might that help be, Admiral?"

"Two Victor Class attack submarines are in route. They should be at your disposal within the next twenty four hours." Veklenko looked at his watch. Their talk had ended.

"Viktor, walk me to my plane."

Admiral Alensandr Veklenko squeezed through the narrow fuselage hatch of the Beriev seaplane. He turned to Belous. "Viktor, the Soviet people are proud of you." He smiled warmly. "With what I have said, you must have a great deal to think about. I am leaving

194

possibly the most important series of tests we have ever conducted in very capable hands." He saluted Belous and slammed the hatch shut.

Slowly, Belous stepped back on the dark-green flight deck as the plane maneuvered its bulk up to one of the steam catapults for launching. Belous turned away and shivered in the cold arctic summer air. He had never known such great confusion. What had he done? What had he become? Maybe—"

"Captain, sir."

"Yes." Belous digested the face of one of his aides. "Yes, what is it?" he snapped.

"The *Admiral Isakov* and destroyer *Provorny* are about to commence an antisubmarine drill. You said to include you in helping to coordinate the search for targets."

"Yes, I did say that." Belous looked up at the towering island structure before him. A testament to Soviet naval strength. And now they wanted him for admiral!

"We will be able to take out any American, Japanese, or Chinese submarine that comes sniffing about, right, Captain?"

"What? Oh, yes. We can take out any sub that gets too close." Belous stared vacantly across the flight deck as Admiral Veklenko's plane launched into the gray mist of Lisinskaya Bay. The admiral was correct. He did have a great deal to think about.

26

"Wardroom, Control."

Commander Burkhart reached from his chair and flipped the station-to-station intercom. "Wardroom here."

"The new base course for Station Bonnie is two nine three degrees true, Captain."

"Very well, Irish. What's our arrival time at Bonnie?"

"Ah, the ETA is 0430 hours tomorrow."

"Is the old lady holding up? Has that crack in propulsion gotten any worse?"

"No change, Skipper. We're watching it closely."

"Nice work, Irish, in finding that damn coffee stain on the chart. One hella've job of navigating."

"Thanks. We're entering the deepest finger of the Chinook Fracture Zone. The charts warn of deep oscillation waves. It could get very rough and with the problem in propulsion—why take a chance. Request permission to take her to eight hundred feet for the next seven hours."

"Permission granted for eight zero zero feet." Burkhart flipped off the switch and looked at the electric clock on the bulkhead across the compartment. It read

0917. Burkhart looked over at David Lathrick who had a series of papers spread out before him. He was drumming his fingers, trying his best to keep quiet.

"Captain, didn't you tell Niven and Sorrell about this 9:00 A.M. briefing?"

"I did, Dr. Lathrick. It was Niven who called the meeting. I'm sure there's a good reason why they're late. They'll be here momentarily." He smiled at Lathrick. "We literally have all day for this."

Lathrick ignored the comment and had already dropped his eyes to his papers. A sharp rap at the door forced Lathrick's head up.

"Come," said Burkhart.

Winebelly Burns, *Skate*'s cook, backed into the wardroom with the backside of his white apron. He was carrying a tray of freshly baked and glazed doughnuts stacked high, and two silver pots of coffee.

He looked up impishly at his captain, with his curly red hair sprouting beneath his white baker's cap. "I thought you might like some refreshments, sir."

Burkhart's face lit up. "Perfect, Winebelly. Just what we needed. I heard you practicing on those bagpipes last night." Burkhart wrinkled his brow.

Winebelly laughed. "Oh, it wasn't me, sir. I was teaching some of the lads how to blow the bag. It takes a lot of practice to keep the windbag filled with air, aside from playing the pipes. That's why it sounded so awful. You shoulda heard me play when I first started—"

The metallic voice of Executive Officer Irish Brennen over the bulkhead intercom interrupted Winebelly's moment with his captain.

"Now hear this. This is the control room. Rig for deep submergence. Secure all loose gear. Rig for possible turbulence and large angles. That is all."

"Excuse me, Winebelly." Burkhart reached over

197

and flipped down the station-to-station intercom switch. "Control, wardroom."

"Yes, Skipper."

"Because of the potential for radiation leakage in propulsion, Irish, I want you to ease the electrical load in the boat by shifting ballast trim and all drain pump systems from parallel to series operation. I just don't want to take a chance when we're that deep."

"Aye, aye, Skipper."

Burkhart turned back, but Winebelly had discreetly withdrawn as Jake and Brahma Sorrell appeared in the wardroom. The deck canted down in response to a ten degree down bubble, forcing them to stagger to their seats and hold on.

"Just in case you hadn't heard, we're going deep to escape some upper level undersea waves. Where the hell have you been? It's your war party." Burkhart looked sheepishly over at the bulkhead clock.

"Brahma and I had a strategy meeting. Sorry we're late."

"Where's Levy?" Burkhart squinted his face.

"He's on his way. He wanted to make some last-minute adjustments to the diesels."

"We could wait until tomorrow if it would be more convenient." Lathrick tried to sound friendly.

"Not a chance, gentlemen," Burkhart grunted. "The weather calls for six-foot seas and we're going to be running on the surface. There's going to be a lot of stomach problems and green faces until we get our sea legs. This is the best time." There was a finality in Burkhart's voice, as Levy, his overalls covered with grease, quietly entered the wardroom. Silently he took a seat next to Lathrick, slinging his UZI behind the chair.

"How are the diesels, Mr. Levy?"

"I've done what I can. They shouldn't miss a beat."

Levy raised his hand and eyes expressively, then found Brahma Sorrell measuring him.

"Something wrong?"

Sorrell slowly filled his pipe with tobacco. "Not a thing, Levy. I just want to welcome you aboard the boarding party." His massive hands continued to play with the pipe. Let's give them a show they'll never forget." His mouth parted in an ugly smile.

David Lathrick cleared his throat. "This briefing is to give you some idea of the hardware and machinery we'll see when we board *Minsk*. It might save us a few precious minutes in searching *Minsk*'s hangar bay for our prize."

"Fair enough." Niven had decided to humor Lathrick until the job was finished.

Lathrick stood and backed to a small blackboard. Arrogance was no longer firmly rooted in his voice. It had been replaced by something that Niven couldn't identify or touch.

"The physics of the Soviet beam gun are awesome. Truly awesome. The Russians have learned to bottle thunder." Lathrick went on to discuss air-cored betatron accelerators, massive magneto explosive generators, and firing tables. No one in the compartment understood the conversation except Lathrick.

"Most components in this weapon are named for their Russian inventor, E. E. Pavlovski. This man is also credited with inventing the multi-channeled ring switch." Lathrick was making an effort to reach his audience, to make them understand how the weapon functioned.

"Dr. Lathrick." Niven tried to sound patient. "Just tell us where the switch is located. That's all we have to know."

Lathrick nodded. Niven was certain he'd hurt the scientist's feelings, and felt sorry for it. "I know we had our problems when we met, Doctor, but that's behind us." Niven smiled.

"Yes, I see. It's just so very fascinating."

"Please go on." Niven nodded.

"Once the created energy leaves the generators, it is pulled through power cables by electro-magnets into a device which acts to stabilize the raw energy into pulses. Each pulse contains one trillion volts or thereabouts."

"Christ, I wouldn't want to put my finger into that socket," Sorrell quipped. Everyone laughed. Even Lathrick smiled.

"Once the energy is converted to pulses, it is rammed into one end of a long tube that we believe runs the entire length of *Minsk*'s hangar deck, about six hundred feet."

Lathrick turned his back to the board and drew a series of diagrams. "At this point the pulses are traveling at a velocity close to the speed of light. The pulses are then fired from the end of the tube through a firing nozzle."

"Where is this gun nozzle?" Niven sat up.

"We believe the Russians have constructed a small elevator to lift the gun barrel above the level of the flight deck, for firing at targets."

"Where is the ring switch, Doctor?" Niven was still patient.

"Yes. The ring switch. It is located here." He pointed to a small chalk box on the board. "It is located next to the generators. It is really the brains of the entire gun. By computer, it tells the generators at what speed and rate the pulses should be released into the gun barrel. This is a tremendous amount of energy at one time, equivalent to several small nuclear explosions. All this is metered out at a steady state by the switch."

"How big is the ring switch?" Sorrell asked. "Can we carry it out of there?"

Lathrick nodded. "Yes. Soviet science has found a way to take that ring switch, which should be the size of a small house, and reduce it down to the size of a portable TV."

"What's it weight?" Niven rubbed his face.

"We think about twenty to thirty pounds." Lathrick cupped his hands together. "Once we find out how they have accomplished this feat, we can duplicate the weapon. Without this ring switch, it will take another five to seven years to catch the Soviets." His eyes caught Niven's stare. "We need that switch at any cost, Mr. Niven."

"Captain Belous will lead us right to the area of the hangar where the switch is located," Niven said. What tools will we need?"

"Very simple. Wire and bolt cutters and hacksaw."

A hacksaw! Jesus, Niven thought. Killing high tech with a hacksaw. Crabby would have loved to hear that one.

"It shouldn't take any more than five minutes to cut the switch away from the weapon."

"Just how damn powerful is this beam gun?" Burkhart looked pale.

"Very powerful, Captain. We think, with proper radar assistance, the gun can fire a six-inch-wide, destructive beam, and hit a preselected target on the moon. Obviously, everything in between, including satellites, space shuttles, and incoming missile warheads can easily be destroyed. We believe it can fire about two thousand pulses in about three minutes. That's a great deal of killing power."

A heavy silence overtook the men sitting around the table. Niven reached for a doughnut, when the entire table bucked upward, then slammed down violently, tossing papers, hot coffee, and people all about the wardroom.

Somehow Burkhart stood in the violent rocking motion and dove for the intercom when it came alive. "All compartments report damage. DC parties stand by. We've hit a large maverick undersea wave."

At last the rocking motion subsided and the red leatherette chairs were righted. Burkhart paused at the wardroom door. "I've got to lay up to the control room." His face broke into a slight grin. "Welcome to the Bering Sea, gentlemen. I think she is bidding us hello." Then he disappeared into the companionway.

The wardroom intercom squawked again. "Now hear this. Movie tonight in the crew's mess at 1600. THE FOG. There'll be free popcorn and Cokes. That is all."

"It begins in earnest tomorrow." Niven looked about the table. "We'll be on the surface as a Russian sub. Maybe a movie might be a welcome relief tonight. In the next few days, we'll need every bit of strength, both mental and physical, that you could imagine. Niven could see David Lathrick's mouth begin to quiver slightly. He was scared to death.

27

"It's time. I'm going to find out how damned good we really are. Once we're on the surface, all bets are off. We'll be just another hunk of shark bait in Russkie's pond." Burkhart rubbed his hands together at the plot table.

Jake grinned nervously, forcing the lump down into his stomach. The months of planning. All those months with Ellie and all those damn ghosts.

"You ready, Jake boy?"

Niven felt his head nod.

Burkhart double-checked the bulkhead clock. One last time he glanced around the control room at his silent crew, the tension fueling their muscles as they moved about in dark-blue Soviet poopie suits.

"Stand by, Irish." His voice carried a defiant hush.

"Ready, Skipper."

"All right, here we go! Take her up. Chief of the Watch, sound surface alarm."

Russotto smiled from his position behind the dive board operator. "Aye, sir." He reached over and pushed a large chrome button on the railing of the stand.

AH OO GAH AH OO GAH.

"Surface. Surface," Russotto ordered firmly.

Burkhart took one last look around the compartment. "Shut the vents. Pump from auxiliary to the sea." Each order was repeated by Russotto as telephone talkers relayed the information to the necessary compartments and spaces throughout the boat.

"Blow negative to the mark. Rig in the sound heads. Full rise on the planes."

A hissing sound of high pressure filled the compartment as air was forced into *Skate*'s smaller tanks surrounding her pressure hull.

"She's rising very sluggishly, sir." It was the officer of the dive standing off to Burkhart's right, behind the helmsman.

"Blow main ballast to the mark," Burkhart responded and the order was repeated. A tremendous gushing of air filled the control room as *Skate*'s main ballast tanks were emptied of water with high pressure air.

"Very good, sir. She's rising beautifully."

When *Skate* reached one hundred feet, the diving officer began to count off feet from the depth gauge in a steady cadence. "Ninety. Eight-five. Eighty. Seventy-five. Sixty—"

Burkhart put it from his mind when he was convinced *Skate* was smoothly rising to the surface of the Bering Sea.

Slowly, then with more force, *Skate* began to roll and pitch to the cadence and wave power of the surface above. Without a word, Irish Brennen moved closer anticipating the next command.

"Up scope." Brennen jerked the pickle of the small attack scope and slowly the stainless steel barrel as thick as a telephone pole rose from the deck below. Burkhart grabbed and flopped down the training handles when, they cleared the scope well and wheeled the scope around a full 360 degrees while on his knees.

"All clear on the surface." Burkhart took a long, deep breath and smiled down at Jake. "Down scope. Secure pumping. Rig in the bow planes. Irish, take the Conn. Give me an ALL STOP bell on both engines."

"Not too damn bad for openers. In fact, a bit of a relief. The surface looks pretty smooth. Maybe a three-foot swell with broken clouds. I still wish to hell we had fog, but all things considered, I'll settle for this," he said cautiously.

"The sail is clear, sir," the Diving Officer looked over at Burkhart.

"Very good. Chief of the Watch, crack the hatch!" Quickly Russotto scrambled up the ladder in the control room, seized the hatch handle, and spun it around causing the steel fingers gripping under the hatch seat to relax their hold. Under pressure from a heavy spring, the steel hatch swung slightly off its seat, forcing air from the pressurized atmosphere within *Skate* to escape through the narrow opening with a swishing sound.

"All clear, Captain," Russotto called down from the ladder, waiting for the next command.

"Very good, Chief."

"You look pretty stupid in that Russian jumpsuit and sable hat."

"The hat is called a *shapka.*" Niven smiled tensely. "Birds of a feather." He handed Burkhart his rimless black fur officer's hat adorned in the center forehead with a large gold five-pointed star surrounding a hammer and sickle insignia. "Just for you. Real dyed Siberian squirrel." His voice was devoid of humor. They both fell silent and quickly donned dark-blue fur-lined parkas and gloves.

"Okay, Chief, open the hatch."

Russotto swung the large hatch open and locked it in a standing position as a small, remaining gush of freezing seawater poured down on him.

"Hatch open and secured, sir." Russotto then scrambled up inside the sail and opened the access hatch to the tiny cockpit bridge atop the sail.

Jake followed Burkhart up the ladder into the cockpit as the twenty-five degree cold summer air slapped at his face and grabbed at his lungs. For a long time he squinted into the muted sunlight until his eyes adjusted.

"Control, this is the Bridge. I've got the Conn. Put the low pressure blowers on the tanks for ten minutes. Raise and activate radar and satellite masts and keep a sharp eye out for targets. Maneuvering, Bridge. Stand by for orders."

Burkhart paused and looked at Niven. "Well, we're off to the Bering War. Propulsion, Bridge. Bring main engines down one hundred percent. Open main induction valve."

"Bridge, Propulsion. Aye, Captain. Bringing her down all the way. Main induction open."

"We off nuclear power, Charley?"

"That's right. Now let's see if Levy can earn his keep. Maneuvering, Bridge. Put main engines on the jacking gear. Fire up and shift the load to both surface diesels."

"Bridge, Maneuvering" came the metallic voice over the bridge intercom. "Main engines on jacking gear, ready to answer bells on diesels."

Loud popping noises drews their attention to *Skate*'s stern, as dark-gray smoke billowed out of the engine room vent system. "Welcome back to 1942, Mr. Niven. Let's see if those Russian potato mashers really work."

"Yeah, it makes you yearn for Ballast Point, a nude over the bar, and unblended Scotch."

"Bridge, Control. Skipper, NAVSAT satellite confirms coordinates. We're sitting right on top of Tenchi Seamount, six thousand feet beneath our keel. When we proceed, the new course of Lisinskaya Bay, Bering Island, is three four degrees true."

"Very well, Irish."

Burkhart turned to Jake, staring out at a dark green ocean watching small waves lap against the hull and bows of *Skate*.

"Is Sorrell in the radio room?"

"He's been there waiting since we surfaced."

"Radio, Bridge."

"Radio here, Captain."

"Is Mr. Sorrell there?"

"Aye, sir. He's standing by, awaiting your orders."

"Put him on, please."

"Sorrell here."

"You're up to bat, Brahma. The satellite scoop is active, so plug in your magic tape, find your correct frequency, and let's go on with this bits and frames business."

"I'll get back to you, Captain."

Burkhart turned to Niven. "Mind if I butt in to your business?"

"Sure. What's troubling you?"

"Is there a problem with Sorrell? The last couple of days he's been a real bastard."

Niven pushed out a breath, looking over the sail down at the bows. "No real problem. He's just very edgy that I invited Levy to join the boarding party. He thinks he can handle everything himself." He raised his eyebrows to Burkhart. "But considering the magnitude of the project—" His voice trailed away and Niven shrugged.

"We're all under a hardass strain."

Burkhart nodded silently.

"Captain, this is Sorrell," the intercom blared five minutes later.

"Go ahead, Radio."

"We've got it! That tape did the trick. Jesus, it was a piece of French pastry. Is Niven still with you?" God, I can't believe it! Is Niven topside?"

"Affirmative."

"Permission to come up, Captain."

"Permission granted."

Niven's face brightened with relief. "I've just elevated shaking knees to a new art form."

"Maneuvering, Bridge. Make turns for eighteen knots on diesel power. Ease up, Jake boy, it's a long bus ride."

"Aye, aye, Bridge. Answering bells for eighteen knots on diesels."

Both men felt an unfamiliar rumbling and vibration beneath their feet as the twin bronze propellers dug into the Bering Sea under conventional power. Noticeably, *Skate* began to roll as she plowed ahead.

"Control, Bridge. The new course to Lisinskaya Bay is three four four degrees true."

"Aye, Captain, the new course is three four four. The helm is coming about to the new course."

"Permission to come on the bridge," Brahma Sorrell's bald head popped through the hatch. His grin was ear to ear.

"Granted."

With difficulty, Brahma squeezed through the hatch and donned his black fur hat. "I'm glad I don't do this for a living." He handed Jake a yellow sheet, then reached over and gave Burkhart a folded flag. "Christ, we did it, you crazy bastard!" He slapped Niven's back with a thunderous clap.

"We better put up our Russian battle flag." Burkhart unfolded the white ensign with a thick blue band at its bottom. The white field was emblazoned with the red star, hammer, and sickle. "If my wife and boys could see me now," he grunted, raising the flag on the staff behind the cockpit.

Carefully, Jake studied the broken naval code as Sorrell dropped back down the hatch. "Radio needs covering since we're now in Russian waters." He laughed softly and disappeared.

"Hot off the decoder, Charley, straight from that Russian satellite. Take a look:

SOPKA NAYAR'PR. SREDAH' CHO'RNY DROST.

AHDEEN' AHDEEN' DVA DE'VET AL-MAHS'

VOLCANO GREEN. WEDNESDAY BLACK-BIRD.

ONE ONE TWO NINE. DIAMOND.

Burkhart nodded. "Just a simple sequential code spit out randomly by their computers. Impossible to break or anticipate. War is such a damn simple process, Jake boy."

"It's a testing of the spirit."

"You're still some damn poet, Jake, even in this lousy corner of ocean."

They fell silent and watched silently as *Skate* continued to pick up speed, heading toward a horizon of billowing clouds ringed with a pinkish halo. The brisk sea breeze, blowing hard and clean across the exposed deck, pushed at their faces.

Burkhart turned and smiled. "It's hard to believe the sun never sets here in summer. Smell that air."

Jake nodded and felt his muscles uncoil for the first time in months. For a moment he found a certain measured peace in the Bering Sea. "The sky is so open. What an incredible beauty. Ellie has a favorite poem by Tennyson. "Locksley Hall":

> 'For I dip into the future, far as the human eye could see.
> Saw the vision of the world, and all the wonder that could be:
> Saw the heavens fill with commerce, argosies of magic sails,
> Pilots of the purple twilight—'

"I forgot the rest. Pilots of the purple twilight," Jake repeated softly. He leaned forward and rested his weight against the cockpit, as the diesels at last found their own throbbing meter.

Burkhart gawked at him. "You're some bloodhound. To put this together, then quote poetry. You're an experience. A damn blend of flesh and knife."

Burkhart raised his glasses and scanned the distant horizon. "What the hell makes you tick?"

"Who knows. The scarred psyche. The restless eyes resting on the broken and bent nose." Niven grinned. He hadn't meant to, it just came out that way.

Burkhart stopped and checked the compass heading through the vertical sighting arm. "How'd you get that slice in your chin?"

"I showed up one morning in Providence unexpectedly, and my ex-wife was entertaining. We got into it and when the guy left the house, she flew into a rage. I should have, but she was the one. Well, when it was over she had tried to slice off my chin with a bar knife and that finished the marriage. Not very dignified for old-line Rhode Island, eh, Charley?"

Burkhart shrugged. "I can't miss what I never had. Annapolis and a working-class family never afforded us many luxuries, Jake boy. After the war, my dad couldn't do much—"

Suddenly, Burkhart looked up and stared at Niven. "When this is over and if we've survived to talk quietly about it to each other, I expect us to do just that. Don't pull another 'Nam on me and bug out for another ten years."

"You get us there and you've got my word."

"Where the hell does Ellie fit into all this?"

Niven thought for a moment. "She's my future. I've grown up enough to appreciate someone like Ellie."

"I think so, too, Jake boy."

"Let's talk business for a minute, Charley." Niven's voice grew cold. "The operational orders call for thirty minutes aboard *Minsk*. I want forty-five." Niven paused and rubbed his cold nose with a gloved hand." Now understand this. If we're not back within that time limit, we're not coming back. It's that simple."

Burkhart nodded.

"Good." That being the case, you get the hell out. I've never been more serious about anything in my life." He hardened his glare to make certain Burkhart understood, then shifted his eyes to the vastness of the northern ocean and a horizon he couldn't see.

28

Brahma Sorrell unzipped the white canvas ditty bag and carefully removed a small machine pistol with a wooden handle. The smell of gun oil permeated the compartment.

"Take it, Dr. Lathrick." Sorrell thrust the gun into his hands. "Get the feel of it." Brahma stood up, aware of Lathrick's discomfort.

He smiled inwardly. "Have you ever held an automatic weapon in your hands, Doctor?"

"No." He shook his head nervously.

Towering over Lathrick, Sorrell reached down and took the gun away. Expertly he flipped down and locked the metal shoulder stock. "You hold the stock against your shoulder and just squeeze."

"All right, Brahma, leave him alone!" Jake leaned back against the desk in the stateroom. "All he wants you to do, Doctor, is understand how to fire it in case of an emergency."

Lathrick blinked and his mind whirled with a thousand horrid possibilities. "What emergency? I'm not trained to use firearms!"

"That's just the point. You don't have to be trained

to use an automatic weapon. You just aim it in the right direction and spray it."

"Like killing bugs on your patio with a spray can," Brahma teased.

"Shut up, Sorrell," Jake snapped. "Sometimes you've got the intelligence of an out of control beer truck." He glanced sideways at Lathrick. "He's right, Doctor. It's just his animal methods that are hard to digest." He took the weapon.

"It's called a Skorpion machine pistol, manufactured in Czechoslovakia." Jake reached down into the bag and pulled out a steel clip and held it up to Lathrick. "This is called a magazine. It holds twenty shells."

Jake shoved the clip into an opening in the belly of the machine pistol and pointed a finger at the selection lever above the rear handle. "This selector tells you how fast you want the weapon to fire." He smiled at Lathrick and felt sorry for the man's fear.

Akivor Levy reached into the bag and lifted out another Skorpion. "Fine weapon and light as a feather. I've never fired one before but I've heard its rate of fire is tremendous."

"It's perfect for our needs. It fires so quickly, it sounds like a zipper." Jake reached into the canvas bag again and withdrew a thick steel tube.

"For this operation we're going to use silencers or noise suppressors." Quickly Jake screwed the tube into the short barrel of the weapon. "With this, the Skorpion hardly makes a sound."

"I didn't think this would be my area of responsibility, Niven." His voice took on a pleading tone.

"Relax, Doctor. You're not going to carry a weapon, but I want you to know how to use it if need be."

"I still don't see—"

"I think Langor undersold the job. You're not going to take high tea on that carrier! There's just no guarantees."

"I suppose you want me to leave the UZI behind?"

"Yes, Akivor. If we lose weapons, or have to leave them behind, they won't be tied to the United States. At least not for a few hours. It's a minor touch, but the more confusion, the more time we'll have on the way out."

The stateroom cleared and Jake repacked the weapons. "I can't find my Tokarev pistol. Have you seen it, Brahma? The thing has always been good luck—"

Distracted, Sorrell cocked his head. "What?"

"The pistol that Lykov gave me years ago. I swore I packed it before we left." Niven raised his hands in frustration. "With all the tension and confusion I only thought I packed it."

"Sorry, Jake. You see how you need me to take care of your dumb butt."

"All hands. All hands," the intercom squawked in the cabin. "Aircraft dead astern. Bearing one six four, range fifty miles. Closing fast. Battle stations surface! Battle stations surface! This is not a drill!"

GONG GONG GONG. The shrill alarm echoed through the boat as crewmen scrambled to their stations. "Close and dog all watertight doors."

Niven and Sorrell stepped into the corridor as crew members pushed past. The dull slamming of hatches could be heard everywhere. "We better go forward or we're going to be stuck here for the duration," Sorrell offered. "We need to be in the control room."

"I agree." Jack widened his eyes at Sorrell. "I wonder if that target is Belous's way of saying he changed his mind?"

Niven found Burkhart at the radar scope, watching

the electronic blip of light move towards the center of the radar dish.

"Russian?"

Burkhart turned on Jake, his face a brooding mesh. "Don't know. We'll just have to sweat it out. We're so goddamned vulnerable on the surface. Now I really feel for those World War Two boys." Burkhart stepped behind Jake onto his periscope stand and picked up the station phone.

"Bridge, Control. Where's the target, Mead?"

"Bridge, aye. No visual contact yet, sir."

"Look alive, goddammit! That target should be in sight very soon. Keep me informed."

"Aye aye, Captain."

Burkhart stepped off the stand. "My gut is working overtime. They're probably coming to kick our butts."

"They can't know, dammit. Don't be so paranoid."

"Look who's talking." Burkhart laughed darkly.

"I asked for that—"

"There's so many places along the way when someone could have pulled the plug."

"I'd know, dammit. I'd know." He thought of Crabb and shivered.

"You could be wrong." Jake could smell Burkhart's breath of stale coffee. "Possibly your friends in Moscow have known from the day Belous gave the decoding tape to Sorrell in Africa. I don't know all the details, Jake, but I'm not stupid. Take a look at that target closing us!"

Burkhart turned away and jammed his hands into a Russian parka. "Plot, what's our ETA to the first contact with the Soviet warships protecting Lisinskaya Bay?"

The assistant navigation officer hesitated, then looked up. "We should make hard contact with our first Russian frigate in about ten hours."

215

Burkhart grunted and scrambled up the ladder to the cockpit with Jake in close pursuit. The complexion of the sea had given way to a pea-green froth dotted with whitecaps. The hostility was punctuated by a dead gray sky.

Skate plowed ahead and her bows rode deeply into well-defined troughs that threw wash and spray over her decks and leading edge of the sail as she fought the Force Seven winds. Each time *Skate* dropped into a wave, her stern rose exposing her twin bronze propellers. Shuddering waves of energy passed through the pressure hull until the next wave forced her stern back down into the sea.

Somehow, the ocean sensed *Skate*'s primitive urgency as the boat pushed north into the Bering and closer to *Minsk*. A large black Albatross circled *Skate,* searching for a place to rest, then suddenly veered away, allowing the gale winds to push her toward Asia.

"Where's the target, Mr. Mead?" Burkhart surveyed the back of Spike Mead's head, turned toward the stern of the boat.

"Bridge, Control. Target closing fast, range fifteen thousand yards. Bearing is now one six two. He's coming right up our ass, sir!"

"Thanks, Control. Still searching."

"There he is!" Mead shouted hoarsely two minutes later. "Five points off the starboard beam. Just a black speck."

Burkhart pushed the binoculars to his face. "Can't tell yet. High wing. That's all I can make out."

"Radio, Bridge. Any signal from that plane?"

"Negative, Captain."

"It's a Lockheed Viking, sub hunter!" Mead screamed out as relief flooded his voice. "I can't make out any squadron number or insignia."

In another three minutes the stubby Viking thundered over *Skate,* less than fifty feet off the ocean. On one pass, the sub hunter had to climb to escape hitting the top of the bridge cockpit.

"At least we've fooled the United States Navy," Burkhart shouted to Jake after that near disasterous pass.

"We haven't fooled anyone."

"What the hell does that mean?" Burkhart screamed to make himself heard.

"It's the heavy hand of Admiral Brandon Langor checking up on us," Jake yelled back, as the Viking's gray-and-white belly flashed over their heads with its cameras rolling. "This is a fond farewell from the comfort of Norfolk." Jake shook his head and laughed sardonically. "The bastard wants to be certain our diapers are pinned on straight."

The Viking swooped in low on a final banking turn, waggled its wings and flew off to the south. A large four-leaf clover adorned her tail.

Burkhart waited for the jet to finish the noisy pass, then flicked down the intercom. "Control, Bridge. Pass the word. Stand down from general quarters. That target is a confirmed friendly. Repeat. The target is a friendly."

"Aye, aye, Bridge."

Spike Mead turned and the binoculars fell to his chest, forcing Jake's mouth to drop. His right eye was a puffy narrow slit and the entire area beneath was an angry hue of red-and-purple skin, stretching far below his boyish cheekbone. The black fur Shapka hat and cold air only accentuated the vivid colors against his white skin.

"Who the hell did you run into?"

Mead hesitated for a moment. "Ah, a hatch handle. It looks worse than it really is." He turned slightly and nodded seriously at Burkhart.

"Captain?"

"Yes, Mead."

"That detail I was assigned has been completed. I've talked to the people involved and they've got the message. I also squared away that Russian seaman with Lopez in the ship's laundry. He can't do any harm back there."

"Very good, Mead." Burkhart raised an eyebrow. "What about that form we discussed. Has it been completed yet?"

"I tore it up. I decided it was in the best interests of the boat."

Burkhart nodded as he reached down for the hatch. "We're going below. I'll have Winebelly send up java and something to eat before it mildews. Make certain you get some extra eyes up here to stand the watch."

Mead smiled. "Aye aye, sir."

Inside the warmth of the control room, Jake turned to Burkhart. "We're getting very close. I think we should have quiet in the boat from this point on, except for essential orders. Sorrell is still in Radio, Levy is planted in the engine spaces, and I'll stand by here in Control, to pass the word in Russian if that becomes necessary."

Burkhart nodded to Irish Brennen. "Quiet boat, Irish. I only want essential talk and I want that in a damn whisper. Teach the crew how to point, if you have to, but no screwups now."

Niven made his way to the navigation stand and carefully reviewed the chart of the Soviet warships protecting *Minsk* at Bering Island.

"Let me show you something," Burkhart moved around the plot table. The strong surface action forced them to hold the edges of the steel table. "Hell of a time to ask, but how accurate is this chart?"

"When Sorrell picked up the Soviet Fleet decoding

tape in Africa, Captain Belous handed him a copy of this map." Niven searched Burkhart's intense eyes. "Belous wants out, so I assume it's accurate."

"You assume." Burkhart rubbed his neck. "Well, hoping for the best, here's what I'd like to do." He traced a pencil in a gentle zigzag between the frigates *Shakal* and *Lev.*

"This is where I want to hit that screen." Burkhart looked around the plot. "Belous indicates these two targets are old Riga class ships, built twenty-five years ago. When we draw within range, Sorrell will send a Russian MAYDAY along with the fleet recognition code."

"I thought the orders called for using the code only when directly challenged."

"I decided to change it, Irish. A captain's choice. I want to take the action right to these vodka sailors. The more aggressive we are, the better our chances."

Burkhart took a hand off the edge of the table and rubbed his face. "Irish, this is no ordinary OP. We're gonna need all the luck that we can get and that's how I see it." He flashed an icy smile.

A deep wave trough forced the small group to hang on as *Skate* skidded down, shuddered, and then rose, throwing tons of water cascading across her bows and decks.

"Well, gentlemen, I think we're going to find out about *Skate*'s sea-keeping qualities and how well General Dynamics put her together."

"Control, Bridge," came the metallic sound of Spike Mead's voice from the cockpit.

Irish Brennen stepped up on the periscope stand and flipped down the station intercom. "Control, aye."

"We're building a pretty good layer of low clouds and fog up here, Mr. Brennen. Request another pair of eyes topside and tell the captain to have Radar look sharp. Another hour or so and we'll be in a soup."

"Aye, aye, Bridge, the captain has the word. We'll keep a sharp eye out." Brennen flipped off the intercom and turned to Burkhart, who had heard the conversation. "The kid's really squaring his act, Charley. I don't know what the hell you said to him, but his performance has risen dramatically. He's been on that bridge for the last eleven hours and he's still going strong."

"I always knew he would work up to his potential." He blew out a cloud of smoke. He looked around the control room. "Thank God for that fog. How about helping me out, Jake boy, and stand a watch on the bridge with Mead?"

"Why not. A two-hour watch would give me a chance to collect my thoughts."

Burkhart nodded silently.

"After I come off watch, I'll start final preparations for the boarding party."

29

"Contact! Sonar signature confirms it's the Soviet frigate *Shakal,* six miles north northwest our position. He's moving slowly on station." Burkhart felt his voice waver within the confines of the tiny radio compartment jammed with equipment.

"Weather reports broken clouds and light fog at Bering Island." Burkhart squinted his eyes at Jake Niven but wasn't sure why he added that meaningless information. It wouldn't help.

Tersely, Jake nodded and rubbed the smooth tips of his fingers together. He acknowledged it was symbolic of cracking the world's largest and most well-protected safe. Brahma Sorrell bent over Jake's shoulder and exhaled a stinking mix of pipe smoke and fear.

"Okay, fuse puller, it's time," Sorrell prodded in a whisper.

Jake swallowed and depressed the talk button on the mike of the transmitter.

"Vneemah'neeye! Vneemah'neeye!" The sudden terror of the moment sucked his tongue into the back of his mouth, as the Russian choked in his throat. *"Mai Den, Mai Den. Mai Den. Mai Den. Gde kahrah'p, gde kahrah'p. Kahrah'p tree tree ahdeen'. Kahrah'p tree tree ahdeen'.* Atten-

tion! Attention! Mayday. Mayday. Any ship, any ship. This is Soviet submarine *Severyanka,* three three one. This is Soviet submarine *Severyanka,* three three one. We have an emergency!''

Gingerly he placed the small mike on the radio table and folded his trembling fingers into a steeple, holding up his nose as he stared at the round metal speaker, waiting for it to come to life.

A low-pitched empty static hiss filled the compartment.

''Bastards,'' Sorrell swore.

This time Jake grabbed the mike more forcibly. ''Mayday. Mayday. Any ship. Any ship. This is Soviet submarine three three one. We have—''

''Tree tree ahdeen',' '' the speaker crackled. ''This is frigate *Shakal.* This is *Shakal.* We have you on radar at five miles south our position. Over.''

''Shakal, we acknowledge your transmission.'' Jake looked quickly down at a sheet of paper holding the Soviet fleet Recognition code.

''Volcano green. Wednesday blackbird. One one two nine. Diamond. Over.'' Jake's mouth popped open.

''Three three one. Do not transmit in the clear. Use your scrambler for all further voice transmissions. Over.''

''Jesus!'' Jake looked up at Sorrell with compressed lips as he tried to clear his mind.

''Three three one, acknowledge on scrambler. We will not accept further voice communication in the clear. Over.''

Jake rubbed his pounding temples. ''Fuck it.'' He hesitated, thinking it through. *''Shakal,* '' we have a critical emergency. Scrambler is inoperative. Repeat, due to severe electrical fire and engine problems, scrambler is inoperative.'' Jake's Russian smoothed just a bit.

"Will you assist or direct us to nearest repair vessel in area? Over."

Jake blew out a hot breath that burned the delicate mucous membranes inside his nose as the speaker hissed with dead air.

"What now?" Brahma whispered.

Niven held up a hand. "I'll just keep pushing the bastards until—"

"Three three one, acknowledge in the clear. Over."

"Go ahead, *Shakal*, we copy. Over."

"Advise you proceed Petropavlovsk for assistance. Will request ocean tug to rendezvous with you for towing. Please advise rendezvous position. Over."

"Dammit!" Jake pounded the table. "That bastard Belous sure didn't give us the straight info about penetrating the screen. Or maybe—"

"Or maybe there's been a change in plans," Burkhart said. "Maybe he's a bookman."

"What would push you to disobey orders?"

Burkhart shrugged. "Something that would create a damn stink with my superiors. Big enough to fuck up my career, if I didn't back down. For our own survival we have to assume that Belous is still a go and bookmen are bookmen."

"I've got to squeeze that *Roos'kee Kapeetah'n's* nuts until he screams." He rubbed his freshly shaved faced.

"*Shakal*, this is *Severyanka* three three one. Over."

"Go ahead, three three one. We now have you fixed and locked."

Niven wiped at the sweat glistening on his face and neck and looked over his shoulder at Brahma Sorrell, his face swelled with tension.

"Try again, Jake."

"*Shakal*, urgent you understand, situation critical. Ocean towing is not possible. We are unable to proceed any great distance for assistance. Petropavlovsk is not possible. Repeat. Cannot make Petropavlovsk. We are in danger of floundering, if wind and seas continue to build." Jake hesitated and rubbed his nose, thinking through, in Russian, his next critical statement.

"If you cannot assist, we will contact American destroyer, ninety miles south of my position. We are carrying classified instruments and documents from extended patrol. Do you fully understand my situation, *Shakal?* You must lend us assistance. Over."

"Stand by, three three one."

"What about his radar, Jake? A simple sweep will tell them there's nothing of ours in the area!" Sorrell sounded frightened.

"What the hell's going on?" Burkhart had listened to the Russian he didn't understand, and then the dialogue with Sorrell, and he was angry.

Niven ignored him.

"Brahma, I told you before that *Shakal,* or those other Riga class frigates, were the weakest link. Their damn surface radar is a relic and can't penetrate more than forty, maybe fifty miles, at maximum range. They were put there to keep out fishing boats, not a Trojan Horse. *Shakal* has no idea what's beyond that range and won't take the chance to check with more sophisticated ships in the screen about a random American destroyer that far away." Jake wiped at his dry mouth.

"Christ, who gave you a crystal ball?"

"I'm betting *Shakal*'s captain wants to keep this thing as quiet as possible."

"If you're wrong, we're dead." Sorrell looked down.

"I agree with Jake," Burkhart added. "But it's still some damn bluff."

Jake drummed his fingers. "Right this second, *Shakal*'s captain is cursing his bad luck, I hope."

"I tell you, he's going to check with his flotilla commander for advice on how to keep sub three three one away from the *Amereekah'nets.*'' Sorrell folded his ugly face.

"The whole damn thing is a gamble,'' Jake countered. "It was from the start.'' He sounded very tired. "I'm gambling that right now *Shakal*'s captain is on the horn with his test force at Bering, to see whether or not repair ship *Dniestr* wants to help. I don't see that he has any other option. I hope Captain Belous is staying close to his communications center.'' Jake rubbed the back of his neck as the radio static continued to hiss its empty message.

"Three three one, stand by. We acknowledge your critical situation.''

Jake Niven crossed his fingers. He wondered if Sorrell could see the pulse pounding in his neck.

"Three three one. Over.''

"Go ahead, *Shakal!*'' Niven's voice cracked in Russian.

"Three three one. We have located repair ship *Dniestr* inside restricted test area, at Lisinskaya Bay, coordinates fifty-four degrees, forty-three minutes north, a hundred sixty-six degrees, thirty minutes east. *Dniestr* has agreed to assist you. Location is approximately twenty-one miles northeast your present position. Can you clear that distance, three three one? Over.''

Jake jammed a thumbs up sign in relief. "Stand by, *Shakal.*'' He released the talk button on the mike.

Burkhart intently watched the relief flood over Jake's damaged face. "Well?''

"The bastard fell for it,'' Jake said quietly. "He wants to know if we can make it twenty-one miles to *Dniestr.*'' He couldn't keep the sarcasm out of his tone.

"For Chrissake, answer an affirmative before he changes his mind!'' Burkhart took a deep breath and squeezed Brahma Sorrell's massive arm.

"Shakal, this is three three one. We can make repair ship *Dniestr.* Repeat. We can make repair ship *Dniestr."*

"Three three one. Do you have necessary charts? Over?"

"Affirmative, *Shakal."*

"Very well, three three one. You are officially cleared to proceed through restricted test area to repair ship *Dniestr,* twenty-one miles northeast your position. You will rigidly follow these transmit orders. One: only your captain and political officers will be allowed on deck as you proceed. Two: you will follow course zero six zero through remaining screening force. Three: you will anchor no farther than one hundred meters from *Dniestr* and report immediately by radio to *Dniestr* for further instructions. Enlisted personnel will not be allowed on deck as long as you are within boundaries of restricted area. You will use frequency nine seven point three for all further communications. Do you acknowledge and fully understand, three three one? Over."

"We copy and acknowledge, *Shakal."* Niven's voice took on a new determination. "We thank you for your kind assistance. Will buy you a peppered vodka, *Shakal."*

"Do svidanya, three three one. Over and out."

Jake flipped off the transmitter's power and slumped in the hard chair, mentally drained. "What time is it?"

"0718," Burkhart responded, backing out of the radio compartment, to take charge of the course change to Lisinskaya Bay.

"It's time, Jake. We better change into our uniforms."

226

30

"Sonar, how we doing?" Burkhart dropped his voice to a whisper as he kneeled on the steel cockpit deck and peered down the hatch at the young face of a telephone talker.

A moment later the talker, with an acne-scarred face, called up to Burkhart. "Captain, low rumbling turns on the bottom, bearing zero one one, range five zero zero yards."

The talker momentarily bowed his eyes from Burkhart and pressed his hand to his earphone. Finally he looked up. "Sir, Mr. Mead has ID'd the screws. They're from a Victor Class attack sub at creep speed, at a depth of four five zero feet. He's moving away from us. Engine room reports extra oil smoke as you ordered, sir." The boy smiled up, but Burkhart had already pulled himself up to his feet.

Burkhart pushed down on his black sable cap to make certain it was in place.

"If you don't mind me saying, Skipper, we sure look stupid in these Russian uniforms." Chief Jerry Russotto's face erupted into a crooked smile.

Burkhart ignored the comment, then asked in a whisper, "How's the boarding party?"

"Niven checked out all the weapons and is now getting them dressed. The crew sure has a lot of respect for those guys. Know what I mean, sir?"

Burkhart smiled. "I know what you mean, Chief." He checked his watch. 0745.

"How long, Skipper?"

"Our ETA to repair ship *Dniestr* should be about 0845. Go below and see how things are coming along?" he whispered.

Russotto turned and disappeared down the hatch ladder.

"Bridge, Radar. Large target, bearing zero two eight, range five double O," the intercom blared metallically.

Burkhart jumped for the intercom switch. "Get off the damn fucking box, you stupid shit!" He tried to keep his voice hushed. "Doesn't anybody on this goddamn boat ever get the word? If they put sound gear on us, we're gonna be stewed deck rats!"

The young fur-capped lookout who had taken Russotto's watch looked very embarrassed.

"Yes, sir," he responded faintly, but there was a slight defiance in his voice. "We're not at war and are still in international waters, ain't we, sir?"

Burkhart squinted. "It's one hell of an argument that could keep the World Court busy for a year, but there's only one problem."

"Sir?"

"There wouldn't be enough left of *Skate* and us to fill a teacup for evidence." Burkhart pointed to the massive black shape growing out of the distance and raised his binoculars. "Jesus Christ!" He whistled softly. "That would be the missile cruiser screen."

"Her pennant number, sir, reads five four five." The young lookout dropped his field glasses against his parka and pulled off his gloves with his mouth. On the small steel bench at the forward bulkhead of the cockpit, he flipped open a thick Soviet recognition manual.

Burkhart kept his back to the youth as he stared at the cruiser sliding into range.

"What's her class, sir?"

"Kresta Two," Burkhart answered without turning.

"Here is it, sir. *Admiral Makarov,* eight thousand tons fully loaded. She's brimmed to the teeth with antisubmarine weapons, and her speed is in the thirty-three knot range." He hesitated. "I see what you mean, sir. They could eat us for breakfast."

"Something like that." Carefully, Burkhart watched as the *Admiral Makarov*'s sleek, angry silhouette came fully into view. "She's all business," he mumbled. Burkhart kept the glasses trained on the *Makarov*'s bridge, waiting for a light signal. The Soviets depended on blinker light communications to counter American electronic surveillance satellites. Finally the missile cruiser was a small gray smudge on the horizon and Burkhart allowed himself to breathe.

"We've made it this far." Burkhart squatted at the access hatch and peered down at the telephone talker. "Pass the word," he called down quietly. "We're into the Dog Bowl."

The talker looked up with a relieved grin. Burkhart had briefed the crew and they all knew The Dog Bowl meant security, at least from the defensive screening force. The talker looked around the control room and Burkhart saw his mouth form the words and he heard faint wisps of restrained comments and hoots from below.

Burkhart rose to his feet and turned back to the young lookout. "If it scares you now, just wait."

Niven tried to down a cup of strong black coffee but the taste made him nauseous. He placed the tan ceramic mug on the linen-covered dining table in the wardroom and slowly scanned the boarding party. Brahma Sorrell was in the final stages of changing into the dark-green uniform of the sub's political officer. For a long moment, Jake held up a heavy, large dark-brown envelope. At last he ripped open the flap as a knock at the door distracted him.

"Wardroom is off limits for the next half hour," he called.

"Mr. Niven, this is Chief Russotto. The skipper sent me down to see how you're doin'."

"Come in, Chief." Jake placed the envelope back on the table.

"Can we get you people anything?" Russotto allowed his eyes to search the wardroom. Each man from the boarding party was in various stages of dress. Three *Skorpion* machine pistols, steel bullet clips along with combat knives, littered the table.

"Hey, Russotto, how's your boat? You better make sure we get there." Akivor Levy smiled evenly and Jake wondered how in the hell he overcame his fear.

Russotto raised a fist. "Those Russian rock crushers are your responsibility, Mr. Levy. If we don't make it, it's your fault, not mine." Russotto looked around a bit longer, forced small talk with the men, and finally left the wardroom when the tension ran him down.

Jake picked up the envelope. "Give me your attention. I have our ID's and dog tags here." Carefully he spread the array on the table and matched the metal tags on neck chains with the light-blue laminated photo identification cards belonging to the Soviet Navy.

Niven surveyed the wardroom, and after a pause made his way to Brahma Sorrell. He nodded at his old friend.

"You ready?"

"I suppose." Sorrell stifled a yawn with a hand.

"No wonder." Jake shook his head. "You babbled in your sleep all night."

"Yeah?" Sorrell smiled lightly with big, heavy eyes. "I must have been thinking about today, but I thought I slept like a baby," he said sarcastically. "It's not as if I do this kind of thing every day."

"What the hell is Vladimir thirty-one? All night 'Vladimir thirty-one' and something about 'columns.' " Jake raised his eyes. "What the hell's it mean?"

Puzzled, Sorrell stroked his beard. "Who the hell knows? After a while all this shit runs together. Finland. Heavy dreams. Peking. Tired sleep. Kabul." He shook his head in disgust. "Now I'll lose my concentration trying to analyze what I goddamn say in my sleep."

Niven touched him lightly on the shoulder. "Do it tomorrow. I'm sorry I brought any of it up. I need all of you today. Listen, old friend, I don't want to make this a Knute Rockne locker room dance, but I couldn't have conceived of this operation without you. I can't smile because I'm too damned frightened right now." Momentarily, Jake looked away, then brought himself back.

"Your name for the next hour or so is Alexie Gushin. Your rank is *starshiy leytenant* in the KGB, attached to this boat as political officer." He handed Sorrell his ID card and dog tag, and nodded meaningfully, without a word.

Finally Niven made his way to David Lathrick, sitting and staring dully at the bulkhead. "Well, Doctor, we're almost there." He searched Lathrick's delicate face. The man was in a state of emotional terror.

"Once we're aboard you're not going to speak to anyone, is that understood? If you are put into the position of talking, just alternate *Da* for yes and *Nyet* for no."

Lathrick parted his dry lips and forced himself to repeat the simple Russian words.

"Is there anything I can do for you?"

Lathrick shook his head, tried to laugh, but couldn't. "How do I keep my legs from shaking off my feet?"

"Try standing on them, Doctor."

Lathrick nodded his head in little wooden movements.

"Well, it really doesn't matter, Doctor." Jake swallowed into the lump in his own voice. "What does matter is your ability to get that ring switch. Are your tools ready?"

"Yes, Niven. They're in the bottom of the canvas bag." He pointed to the table. "I want to ask you something?"

Jake raised his eyes. "What?"

"Will there be shooting?" Lathrick nodded toward the machine pistols laying on the table and his voice twisted up an octive. "I mean, I have a family."

"We all do, David." Niven took a breath and thought of his daughter and Ellie. Just as quickly he blocked them out. That kind of distraction would get them all killed, or worse, captured.

"David," Niven said reassuringly. "Take a deep breath and try to relax before we jump off. Sorrell is a damn street Neanderthal. He dances on everyone's head." He patted Lathrick's shoulder. "Nothing is going to happen, I promise." Niven felt his hands reaching for Brandon Langor's throat for having selected a man of Lathrick's emotional makeup.

Lathrick swept a hand through his hair. Niven could see the anxiety floating just behind his eyes.

"Sit down, David, close your eyes and breathe deeply," Niven commanded. "It will help."

"I'll try, Niven. I'll try. What do you think the Soviets will do in response to our stealing the ring switch and one of their ranking naval officers?"

"They haven't consulted me, David," he replied quietly. "Let's not try and think about it. It doesn't help."

"Will there be shooting?" Lathrick couldn't leave it alone.

"Honestly, I don't know. The real point of this operation is not to start a war but to slip quietly through a crack in their armor, steal the gadget, jump back in *Skate*, and get the hell out. The name of the game is speed and stealth." He paused and widened his eyes at Lathrick. There just wasn't much more he could do for the man, short of carrying him on his back.

"Look, David, I have every intention of going home and I have every intention of making certain you come home with me." He smiled and handed Lathrick his ID card and dog tag.

"Your Russian name is Petr Ivanov. Your rank is *leytenant*. You are the boat's assistant engineering officer." He examined Lathrick's intelligent face. "Just keep your mouth closed, get the switch, and I'll get you home."

Something caught Jake's eye and he looked down at Lathrick's arm. "Take off that watch, Doctor. I mentioned it before, but I suppose you overlooked it. We're all a bit tense, my friend. The fact is, a gold Rolex would be impossible for a junior Soviet officer to come by, even on the black market. Someone will ask you in Russian to explain where it came from and your English answer might be embarrassing."

"Yes of course." Lathrick offered as he sat down heavily.

Jake moved to another corner of the wardroom and found Akivor Levy, already fully dressed and sitting quietly. During the past months he had come to admire Levy's professional skills and calm, quiet strength.

"Well, MOSSAD, you ready to jump off?"

Levy looked up and studied Jake's face for a long time. "We both understand the fear, don't we? I can easily read it in your face." Then he answered Jake's question.

"I suppose. My stomach has turned itself inside out. That means I'm ready."

"Yes, I know, Akivor."

Levy lowered his voice to a whisper and held up a thick hand tinged with black grease under the rounded fingernails. "What else can I say?" He smiled warmly.

"It's like a bank." It felt good for Jake to talk to someone who understood. "It's very easy to get in, tough to get out."

Niven handed Levy his ID and dog tag. "You are Feliks Kalinin with a rank of *starshiy leytenant* and you are my senior engineering officer."

"The stripes on my uniform told me my rank, and who are you going to be at this masquerade ball?"

"I'm Oleg Nkolai, Executive Officer of the Soviet submarine *Severyanka*, three three one, with proper ship papers and operational orders."

Levy opened his palms, then swept a hand around the wardroom. "Where did these uniforms and dog tags come from?"

"The tags and name identifications came from the Golf submarine we dragged up from the Pacific and these uniforms from a source in East Germany. If you pay enough, there's nothing you can't have."

"Everything but a Soviet ring switch to make a beam weapon with." Levy moved his restless eyes over Niven.

Jake moved his mouth and jaw, just as a knock at the door turned his head.

"It's Brennen," the voice came from behind the door.

"Come in, Irish."

"We have the tracking ship *Komarov* in sight. *Minsk* and *Dniestr* shouldn't be far away." His eyes were very wide as he waited for Jake to say something.

"I'll come up to the bridge and Sorrell will go back to Radio." Jake turned to Levy. "Akivor, station yourself in the engine room." Jake looked at the bulkhead clock. It read 0823. "We'll meet in the control room as soon as we drop anchor."

He glanced over at Lathrick, standing in the corner, as Levy and Sorrell departed. "Doctor, you come with me and station yourself in the control room. For emphasis, Jake gently took Lathrick's arm and directed him to the table.

"Here, David, you take the canvas bag." Niven picked up the machine pistols, slung them over a shoulder, and started for the door. "Now, David. It's time," he heard himself say. Niven circled back behind Lathrick and guided his elbow through the open door.

31

"Permission to come on the bridge," Jake called quietly as he popped his head through the access hatch.

"Come." Burkhart's eyes never dropped from the horizon.

Jake leaned over the port cockpit bulkwarks and raised his binoculars. The tracking ship *Komarov*, the size of a Caribbean cruise liner, her silhouette dominated by three large radar domes, slid by at five hundred yards. *Skate* was bucking mildly in the swell as she sailed into the belly of the Soviet Task Force.

"Anything from that Victor sub?" The words vaporized into the Bering chill.

"No." He pushed out a breath. "I just keep waiting for the bubble to burst."

"Niven swept a hand around across the misty gray-green horizon. "It's a crazy sensation."

Burkhart looked at him. "Pure understatement," he whispered. Burkhart raised his glasses to starboard and scanned the ocean at a point where he thought water and sky should meet. Usually, there was an invisible geography to the ocean's surface that seamen knew by feel and smell, but not here. This was a place where clear distinctions and finite boundaries blurred—there was no horizon. "We just have to step lightly and not wake the bastards."

"This difficult for you, Charley?" Niven suddenly asked.

"No. I've waited my entire adult life for this battle test." He smiled at Niven. "You just can't tell a virgin what it feels like."

"A mission like this can pulverize all the best instincts a person has."

"I'm still a virgin—" His voice faded into the throbbing of the diesels as he squeezed his eyes into the binocular's eye cups.

"Not for long," Niven said quietly. "Two ships, broad on the port beam. One of those babies has to be *Minsk*, the other the repair ship *Dniestr*. How come radar didn't report?"

"I shut it down. I don't want any more mistakes on the squawk box."

Burkhart squatted at the hatch and called down to the talker. "Give me more smoke. I want more damn smoke on these diesels! Let's make it really look like we're wounded." He eyed the young talker down the hatch. "Don't keep repeating my orders, just pass the word."

The talker nodded solemnly.

"Make turns for fifteen knots and come left to zero two zero, true." Burkhart watched the talker's lips move into his breast mike, then he looked up and nodded. Burkhart rose to his feet and could feel the boat's center of gravity shift as the bows began to swing more to port.

"We're entering Linsinskaya Bay," Jake called out quietly as *Skate* plowed ahead into the large half moon-shaped natural bay, dominated by a great barren mountain range of rock and ice that formed Bering Island.

Burkhart squatted again at the hatch and called down to his talker. "Keep that smoke coming and make turns for ten knots."

"There she is, Charley." A twinge of excitement coursed through his voice."Jesus, she's huge! All one thousand plus feet of her." Jake refocused his glasses and through the grayness, spotted her pennant number, 117 in large white block letters, emblazoned on her gray hull.

"She looks like a magnificent death machine with that narrow clipper bow," Jake whispered aloud, his eyes glued to the binoculars. "I count three blue Yak jump jet fighters on her flight deck, along with two helicopters. The fighters have to be strictly window dressing for our orbiting sky spies. Right now there's just no place on that carrier for fighter operations."

"Look how low she's riding at anchor," Burkhart added. "I'll bet her displacement with all that particle beam hardware aboard has swelled to sixty thousand tons."

Minsk was a shocking experience for both men. Her lines and superstructure were massive yet sleek and there was an overall frightening, brooding quality about her. A certain mystic tension like a Rodin sculpture. *Minsk* was just a different kind of ship than they had ever seen. A live presence that tested their limits. *Minsk* didn't have the squatty rectangular look of American carriers; rather, she was knife sleek in the bows, a look that only added to her menace.

Aft of the bows, *Minsk* flared out dramatically into the fullness of her one hundred thirty-five-foot beam, dominated by a hugh island structure, replete with a full array of electronic aerials and scoops that only added an efficiency to her lines. Offset to the left of the island, the green flight deck swept aft to the broad fantail.

238

Cautiously, Niven lowered the glasses, forcing used air from his lungs in steamy breaths.

"Captain," a soft voice floated up from below. Burkhart crouched at the hatch and peered down.

"Dr. Lathrick just threw up all over the plot table down here and seems in pretty rough shape."

"Jake!" Burkhart turned on his heels. "Poor damn Lathrick is puking his guts out all over my control room."

Niven looked like someone had just shot him in the chest. "Jesus, not now!" He lurched for the hatch and scrambled down the ladder to the control room, where he found David Lathrick leaning over the plot table, wretching what he hadn't already tossed up all over the table and surrounding linoleum deck.

The entire control room reeked of a horrid-smelling mixture of bile and undigested food. Lathrick's face was a mess, but, fortunately, his uniform was relatively clean of vomit.

Finally, after a final dry retch that seemed to come from his toes, Lathrick vaguely acknowledged Niven standing next to him, but his eyes carried a far-off glaze. His skin had dissolved into the color of dirty snow.

"What happened, David?" Niven muted his voice into a soft mixture of father and nurse. He had only a few minutes to put Lathrick back together. "What happened?" Niven repeated softly.

"Terrible stomach cramps. Breakfast," he moaned, coughing up a residue of phlegm and stomach bile.

Gently, he picked up Lathrick's head with his hands. It was one of the bravest things he had ever done, but the moment called for something extreme. Lathrick was a mess and they were out of time.

"Listen to me. We're going to cross to *Minsk* in a few minutes. Do you hear me, David?" Slowly, Lathrick's eyes began to focus. He was going to have to baby the man across that gulf of ocean. "Good man, David. Good man."

Two large tears rolled down Lathrick's cheeks. "I'm scared, Jake. I'm damn scared."

"We need you, David. We're all depending on you."

Lathrick's small animal eyes focused on Niven.

Niven sucked in a breath through his mouth to counter the foul stench surrounding Lathrick. "The United States needs us right now, David. Los Alamos is waiting for what only you can bring back. You'll make us all proud."

"I've always hated guns. When I was a child, I had a BB gun and accidentally shot a bird—" His eyes narrowed again.

"I know, David. The guns we are carrying are just a precaution. Niven tightened his hand vise, holding Lathrick's head just as if he were cradling and soothing his daughter. He had to somehow cut through the man's paralyzing fright.

"But Admiral Langor promised me that Russian captain would take care of everything." His voice rose to a simpering whine.

Jake smiled. Langor was good for something after all. "Admiral Langor was right. Captain Belous will take care of us." Jake swallowed. He was out of time. "You'll see, David. I promise he will. Do you think I would go if I thought something was going to happen to us?"

"I suppose not. I'm, ah, not very good at this physical aspect of the mission. I thought it would be much easier—"

"Here, Doctor." Niven looked up and found corpsman Al Ginepra standing above them. Jake nodded and the corpsman squatted.

"Here, take this, Doctor. It's a stomach relaxer. It will help the cramps."

Ginepra held the small folding paper cup to Lathrick's lips as he downed the small orange capsule. Sensing the moment, Jake reached down and pulled Lathrick to his feet. It was now or never.

"Better, now?"

Lathrick tentatively nodded. "Yeah, I think."

"Mr. Niven, sir," the talker stationed below the open hatch called. "Captain Burkhart wanted me to tell you Sorrell has initiated contact with the repair ship *Dniestr.*"

Jake stiffened and turned to Lathrick. "It's almost time to go, David. We'll do this together."

For a moment he moved away to Brennen and motioned him down from the periscope stand with a finger. "Get Levy up here from the engine room on the double," he whispered. "I don't want Lathrick left alone. I've got to get back to Radio, so have your corpsman stay with him until Levy gets here, then fill him in."

Jake returned to Lathrick, who with the help of a sailor was cleaning up his clothes. Luckily he hadn't yet put on his parka, which would hide the mess, if not the odor.

"Be right back, David." He patted him softly on the back. "It happens to us all." Then he disappeared aft toward the communications compartment.

Niven bumped into Sorrell, who was hurrying forward through the narrow corridor. "We're up, Jake! Belous came through. Right on the money. As soon as I initiated contact with *Dniestr,* Belous patched into the conversation. He's sending a barge over for us."

"But we're not even in position yet." Niven was momentarily off balance.

"Like hell we're not! Burkhart just set an anchor detail." Sorrell looked strangely at him. "Where the hell have you been hiding?"

He blew out an exasperated breath. "With my friend Lathrick. He just spilled his cookies all over the control room."

"We're dead without him! We've come all this way for nothing. He's got to go," Sorrell stammered.

"He'll go. I'll have Levy hold his hand all the way across. We all will."

Sorrell nodded. "Let's get up on deck."

32

The boarding party stood huddled against the cold in a small isolated cluster on *Skate*'s flat steel deck. For insurance, Akivor Levy held a powerful hand under Lathrick's arm, while Jake settled his gaze on the massive carrier, riding peacefully at anchor, five hundred yards abeam of *Skate*. Slowly he shifted his eyes to the choppy green waters of Lisinskaya Bay as a small gray abstraction approached and grew into an open utility barge.

Burkhart looked down from the cockpit and caught Jake's gaze, then slowly held up a thumb for luck. Jake pressed his hands together and jiggled his head, anything to burn off the adrenaline. He felt inside the parka for the Skorpion machine pistol, lying flat against his hard belly, hoping the bulky jacket hid its outline.

The boarding party, deck line handlers, and Burkhart, all stood transfixed in a queer frozen moment as the Soviet boat slowed and idled its way uncertainly toward the canted hull of *Skate*.

Assessing the dilemma, Burkhart quietly called down to the control room to bring *Skate* down another three feet by controlled flooding of seawater into her trim tanks. Rapidly she dropped to meet the barge with a deep gurgling sound from water pushing compressed

243

air from the filling tanks. Burkhart looked down at Jake and raised his eyes.

While the Soviet coxswain drew his craft alongside, sailors in the bow and stern of the open boat received mooring lines from *Skate*'s deckhands, dressed in regulation Soviet Navy work uniforms.

A young, dark-faced sailor in the aft section of the barge smiled and waved a hand.

"Zdrah'stvooite!" he called out above the rumbling engine.

Hello yourself, Jake said to himself, thinking that was a stupid way to start a war, then called back *"Rah'da vas vee'det."* It wasn't a lie. He was glad to see them.

Niven turned his head and scrutinized his people for the last time. Levy was firmly guiding Lathrick as they moved toward the gunwale of the barge. Levy silently met Jake's glance and understood. The weakest would go first.

With a helping hand from the young Russian sailor, Levy and the Los Alamos scientist found themselves standing on the open, aft deck of the barge. Niven drew a deep, cold breath and felt his pulse quicken as he assessed the Soviet seamen. From this point on, every nuance might be an obstacle to HAWKSCREECH. The glance of an eye or a slight body movement could be the difference between life and death.

The Russian seaman spent their energies trying to avoid ramming their fiberglass barge into the sloping steel-skinned ballast tanks surrounding *Skate*'s pressure hull. A careless move in the steep swell would quickly crush the small boat against the submarine. The sailors didn't seem to care what the cargo was, as long as they brought back an undamaged boat to *Minsk*.

Jake glanced over at Akivor Levy, who nodded slightly. Good. Lathrick was holding his own. Niven sucked in another breath of arctic air. It was working, so far. He looked up at the approaching form of *Minsk* and felt a special tingle in his fingertips.

Carefully, Jake talked himself down to subdue and control his rush of animal energy. This was thinking man's combat. Not the old frayed and pained Vietnam instincts and images of burning hooches and the punishing smell of river stench.

He watched with a passive expression while Brahma Sorrell waited for *Skate*'s deck and gunwale of the barge to meet, timed it perfectly, then easily jumped. Niven took one last look up at Burkhart's open, expectant face, then leaped into the Russian launch.

"Ee-d' Yom!" shouted the aft deckhands as the hemp lines were cast off and tossed back onto *Skate*'s deck. Suddenly they were rumbling to the beat of the small open boat, toward a giant ghost off in the distance. Niven watched the helmsman swing his bows around and gun the engines as the barge knifed through the seas. For longer than he could remember, he had thought about this moment.

Brahma Sorrell stood with his legs apart to take the shallow motion of the waves. He had stationed himself next to both deck sailors, silently staring across the water at the rapidly growing *Minsk.* They still didn't seem the slightest bit curious. If trouble arose, Sorrell would be in a perfect position to neutralize them.

Jake turned his eyes back to *Minsk,* which was growing larger by the minute. Crossing the small gulf of cold ocean symbolized a crossing into another world. A world of dark alleys, rigid controls, and brooding silences, punctuated only with knowing eyes and footsteps. This was the world that Jake knew so well and this had been the world of Vasili Lykov.

He lifted his deep-set brown eyes and stared at *Minsk.* He couldn't help being drawn to her. She was compelling and menacing with a bold red star emblazoned on the tip of her bows, offset with large white Cyrillic script letters spelling out *Minsk*. He shivered at the thought of the particle beam weapon buried deep in her steel gut.

Jake started, as the rhythmic beat of the barge's engines slowed. Barely moving, the boat glided to the midship's landing platform of *Minsk* and Jake felt a strange silence fold over them. Orders to a painting and chipping detail blared over *Minsk*'s public address as the barge idled and then bounced against the platform.

Akivor Levy already had David Lathrick on his feet, while Sorrell moved cautiously behind the entire party. Slowly, he placed a hand inside his parka and rested it against the stock of the machine pistol.

"The orders," Sorrell whispered in Russian.

Jake nodded and pulled out the forged operational orders and ship documents that would be presented as a formality to the officer of the deck.

Silently, the barge was secured and they disembarked. Jake took one last look at the boat as it rose in sympathy to the ground swell in Lisinskaya Bay. He picked up the canvas tool bag and motioned them all ahead. Cautiously, they climbed the accommodations ladder to a main gathering area that served *Minsk* as a cargo elevator. Niven blanked his face and braced for a salute from the scowling young Soviet officer of the deck.

The *mladshiy leytenant*, junior lieutenant, saluted smartly as Jake took two short steps to meet him. The officer was young, probably not more than twenty-five, and his eyes were squinting and restless, as he regarded each member of the boarding party.

"Welcome aboard *Minsk*, sir." Niven stood smartly and returned the salute, pivoted a quarter turn to his left, and saluted the Soviet colors.

"Permission to come aboard?"

"Permission granted."

Jesus! He'd done it. Cautiously, he took stock.

Jake noted the officer's smooth polished speech, indicating he was well educated, probably at Frunze Naval Academy in Leningrad or Nakhimov Black Sea Higher Naval School in Sevastopol.

Forcing himself to breathe slowly, Jake calmly handed him the submarine's forged documents, nodded severely, and then stepped aside watching anxiously as Levy and Lathrick went next.

Levy snapped a crisp salute, then surprisingly pulled out his ID card, shoving it in the OOD's face. The Russian officer examined it, grunted his approval and Jake silently thanked the Israeli. Levy had taken away the Russian's momentum.

"Let's hurry this up, we're late, dammit. We don't have time for this," Levy commanded.

Somehow Lathrick summoned up enough energy and saluted. The *mladshiy leytenant* stood almost on top of Lathrick when Jake saw the shape of the Russian's eyes change.

"Excuse me, sir."

"What's the problem, Lieutenant?" Jake raised his voice. "I said, what the hell's the problem here?"

The Russian turned to acknowledge the command, then glared down at Lathrick's wrist. Lathrick had forgotten to remove the gold Rolex, which stood out like a beacon.

Niven and Levy noticed the watch at the same time. In an instant Levy moved between the men, but the Russian stubbornly thrust his hand around Levy and grabbed Lathrick's wrist with an iron grip.

Sorrell took a step, but Niven shook his head.

"We're not here to compare watches, Lieutenant!" Niven cut him short. "We've been ordered aboard your vessel by your commanding officer, Captain Viktor Belous. I'm Executive Officer of that submarine, the *Severyanka*. We have a severe engine problem and we've been fighting to stay alive for the past forty-eight hours. We are damn tired right now and you're out of line! I said I was tired."

The officer snapped to attention. "I know who you are, sir, but—"

Niven saw the burning eyes, silently hanging on to that damn Rolex. He carefully fingered the knife handle and cursed his luck when suddenly Levy threw his arms around the officer in a half beer hug and pulled him away from the group.

Levy grabbed the officer by his cold cheeks and squeezed, leaving white marks. His Russian was informal, even brotherly.

"These fucking senior officers don't give a shit about us. They act like peasants." Levy nodded his head. "What's so special about a goddamn watch?" Levy was smiling and moving his arms as best he could in the bulky parka.

"What can I do for you, Lieutenant? Hurry and tell me because your captain will not wait much longer." He showed his white teeth in a caring smile.

The Russian officer looked down, forcing Levy to raise the man's chin with his gloved hand. "We're educated men, *Leytenant*, don't act like a fucking beet farmer from Tadzhikistan. Tell me."

The young officer, with the wisp of a smile on his lips, looked up into Levy's intelligent, caring eyes. A con game with an amateur. If only he knew Levy was a Jew. The thought forced Levy's smile to grow even more intense.

"Do you have any alcohol?" His voice was a confident whisper.

"What?"

"Alcohol. You must have grain alcohol aboard to service your delicate instruments."

The son-of-a-bitch *leytenant* was grasping for leverage with the force of a young street pusher. But alcohol?

248

"What about cleaning fluid or torpedo alcohol?" His eyes grew wide. "I'll take anything, even solvents. I don't know about your submarine, but here on *Minsk* our lives are rigidly controlled and it is very lonely. We drink what we can to escape—"

Levy glared at him sternly.

"If you can't get me alcohol, do you have any blue meat coupons?" He raised his eyes and showed Levy just what an amateur he really was. "My parents live in the industrial city of Kazan and they are rationed to seven hundred grams of meat and sausage a month. The bastards in Moscow get everything."

Levy almost felt sorry for him. If he couldn't steal for himself, at least he would steal for his parents.

"I can help you. How about a gallon of ethyl alcohol if you keep quiet about the damn watch?" He flashed another brotherly smile and squeezed the Soviet officer's lean shoulders with a burly arm.

"A gallon!" His stiffness melted.

"We'd better be taken to Captain Belous or you won't get your gallon and we'll all end up on our asses as *Siberyaki*."

"Yes, I'd better take you to the captain," he repeated. "I was instructed to see you to his in port cabin, just aft of the bridge."

Levy bridled inside at what was probably routine blackmail and guided the Russian back to the others, then slowly announced: "The lieutenant and I have come to an understanding. I've decided to lend my young friend a gallon of alcohol in exchange for his silence regarding the gold watch." He smiled knowingly at the Russian officer. "But right now we have to hurry, because Captain Belous is waiting for us."

Niven took a deep breath and released his grip on the knife handle inside his parka.

The officer hurried the four men up a stairwell

crowded with a work party and they emerged topside on the massive green flight deck. Jake swept his eyes from the glass-windowed bridge, high on the superstructure, to a Yak fighter tied down near the fantail. A large white Soviet flag was painted to the dark blue fuselage.

Suddenly out of the corner of his eye, Niven saw two very large Soviet naval infantrymen moving double-time across the flight deck toward them with their well-oiled Kalashnikov carbines glistening dully in the impoverished northern sunlight. Sorrell and Levy had seen them, too.

Maybe the naval infantrymen, looking like angry Cossacks in their bulky navy-blue greatcoats, black combat boots, and fur shapka caps, were heading elsewhere, Niven rationalized. Christ, *Minsk* had to have a crew of at least thirty-five hundred people, and discipline had to be a problem, if the officer of the deck was any indication.

He swore to himself. There wasn't any doubt now. The Cossacks were heading for them, trotting at a perfect angle to cut them off before they reached the Island superstructure. Casually Sorrell dropped back and fell into step with Jake, careful never to take his eyes off the Kalashnikov's bouncing on the chests of the approaching guards.

Sorrell spoke Russian, barely moving his lips as they walked. "This is some place for a firefight. What do you want to do?"

"Keep moving, dammit! Move!" Niven grimaced. "Move and keep your mouth shut. Let our alcoholic junior officer, who wants his gallon of joy juice, work it out. It's all we have." Jake motioned him to take his place in front of him. He glanced at the Cossacks, not more than twenty feet away now, and could feel the heat flushing into his face.

"Sir?" shouted the smaller guard, with strong Mongolian features and the hooded eyes of a lizard.

The Russian officer stopped short. Jake coiled his moving body and reached under his parka, easily finding the safety of the Skorpion with his fingers. He had grown furious.

The larger naval guard stopped eight feet away, planted his feet, and gripped the Kalashnikov with his gloved hands. His vague head was the size of a medicine ball.

The nightmare was coming alive; trapped and exposed, with no way out. All that was missing from the dream was Vasili Lykov, coming back from the dead.

"Captain Belous sent us down from the Weather Bridge, sir. He wants to know what's holding up that submarine crew? He saw the barge come alongside some time ago."

"What the hell does it look like, Michman?" The Russian snarled at the Mongol. "I will guide them to Captain Belous just as fast as our legs will carry us. You go about some other business. Is there anything else?" The Russian officer stood ramrod straight, waiting.

"No, sir," the Mongol grunted, then turned away and motioned to his mate. Quickly they turned and trotted off.

The Russian officer thrust up a gloved hand and twisted his thumb between his second and third fingers, then clenched his fist. The sign of the fig. *Fig v karmane.* The Russian hand sign of fuck you.

"Captain Belous's private, salivating guard dogs. We call them *Dezhurnaya.* Belous's old snooping women." The Russian smiled for the first time, revealing ugly steel fillings in the bottom row of front teeth. "The privileges of *nachlastvo* and Party membership. They're all jingoist fuckers."

He smiled at Akivor Levy, who shook his head, agreeing as violently as he could. Comrades in arms, Levy grinned inside. The irreverent booze hound and the Jew. If only his MOSSAD associates could see him now.

They were led through a small hatch into the starboard Island structure, rising twenty stories, from keel to the top of the radar mast. An empty elevator sped the boarding party to the bridge deck level, and finally to the cabin marked CAPTAINS IN PORT CABIN in bold Cyrillic letters.

The young officer knocked loudly on the steel door, turned to Levy, and nodded soberly, silently telling him that sometime within the next twenty-four hours one gallon of pure rotgut was due aboard *Minsk*.

Levy nodded with a taut smile.

The officer turned to Niven.

"I hope your papers are in order or Captain Belous will have your ass, sir. He expressed great displeasure all morning about your submarine intruding into a restricted testing area."

"Shto'?" came the rich but suspicious voice from behind the compartment door.

"The officers from the submarine are here, sir.'

"It's about time. Send them in!"

The young officer opened the steel door by pulling it toward him and then extending a beckoning hand.

The Russian officer caught Levy before he entered Belous's cabin. "As you know, sir, black market goods are an indiscretion for naval officers. I expect that gallon aboard by this evening in care of Mladshiy Leytenant Ernst Kosov." He smiled sullenly at Levy.

"I'll have it here within two hours." Levy shrugged and followed Lathrick into Captain First Rank Viktor Belous's cabin.

33

Viktor Belous, *Kapitan Pervogo Ranga,* stood rigidly still, legs drawn apart, his crisply pressed dark-blue uniform offset with gold piping. The only ribbon adorning his left breast was the Order of Lenin, with two clusters for bravery in the Great Patriotic War.

Niven stepped forward to attention and saluted, waiting for the hatch door behind him to slam. He could feel the unchanneled tension arcing about the large, well-decorated cabin. It had to be a difficult moment and he was close enough to smell Belous's sour, nervous body odor.

"Kapitan Leytenant Oleg Nkolai, Executive Officer of submarine *Severyanka,* three three one, reporting as ordered, sir," Niven announced.

Belous grunted as Jake stared into his gray, heavily lidded eyes. So this was Viktor Belous. He had burned Belous's image and history into his mind. Age, fifty-eight. Height, five foot nine inches. Weight one hundred seventy-five pounds. Massive burn scar on left forearm. Black, wavy hair, thinning on top. Graduated from Frunze Higher Naval Academy in 1943 and became a war hero a year later when the motor torpedo boat he was commanding made a suicide run to protect a convoy and sank the German destroyer *Z-24* near the Kola Inlet. He advanced in rank and trust with the Party and Admiral Flota Sovetskgogo Soyuza, Sergei Gorshkov and the Soviet Admiralty. Belous was an imposing man.

The dull slamming sound of the compartment door brought him back.

"What are you staring at?" Belous demanded, his Russian gravelly and strained.

Niven shook his head. "Nothing, sir."

Belous brushed past him and approached Sorrell. "It has been a very long time since Africa, Sorrell." Belous somberly shook his head and looked up at the heroic portrait of Nikolai Ilyich Lenin guarding the rosewood-paneled cabin. Belous turned again with his hands on his hips and inspected each member of the boarding party.

"Can we talk in here, Captain Belous? We must hurry!"

"You must be Niven, correct?" There was a great caution in Belous' eyes that was accentuated by his commanding but wooden movements.

"Do you have the other half?"

"Yes. Quickly please, Captain!"

Niven unzipped his parka and the Skorpion jiggled free on its strap, forcing Belous's thick eyebrows to arch, but he said nothing. He reached into his uniform pocket and pulled out a piece of neatly folded cloth wrapped in a thin plastic watertight bag. Quickly he pulled the cloth free and handed it to Belous, who examined it carefully, finally comparing its torn edge with a mate.

"Can we talk freely in here, Captain?" Belous was purposely delaying.

Belous looked up from the cloth, his eyes and expression having lightened. "Yes. That is why I had you brought in here."

Jake nodded. "Is that the correct cloth?" He reached out and flicked off the safety on the machine pistol.

"Yes. That is the same Gucci scarf I bought my wife in London." Niven could see the genuine pain in his face, accentuated by the deep lines and bags holding up his eyes.

"Let's move it, Captain," Sorrell snapped. "There will be plenty of time for Rodeo Drive if we can get the hell out of here."

Niven raised his eyebrows at Belous. Then he pulled a cheap Pobeda Russian pocket watch from his jacket. "We have only twenty-five minutes. Then our taxi has been instructed to leave." He glared at Belous.

"Do you have the Da Vinci "Madonna Litta" aboard your boat?"

"Yes." Niven had to move him or kill him. "The same painting your wife viewed in the Hermitage." He clenched his teeth, trying to spill off the rising tension. "We're out of time. We've met every part of our end of the agreement."

Still Niven saw the hesitation in Belous's eyes. The nightmare was taking on shape and form. "This is what your wife Anna would have wanted. Commander Crabb told me the story of London."

"How is Crabb?"

"Very dead, Captain. The same dead that we will be if we don't move out to the beam weapon bay."

"I am no less a Soviet naval officer than before. I—"

Niven held up a hand. "Goddammit, not now! This has gone far enough." Niven raised the machine pistol. "We go now or we fight our way out." His stomach tightened.

Belous studied Niven for a minute with curiosity. "My wife died alone. That is reason enough. That Da

255

Vinci was her obsession." He smiled darkly. "Now it is my obsession. It is the only earthly link I have left with her. It became our child of love in Leningrad. Our summer evenings on Yelagin Island strolling through Kirov Park. Our home in the Yevropeiskaya Hotel is cold and dead."

"I have traveled Kirov *Prospekt* north to the Neva Delta and the Kirov Islands. The Kirovs are the most beautiful part of Leningrad. Now, Captain Belous!" Niven coaxed.

Niven watched his face and decided that when Belous was young and before gravity and grieving had rounded the once sharp facial features, he had been very handsome. His skin still had the tautness of a much younger man and his nostrils still flared with a certain unspoken defiance. It would be a shame to have to kill him. He wasn't used to being challenged on his own ship.

"The ring switch, Captain."

"Yes, it is time." Suddenly he smiled. "They want to give me a Star." He looked about the plush cabin. "It is time."

"Any last belongings you want to take along?" Sorrell asked.

Belous pointed to a leather reading chair in the corner of the cabin with a small nylon tube bag.

"What about security?" Niven asked, paying very close attention to Belous's movements.

"The weapon and support facilities are set up in such a fashion that, except for the special elevator that raises and lowers the gun nozzle, there is only one entrance and exit. There were others, of course, when the weapon was being constructed, but they have all been sealed off."

"How about once we are inside the gun room?"

"The operational scientists and technicians are in

256

Vladivostok for a special meeting and will fly back to the ship in the morning. The meeting has been planned for months. It is today or never."

"Today, Captain." Niven raised the machine pistol.

"Before we leave, there is something that we must do, Niven, to give us the lead time through the screen. It will only take a moment." Belous extended a hand and pointed toward another hatch at the forward section of the cabin.

Niven stood his ground watching them all.

"The weapon stays here, Niven. You cannot take it on the bridge." Belous tried to smile.

"I'll cover you from outside the hatch," Sorrell said.

Jake nodded and removed the machine pistol. "Let's go, dammit!"

"This better not be a setup, Captain." Sorrell furrowed his ugly face.

"If it is, kill him first," Niven said coldly.

Anger flared in Belous's nostrils. "I am the captain of this vessel. My whereabouts are closely monitored. I must create a fiction for leaving *Minsk*."

Jake motioned toward the hatch.

"Fine, Niven. Through that hatch is the bridge. There are probably nine men in there, including my first officer." Belous paused. "I am going to embarrass you."

Jake's entire body tensed.

"Just act embarrassed, Niven."

Belous opened the hatch and marched onto the bridge. His arrival was announced by another infantryman stationed just inside the hatch.

"Captain on the bridge," he shouted crisply.

Belous strode forcefully to his bridge chair, set high on a single steel swivel leg welded to the deck, that gave Captain Belous a sweeping panorama of *Minsk*'s battleship clipper bows and the green angled flight deck below through a series of windows, both forward and to port. Niven allowed himself the liberty of quickly examining the Soviet bridge.

Next to Belous's command chair stood a rather small steel helm or ship's wheel, that Niven surmised was computerized with an auto-pilot, based on the series of black metal consoles built under the helm. Dropping down above the ship's wheel from the overhead was a large gyrocompass and what looked to Jake to be a powerful Doppler radar console. Farther to the left of the ship's wheel, stood another bank of consoles containing a large green-faced rate of turn indicator, engine revolution counter, knot meter, rudder angle indicator, and a satellite navigation and communications system.

Niven looked up to find every eye on the bridge riveted on him. Certainly, the bridge staff knew a great deal about the submarine sitting off her port beam.

Belous secured himself high up in the chair and for a long moment ignored Niven. Belous examined a clipboard, turned and said something quietly to an officer Jake assumed to be the executive officer. After a few more long moments, his ears picked up the audio rhythm of the bridge—the usual electronic chatter, a continual sound of communications with various parts of the ship as well as with other ships in the screening fleet. Niven was amazed at just how busy the compartment seemed, although *Minsk* was anchored. The sea had begun to rise and the radio traffic was mounting in response.

"Are you enjoying yourself, Kapitan Leytenant Nkolai?" Jake jerked his head at the sound of the loud, sharp, commanding voice. Every head turned to meet the command in stony silence, then gradually the noise returned to fill the vacuum.

"Sir?"

"You have totally disrupted this secret test area by disregarding orders and pushing past the frigate *Shakal*. Well?" Belous's jowls were shaking and his face had turned purple with rage.

"We have an emergency—"

"Are you retarded?"

"No—" Niven stumbled over his Russian.

"Answer the question," Belous hissed with disgust. "What was so important about a broken down pigboat intruding into restricted space? I could easily have your ass, mister."

"Yes, sir. We were in danger of floundering. We are in transit from our duty station in the Maldive Islands in the Indian Ocean, via a refueling stop at Cam Ranh Bay, to Petropavlovsk. We collided with a Chinese fishing boat and lost our power. At one point we experienced a massive electrical failure and drifted without diesel or communications power. We drifted off course until we generated enough power to maintain steerage," Niven offered weakly.

"You have all our official orders and ship's documents."

"You drifted a hella'va long way," Belous quipped suspiciously, "but I will personally check this out."

"We feel fortunate to still be afloat, sir. For a period we had no control—"

"Indeed. Don't you have qualified technicians aboard? Has the Soviet Submarine Force become incompetent?"

"Sir," Jake protested, his voice cracking, "we needed critical parts to make repairs. The damage to our stern is clear."

"Yes, yes." Belous raised a hand and turned his head away. "I've heard all that. You're babbling and falling all over your own words. Talking with you is like talking to a wall." Belous hesitated and picked his nose with contempt while staring into Jake's eyes.

"Besides, when you anchor a ship, it's customary to break out your jack. Ah, I'm tired of my time being taken up with this incompetence." Belous turned and scrutinized the faces of the men on the bridge.

Jake forced himself to hold a dumb gaze on Belous. His heart was pounding in his neck.

"I'm going to make an example of you," Belous shouted.

Jake felt every face staring at him, waiting for the ax to fall. He reached for the knife in his pocket.

"I don't understand, sir?"

"I'm going to escort you back to your submarine and you will personally demonstrate for me exactly what your problems are, and I hope for your sake and the sake of your children I find the problems as real as you say. You have completely disrupted my morning routine."

"Yes. sir," Jake lowered his eyes and released the knife.

"I certainly hope your captain runs a taut vessel."

Belous turned to his first officer, standing discreetly out of range. "Kapitan Bruslov, I will be leaving *Minsk* for the remainder of the morning watch. This submarine is going to take me for a little shakedown cruise so I may judge for myself just how wounded they really are. Then I will examine their log and documents in depth. You will assume command until I return. Is that clear?" he bellowed.

"Yes, sir. I understand."

"I'm glad someone does!" Belous jumped off his chair and turned his head about the bridge. Then in a fit of pique he stomped through the hatch back into his in-port cabin, and the infantryman yelling in circus style, "Captain leaving the bridge." The slamming hatch ended the drama.

Belous sucked in a deep breath. "You did well, Niven," he whispered. "You did very well."

"So did you." Niven wiped his nose.

Sorrell approached. "Christ, Jake! Get the lead out!"

Niven shook his head and nodded to Belous, who shuffled past Levy and Lathrick out the other hatch. He instructed his private guards to stay put and await his return from the submarine. The Cossacks braced and saluted smartly.

Belous pulled a key ring from his trouser pocket and inserted a key into a private lift lock near the cabin. When the elevator door closed he pushed 001 DECK.

34

The lift door slid silently open and Belous led the way down a narrow, poorly lit companionway. The corridor dogged to the right and Niven looked about as they passed through a series of watertight doors. In case of a foul-up they would have to find their own way back.

Niven followed close on Lathrick and Levy's heels. Lathrick seemed to be holding his own, but he shuffled as a sickly old man and often Levy would help him along with a powerful arm.

The group stopped short at a compartment hatch marked by a large black-and-white sign, *"Fhot vas-pr'ish' Cha-yit-sa,"* No Admittance. Two naval infantrymen braced and saluted Belous. He nodded silently with a crusty expression, signed a clipboard, then checked his watch and wrote down the time next to his signature.

One thickly built guard pulled down a large locking mechanism, and the steel compartment door swung out.

They entered through the hatch into a brightly lit hangar, a cavernous steel chamber that reminded Jake of the blimp hangar at North Island that housed the ghostly remains of the Soviet Golf Class submarine.

Niven edged up to the shorter Belous and scrutinized him. "How alone are we, Captain?"

"Quite, Niven. Welcome to Operation Flashlamp," he announced darkly, waving an arm around the hangar bay.

"It looks like Frankenstein's laboratory."

Belous looked puzzled. "I don't know what that means, but in fact, this hangar bay is the devil's furnace." He pointed down toward the deck. "Beneath our feet is a steel chamber that was installed during a standard refit last spring. It took me three months to find out its function. They removed the midships magazines to put it in. That's where they explode the small nuclear devices to give this weapon its needed energy push. That energy from the device is then channeled up here to power the beam generators."

"I don't want to talk now, Captain. Please understand. I'm not here for a physics lesson."

Niven then made certain the hatch was closed. "Let's go, dammit!" He could feel his hands trembling. "I want to be out of here in ten minutes." He examined Lathrick's face and shook his head. "David, you're doing just fine. Just show Levy what you want cut out of this damn machinery and he'll do the rest."

"I'll patrol the machinery area, Jake. You take the hatch area, here. You can keep an eye on Belous," Sorrell offered.

"This is incredible," Lathrick whispered. "My God, they're advanced! After I take the ring switch, I must take pictures of this compartment. This is the most astounding thing I've ever seen!"

Niven wheeled and searched the cavernous steel chamber. He gauged the overhead ceiling at sixty-five feet.

"All right, move out!" Niven snapped. "Levy, you shove off now! Sorrell, take off!" He was talking in a whisper. He eyed Sorrell. "Circulate, Brahma. You know what to do."

Simultaneously the parkas came unzipped and the machine pistols, with their thick silencers, glistened in the bright lights of the hangar bay.

"Flick off your safety and chamber a round," Niven reminded them, as the boarding party hustled off into the jungle of equipment. Unconsciously, his gun finger lightly stroked the trigger of the Skorpion, waiting.

There was an eerie silence in the chamber and Niven, once out of his line of vision, followed Levy's progress from the voice echoes bouncing back, from deep within the bowels of the weapon.

"Hurry it up, people," Niven called out in a hushed tone as he glanced sideways at Viktor Belous.

"Your Russian has just a hint of a Polish accent, Niven," Belous said as his strong eyes bored into him.

"Not now, Captain," Niven said sharply. "That was your show up there, down here it's mine. Later, on the sub, if we have the chance, we can talk." He turned his back and stared into the weapon.

Carefully, Niven surveyed the chamber as he waited. Miles of fist-sized, rubber-coated power cables littered the deck spaces, amidst the maze of curved stainless steel piping and banks of meters set up every twenty feet. Niven found what he thought was the betatron accelerator, massive by conventional standards. It must have weighed seven thousand pounds. A series of generators, squatting on firing tables looked large enough to handle hydroelectric power from Hoover Dam. Lathrick had called them Pavlovski Explosive Generators and it was their job to give the bursts of beam energy the first real push toward the speed of light.

Niven looked past a plumber's nightmare of chrome piping, steel bottles, and translucent control panels, to the beam gun's massive computers. Just beyond lay a compound surrounded by chain-link fence. Partially hidden from view, Niven reasoned that their jeweled prize, the multi-channeled ring switch, lay somewhere in that maze of hardware and copper coils.

The ring switch metered out the enormous amounts of energy and then rammed it into the barrel of the gun that ran the length of the entire hangar deck. One section of the barrel had been removed for servicing, and he noticed a series of chrome tubes rising out of the bottom of the barrel. They had to be the drift tubes that guided the energy as it raced down the barrel toward the firing nozzle at the speed of light. The barrel carried the girth of a section of the Alaska pipeline. It wasn't hard imagining its beam of destructive energy hitting a target as far away as the moon.

He strained his neck to see around the equipment into the area where Lathrick and Levy were hopefully cutting out their prize. "Get the damn switch," he called out again softly. "No ring switch, no beam weapon," he mumbled to himself. Niven checked his watch. His boarding party had been in the gun room for ten minutes. The schedule was falling apart.

A noise forced Niven's head to the right. His hands squeezed the wire stock of the machine pistol as he aimed the barrel of the automatic weapon at the sound.

Suddenly, Belous broke the heavy silence. "You have judged me a traitor of my homeland, haven't you, Niven?"

"What? Oh, Jesus, not now, Captain. Please!" Niven, stretched to the breaking point, nervously scanned the chamber.

"Hurry it up!" Niven yelled out impulsively. He mashed his jaw and turned to Belous. "I'm sorry, Captain."

"I'm certain your people will get the device." He smiled reassuringly at Niven. He wanted to talk. To boost his own sagging spirit and sense of right and wrong, but Niven wanted no part of it.

Compulsively, he checked his watch. Only a minute had passed since the last check. Damn! What was taking so long?

"Have you been to Colombe d'Or, in the south of France?" Belous asked. "It's near a little village called St.-Paul-de-Vence. Anna used to love it, when we were on holiday from London—"

"Not now, dammit!" Niven wanted to crush his throat for talking. He wanted out. He wanted the ring switch, his money, and Ellie. A goddamn life! He was entitled. He'd earned it! He peered back into the maze of machinery. They were almost out of time!

"It will be over soon," Belous offered.

"You're wrong, Captain Belous!" the harsh voice shouted in Russian. "It's all over now!"

35

Niven dropped flat on his belly, the machine pistol trained toward the alien sound. For a split second he stared and then his body slumped involuntarily.

In an instant the shadow was on him, kicking the Skorpion out of his hands with a blinding force.

"Surprise, Jacob! Time to pay your dues, asshole."

"Sorrell? What—" Jake sucked in a breath, off balance and uncertain.

"No joke, old friend. It's finished." Sorrell stood over Jake Niven, holding a silenced pistol leveled at the top of his head.

"Chrissakes, Sorrell!"

"Ny name isn't Sorrell."

Slowly Jake pulled himself to his knees, testing his comprehension, but the shock was blocking his mind.

Jake swallowed. "What—"

"My name is Misha Lykov." He hesitated and stared at Jake. "You killed my father. You remember, Jake. It was a cold day last spring, in the Gulf of Finland, when you blew my father away. General Vasili Lykov."

Jake pulled himself to his feet, shaking it off. It just wasn't happening. "We're out of time, Brahma. Get

Lathrick and Levy and that damned switch! We're on our way. Burkhart's waiting!"

"The fantasy is over, Niven. Look at the damn pistol, you bastard. The special manufacturing logo from Tula Arsenal. My father's name engraved on the slide stop. Your special silencer." He shook his head. "My name is Misha Lykov, Colonel in the Glavnoye Razvedyvatelnoye Upravleniye."

"The GRU?"

"That's right. The Soviet General Staff, just like my father. Your ghosts have come to life. Look at the pistol. Your darkest nightmare has come to life and you'll never see home again."

It was Jake's Tokarev that had turned up missing. He shook his head, still not wanting to believe it.

"I've waited a long time for this moment."

Jake stood silently and desperately searched Brahma Sorrell's face. But there wasn't a sign of Sorrell anywhere in the hard edges of his eyes. Sorrell had metamorphosed into another being. The fierce eyes grew hostile. The face took on a flat, hollow look. The voice grew unfamiliar. Sorrell had shed the last layer of dead, molting skin.

"It's very simple, Jacob. Very simple. Six months after you and my father set up a working apparatus and then the shop in Rome, I was activated to infiltrate your leak-proof Task Force 157. My father was a suspicious man. You don't spend your childhood working under the likes of Yan Berzin and Laurenti Beria at the Cheka Registry, and then, of course, early adulthood with Richard Sorge in Japan, without learning just how vicious political and military life is in the Soviet Union. I was his ultimate, incorruptible life insurance.

"By the time I was fifteen and had given up on Phys-Mat School, my father enrolled me at the GRU's Sanprobal Military Academy in the Crimea. By the time I was twenty, I was leading an elite unit of Spetsnaz troops, assassinating Warsaw Pact opponents in Poland and Hungary. On one occasion, we attended a Warsaw Pact sports competition in the town of Szeged, Hungary, disguised as a Soviet Army wrestling team. We won the competition and murdered three local officials before leaving. A year later my father sent me to the United States to join the Navy, waiting as the ultimate mole for an assignment. Creating a background and a personal life as a Navy chief was easy. Your security checks are shit.''

A shrill squeaking broke the eerie quiet.

''What the hell was that?'' Lykov looked quickly at Captain Belous. The rapid squeaking started, then stopped again.

''Captain, what is it?'' Lykov's voice had grown cruel. ''It's your ship. It *was* your ship.''

''I don't know.'' Belous shook his head, resigned to the inevitable triumph of Soviet State Security. He had seen it all his life.

''No matter, Captain.'' Lykov glanced over his shoulder, but the surrounding area was still empty of Levy and Lathrick.

Niven swallowed and began to recover his equilibrium.

''Your father knew about HAWKSCREECH?''

''Every step of the way.'' Misha Lykov waved the Tokarev in Jake's face. ''My father had been aware for a very long time of Chebrikov and the KGB's drive to have him liquidated, or at the least removed from the scene. When HAWKSCREECH fell into his lap, it was a perfect opportunity to regain the ultimate leverage with the Politburo. The Da Vinci was a cheap price to pay.''

Lykov stepped back and steadied the Tokarev at Niven's head.

''Before you killed my father, we had planned to

take you, this bastard Belous, and your technical expert back to Moscow for a public trial. It was all planned to be a perfect coup to neutralize Chebrikov, save my father's retirement, and pave the way for my return home. Now, you and this fucker, hiding behind your skirts, will save me from Chebrikov and his goons. It's all that I have left; my ticket home."

Vaguely, the pieces began to fit, despite the fact that Niven's mind was still reeling. The holes in Sorrell's life. Everyone, especially in their business, had gaps and holes. Damn! Then it all had begun to focus with sickening clarity. Every American operative he knew spoke Russian with a Polish accent, but Sorrell spoke it without any accent at all.

"What about *Skate?*" Niven asked numbly.

"A sticky question. To take or sink *Skate* might push the United States over the edge. Besides, after knowing Burkhart, he'd probably ram *Minsk* and raise all kinds of hell before pulling the plug. No, Jake, my plan is to let *Skate* escape." Lykov looked at his watch and smiled again. "I've got what I want. Just a little longer, Jacob."

"That's why you screamed your head off about Levy making the trip across to *Minsk*. It was all so clean until I screwed up by involving an Israeli."

"Ah, that quick mind of yours. But I'm a realist who learned to salvage opportunities. Levy can only add to the overall impact this overt act of war will make on the world court of opinion, to say nothing of the impact this will make on the Kremlin." Lykvo smiled. "I've brought a great deal of useful baggage to this ship. From the time I was old enough to walk, my father taught me to be flexible. He'd say, 'In the field use only what you have. Make every adversity work for you, and above all, be patient and wait for your moment.' "

"And this is your moment," Niven sneered as he

stared at the silenced barrel of the automatic. "I assume that talking in your sleep had some—"

"Yes," Lykov interrupted. "Columns refers to the Hall of Columns in Moscow, where your trial will take place. Francis Gary Powers was tried there in 1960."

"And Vladimir?" Jake raised an eyebrow. It was all falling into place. He'd been the village idiot! Christ! How hard he had worked Vasili Lykov to make the trade for the Da Vinci. He had sacrificed Koslov for no reason.

"Vladimir is going to be your home for a very long time. It's Vladimir thirty-one, a very special prison one hundred fifty miles east of Moscow. The watery soup with floating fish eyes. The usual comforts of home. Just close enough for me to visit. What's the matter, Jake? You'll like the *gulags.*"

"You nailed Crabby, didn't you?"

"Yes. The old Englishman fucked up. I wanted him to kill Crabb before your eyes. A nice mark of revenge. Turn the screws, as it were. I killed him on my vacation. The poor bastard never saw it coming. I liked him. It was quick and humane. You look ill."

Jake nodded. "Yes, I'm ill," he said.

That was it! he screamed at himself. He can't stop talking about himself. Lykov was compelled to bare his soul. These secrets had been pent up for so long. A need to explain himself. A weakness! Otherwise those armed Navy infantry would have been called in long ago.

"I know what you're thinking!" Lykov barely turned his eyes and scanned the area where Lathrick and Levy would emerge from when they had finished removing the ring switch. Lykov could finish them long before Levy could get off a burst of fire.

Slowly and carefully, Lykov backed over to the steel compartment door, careful to keep the Tokarev aimed at Niven and Belous.

"Don't think I won't like to use this on you, old friend. I would enjoy killing you with the gun my father had presented to you as a gift. A red hole right above the bridge of your fucked-up nose, or maybe in the spine, to cripple you."

Lykov was still talking, vomiting up all those years of keeping the lie. Involuntarily releasing himself from the burden.

"Your father was a sick old bastard, Misha." Jake laughed. "I did the ass fucker a real favor. At least it was quick."

Lykov winced, as if Niven had snapped a fist into his solar plexus. "My father had more grudging respect for you than any other man, except Joseph Stalin."

"Great company," he quipped. "Yosif Dzhugashuili Stalin, that little murdering Georgian pimp, with a pocked face and deformed left arm. There's two million good Russians still sitting in the labor camps he set up."

Niven rocked his head. "Yeah, I can see Vasili and Stalin clinking glasses of their favorite red Georgian wine, Kinzmarauli, after the Great Patriotic War, discussing the monthly body counts of political prisoners. Christ, Stalin and your father turned the bitch motherland into a bloody Gestapo torture chamber. How many purges, Misha? How many millions of innocent people died at the hands of your father and his mentor, Stalin?"

Niven spit on the studded steel desk. *"Pah'ra zho'lty mesneek!"*

"Yellow bastards, were they? Smart talk, *boychik*, won't help your ass one damn bit! You told me the day you killed my father, he was too old and too tired, and you slipped into that gap and took him. You arrogant prick! You let me slip right past you!" He laughed, waving the automatic.

"You mean you slipped behind my back and buried the knife, covered with pig shit. A real chocolate-covered snake."

"I'll throw some of that pig shit on you when I bury your dead ass in Novodevichy Cemetery, right next to Khrushchev."

Niven took a fluid half-step to his left, slowly crouching his body. Captain Belous jumped out of the way, momentarily distracting Lykov's eyes.

Reacting as quickly as he thought, he whipped out the Kruithoorn knife, the short squat blade gleaming in the bright illumination of the hangar bay deck.

Lykov wheeled the Tokarev around. "Freeze! I don't want to kill you. Not yet!"

Keep him talking, Jake thought. Start circling. Measure him. "You can't kill me." He snapped his fingers. "Puff! No Jake Niven, no circus. I'm the star."

Suddenly, Lykov stood straight up and leveled the automatic. "Nice try, Ashbal. I'll buy your first wheelchair. Too bad you'll never see your daughter again. Watch her grow into womanhood." He squinted his ugly face at Niven.

"Too bad you'll never see your unborn child." Lykov smiled.

"What?"

"But I'll never see my father again. A fair exchange, don't you think, Jacob?"

Niven shivered. "Unborn child?"

"I read the letter Ellie sent along with you. Very interesting. She's been pregnant for the past three and a half months, you stupid shit." Lykov smiled again. "And she's going to have it." Lykov looked to his left to mark the progress of Lathrick and Levy.

"You're never going to see your love child or the letter. It was actually quite touching. The modern American woman, building a career and having a child

273

with the man she loves. You should have married her and made an honest woman out of her.'' He laughed from his throat.

Niven shivered as another wave of shock and regret swept over him. Their child! Ellie carrying their child and the emotional burden alone! Ellie wanting a future.

Niven's pulse hammered at his temples. He knew the man was close to squeezing the trigger and he knew that Lykov would go for a crippling shot. They had been as close as brothers and he knew. He watched helplessly as Misha Lykov widened his eyes in that special way and anger clung to Niven as a heavy mask as he waited for the pain to tear into his knees and spine, severing and killing those millions of precious nerve endings.

Jake looked into Lykov's pink, ugly face and saw the laughing eyes. Lykov was playing with him and suddenly Jake felt an anger surge through his body. But he knew that Lykov was the best shot he'd ever seen.

''Come on, poet, say something appropriate while I shoot you into a cripple. The kneecaps, then the spine. You've had your last woman and your last hot crotch. You'll know what it feels like to live the rest of your life with a numb, empty sack. That's the Lykov legacy to you,'' Misha Lykov taunted.

Niven felt his blood rush to his head.

''Your friend Levy and his weak little charge, Lathrick, should be coming my way soon.'' Lykov stopped laughing and nodded with the gun. ''I'll take the Israeli first. I can't take a chance with him. He's too damn dangerous. Then I'll play with Lathrick's fear.'' Sorrell shook his head. ''I don't even feel sorry for you, Jake. You've just run out of time.'' He raised the pistol with both hands and took aim.

36

Jake feinted to his right and dove left at Misha Lykov, holding the knife in a locked fist, but the head fake wasn't nearly enough to trick the burly but quick Lykov. Jake flew by Lykov, but at the last possible second hooked his free hand around Lykov, pulling him off balance. Lykov tumbled backward, hitting the steel deck in front of Jake's feet. The force of his body hitting the deck jerked the Tokarev from his hand.

Swiftly, Jake regained his feet and sprang headfirst landing on top of the stunned Lykov, smashing an elbow up into the bottom of Lykov's jaw.

Groggy but still strong as a bull, Lykov grabbed Niven's throat and pushed up, to back the smaller man away. At just the right moment, Jake countered the stronger force and whipped around his knife, thrusting for Lykov's throat. Lykov saw the glint of the blade and bucked his body. He quickly followed with a short, chopping left to Jake's jaw, knocking him backward. The knife tumbled harmlessly out of his grasp.

Quickly regaining his balance, Niven bounced back on Lykov's body, this time reaching for his thick beard. He came up with two solid handfuls, slamming Lykov's flushed red face into the deck with a sickening thud. But Lykov pushed back, his neck muscles as strong as Jake's entire upper torso. Again, Niven smashed his head into the deck plates, but this time Lykov, reacting with only a groan, rolled right, forcing him over.

Before Jake could stop him, Lykov had muscled their bodies over to the Tokarev. With his free hand, he tried to stop Lykov from reaching for the automatic, but just couldn't bring enough strength to bear.

Suddenly the automatic was back in Lykov's massive hand.

From somewhere, Niven mustered up enough strength to hold off the gun with one hand and jam Lykov's head back against the deck with a cracking thud. Lykov's eyes rolled up into his head. Their hands and forearms, locked in an Indian grip, slammed to the deck, discharging a round of the Tokarev with a whining thump. To be certain, Niven pounded Lykov's massive head twice more into the deck, dimly aware of a sharp, moaning sound.

Jake rolled off Lykov's body, exhausted and gasping for breath. Slowly he turned his head and saw Akivor Levy tending to David Lathrick, thrashing about in pain.

"The shot hit your scientist," Belous called out dully over his shoulder.

Niven, pained and bruised, pulled himself to his feet and staggered toward his boarding party. "Did you get the gadget? The ring switch?"

Levy picked up his head and pointed silently to the bulging canvas bag. "It was damn difficult to cut free." He tried to smile.

Jake leaned down over Lathrick. "How bad is it?"

"What the hell happened with Sorrell?" Levy ignored Niven's question, intent on his own agenda.

"Sorrell is a Soviet operative. Has been all along,"

Jake groaned, still fighting for breath. "This was supposed to be the great trap. I was headed for a public trial and you were going to be fed to the fish. Now let's get the hell off this damn ship!"

"Bastard." Levy flared his hands. His face mirrored Niven's shock.

"How bad is Lathrick?" Jake asked again.

"The poor bastard. Not much blood, but he took a heavy slug in his side with plenty of push behind it. He's probably all torn up inside. If we hurry, I think we can get him out of here."

With a great effort, Niven quickly retrieved his Tokarev, and watched as Akivor Levy bent over Misha Lykov's neck, feeling for a pulse. "Bastard's still alive. Not by much, but still alive. Finish him off, Jake!"

Niven looked down and studied the massive head of Misha Lykov as it lay in a bright red pool of blood.

"Kill the bastard, Jake!"

"No. He's dead already. Let him slip away on his own. There's no security here, and by the time they find him tonight or tomorrow morning, we'll be almost home." The thought of killing Sorrell, no, he meant Misha Lykov, forced Jake to shiver. His anger was gone. He was only filled with betrayal. He couldn't kill another Lykov.

"Niven, come here!" Belous demanded, but Jake was watching the compartment door, wondering if the Cossacks outside the hangar bay had heard the silenced gunfire.

Another sharp squeak echoed through the hangar, this time followed by a scampering sound of feet.

Niven crouched and leveled his automatic at the approaching sound. "I'll take the sound, just get Lathrick on his feet. We have to get out of here!" he whispered to Levy.

"The doctor is still conscious, but very weak," Belous called out softly.

"How damned often is this hangar bay patroled by your security people?" Niven demanded, with panic rising in his voice.

"Not at all. A hijacking at sea wasn't expected." Belous checked his watch. "We have until late today when the technicians turn everything back on."

"Like hell we do!" Jake whispered, still watching the direction of the sound. "We've got less than seven minutes before Burkhart steams out of this bay!"

The squeaking grew louder and then a shaggy brown ship rat, the size of a large cat, waddled out of the shadows of a large generator and casually climbed atop the unconscious Misha Lykov, exploring with his long gray whiskers.

"Jesus!" Jake recoiled numbly, as the rat, with his long, wet tongue, darting, intelligent black opal eyes, searched Lykov's belly, dragging the pink tail on the deck. The rat reached Misha Lykov's bearded face and defiantly showed his sharp, moist, hooked teeth.

"Let's move Sorrell, or whoever the hell he was, behind those generators," Belous commanded. There wasn't the slightest hint of panic in his voice. "It will give us time—"

"I thought there wasn't any security here in the chamber?" Niven stiffened.

"There isn't, but what if a technician stumbles in and finds him? A number of people are cleared for the chamber."

Niven moved as quickly as he could, first kicking the large hissing rat off Lykov's body. "Sorry, pal, we're just putting your dinner in a dark, cozy place. *Bon appétit,*" he said, pulling Misha Lykov into the shadow of a massive generator.

"Speed, dammit!" Niven hissed at Belous. "We

have to hurry!" He thought of Sorrell and fought down the shock. Instinctively, he began pushing Belous towards Lathrick's side. "Hurry, dammit!"

Niven bent over Lathrick and felt his skin. It was cold and clammy. Lathrick was going into shock, but he was still conscious, if just barely. Gently, they lifted him to his feet.

"We're taking you home now, David." Niven looked into his glazed, dull eyes and knew Lathrick was beyond hearing. "I'll take the ring switch, you two grab Lathrick," he commanded hoarsely, pushing them toward the compartment doors. Niven took a deep breath, trying his best to fight the panic eating at the insides of his throat.

Belous swung open the large compartment door. "Hurry! There's been a terrible accident! We need your help. These Party members are visiting from that submarine. This man took a bad fall. We have to help them to their launch. They have their own medical team in the sub."

The Cossack guards nodded stiffly, then tentatively stepped into the compartment. "Move it!" Belous screamed as the guards took Lathrick from Akivor Levy.

"Follow me," Belous sternly ordered the guards, who dared not question their commander. "We must hurry!" he urged as they stepped into the narrow corridor.

"Captain, sir?" one guard called to Belous.

"What is it?"

"I cannot leave this security area unguarded."

Niven turned his body and put his finger on the trigger of the Tokarev in his parka.

"Of course," Belous said quickly. "You remain at your post and once we get this man aboard his ship, I'll send back your mate."

"Very well, sir." The guard saluted as they started down the empty corridor toward the midships landing platform.

Niven couldn't swallow. He forced himself to look at the Russian pocket watch. It confirmed what his guts were telling him. They were out of time! It was impossible. It was over! Right that very moment, Burkhart would be putting propeller wash across his rudder and turning *Skate*'s bow toward the open sea, to take his chances. Somewhere in the back of his mind he heard Belous exhorting him on, pushing them all. What was the point? HAWKSCREECH was dead. Jake Niven had lost.

37

Burkhart jammed the cheap rum-soaked crook cigar back into the corner of his mouth and continued to pace the periscope stand. Abruptly, he stopped and leaned against the railing next to the attack scope. After a long moment of grinding the delicate juices from the wet end of the lighted cigar, he glared down at Irish Brennen and Chief of the Boat Russotto.

"Tell me, again, goddammit!" Burkhart tried to keep his voice down, but the temper was evident. Niven had dissolved into thin air and now *Skate* was acting up.

"It looks damn bad, sir. We found large cracks in number three boiler tube, inside the primary loop of the reactor. The steam is radioactive, so we can't get in there to be certain what other damage there might be. That's yard work. No radiation leakage yet, but I'm damn certain that sooner or later—"

"Damn!"

"There's more, Skipper."

Burkhart curled his lips and shot out a cloud of brown smoke. "Well?"

Brennen swallowed. "It's in the clean steam system."

"Go on," Burkhart snarled. The pressure had affected them all. They had never seen Burkhart that angry.

"Ah, we found a very serious crack in another silver-brazed joint, leading to the port side circulating pump. It looks like someone got careless at some point in the past and exceeded all the heat-up curves in the primary loop." Brennen looked up into Burkhart's tired blue eyes.

"Jesus H. Christ!" Burkhart snapped. "What the hell's the matter with you, Russotto?" He slammed a hard fist into an open hand and looked past Brennen to Russotto. "Whatever happened to defense in depth on this boat?"

"Sir?"

"Don't give me that sir shit, Russotto. I've known you too long for that crap!" Burkhart leaned his red face forward until he was very close to Russotto's face. "I depend on you, goddammit! I set that propulsion search detail right after we left San Diego, and you come to me now!" Burkhart widened his eyes and both men could see the little hairs bristling on the back of Burkhart's neck.

"Look, sir," Russotto straightened his back, "there ain't no defense in depth left in this old boat. *Skate's* too damned old for backup systems." He threw up a hand in frustration. "It's like trying to keep the Golden Gate Bridge painted. A patch here. A patch there. Just can't be done, the way the book says. For God's sakes, sir, *Skate's* older than most of these kids serving as her crew. We're doin' the best we can."

Russotto and Brennen lowered their eyes.

"Why'd you wait until now, smack in the middle of the Dog Bowl and the Soviet Navy, to tell me?" Burkhart poked a thumb into his own chest. "I'm the bus driver here, goddammit!"

282

"We just found the cracks, sir," Russotto offered weakly. "In *Skate*'s condition, she ain't even worth refitting."

"You sure took your sweet time. It's like that damn cannibalized Mark 37 bouncing around in torpedo reload. It took a week to find and secure it properly when it could have been done in two hours." Burkhart blew out another cloud of cheap cigar smoke." He was finally beginning to calm down.

"I know, sir. But, Jesus, I've had the boys working overtime on this. There's a lot of miles of plumbing, piping, and joints to inspect and—"

"Look, Skipper, Russotto and I have had our differences, but not on this. Brennen set his chin. "Christ, in our propulsion system alone, there are over three thousand silver-brazed joints."

Burkhart held up a hand. He couldn't help but smile. These were his people and his boat and they all cared beyond reason. "I'm sorry, gentlemen. We all care and I know you've both done one hella'va job and I appreciate—"

"Sir?" interrupted a message runner stationed in the Radio Room.

"What?"

"That Soviet repair shop, *Dniestr*, is hailing us on the RT. That's all the Russian we can make out."

"Damn!" Burkhart rubbed his chin. "The radio telephone now—the boarding party is twenty minutes overdue and my boat's falling apart."

"We've been in worse straits before, Skipper."

Burkhart raised an eyebrow, then smiled darkly. "I wanted a battle star. Well, no one lives forever—"

Quickly he ran through the options. He was out of time, according to Niven's own instructions. He'd have to communicate with that Russian repair ship as quickly as possible, if *Skate* had any chance at all, running back through the Soviet screen. Jake and the boarding party had been swallowed up inside that Russian sewer. How much longer would it be before a move would be made against *Skate?*

Maybe *Minsk's* officers were checking with Fleet Operations or the Admiralty, to see what to do with *Skate.* Burkhart rolled the cigar in his mouth. For a moment his mind flashed back to his friend, Lloyd Bucher, captain of the ill-fated *Pueblo* spy ship. Bucher and *Pueblo* had been at the wrong place at the wrong time without weapons to defend themselves in North Korean waters.

Burkhart searched the faces of his men. He'd have no choice, if HAWKSCREECH was down the toilet. He couldn't fight it out and capture was out of the question. There would be no choice but to fulfill his promise to Admiral Langor. He'd pull the plug and take *Skate* to her death. Again he looked across the crowded control room. The young faces of his crew were locked on him.

"Maybe it's time to get the hell out, Skipper," Brennen said quietly. "It's as if *Minsk* just swallowed them up. We can make it."

"What shall I do, sir?" the runner from Radio asked again.

Burkhart rubbed his thick neck. "I'll be damned if I'm going to quit now. We've come too far to pack it in," he said as he reached for his parka on the periscope railing.

"Any other problems with the boat that I should know about, Chief?"

"A sticky reducer valve in Main Ballast Tank Six has been repaired."

Burkhart turned to the runner and smiled tautly. "Tell Radio to jam that signal, destroy the radio telephone, whatever hell it takes!" He held a thumbs-up sign to his crew as he stepped off the stand. "Irish, get that Russian seaman we picked up, topside with a blinker light tube and a .45 automatic, on the double.

Spike Mead squinted and smiled, but he looked like a freak, with his eye and cheek colored a dirty yellow and purple.

"You a gambler, Spike?"

"I've done my share, Captain. Why, sir?"

"Watch this." Burkhart lighted a fresh cigar. "They say that five-card draw is the purest form of poker and—"

Brennen popped his head through the hatch with light tube and pistol. The Russian seaman Petr Deriabin followed closely behind. He took one look at *Minsk* and his eyes filled with shock. He turned to the sound of a foghorn from one of the repair ships off in the distance.

"We need your help, Petr." Burkhart smiled and put his arm around Deriabin's shoulder. "We need you to signal that repair ship over there." He pointed to *Dniestr*. "I know you know Soviet naval light procedures." He made certain Deriabin saw the shape of his eyes. "I speak and can signal in Russian, but not as quickly as you can." He saw Mead's mouth drop.

The Russian swallowed. "Can do for you," he nodded, but his voice was flat. He was confused, but it wouldn't last. "Have signaled when in Soviet Navy." He blinked and his eyes took in Burkhart and Mead's uniforms. "What is the reason you—"

Burkhart stuck the .45 automatic in Deriabin's ribs. "If you want to live and get back home, do what I say! You understand?"

"Yes, Deriabin understands."

"I can signal in Russian and I understand the lan-

285

guage. If you don't say exactly what I tell you, or decide to add something extra, I'll blow a six-inch hole in your side. Do exactly what I say and you'll live," he repeated. "For emphasis, he painfully twisted the gun into the Russian seaman's ribs.

"I do what you want. Proper call, identify, break sign, ah, message and ending. Okay, sir?" Deriabin's voice was no longer flat. It was high and frightened. "No other things."

"I have nothing to lose." Burkhart brought his face very close to the Russian. "If you fuck up, we all die, you included."

"I understand what necessary." Deriabin's lips trembled.

Burkhart scribbled the message on a blank tablet. He watched the fog bank rolling toward them and hurried. "After you send, I'll give you the tablet and you can write down the response. You understand?" Once again he shoved the gun into Deriabin's belly.

"Yes! Yes!"

Burkhart handed him the battery-powered black metal tubular blinker light.

"You hold for me, Captain, the message book and I use the signal lamp." His hands moved with a tremor as he slowly began to translate from English into Russian and then into the proper sequence of dots and dashes.

U-N-A-B-L-E T-O E-F-F-E-C-T-I-V-E-L-Y
R-E-C-E-I-V-E T-R-A-N-S-M-I-S-S-I-O-N D-U-E
T-O E-L-E-C-T-R-I-C-A-L P-R-O-B-L-E-M-S
W-H-A-T Y-O-U-R M-E-S-S-A-G-E G-O
A-H-E-A-D

A-R A-R

"What else, Captain, you want me to send?"
"Send it until they respond. It's damned difficult to

signal at sea. Tougher still in this garbage weather."
Burkhart looked down at the gun in his hands and then
into the Russian's face.

Deriabin began signaling again as Mead raised his
glasses and scanned the *Dniestr*'s squat smokestack and
then the tower-like bridge structure of the repair ship.
After a short search he found the tiny signal lamp
structure on the wing of the bridge. He spotted two
men moving about the wing, but the signal lamp was
still dark.

"Nothing, Captain."

"Keep sending, Petr!" Burkhart commanded.
"Come on, dammit!"

Mead looked into Burkhart's worried face and then
raised his glasses to search again. After a long silence
and an intensifying wind that rolled *Skate* on her beam,
Dniestr's signal light came alive across the water.

"There she goes!" Mead called out.

The Russian picked up the pad. He had to squint to
make out the signal as Burkhart tightened his grip on
the automatic. He glanced over at *Minsk* and prayed
that Niven was still alive.

R-E-Q-U-E-S-T B-O-A-R-D-I-N-G
P-E-R-M-I-S-S-I-O-N
S-U-R-V-E-Y D-A-M-A-G-E T-O
E-X-P-E-D-I-T-E R-E-P-A-I-R-S
G-O A-H-E-A-D

A-R A-R

Burkhart read the message. "Tell them to wait.
Damn!"

Petr Deriabin held up the lamp, and aimed it at
Dniestr's signal bridge, and flashed out the message.

Burkhart rubbed his stubbed chin with a cold hand.
For a moment he surveyed the view from the cockpit.

The weather was definitely closing, the wind had increased to twenty knots, and the swell was growing. Was he waiting for a dead man?

"If the boarding party ran into trouble on *Minsk,* at least the word hasn't been sent out to *Dniestr* yet."

"We don't know that, Mead." He thought about it. "Maybe yes, maybe no. Prien's luck, dammit! It's all we have left." He raised his glasses to *Minsk,* looking for any sign of his people.

"Come on, Jake boy, don't let me down."

Mead stared at Burkhart, chewing on a slimy stub of a dead cigar, and fully understood the weight of his dilemma. "Mr. Niven seems like a very resourceful type, Captain. We've sure come a long way to leave empty-handed. Wait him out, Captain," he said softly.

Slowly Burkhart grunted and looked over toward *Minsk,* looming ghostlike and evil out of the closing fog, which only added to his resolve. Quickly he scribbled another message on the pad and held it up for Petr Deriabin.

C-A-P-T-A-I-N M-I-N-S-K E-N-R-O-U-T-E T-O
I-N-S-P-E-C-T O-U-R D-A-M-A-G-E A-N-D
C-O-N-F-E-R W-I-T-H C-O-M-M-A-N-D-I-N-G
O-F-F-I-C-E-R C-A-N-N-O-T A-L-L-O-W
Y-O-U T-O B-O-A-R-D A-T T-H-I-S T-I-M-E
G-O A-H-E-A-D

A-R A-R

Burkhart and Mead watched each other breathe in short, nervous spurts of steam, marooned in the present, as they awaited *Dniestr*'s reply. It came quickly.

* * *

U-N-D-E-R-S-T-A-N-D Y-O-U-R
S-I-T-U-A-T-I-O-N A-N-D P-O-S-I-T-I-O-N
P-L-E-A-S-E A-D-V-I-S-E W-H-E-N
B-O-A-R-D-I-N-G P-O-S-S-I-B-L-E G-O-O-D
L-U-C-K E-N-D T-R-A-N-S-M-I-S-S-I-O-N

Burkhart read the message to Mead and tossed the soggy cigar butt over the side. He lifted his glasses and studied *Minsk*. She was still brooding and quiet. Through the mist, Burkhart could barely make out the barge at the bottom of the accommodations ladder. There wasn't a sign of life.

"Are basketball players God-fearing, Mead?"

"What?"

"Pray for a higher luck, Spike. I don't want any atheists on my boat right now." Burkhart pulled another cigar from his parka and ran it under his nose.

Skate suddenly rolled and they hung on for their lives.

"Sir, she's moving! Dragging her anchor in the swell."

Mead, set a sea anchor detail, on the double! That will slow us down, hopefully long enough to take Niven's party aboard." Burkhart tried to sound hopeful.

"On the double, sir." Mead quickly disappeared through the hatch, knowing that Burkhart was on the verge of giving up Niven for dead and pulling out of Lisinskaya Bay. He shivered at the prospect. They all knew Burkhart and what that meant. If he couldn't slip through the screen of Soviet warships, Burkhart would take *Skate* down with all hands aboard.

A powerful force seized the Colt .45 in Burkhart's hand. "I go home now! I go home to Soviet Fleet!" Petr Deriabin forced the gun all the way over until the barrel was pointing at Burkhart's eye. "Not great distance. I go home," he grunted as his powerful hands working as one peeled Burkhart's fingers from the trigger of the Colt.

"Get your hands off, you bastard," Burkhart groaned, but the youthful Russian had the leverage and the stamina.

"I kill you to go home!" Deriabin lunged forward and Burkhart fell back against the Sail bulwarks. Burkhart stared into the Russian's eyes as he felt the gun helplessly slipping out of his grip.

"No, you bastard!" Burkhart lowered his body into a crouch, dragging the Russian down with him. He still had the weight and used it. Deriabin lost his balance and the Colt slipped out of his hands. Burkhart whipped the automatic around and fired at point blank range into Petr Deriabin's stomach. The force of the explosion pushed Burkhart back into the back of the cockpit. He looked down at the Russian, with a large ugly red tear in his parka. It must have measured five inches across.

"Go home. Go home!" A large mouthful of blood vomited from his mouth and he fell to the cold steel deck with his dead eyes staring up into Burkhart's face.

38

"Hurry, for God's sake!" Belous urged them sharply. Inside he may have been panicked, but his face and voice didn't show it.

Jake pushed his eyes down the narrow corridor and surveyed the functional clutter of snaking steam pipes, sprinkler systems, and polished brass fire hose fittings, all secured to the overhead. Every twenty feet the clutter was interrupted by watertight doors. *Minsk* was solidly built. Nothing fancy or sophisticated, just a mammoth steel-plated hull, built to take considerable punishment.

Wire mesh damage control lockers lined every bulkhead, holding standard fire hoses, portable foam extinguishers for chemical fires, and hooded flame suits. Thick black rubber biological warfare suits also hung inside the lockers.

Belous moved faster now, rushing them down under the Beam Weapons hangar bay, deep into the ship's bowels beneath the waterline, along shaky steel mesh catwalks, and through what seemed an endless series of cold, damp corridors, hatches, collision doors, steep narrow stairwells. After a few minutes each corridor and companionway looked the same, and after another series of turns, Niven couldn't be certain which direction they were headed. At one point, when a corridor had been empty of sailors, he dropped back off the pace, and quietly laid his Skorpion machine pistol behind one of the fire hoses. It was too cumbersome and he preferred his automatic, keeping one hand on its butt in his jacket pocket and the other lugging the ring switch bag, carefully watching ahead.

David Lathrick had grown progressively weaker and at last an angry red smudge stained through the right side of his parka, below his ribs.

Niven continued to trail them as Lathrick leaned more of his weight from Levy to the Soviet infantryman, who was beginning to struggle. The guard's discomfort in Belous's presence was apparent, which blurred, or at least delayed, any immediate conclusions he might draw.

They turned into a short, dark companionway and then began climbing what would be up through three decks. They were all out of breath, and by watching Lathrick's sagging body, Niven knew he had lapsed into unconsciousness.

Suddenly, Levy stumbled, pulling the guard and Lathrick backward. Levy's incredible arm strength broke their fall as he reached out and grabbed the steel railing with his free hand.

"Hurry it up! Keep him on his feet!" Niven urged through clenched teeth. "We're not going to die down here, dammit!"

The boarding party heard them before they saw the Russian sailors. Suddenly they were engulfed. A traffic jam of grumbling Russian seamen crushed past them on a narrow stairwell. Levy shoved Lathrick's head straight up, to give the *Minsk* crewmen the room they needed to squeeze past. Poor damn Lathrick.

Niven shuddered inside, but he wasn't going to die—

at least not yet. How long had they been climbing out of *Minsk?* It seemed like hours. Maybe even days. He had never lived his life anywhere else, except entombed in *Minsk*'s damp gray steel maze.

He had to see his Ellie, his unborn child. His Danielle. He held those images in a small walnut-sized island of hope. One foot in front of the other. Keep climbing. At least you're going to die in the daylight. Not in this bastard tomb!

As Niven pushed himself and the boarding party in front of him, he just climbed and pushed his people to climb. He gripped the ring switch tighter. They'd have to pry his dead fingers from the bag with a screwdriver. Niven was using his fear—everything he had, to keep his sanity as he pushed them on. Suddenly, he shivered and his mind wandered to Brahma Sorrell. He shivered again, cursed himself, and felt alone without hope.

Jake shivered again. Still, a part of him wouldn't believe what had happened in the hangar bay, but his entire body ached from the encounter.

"We're almost up to the portside loading platform," Belous turned and called back.

"Jesus!" he muttered, checking his pocket watch. His heart plunged to the bottom of his feet. They had been aboard an hour and ten minutes! It was over. *Skate* was gone. He knew Charley Burkhart and he knew what he had ordered him to do. 'If I'm not back in forty-five minutes, I'm not coming back.' He checked the watch again. *Skate* had slipped away to meet her own fate and there wasn't even room in his mind for one last, comforting fantasy.

"There's light ahead," Belous called back.

Belous's glimmer of light didn't matter. He knew Burkhart's ultimate fear of capture. By now, *Skate* was moving out of the Dog Bowl. He had pushed HAWK-SCREECH beyond human limits and failed. All those

293

terrible emotions and fears that he thought had died since his River Days in Vietnam were on him again, as an aroused and hungry python, coiling and crushing his windpipe. A python named Misha Lykov, dropping down on him from the trees, striking him when he was most vulnerable and alone. He must have been blind.

What about Ellie—her soft warm smile, her secret, and the letter he would never see. He tried to smell her fragrance, but he had lost her scent somewhere in *Minsk*. The feel of her soft black hair, gone forever. She would never even know what happened to him. He thought of her agony and cursed himself. He might have escaped Vasili and Misha Lykov's well planned trap, but how far could they get now? Without *Skate*, where could they go?

Niven felt his hand tighten around the cold steel handle of his Tokarev, with the small Soviet star making an impression in his palm. Maybe he should give up the surface and head back down to the weapons bay, to demolish what he could of the beam weapon. His death had to have some worth!

Someone was talking in the back of his mind. They passed through a large hatch and Belous turned, babbling in Russian. Think in Russian, goddammit! There was more light, although it was very murky. Niven strained his eyes and saw the trail of blood that Lathrick was leaving behind.

"The elevator platform, Niven. We've made it," he heard Belous say.

Out of the corner of his eye Niven saw that young, alcoholic Officer of the Deck with a passion for gold watches. God, it had been just over an hour ago since that bastard confronted the boarding party. It seemed like a lifetime since Niven had seen those hungry Russian eyes.

Jake's feet moved quickly, as he overtook Akivor Levy and the exhausted Soviet guard, shouldering David Lathrick. Niven dared a fast look. Lathrick's head wobbled like a dead puppet. With his body, Jake was pushing them ahead by instinct. He refused to allow himself to think about *Skate*.

The light grew stronger and then they were in the open spaces of the elevator platform. His feet kept pushing him closer to the chain railing as the salt air and heavy dampness slapped at his face.

There it was! He shut his eyes, then opened them again. It wasn't wishful thinking. Across the water, obscured into a soft blur by the closing fog, *Skate* rolled in the rising green sea as a black sliver. It was the most wonderful sight he had ever seen.

"I love you, Charley Burkhart, you gutsy bastard," Jake mumbled, leaning out over the wet chain. He looked again across the water at Bering Island and his hopes of escape dissolved into a crushing despair.

39

Skate was signaling *Dniestr* with a blinker light! A sudden panic gripped Niven's stomach. There wasn't anyone in Burkhart's crew who understood Soviet Navy blinker signals. He leaned far out over the railing but still couldn't make out the message, just that it was continuous.

"Attention on deck," yelled the Officer of the Deck as he caught sight of Belous coming toward him from the passageway. He rammed his back straight, throwing a crisp salute toward his commanding officer.

"This man is injured!" Belous shouted back at the OOD, ignoring his salute. "Help us down the accommodations ladder immediately."

Gently, the OOD lifted Lathrick's dead weight from Akivor Levy, then awkwardly started down the ladder assisted by the naval guard. Lathrick's condition had soured and his skin had turned a lifeless ash. Niven thought he saw his eyes roll back into the top of their sockets but couldn't be sure.

At the bottom of the platform, Niven scrambled into the rolling launch first, and then set about anchoring the ring switch bag against the bulkhead of the small wheelhouse. He then turned and pulled Lathrick's limp body into the barge with the help of the Russians. Carefully, they laid him on a long wooden bench. A deep swell rolled the launch and Niven stumbled against the bulwarks, but checked his fall by jamming his foot into a tarnished brass scupper that served to drain water from the deck to the sea.

"Pash-l'i-t'i za-dok-ta-ram!" the hovering OOD screamed at the infantry man, who had retreated across the deck, not wanting to become further involved.

Send for a doctor! Niven shot a threatening glance at Levy.

"Where the hell's the launch crew?" Belous shrieked at the OOD.

The OOD went pale, then without answering, raced up the steep accommodations ladder to find them.

"Goddamned stupid bastards," Belous screamed after him in frustration. "At times I'd like to put this whole damn ship on report." He turned to the guard, who instantly turned his eyes away.

"What the hell are you staring at, rating?

"Nothing, sir!" gasped the naval guard.

Niven turned his head and could feel his whole body shaking. They were so close. He again exchanged silent, agonizing glances with Akivor Levy, who was thinking the same thing. We're back from the dead, and now there's no crew. Simultaneously, both men turned longingly toward the submarine.

Slowly Jack backed away from the Cossack guard, toward the wheelhouse, when an iron grip caught hold of his arm.

Captain Belous had read his mind.

Slowly Belous shook his head. "Be patient. Be patient," he whispered in Russian to Jake. "We've come this far. If you steal this launch you'll kill every chance for escape we have. I want that Da Vinci painting, Niven! I won't die without spending time with it. I've

297

given up too much!'' His strong fingers were digging into Jake's arm to make his point.

"We need at least two hours lead time through the screening force to escape alive, Niven. Don't victimize us.'' Belous fixed a steel glare on Jake until he felt Niven's muscles relax.

"Very good. Just let me handle it!'' He was very close to Niven's tired face. "I am still captain of this vessel. Do you understand?''

Jake returned the gaze, then slowly nodded, expelling a steamy breath.

Belous strode to the waiting infantryman. "Thank you for your help. Now you had better return to your security duty.''

"Yes, sir.'' The Cossack saluted and stepped off the barge, relieved to depart his captain's presence without having been disciplined.

Jake made his way to Akivor Levy, who had seated the unconscious David Lathrick with his head slumped over.

"Hold his damned head up, Akivor.''

Levy shot him a disgusted look, then let Lathrick slide back to a prone position. "You sit here,'' he whispered sharply, "and let him bleed all over you! The poor man is dying. Give him some peace.''

The young Russian OOD was still hovering, making his presence obvious. Finally he climbed back into the barge and approached Niven. "There are some new conditions,'' he said sternly, turning halfway to keep an eye on Captain Belous. "I expect that gallon of alcohol sent back aboard when the launch returns from your submarine.'' His knowing eyes darted back and forth as he spoke.

"Do you?'' An anger welled up in Niven that he was powerless to control. Instantly, he looked at the man and smiled openly, rubbing the cold from his once damaged nose. His bruised and hurt body ached in the tense cold, which only added to his rancor.

"I ought to put your ass in the water right now, shitface." He kept smiling at the OOD, whose face sagged with a disbelieving expression. He was hearing the words, but Niven's body language was disarming him.

"The alcohol?" the OOD repeated, off balance. "The gold watch?"

"Fuck your sister," Jake whispered.

"What?"

Niven motioned him closer with his best and most intense smile. "When I'm done with you, you'll be cleaning slop jars and peeling frozen farts from the walls in Murmansk."

He watched the petty defiance grow in the Russian's young, arrogant face. "You can't—"

"You're right. I can't."

With a friendly gesture, Jake reached out and put his left hand on the *mladshiy leytenant's* shoulder, then with a quick reflex action snapped a short crunching fist up into the upper stomach of the OOD. The unexpected blow made the sound of a shattering watermelon, slumping the Russian forward into his body.

Dancing the groaning Russian officer around, Niven sat him down hard on one of the cold wet benches lining the aft section of the launch.

"You're an asshole," Jake whispered in his ear. "You were promised your ration, but you pushed too fucking far."

Niven felt his hands trembling with anger, and out of the corner of his eye he saw Captain Belous approaching.

"If I give Captain Belous the word, you're a dead man." Still smiling broadly, he grabbed the officer's face with a gloved hand and pulled it toward him.

"You see, there was no gold watch. It was a figment of your imagination. An hallucination." Niven thrust an arm around the Russian's middle and held him up. He was having trouble catching his breath, making short, grunting empty bellow sounds, trying to refill his protesting lungs with cold air.

If the young Russian protested again, Niven would snap the knife into his heart and take his body back aboard *Skate*. Staring at the Russian, Niven's mind rubberbanded to the deep-blue summer sky, scented green pines, and lazy sloops under full sail, dotting La Jolla Cove. Ellie standing on the redwood deck, the sea breeze lifting her hair. That was his only goal as he looked into this strange young man's alien face.

"What the hell are you still doing aboard this launch, *Leytenant?*"

The OOD glanced watery-eyed at Niven and hesitated. The Russian had probably already sold three quarts of the promised alcohol, Jake mused.

"Answer the captain, *Leytenant.*"

The Russian was laboring to pull in enough air to breathe, let alone speak.

"Lending a hand and helping out, sir." It came out as a gasping moan.

"Are you ill?" Belous eyed Jake suspiciously.

The OOD shook his head.

The engines began to throb under their feet as the coxswain developed enough courage and turned back over his shoulder with a questioning expression, looking through the opening of the small wheelhouse.

Niven stood and pulled the OOD to his feet.

"Back to your post now, *Leytenant.*" He held up the OOD's shoulders and walked him uncertainly across the deck to the landing platform. There was only the slightest resistance to Jake's grasp, which saved his life.

As the OOD stumbled off the launch, Jake offered a

teasing, cruel hope. "I'm sure we'll be here long enough for us to send over that special order this evening." He forced another smile, patted the OOD's arm, and watched as the lines were cast off fore and aft. The launch moved unsteadily into the rising sullen gray-green swell of Lisinskaya Bay, and Jake watched *Minsk* grow smaller and finally dissolve into the thickening overcast. He thought of Sorrell, or was it Misha Lykov, and shuddered inside.

40

"Captain! Broad on the starboard bow!" Spike Mead mashed the binoculars into his eyes until they hurt. Out of the rolling mist, the Soviet barge, looking small and helpless against the foaming seas, slid and bobbed toward *Skate*.

"Jesus. Thank you, God!" Burkhart muttered as his heart pounded in his chest.

"The barge is closing fast, one point forward of the starboard beam," Mead called out.

Burkhart crouched next to the sail hatch and called down, "Pass the word, we have the boarding party in sight. Tell Mr. Brennen to pass the word to the engine room to crank up the diesels."

"No shit, sir?" The talker looked up hopefully, then his young face erupted into a grin. "The boarding party's comin' home from shark castle!" the talker blurted out in the control room. Cheers and hoots swept through the boat.

"Knock it off, dammit!" Burkhart called down. "Just pass the word by messenger to crank up those rock crushers and stand by to get underway."

After two frustrating approaches at *Skate*'s starboard bow, the utility barge was forced to back away in the rising swell of Lisinskaya Bay. The young coxswain, troubled by the tricky current, stood out from *Skate* and circled her stern to the leeward. Finally the boats came together. Lines were quickly thrown and the barge was secured to *Skate*, despite the vicious pitch of the sea. Niven gauged the rise of the barge to *Skate*'s, then leaped with the ring switch bag into the hands of the deck crew.

"Let's go, dammit!" Niven motioned for Belous to cross over. A moment later Niven was back in the barge to help Levy with David Lathrick. A large swell rolled under the shallow-bottomed barge, sending them all sprawling to the deck.

Jake reached down and gently lifted Lathrick's head. A bright ribbon of crimson trickled from the corner of his waxen lips.

"I'm sorry, David," Niven mumbled softly in Russian. "You knew, didn't you. I'm so very sorry." Then both Levy and Niven muscled him to *Skate*'s deck, as a swell funneled a geyser of icy seawater between the boats, drenching them all. A moment later they were all down the aft hatch within the safe confines of *Skate*. Down into the warm stink of diesel oil and lubricants.

"Welcome aboard *Skate*, sir." Burkhart raised his hand in salute.

"Thank you, Captain, I accept your welcome." His English was thick with fatigue.

"Charley, get your corpsman back here, fast. David Lathrick's been wounded." Jake motioned toward Lathrick, lying crumpled in the corner of the engine room spaces.

"What the hell—"

"For Chrissakes, get him!"

"Irish, get Corpsman Ginepra back here, on the double. We've got a wounded man."

"Don't trouble yourselves." Levy raised his eyes from Lathrick. "He's dead."

Burkhart surveyed the remains of the boarding party and their silence. "What the hell happened over there? Someone speak to me. I can't sit here all day and wait for Sorrell. Where the hell is he?"

Jake shrank back silently into his parka and met Burkhart's steady gaze with silence.

"What's going on here? Where the hell is he? We can't sit here all morning, for Chrissakes!"

"Dead. He's dead, Commander Burkhart," Akivor Levy offered. "He was a Soviet operative."

"What the—" Burkhart riveted his gaze on Niven. "I don't understand. I thought you knew this man for ten years? "What the hell are you telling me? Was this whole goddamn operation for nothing?"

"No." Jake pointed feebly to the canvas bag sitting by one of the diesel mounts. "We have the ring switch."

Burkhart motioned to Lathrick and rubbed the hairs standing up on the back of his blushing neck. "What'd you do, start a war on *Minsk?*"

"Almost, but not quite." Niven raised his eyes. "We got the job done. Now it's over."

"Not quite, Jake boy. Not quite." He smiled for the first time at Niven. "It's good to have you back. For a while, we thought we'd lost you."

"I thought so, too." He slapped Burkhart's back. "Thanks."

"Now, let's move! I've got a hundred lives in my hands and I still have to take this old girl through a screening force, just waiting for the word to cut us into fresh hamburger. And unless I make it, that bag of circuits and microchips isn't worth toad shit to the United States or Marblehead Langor."

"Your mission has not yet been jeo—jeopardized."

304

Captain Viktor Belous stepped forward." His English was labored as he searched for the words. "We have enough time before Fleet Headquarters becomes suspicious and starts a search. If we hurry, we can proceed through the Task Force."

"Get that Russian sailor up here, Charley. He'll help the captain with his English and Russian."

"Not possible, Jake boy. He's in Winebelly's freezer with a five-inch hold in his side." Burkhart mashed his face. "We needed him to signal that repair ship, then he decided it was time to go home—"

"Trouble with the rock crushers, sir," Russotto called out from across the compartment. "Can't get 'em started. We've tried everything, but there ain't much diesel experience aboard."

Silently Akivor Levy rushed through a narrow opening separating the engine mounts to a large air compressor.

"She starts beautifully, maintains pressure, but the main engines won't kick over."

"Dammit! I didn't just go through hell to have this happen." Levy, tired and soaked, shed his parka and machine pistol and stooped to examine the air compressor, needed to start the main diesels. For a moment he surveyed the machinery, which was coated with a film of oil and ran his thawing hands over the warm cylinder head, feeling mystically for some ill.

"Hit the starter again."

Russotto pushed the starter button and the pressure rapidly built in the tanks. "Come on, you bastards," Levy yelled above the noise. "Don't fuck me now!" The needle on the side of the tank stopped at one hundred ninety pounds. With a surgeon's touch, Levy tapped the glass gauge. The needle held rock steady.

"Three hundred pounds, Russotto. I told you—" Levy, shoving away his fatigue for a few critical moments, rose to his feet and reached for the air switch, making an adjustment. Quickly, he nodded grimly at Russotto. Despair and tension circled his eyes.

Russotto opened a large chrome wheel that forced highly compressed air into the half-working cylinders. Both Russian engines rotated, with a sharp ear-splitting explosion and Levy held his breath. When he died, he wanted to be home in Israel—close to his dead wife and children, not here on a submarine at the end of the world!

At just the right moment, Levy nodded at Russotto, who hit the fuel injection switches for both engines, allowing a fine spray of oil into each cylinder.

He closed his eyes and prayed. A moment later, *Skate*'s engine room exploded with the vibration, noise, and stench of raw power from the hammering diesels.

Levy smiled over at Russotto and grabbed a familiar rag from a closed bin. Slowly he wiped a smear of oil from his palms and fingers. ''Make certain the air pressure in each cylinder doesn't rise above five pounds or we'll have hell to pay,'' he shouted to Russotto.

''You got mine and every guy's vote for all-time guts. This boat is damn proud of you!''

Levy nodded. ''Just tell your captain to get us the hell out of here before those bastards run us down!''

41

Skate forged sluggishly ahead, rolling into the seas, a slender ghost in a protective fog.

Shifting his knees to compensate for the roll, Charley Burkhart flipped down the squawk box speak lever in Niven's stateroom.

"Control, this is Burkhart."

"Control, aye, Skipper," blared Brennen's flat, metallic voice.

"Keep your turns at five knots. Remember, we're out for a stroll while the Soviet Captain checks us out. Just keep it nice and easy. We're gonna waltz out of here with a soft smile. Steady on one five two."

"Aye, aye, Skipper. Nice and easy she goes, one five two is the new heading."

Burkhart turned as Jake entered the cabin. He was holding a twenty-inch-square package surrounded with flat protective foam, overlayed with thick corrogated cardboard. He slid past Burkhart and silently handed the package to Captain Viktor Belous sitting on the bottom bunk.

"Your Da Vinci, sir."

Belous looked up with his sagging Russian face, then savagely tore the protective wrappings from the painting. "Did you know that I grew up with masterpieces all about me?"

"That's what Crabb told me."

Belous didn't hear him. "In 1931, my father negotiated the sale of Raphael's "The Alba Madonna" to Senator Andrew Mellon." He fell silent, examining the five-hundred-year-old tempera-on-canvas Da Vinci masterpiece.

"Look at it, Niven." Belous's voice was barely audible. "The delicate sweep of the child suckling her mother's breast. Only possible with the Italian tempera and Leonardo's brilliance. The concept behind the technique. That was Da Vinci!" His voice rose strangely. "Ahead of his time. A true pioneer." He had detached himself.

"The line, Niven. Look at the line." He pointed with a large strong hand at the chubby foot and leg of the child. There was poignancy in his voice. "The boldness of proportions in the left leg. The delicate reddish curl of the child's hair."

A great sadness swept over Jake. This stranger. This man from a different world, trying to link himself to his dead wife through a mystical five-hundred-year-old image of a child, wrapped in the last illusion of his life. It was the child Belous and his wife never had.

"Look at the blues of the composition, dominating the ivory hues of the flesh. Remarkably expressive! The red of the madonna's gown, the closeness of the mother and child."

Belous hesitated and rubbed his face. "Relief now filled out the fleshy pockets and soft planes of his face. He seemed to be telling Niven without words that he could rest. Belous raised his hand and swept it delicately in the air. "This is truly a portrait of the Milanese period—with perfect form. Very strong Lombard elements."

Belous dropped his eyes back to the painting like a stone. "Anna says . . ." he paused and cast his eyes down heavily. "My wife wrote me before her death," he carefully corrected himself, "that in 1865, Tsar Alexander II purchased the masterpiece for the Winter Palace from Viscount Litta, thus the name 'Madonna Litta.' My wife was as soft and as beautiful as this madonna."

Belous fell silent, his eyes vacant, lost somewhere in the collapsed horizon and image of the painting and the memories of his wife. Niven swallowed and Ellie danced into his mind, forcing him to shiver from the ache.

A loud knock at the door broke the spell.

"Yes?"

"The captain would like you in the control room, sir. We're heading out of the Dog Bowl, aiming right at the teeth of the Soviet screen."

"Be right there."

"We are going?"

Jake nodded tensely. "Yes!"

"I won't deny that the odds are against us, but the screen isn't expecting this," Belous offered. "We still have surprise on our side."

"We'll see!" Then Niven was gone.

42

The arctic fog, fueled by the warmth of the Japanese Current and the cold of the Kamchatka Stream, spread a thick blanket over the eastern approaches to the Bering Sea. As *Skate* plowed toward the Russian screening force, a howling *Williwaws* wind piled the seas before them.

"Control, Bridge."

"Control, aye." Burkhart moved close to the metal speaker.

"Russian cruiser *Admiral Isakov* is broad on the port beam. Range estimated at four zero zero yards. She's putting just enough propeller wash across her rudders to keep her on station. I see some movement, but it's hard to really tell with fog closing down visibility. Request radar assistance. Keep your heading steady on one nine five, true."

"Steady on one niner five, she goes, Mr. Mead. No radar just yet. I'm risking enough just using intercom. Let's just keep giving them as little as possible to think about," Burkhart called. "Keep it brief, but keep me advised. We're only in the eye of the storm. Don't let it fool you." For no logical reason, Burkhart found himself whispering, as if that could hide them from scanning by Soviet electronic ears.

He pulled a fresh cigar out of his shirt pocket and ran it under his nose. After a reflective moment he checked the bulkhead clock on the periscope stand.

Two hours, twenty minutes, since hauling in the sea anchor and "softly waltzing" away from *Minsk*. Two hours twenty minutes, wallowing on the surface, zig-zagging, playing benign sound signature games with those surface ships and the two bottom prowling Russian submarines, constantly probing anything suspicious with their sonar.

Once the fog and ocean depths could have provided a safe haven for *Skate*. Now the mask of deception was only psychological. *Skate* couldn't hide. High tech sensors could even track *Skate* from the tiny trace elements of radiation emitted by her nuclear reactor. And here they were, pounding along on the surface like it was 1945.

Two hours, twenty minutes. Burkhart laughed darkly to himself. The operational orders had called for *Skate* to be through the screen by now, running on nuclear power, in the depths of the Aleutian Basin, hopefully out of reach.

Admiral Brandon Langor's operational orders. The Washington armchair tough guy who'd sucked him in with the disease of greed hadn't taken into account eight foot seas, for a boat built to run submerged, but not on the surface. A boat he couldn't run over fifteen knots in those seas, without shaking her guts out. Closed spaces in a pitching and rolling steel pressure tube accented the overwhelming smell and taste of diesel oil, with mildew permeating their fingernails and even the food they ate.

Irish Brennen's voice, pushing at him from the plot table, forced him back. "—once we clear the Russian

311

frigate screen, we should be home to Station Mollie in about twenty hours.''

''One damn mile at a time, Irish. This bastard ocean, not to mention the Russians, has the soul of a whore.''

Burkhart leaned over the steel table and silently examined the navigation chart of the Bering Sea. Brennen had penciled in a south by southwesterly heading to the Near Islands, a tiny group of ink spots of volcanic rock and ice, where west turns to east, at the end of the civilized world in the Aleutians.

''The Aleutians,'' Burkhart mumbled. A shiver rocked his upper body. His finger swept over the two thousand-mile necklace of cold rock, arcing across the northernmost reaches of the Pacific; stark, jagged remnants of the Bering Land Bridge that had linked the Asian and North American continents until four million years ago.

''In all my years of submarine operations in northern waters, there's never been a sweet smell anywhere in the Aleutian archipelago. Just a cold sour stench. This ocean is bloated with death,'' Burkhart said with a blank stare.

He had never liked the Bering, nor had he ever trusted its tricky currents, compass problems, uncharted shoals and ice flows. But mostly, he had hated the fog-muted sun that always lurked just on the lip of the horizon, as a lifeless orange ball. His father had always called this patch of dull ocean the ''kill waters.''

The superstition he had tried so hard to suppress came back. His father, serving as a young gunnery officer in the heavy cruiser *Salt Lake City* in March 1943, had lost his leg and career when his ship ran into a Japanese task group resupplying their garrisons on Attu and Kiska. The Japanese heavy cruiser *Nachi* caught *Salt Lake City* with numerous salvos, including an eight-inch shell hit on her quarterdeck where Burkhart's father was stationed.

Now Burkhart felt himself being drawn back to that same patch of ocean, to finish his father's business. He was reaching down and grabbing at something soft and frightened within him.

Burkhart bit down hard on the cigar, grunted and shoved that naked thought back into its hiding place, just as a silver heap of ash dropped on the Bering chart. The uneven tip of cigar glowed red as he drew deeply from its comfort. It was the only warmth he felt.

"There's no music in this place, Irish."

"Skipper?"

Burkhart rubbed his stubbled chin as he stared at the chart. "Music. Not a goddamn bit of music in this chicken shit ocean." The cigar glowed red again casting a dim glistening shadow back across Burkhart's impoverished expression.

Brennen cocked his head, "Yeah, Skipper," then ignored the remark when it failed to register.

"Here." Brennen was tapping the chart with a flat-shaped fingernail at the easternmost tip of the Aleutians. "Twenty hours to a safe harbor. That's all, Skipper."

"You make those twenty hours sound so prosaic. "Twenty hours," he mumbled again, turning the words over and polishing them, each time he spoke.

"That's twenty knots submerged."

Burkhart tapped the ink spots. "Distance to Hammerhead Island?""Five hundred forty nautical miles from the outer perimeter of the Soviet screen."

Burkhart blew a stream of smoke in Brennen's face. "How long until we clear the last Russian warship?"

"Another hour and a quarter, then we can wet her down." Brennen waved the flat fingernail below Burkhart's eyes.

313

"Well, that's something I can hold on to."

"We cross back into American territorial waters just north of Stalemate Bank, sweep past the northern coast of Attu Island, then meet the rendezvous ship, an ammunition carrier, in Shemya Pass. We'll transfer the men except for a skeleton crew, then head for the scuttle point."

Burkhart nodded. "Tahoma Reef?"

"The deepest area of the Aleutian Trench. Four thousand fathoms of water and a bottom littered with nerve gas in cement drums from Rocky Mountain Arsenal. There's a special team aboard the rendezvous ship that will pull Skate's reactor core, before she goes down."

Burkhart pulled on the cigar for warmth. "I guess I asked for it, but it still hurts. They're gonna open her seacocks and bury my old girl in twenty-four thousand feet of water filled with nerve gas." His voice was sad. "Right smack in the middle of the Rat Islands."

Burkhart eventually took the cigar stub from his mouth and examined the chewed, moist butt. "There's breaks, hidden shoals, and a murderous current running through Shemya Pass. Damn! There's always the threat of high winds and ice here, even in summer. Christ, the RP is only in nine and a half fathoms." He let out a breath and peeled a tiny strip of tobacco that had stuck to his tongue."

"It's a good plan, Skipper. Admiral Langor's people had put a great deal of time into preparing this. Once we cross the line we're virtually in American waters since many of the islands are defense reservations. The Russians won't dare poke their noses in these areas. Traditionally, it's always been hands off."

"Traditionally, we don't act like pirates in Russian waters, board their aircraft carriers, steal their captain and their secret weapons."

"I still don't see any holes in it," Brennen challenged evenly. "It's all here. What's left?"

"What's left?" Burkhart repeated the question softly.

"I'll tell you what's left," he said ruefully. "The Soviet Navy and Air Force, and if that's not enough to survive, five hundred forty miles of some of the world's roughest ocean with a boat whose operational characteristics are at best questionable."

Burkhart reached for his parka and Russian fur cap slung over the stand railing and climbed the access ladder to the bridge where he found Niven standing watch with Spike Mead. The williwaws had risen to force eight, almost thirty-five knots. The cold air and foaming gray seas, throwing spray over the sail, momentarily revived his spirits. The Soviet battle ensign continued to pop and snap sharply on the staff behind the bridge cockpit. *Skate* was smack in the middle of what seamen called an "Aleutian low," a semipermanent low pressure system that hovered over the entire island chain.

"You're relieved, Mr. Mead. Go below and take some hot java and chow. Winebelly's just taken three pot roasts out of the oven. Eat something before it begins to mildew or stink of diesel fumes."

"Thank you, sir," Mead said gratefully, then quickly disappeared down the access hatch.

Burkhart surveyed the fog-patched surface with binoculars, then broke the silence. "Brennen says your escape route is a natural."

"Yeah, I thought so, too, when I put it together. It's a hella'va lot different when you're right smack in the middle of it, with your guts turning upside down." Niven tried to smile.

"I know what you mean."

They were silent, watching the churning gray sea for

315

the approach of Soviet warships. Only when salt tears formed in their eyes did they dare drop their binoculars to clear their vision.

"I'm sorry for what happened to Sorrell," Burkhart finally said.

"So am I, Charley."

"Well, at least we got what we came for, and I'm damn proud of my boat, regardless of what happens from this point on. We did the impossible! What's your estimate of lead time before the cavalry comes charging out of The Dog Bowl?"

Niven stuck out his chin to the cold. "Who the hell knows? The Soviets are so damned unpredictable." His voice faded into the roar of the wind. Lifting his glasses, he peered out over the cockpit bulwarks, his feet vibrating to the heartbeat of Levy's diesel engines.

"Contact! Broad on the port bow."

Burkhart moved across the tiny cockpit and trained his glasses on a black smudge growing on the misty horizon. "It's a ship all right."

"Must be the frigate *Shakal,*" Niven said tautly.

"She's the exit door." Burkhart raised his glasses to the approaching warship.

"Bridge, Engineer of the Watch."

"Engineering, this is Burkhart."

"Sir, the checklist for restarting the reactor has been completed."

"How's it look?"

"Not too good, sir." The flat metallic voice hesitated. "The silver-brazed joints are filled with hairline cracks all through the piping leading to the fresh water feed pump. God only knows what's really happening behind the protective shield in the boiler tubes." The voice faded.

"You pass the word, Henderson."

"Sir?"

"You light that pile and give me nuclear power for the next twenty-two hours, or we'll never see home again." His voice was incredibly matter-of-fact. "That's the straight shit, mister."

"Aye, aye, sir." Burkhart could hear his breathing through the mesh speaker. "Request permission to withdraw the rods for criticality, to start up the reactor and open main steam valves."

"Granted, Henderson." Burkhart looked out at *Shakal* and shivered inside.

43

The thumping growl of the jet engines bounced off the wave tops, as the squat Kamov antisubmarine helicopter skimmed the surface of the Bering Sea, pushing all out at two hundred twenty kilometers per hour. A sudden down draft slammed the Kamov dangerously close to the white-capped waves, appearing suddenly out of the fog.

The pilot lurched against his nylon restraining shoulder harness and fought to control the helicopter, then when the crisis passed, turned his white crash helmet just enough to exchange a questioning glare with his co-pilot.

"Any damage back there?" he called angrily through his face mike to the two crewmen manning the electronics in the aft compartment.

"Negative, sir, just a little shook up. We thought we were going for a morning swim."

The pilot motioned for the co-pilot to take the controls, then swiveled his head to the seat just behind him.

"It's tough enough being out here in this fog, this close to the surface, but with my throttles rammed to the firewall and no altitude to play with in this cross wind, I—"

"You have your orders," the man in the seat replied coldly.

"We're operating below minimal flight rules as it is. We never should have taken off from *Minsk,*" the pilot protested. Then, loosening his harness, he turned his body more, staring into the menacing, bloodshot eyes offset by the white bandage circling his baldness. Strange tearing bite marks dotted the right side of his face.

"Within an hour we could be flying in zero zero visibility, *Palko'vneek.*" The pilot knew he couldn't push much harder, especially with Military Intelligence. They had ultimate power. They'd have his ass in a ringer for sure.

Colonel Misha Lykov gingerly touched the wound in the back of his throbbing head, which *Minsk's* chief surgeon had hastily closed with forty stitches. The physician was bewildered that Lykov had regained consciousness and had crawled to the bulkhead phone in the weapons hangar bay at all. A lesser man would have bled to death. Now the anesthetic from closing the wound was wearing off, and the blood loss had left him light-headed, tingly, and very nauseous. Only his frenetic obsession to recapture Niven had kept him going. In fact, he had said nothing to *Minsk's* senior political officer, or the senior Flag-rank Flotilla Commander by phone in Petropavlovsk about the coveted ring switch. He would recapture them all using the frigate *Shakal.* Returning the switch would only solidify his favorable return home. It wouldn't be too difficult, give *Skate's* unreliable condition. He, like Niven, knew *Skate* inside and out. He would exploit her every weakness and the weaknesses of every man in her.

Luck and apathy were on his side, at least temporarily. He had lied convincingly enough about the entire affair to *Minsk*'s political and executive officers. All he needed was time, he explained, to keep the nature of the incident localized. Translated into Soviet naval terms, it meant play ball and your careers won't be touched by this stain. They wanted to be convinced, even though the story was rife with holes. He would have another ten hours before the story would die of its own weight.

Incredibly, all they pressed to know was why he'd been on the submarine. Surprise inspection. Not uncommon, especially when morale problems had been reported by *331*'s political officer. *Minsk*'s senior officers were only concerned with their own healthy paranoia. Afraid they were being watched.

The story had to be simple so Misha Lykov could cover himself. He had boarded the submarine in Cam Ranh Bay, Vietnam, on a refueling layover. Final destination was Petropavlovsk for a major refit, when the collision with the Chinese fishing boat occurred. The submarine radioed for assistance and they had been directed to Bering Island, stumbling on the secret test site. At sea, an endangered ship always seeks help from the closest source.

Captain Belous, angry at the intrusion, had gone aboard *331* to conduct a personal inspection. That seemed to be Belous's style, and the senior officers aboard *Minsk* agreed. For some reason unknown to Misha Lykov, Belous had stopped by the secret weapons bay to show *331*'s executive officer something. There had been a fight with one of the sub's officers, and when Lykov regained consciousness, he was alone. There was nothing more to it. But the submarine couldn't get far, with a kidnapped Belous, limping along with major engine problems. The simple lie would buy him the few hours he needed. Lykov knew that he wouldn't get much more.

Then the bureaucratic system would take over and the computers in Leningrad and Moscow would be working overtime. No one wanted responsibility for the incident, so a senior GRU Military Intelligence Officer, namely Misha Lykov, would handle the problem, relieving them of their fear. The Kamov bounced in the turbulent air.

Misha Lykov focused his energy and attention on the pilot, who was staring at the small, angry rat bites on his face.

"Something wrong, *Leytenant?*"

"No, sir!"

"That's fine." Lykov's thin terra-cotta smile dissolved. "How long before we reach *Shakal's* station?"

"She's about seventy-five kilometers due south of our position. If we don't have problems and if the headwinds don't get any stronger, I estimate forty-five minutes to an hour."

Lykov nodded sullenly.

"We should be in search-radar range of *Shakal* in a few minutes. Then I'll radio ahead to *Shakal* to make preparations to accept an airborne passenger, since they don't have a landing platform."

Lykov squeezed the pilot's shoulder. "You won't radio *Shakal* until we're overhead."

The pilot squinted, thinking it over, then shrugged his shoulders. "It's your show, *Palko'vneek.*" He turned back to his instruments and lost himself in the engine noise and shrill beat of the twin counter-rotating rotar blades chewing at the fog and low clouds.

44

Burkhart scanned the empty foredeck of *Skate* as her false bow nosed into a foaming, pungent sea, then rose urgently, throwing off tons of icy water.

"Ready, Charley?" Jake Niven looked up at the leaden sky, wondering if he would ever see it again.

"You think this is easy?" Burkhart shot him a dark look, then leaned over the cockpit speaker. "Control, Bridge. Rig ship for dive. Rig ship for dive. Irish, what's our depth?"

"Fathometer indicates one hundred two fathoms under our keel," the speaker answered.

"Very well. Stand by."

"I never met a man who wanted to die, Jake. Maybe we'll make it."

Burkhart sucked deeply from the chill and allowed the cross wind to sting and water his eyes. "Maneuvering, Bridge. How you doin' back there?"

"Holding together, Captain. We'll be able to pull the cork and answer bells on nuclear power and a full head of clean steam whenever you want."

"Very well, Mr. Henderson. Make ready the jacking gear to disengage diesels and engage steam turbines."

"Aye, Captain, the diesels are disengaged, the port and starboard turbines are engaged. Answering bells on nuclear power. All systems, temperatures, and pressure readings are within tolerable limits."

"Close main induction valves," Burkhart ordered.

Niven was astonished. All vibration and noise ceased and the oily stench of diesel smoke dissolved into the cacophony of the Bering Sea and the wind whipped Soviet flag.

"Scared?"

"Sure." Jake grimaced. "I don't want to let go of the surface and the fresh air."

"There are times we all get the belly quease about submerging. But if the fates let us, *Skate* will get us home, one way or another. They ought to give my *Skate* the Navy Cross for what she's done here."

"She can have mine, Charley."

Burkhart squeezed out a steamy breath and gazed out to sea. "She's the only music I hear in this godforsaken piece of ocean. This crew is a very taut family. *Skate*'s not a slack boat. She's the best in the fleet, by God—" He raised his glasses to the blurred horizon and noticed a chunk of blue ice bobbing in the sea.

"Jake boy. *Skate*'s kinda like a stink, a sonnet, and a Skinner box, all rolled into one." Burkhart smiled faintly. "There's a real music deep in her guts."

"Now who's the poet?"

"Bridge, Control."

"Yeah, Irish?"

"Hydraulic manifold is ready to be unlocked."

"Okay, Irish. Give me an all-stop bell. I want her to settle down. I don't want to drive her under. I'll dive from the Control Room."

Both men scrambled down the inside of the tall sail structure, then Burkhart dogged and secured the control room access hatch with a loud clang.

Burkhart stepped up on his stand next to Brennen and picked up the mike hooked up to the boat's public address system.

"This is the captain. Secure all loose gear and prepare for possible large angles in case of trouble." He paused, collecting his thoughts. "You've all done one hella'va job, let's just keep it together a little while longer and we'll all be stateside before you know it."

He paused again and rubbed his nose. "I'm damn proud to have served with you all."

Jake looked about the control room and the young faces staring up at Burkhart. There was a white silence, punctuated only by the hum of *Skate*'s internal machinery.

"Pressure in the boat," Brennen called out after the trim manifold operator released a long blast of compressed air into the sealed boat from concealed banks of steel air flasks. It caused only a minor rise in atmospheric pressure as each man felt a slight bump in his ears. Any leak in the hull would betray itself before the dive. After a few moments, Brennen turned to Burkhart.

"This boat is rigged for dive and ready to submerge, sir."

"Sound diving alarm."

Brennen leaned over the railing and hit the flat chrome button. AH-OO-GAH. AH-OO-GAH.

"Rig out the dive planes," Burkhart ordered the diving officer. "Make turns for twelve knots," he called out as the telephone talker relayed the information to the maneuvering room, which in turn passed the information to the engineering spaces.

"We have a straight board," Chief Russotto called out. "She's sealed tight, sir."

"Very well, Chief. I'll take the Conn."

"Okay, Skipper." Irish Brennen smiled. He was

back in his element. Back with physical principles and laws he could grasp and finished with *Skate* as a surface pirate.

Burkhart took one last look around the control room, then pulled a fresh cigar out of his shirt pocket.

"Dive! Dive!" he called out. "Make your depth nine hundred feet. Five degrees down bubble. Helm, the new course will be one one two degrees, true."

All the orders were repeated back to Burkhart and then he watched as Russotto opened the hydraulic manifold, in turn releasing the locks on the main vents of the aft ballast and trim tanks. He then followed quickly with the forward tanks. The opening vents produced a tremendous gushing roar of seawater forcing the last remaining volume of air from the tanks, as *Skate* began to settle beneath the Bering Sea.

As her nose sloped downward, a concert of sound and practiced activity under Burkhart's orchestration was growing in the nerve center of the boat.

"Rig out the sound heads, Irish, then I want sonar active, on the double."

Burkhart slipped the cigar out of its cellophane, then leaned out over the stand and looked back to find Spike Mead leaning over his still-dark, passive, and active sonar dishes. "It's up to you, Mr. Mead. From now on, you're our eyes and ears." He smiled approvingly. He had grown to like the man who had emerged from inside Mead in the last ten days.

"Aye, aye, sir. I'll nail every shrimp all the way to the Gulf of Alaska." He grinned back, the flesh beneath his right eye reflecting only a slight trace of purple.

A moment later a minuet of soft pinging began to rhythmically bathe the compartment as Burkhart sat heavily on his red swivel stool between the two periscopes, twirling and wetting down the business end of the cigar.

"Contact! Solid echo return!" Mead's voice jumped over the background noise of the control room as his sonar dish came alive. "High speed screws. Possibly a hundred beats a minute. The target bears one six nine degrees, true. Range twelve miles."

Burkhart craned his neck around the corner and looked into Mead's eyes without speaking. Mead pulled off his earphones and soberly shook his head. "She's pinging like crazy, looking for us."

"Has the target found us?" Burkhart shoved the un-lit cigar into the corner of his mouth.

"I'd say so." Mead looked down at the flat sonar plate again, then looked up. "Her bearing is steady on one six niner."

"Speed?"

"About twenty knots on two shafts!"

Burkhart twisted his face and glanced at the large-faced knot indicator on the bulkhead, above the dive station. It registered twelve knots.

"Brennen, I want emergency turns for flank speed!"

"I wouldn't put that much pressure on the steam plant and rector systems," Brennen protested.

"Make turns for twenty knots, goddammit!" Burkhart snarled, then turned back to Spike Mead. "Any guesses yet as to what the contact is?"

Mead placed one ear cup to the side of his head and stared past Burkhart, listening to the echo. "She's a destroyer or frigate."

"Nationality?"

Mead looked up and shot Burkhart a knowing scowl. "She's a vodka tramp! No doubt about it, and she's closing on us!"

45

"Your mentality is that of a peasant! Just listen to what I want you to do." Colonel Misha Lykov stared into the clear brown eyes of Valentin Markin, Captain Third Class, commanding officer of the frigate *Shakal.*

For an instant Markin looked past Lykov to his political officer, Nikolai Kirov, sitting stoically in the swivel seat on the port side of the enclosed bridge. In response to Captain Markin's glance, political officer Kirov barely nodded, indicating that Lykov had ultimate power and could use *Shakal* any way he saw fit.

"For the record, *Palko'vneek,* I will turn over my detailed sea log to Third Flotilla Commander, Kontro-Admeerah'l Alensandr Gorsky, when we return from this mission." The thirty-six-year-old captain glared at Lykov. He wouldn't allow some military intelligence asshole to drop down out of the overcast from *Minsk,* like some Communist prince, and take his ship away.

Lykov pulled his curved briar pipe from his pocket and slowly filled the bowl from the battered leather pouch. Maybe a smoke would cure the pain in his head. "I apologize for calling you a peasant, Captain Markin, but I have a job to do, and you must assist me." Lykov smiled, mitigating the cruel angles of his face

327

and white head bandage. He stepped forward and laid a large hand on Markin's shoulder.

"What about it, Captain?" It would be easier with Markin's help, but if necessary he would take the ship away from him and assign her first officer to assist him.

Standing at the large chrome helm, Markin turned and looked at the back of his coxswain's head. He'd be a fool to resist any further. "Yes, I will carry out your orders, but there is something I must say, for the record."

The political officer was vigorously shaking his head, but Markin silently waved the protest away. "Some years ago, I was a junior officer on the guided missile destroyer, *Svirepy*, on station in the Gulf of Riga, Glamour duty, as it were. Does it ring a bell, *Palko'vneek?*" He loved his crew and kept no secrets from them.

"Yes, it does," Lykov replied, but his eyes were impatient.

"Good, then you remember the mutiny staged by *Svirepy*'s political officer and a number of her crew." He rammed a fist with a thud into his chest to make the point. "I was locked at gunpoint in a storage locker along with my commanding officer and other loyal members of the crew, while the mutineers turned the ship toward Sweden. The mutiny was barely foiled in time by air units, who threatened to blow up the ship. That action finally forced the ship to come about."

"So?" Bored, Lykov turned and looked out and down toward the narrow bows of the old frigate, the sleek lines broken by two gun turrets.

"So this, *Palko'vneek*. As loyal officers, we were held accountable by the Admiralty and State Security, and here I stand, transferred to the Pacific Fleet and lowly escort duty on this twenty-five-year-old gut bucket. My parents worked their asses off for years managing the Sandunovsky Steam Baths in Moscow to get me into

Frunze, and they can't understand how my career went down the drain, babysitting a generation of rust, masquerading as a warship."

Markin moved close to Lykov and shuddered inside at the awesome size of the man. "Our motherland works off the precept of guilt by association, as if you didn't know. By even chasing these amateur renegades, I could end up cleaning out steam boilers at Komsomolsk shipyards, up the Amur River."

"Not a chance of that happening here, Captain, I assure you." Lykov smiled painfully and pushed out a blue cloud of pipe smoke.

"Fuck your assurances," Markin mumbled and turned on his heels, heading aft into the adjoining combat information center, the electronic heart of *Shakal's* weapons systems.

In the dim red glow of the CIC Markin looked down at the active rippling pattern on the green sonar dish. "How's our target doing now?" Markin looked into the eyes of the young second class petty officer.

"Three three one is submerged and accelerating at a speed close to twenty knots. I wasn't aware she could travel submerged on electric motors at over fifteen knots." He turned his head slightly sideways toward his commanding officer.

'I wasn't, either," Markin replied, stalking back through the compartment hatch onto the bridge. With deliberate care he leaned over the engine telegraph and rang up FLANK AHEAD as a dim set of bells clanged. Then he picked up the engine room telephone, staring ahead at the bows.

"Engine room, give me power for emergency revolutions." His voice was calm, even quiet. He was quite in control of his warship and crew.

"We have your submarine and are tracking it on sonar, *Palko'vneek* Lykov, but something puzzles me."

329

Lykov took the pipe from his mouth. "Yes?"

"She is submerged and her speed is twenty knots. How do you account for that?"

Lykov furrowed his brow. "So? Do I look like a naval engineer?" He laughed, with a heavy note of dismissal in his tone.

"A very flip answer, but not to my question." Markin's voice was still calm and quiet. "You see, this F-class sub of ours is not capable of more than fifteen knots submerged." Markin drew his hands together and cracked his knuckles with a loud pop.

"When will we overtake the sub?" The stitched gash in Lykov's head was pounding and he was growing lightheaded again from the concussion.

The CIC phone gave two shrill rings on the bridge. Markin reached for the receiver and listened intently. Finally he spoke. "Keep me advised."

"Our second mystery, *Palko'vneek.*" Thin frown lines formed at the corners of Markin's eyes. He seemed much wiser than his years.

"I don't care about your little mysteries or anything else other than overtaking and surfacing that sub. Is that clear, Captain?" The snarl in Lykov's voice spilled over inadvertently.

"You tell me then, Colonel!" Markin raised his voice in protest.

"Stop babbling, Captain. Speak your mind."

"My sound people have just informed me that they have picked up the sound of steam turbines emanating from that deep-running sub. Not the sound of electric motors, which we fully expected from a submerged diesel-electric boat not operating on snorkle. Steam turbines mean nuclear power, *Palko'vneek!* Now, what the hell are you drawing me into? I demand to know!"

For a long moment Lykov sucked on his cold pipe, staring straight ahead at the gyro-compass. "This sub was specially adapted with nuclear propulsion as part of an experimental test. That is all I can say." He turned and a long breath rolled from his mouth. "There is nothing more to it."

Markin rolled his eyes. "That's a well-greased response. How easily the lies roll off your tongue." Markin's tone was ice-cold. "But they're words, just fucking words."

Lykov held up a large hand. "No more veiled threats. Just find and force that submarine to the surface, or they will know your name and story on every computer display screen in the Kremlin." Lykov snarled inside. He was sounding more like his father.

"I didn't mean that, Captain." Lykov softened his tone, trying to take the edge off the threat. "I'm under a great strain, trying my damndest to keep Moscow and the Admiralty out of this little mess."

The CIC phone interrupted. "Put it on the speaker," Markin barked to his officer of the deck.

"Range to target is two seven zero zero zero meters. At flank speed, expect to overtake within three hours. Target has changed course to green one three four degrees, true."

"Twenty-five kilometers," Lykov whispered to himself. There was still time to overtake her.

Markin turned away from Lykov and massaged his forehead. After a moment he turned to the quartermaster standing over the small wooden navigation plot table, positioned hard against the starboard bulkhead.

"Change course to green one three four degrees, true."

"Aye, sir. The helm is coming right twenty-two degrees."

Markin and Lykov stared coldly at each other as the ship heeled to starboard and they both could feel her twenty-five thousand-shaft horsepower vibrate through her steel plates at maximum revolutions.

"Steady up on one three four," called out Markin as *Shakal* began to pitch earnestly into the seas with a motion that was so familiar to her. Rising to knife through the tops of rolling combers, then the sudden skidding, as the two-hundred-ninety-eight-foot *Shakal* skied the faces of the waves, shaking to her keel as her screws bit back at the seas.

Shakal, built in 1958 alongside the Ussuri River on the Muraiev Peninsula, easily took the waves and the constant battering of the sea. Usually every human decision made aboard *Shakal* was made in that jarring motion. Every human emotion of her one hundred fifty men was based on the rise of *Shakal*'s bows to meet some new sea, or running before a squal line on a cold ocean. Often, while on patrol, or carrying the mail for the vast Northern Pacific Soviet Fleet, *Shakal* and her crew developed a strange detachment from all other living things.

Markin's knees took the major shock of a large sea that submerged *Shakal*'s bows, then she rose majestically with explosive force, throwing off tons of frothing seawater. He turned his head and stared, first at the gyro-compass, then at the magnetic compass. It was a wise habit built on the premise that at times, this close to the magnetic North Pole, compasses would swing wildly, or hours could be spent traveling a course that wasn't a true reading.

"Steady up on the new course, helm?"

"Aye, sir. Steady as she goes."

Markin could feel Misha Lykov's dominating presence close to him on the bridge. "What appropriate weapons systems do we have aboard to force three three one to the surface?"

Markin turned his head as if he didn't hear Lykov correctly. "Weapons?"

"Weapons, Captain." Inadvertently, Lykov touched the back of his head and a bolt of searing pain shot through him.

"I suggest we overrun the target, then contact her commanding officer by underwater telephone." Markin glanced sideways at Lykov.

"What's the range of the underwater phone?"

"About one and a half kilometers, give or take, depending on sea conditions."

"What about your antisubmarine weapons?" he squinted harshly at Markin.

"Before using weaponry, I must clear it with Flotilla Command. I cannot assume that responsibility."

"I assume all responsibility," Lykov snapped. "What weapons can we use to bring them to the surface, if the underwater phone fails to do so?"

Silently Markin stared ahead through the large rectangular bridge windows with the windshield wipers slowly clearing salt spray.

"Don't fuck with me," Lykov suddenly said softly. "What happened to you after the Gulf of Riga incident was nothing compared to what will happen if you continue to resist me."

There was something about Lykov's expression and a special note in his voice that forced Markin to shiver again. Slowly he drew a breath. He could no longer risk what was left of his career by holding off this fierce animal from military intelligence.

He looked again at Lykov, who was shaking his head, reading his mind and the reluctance in his eyes. "We carry four depth charge projectors aft, a twenty-four-barreled hedgehog, just forward of the bridge, abreast 'B' Gun, and one stern DC, depth charge rail."

"Is that all?"

"I am afraid so, *Palko'vneek*. *Shakal* is not one of the new Navy but build strictly for coastal defense and very limited-escort antisubmarine duty."

Lykov blew out his pipe and refilled the bowl in silence as he thought through the options. Quickly he made a decision. "Captain, I want you to arm those hedgehogs and ready the stern depth charge rail."

Markin swallowed hard and glanced again at the political officer sitting silently in his portable chair. This time he nodded at Markin with his eyes, an old Russian habit. The bastard, Markin thought. Kirov wouldn't dare stand up and be counted with the threat of Lykov hanging over his head.

"Did you hear me?" Lykov repeated, the pipe clenched tightly in his teeth. "Arm those hedgehogs and ready the stern rails."

Markin felt himself once again helplessly being sucked into another black-pooled nightmare similar to what happened board *Svirepy*, in the Gulf of Riga. Russians firing on Russians. The glaze in Lykov's eyes was obvious.

46

The wavering green target echoes continued to spread but came faster on Spike Mead's flat passive sonar plate. The surface target was moving closer.

"How soon, Mr. Mead? How soon will he be on us?"

"If we don't change course again, another twenty minutes, more or less, Mr. Niven. He's really cranking it on. He should be echo ranging again."

Niven nodded solemnly and looked up to find Charley Burkhart watching him from his periscope stand. "What's left?" Jake quizzed softly.

"Nothing," Burkhart scowled, "nothing but to keep trucking straight ahead for Hammerhead Island and hope the good guys don't get screwed over. That's the simple, unvarnished truth."

Burkhart pulled a mashed cigar butt from his mouth and turned it over in his tobacco-stained fingers. "What the hell went wrong, Jake boy? What happened to our lead time?"

"I don't know, Charley." Niven pushed out a breath.

Burkhart stepped off the stand and spoke quietly to Niven so the others couldn't hear. "Langor's taken

away all my live torpedoes. What the hell can I do!"
He mashed his jaw and felt his neck grow red.

"Just surface the boat and I'll kill the bastards with
my spit." His voice got away and echoed across the
control room. Suddenly the compartment erupted in
spontaneous laughter and the tension was gone.

"The target is five miles off our stern and coming
fast!" Spike Mead sang out. "Twin screws, destroyer.
No, check that. A frigate. Noisy as shit. Old machinery. Geared turbines. Two screws."

Burkhart stood deathly still with a hand on his hip.
Perspiration stained his entire upper body as the tension hemmorhaged through his khaki shirt in dark, uneven blotches. His mind was racing. The orders were
specific. Besides, his only weapons had been taken away
by Admiral Langor.

"What options do we have?" Jake asked in a low
voice as he climbed up on the stand.

"Options! Christ, all the options belong to that
tramp on the surface. Unless that guy screws up, we
are going to drop right through the crack without a
whimper."

Burkhart drew a breath and opened his hands like
two plastic Mexican fans. "Maybe she's just trying to
bluff us out." He rolled his eyes.

Burkhart picked up the station-to-station phone and
pushed down the maneuvering room button. "Henderson, this is Burkhart. Squeeze every turn out you
can. Just keep that pile glowing," he barked.

Suddenly his face turned sour.

"Dammit. Very well. Do your best."

"What?" Niven held his breath.

"Jesus! Henderson wants to scram the reactor. He
says more cracks have appeared and there is a danger
of radiation leakage."

Niven balled his hands into fists and felt his belly tighten with fear.

"I've got to shut down the reactor. There's no choice. When I jack over to electric motor propulsion, our speed will be cut to six knots. A damn rowboat could catch us."

"How long do you have to shut down nuclear power?"

"Sorry, Jake. For good." Burkhart looked up toward the steel overhead. "That vodka tramp is gonna have our ass. Chief Russotto to the control room, on the double," he called over the ship's intercom.

Captain Markin scratched his head and furrowed his brow, then looked into the eyes of his sonar operator. "Is it a trick of some sort?"

"No, sir. I don't think so. Probably his sound gear has picked us up and they have decided to surface and for some reason have gone to electric drive." The young petty officer raised his busy blond eyebrows, but said nothing more.

Markin walked five feet in the cramped CIC, to the section marked ASW, antisubmarine warfare. It wasn't really a section at all, or even a space for that matter. It was two flat tables, chest-high, with mechanical arms and a thick pad of velum on each. A seaman was standing at each table and with a pencil was tracing the exact course and every change made by *Shakal* and the target. He cursed softly under his breath, desperately wanting to turn to use a computer like the new antisubmarine escorts use. But the only computer was in his head.

Carefully he traced a long slender finger over the penciled course of the submarine.

"Can I assist you, sir?" the youngster, no more than twenty, asked as he slowly drew another short track of the sub on the white plotting sheet. He smiled eagerly at his commanding officer. Markin nodded and affectionately patted the boy's back.

"Captain, sir," called the sonarman, "we'll be over him in a few minutes at most." He looked into Markin's eyes for some sign of what would come next.

"That's excellent, Captain." Misha Lykov smiled in the dim glow of the CIC, his bandaged head and facial cuts casting a grotesque shadow.

"Three three one's speed has dropped to six knots and he's running on his electric motors." Markin shoved his cap back further on his head.

Lykov nodded silently.

Markin slid his lanky frame to the forward bulkhead phone and called to the bridge, "This is Markin, ring up one-third revolutions on both starboard and port shafts." Satisfied, he pushed another glowing button on the phone wall console. "Number one, I am sorry to disturb your sleep, but our errant submarine has pulled up short and I'm tied down here in CIC. I want you on the bridge because I am going to call battle action stations. When you relieve the OOD on the bridge, have the ASW Deck arm the hedgehog mortars with the sixteen kilo warheads."

"We have a solid target," the sonarman called out. "Echo ranging has her at a steady depth of two hundred seventy-three meters, course steady on one one two degrees, true. Range to target has closed to four thousand two hundred meters." The returning electronic echo sent by *Shakal*'s sonar, bounced off *Skate* and returned as a grating shriek.

Markin looked once again at Misha Lykov, then hit the bridge button on the CIC phone. "Duty Officer, this is Markin. Sound battle alarm, no drill, then inform stern rail depth charge station to arm six fuses for two hundred twenty meters. Number one is on his way

338

up from his stateroom to relieve you. Put the goose to the mousetrap crew, to be sure they are at the ready. They have been slow in the past month's drills. I want hydrostatic fuses on those warheads."

"What the hell are mousetraps?" Lykov was hovering over Markin again.

Markin pushed out a short breath. "The mousetrap is the nickname for the hedgehog mortars. Anything else, *Palko'vneek?*"

Lykov shook his head.

A shrill air horn blasted through every compartment in *Shakal*. Markin had taken her to battle ready.

47

"How much time do we have on the batteries, Chief?"

Russotto nervously rubbed his mouth. "At maximum speed of six knots, maybe two hours, at the outside. The damn batteries weren't built for long durations in nuclear boats, just emergencies."

"This is an emergency, dammit!" Burkhart tried to crowd out the fear and rolled the cigar in his mouth. A hideous screeching echo slammed into the hull with the sound of a wounded elephant, crawled all over *Skate*'s steel skin, then retreated.

"He's echo-ranging again, from almost right on top of us," Mead called out from the sonar stand.

"What's his range now, Mead?"

"Three thousand five hundred yards. He's reduced his turns to nine knots to lower sonar distortion."

The screeching echoes were bouncing off *Skate*'s steel hull every half minute, creating a distracting and nerve-racking symphony.

"Try and ignore it, gentlemen," Burkhart called out confidently to the control room crew. "They're just playing games."

Jake Niven slumped back against the plot table and

340

rubbed his eyes. He looked from Burkhart to Mead, then to the crew, all virtually standing around waiting for something to happen. A soft melancholy had overtaken them all.

"They've gone to battle stations," Mead called out. "I can hear their klaxon."

The sound of Mead's words snapped Burkhart back to full attention. "I want a meeting right now in the wardroom with Niven, our Soviet captain, Akivor Levy, and Chief Russotto." He pointed a large finger at Brennen, standing watch over the dive station.

"Irish, take the Conn. Keep me informed, even if that frigate belches," he snapped, then led his troop forward through the main longitudinal corridor to the officers' wardroom. A messenger brought in Viktor Belous.

Burkhart turned to Captain Belous. "Will that tramp fire on us?"

"The name? Do you know the name of the ship?" Belous pursed his lips and took a deep breath.

"Control, this is Burkhart. Has Mead ID'd that tin can, yet?"

"Yeah, Skipper," Brennen answered through the speaker. "It's a single-stack Riga class escort. Mead's pretty certain, from sound signature, that it's *Shakal*, the frigate we ran across on the way into the Dog Bowl."

"Thanks, Irish." He looked up. "What about it, Captain. Will *Shakal* fire on us."

"He'll shoot to kill and he knows his business. The 'he' is Valentin Markin, Captain Third Class."

"You hear something?" Levy's eyes darted to the door.

It came again. A soft series of knocks.

"Shit," Burkhart muttered. "Come!" he boomed.

A young Latino storekeeper stood in the open doorway. "Can I see the chief, sir?" His voice was barely audible.

"It'll have to wait, Lopez," Russotto called out, looking at Burkhart.

"Just take a sec, Chief."

"Get outta here, Lopez. You're in officer country."

Burkhart held up a hand, then nodded at Russotto.

"Make it fast, Lopez!" Russotto grunted.

Lopez toyed with his dark-blue baseball cap in his hand. "See, they won't let me start up my washer and dryer 'cause we're on the batteries, and the whole boat's screamin' at me for clean skivvies and socks, 'cause they all got jockrot from the damp." His face was deadpan.

Russotto looked at Burkhart again, then waved a beefy arm. "Get outta here, Lopez. Of all the times! I'll come aft and settle it when I'm done here."

The door closed again as Russotto started his apology. "Christ, sir." He held up a hand in surrender.

From somewhere Burkhart found the strength to laugh. "The question before us is jockrot and if we should drown with or without clean underwear."

Burkhart turned to Viktor Belous. "What about *Shakal*, Captain?"

"Captain Third Class Valentin Markin is her commanding officer. He is, ah, very loyal to his men and is exceptionally well liked. He's not an admiral's officer, he's a sailor's officer. His men come first. His fitness reports have been first rate."

"Does *Shakal* have ASROC?" Burkhart eyes grew wide.

"Nothing as sophisticated as rocket-boosted torpedos. She's old, but her teeth are sharp," he said grimly. "Believe me, Markin will kill us, if that is his order."

Burkhart threw his dead cigar butt across the compartment into a metal wastebasket. "Well, I'm the skipper and I'm out of answers. I'm sitting here on the bottom of the Bering Sea, without weapons." He looked around the table. "We might as well be on the moon without air."

Jake held up his hands. "My responsibility. The whole damn thing is my responsibility. Well, Admiral Langor is sitting with his friends in Norfolk, sipping his bourbon and branch water. He's got a goddamn sky spy the size of a Greyhound bus that's been tracking us since we left San Diego. Infrared high resolution cameras, thermal sensors, and God knows what else. Too damn bad it can't show him a picture of the fear in our eyes."

"Captain, it's Mead" came a metallic voice over the intercom.

"Yes, Mead."

"*Shakal* has increased her speed to flank, heading straight for us. She's going to make a run at us."

"Conn, this is Burkhart. Sound General Quarters. Close and dog all watertight doors. Rig ship for depth charge and heavy shocks. Take her down to twelve hundred feet. Rig ship for silent running. Right full rudder!"

"Aye aye, Skipper."

Russotto stood up stiffly, then almost fell down as *Skate* heeled sharply into a turn. "I'm not needed here, sir. I gotta protect my boat from those bastards." He looked up angrily and then before giving Burkhart a chance to answer, opened the door and disappeared.

"The rudder is hard right, Captain," a voice cut in over the intercom.

The sound of a chugging freight train brought every pair of eyes up to the overhead, as *Shakal*'s propellers brought her in for the attack.

* * *

343

"Plee! Plee!" Valentin Markin barked into the phone, from CIC to the hedgehog mount. Instantly he felt the jolt as the twenty-four bombs were fired skyward from the swivel spigot mortar tubes in an elliptical pattern, splashing heavily a hundred meters away from *Shakal.* The hydrostatic fuses that Markin had ordered exploded the warheads when the water pressure registered three hundred thirty-five meters, one hundred feet above the diving *Skate,* as she turned sharply away to her right, heading directly under *Shakal's* keel for protection.

Markin let out a barely audible sigh and looked over at his sonarman, who had removed his earphones when the hedgehogs exploded, but watched the scattering effect appear as circular snow on his scope. "The sub has turned ninety degrees and is heading under our keel."

"Smart move. That's what I'd do," Markin whispered aloud.

"How close did the hedgehogs come?" demanded Misha Lykov through the dim red glow of CIC.

"Very close," Markin said with disgust.

"What kind of damage?"

"The pressure vibrations and shock would break glass gauges, rupture pipes, tear coverings from the bulkhead walls. Who knows, maybe even tear eardrums," he said flatly.

"Would your mousetrap frighten them?" Lykov was smiling, with his tongue darting in and out, tasting the hostile air like a snake.

"You bastard!" Captain Valentin Markin stood up straight from the sonar dish and looked into Lykov's eyes in the dark. "It is the worst fear a submariner can ever have. A complete feeling of helplessness. Those men are Russians down there," he pleaded.

Lykov calmly pulled out his pipe again.

"You can't smoke in here with these electronics."

Just for a moment Lykov grew taut, then relaxed his aching body. It had been the longest day of his life, and it was finally drawing to a successful conclusion.

He smiled softly, looking down at the pipe. "Of course, Captain. I should have known."

Markin pivoted on his heels and started for the forward compartment hatch leading to the bridge.

"We still have business in here, Captain Markin!"

"I think we're done with this business of Russians firing on Russians."

"You're done when I tell you you're done." Lykov paused and scratched his hawked-shaped nose. "Now make ready to fire another salvo of hedgehogs."

"I thought you wanted to surface the sub, not kill her," Markin snapped, his voice filled with anger and frustration.

Misha Lykov popped the empty pipe bowl against the thick flat palm of his hand, then studied Markin's smooth open face.

"Fire another salvo of those fucking mousetrap mortars, or I promise I will cut your throat with my own blade in some dark alley within one week after we dock in Vladivostok!"

Lykov's body, despite his enormous strength, was giving way to extreme pain, and he could no longer tolerate Markin's nipping and chewing, regardless of the difficulties it might cause later aboard *Shakal*.

"I warn you that if you press the attack on the sub too closely, she will turn quickly on us and fire a spread of torpedoes." Lykov's physical presence and biting threat had at last taken its toll. The snap in Markin's protests had turned to harmless pawing.

Lykov slumped his shoulders and brought his menacing face, glistening from the warmth of the CIC and the flush of his head and facial wounds, down close to

345

Markin. In the red glow of the battle compartment, his eyes cast a strange amber glaze that forced Markin to hide within himself.

Lykov hesitated and smiled to himself. Jake would have been proud of the way he'd set the hook in this man's mouth.

"Fire that salvo of hedgehogs, then come about and make ready your stern depth charge rails for a final run. If they won't come to the surface now, we'll kill them."

48

Finally, the blood-curdling death song vibrations subsided from the thick steel hull, but the wild bucking motion continued twelve hundred feet below the surface of the Bering Sea. Jake thought she was shaking herself to pieces as he pulled himself off the cold linoleum deck. He held his breath, waiting for the groaning and squeaking pressure hull to give into the sea, relentlessly probing *Skate*'s skin for a weak spot.

At five hundred pounds of pressure per square inch, a pinhole leak in a weakened seam would rip the skin from a man's bones with the force of a lasar, while the screeching whistle would shred his eardrums into hanging flesh. An agonizing fear gripped his belly.

Finally, Niven opened his eyes, but the hard blackness had sucked out and killed the light. He pulled in to fill his lungs, but couldn't breathe. *Skate*'s air was filled with a thick choking dust from the chunks of cork insulation that had been ripped away from inside the pressure hull by the force of the exploding mortar bombs.

Then it was suddenly quiet. A quiet, free of shattering glass instruments, the shrill popping of delicate sonar tubes, and the sounds of shelving being ripped from bulkheads. All Niven could hear was the steady clicking of the fathometer, sounding the ocean floor. An instrument, trying to find *Skate* a place to die. The control room lights blinked on long enough for Jake to catch a quick strobe frame glance of Charley Burkhart's intense face, hanging over the periscope railing. Then the world went black again.

Another screeching electronic echo from *Shakal*'s sonar collided with *Skate*.

"Emergency lights, shift to the red," Burkhart called out calmly.

"Sonar, what's happening?" Burkhart leaned out over the railing and surveyed Spike Mead, squatting under the sonar dishes with a technician.

"The shock waves blew the tubes. I should have sonar active in another five minutes."

"Very well. When she's active give me a one-eighty sonar sweep off the bow. Just find me that Russian can before she tucks in her stern and makes another run."

"Aye, aye, sir," Mead called back with his head buried inside the sonar console.

Burkhart stepped off the stand and helped Niven the rest of the way up. *"Skate*'s no longer the oldest living virgin. She just got her first battle star." He stared into Jake's eyes, offset against the red glow. "You look awful."

He touched the side of Jake's head and he recoiled in pain. "Nasty cut."

Niven reached up with his fingers and felt the warm sticky blood already beginning to cake near his right temple.

A moment later, the control room was bathed in a conforting red glow, muting the destruction around them.

Burkhart picked up the station-to-station mike. "All

compartments report damage. Damage control parties stand by."

Niven tried to stand but stumbled back to the wildly gyrating deck.

"Trim this boat up, on the double, Russotto! Irish, you handle damage control."

Russotto's hands moved with quick assurance over the ballast control panel levers controlling *Skate*'s ballast, auxiliary, and trim tanks. Through it all, he somehow maintained his balance, flooding a bit in the forward tanks, deballasting midships and aft, then reversing the process. Slowly he fought *Skate* to a standstill as her motion calmed to a gentle rocking, then to a smooth and steady hum at six knots.

"Helm, do you have rudder control?"

"The helm is answering up properly, Captain," called back the diving officer.

"Very well, hold steady on the course."

"Aye, sir, the rudder is amidships and the course is steady on."

"The Germans had a great name for depth-charging. They called it *Blechkoller*. Sardine can neurosis. I'm beginning to understand the feeling, Jake."

Burkhart patiently scanned Niven's worn-out face, his eyes narrowing. "Ideas, Jakey? If something's cooking in that clever squash of yours, spit it out, because that freight train's comin' back in to finish what it started."

"Sonar any minute now, Captain," Mead called out.

Burkhart watched Jake's Adam's apple roll down in his throat like a rusty wheel.

"What's the matter? I thought you sat on the bottom of Vladivostok in *Drum* for a week a while back. No sweat. It all sounded pretty good in Langor's office."

349

He laughed nervously. "You're just as scared as the rest of us."

"You're right. It was nothing like this!"

"This is what they call a dirty groin shot." Burkhart looked up toward the main hatch in the control room.

"I'll think of something." The sweat and fear glistened on Niven's face in the compartment's red glow.

The pinging from Spike Mead's sonar station distracted them.

"Sonar active, Captain. *Shakal*'s increasing speed and has turned on a new heading that will take him back over us! Range to target is now eight zero zero yards and closing! She bears zero four zero degrees, true."

"Very well." Burkhart swallowed and could feel his heart pounding in his neck. He hadn't known this kind of fear in years. He looked over at Jake Niven.

"Well, Jake boy," he said softly. "Now what?"

Niven turned and surveyed the control room in the red dimness. It was a mess, littered with torn insulation, instruments hanging by broken metal straps, and shattered glass crunching beneath everyone's shoes. It looked like an artillery shell had exploded in *Skate*. He didn't know what to say to Burkhart.

"Skipper," called Brennen. "Got a report from the engine spaces that the last set of shocks cracked a hydraulic pressure fitting in the main jacking gear clutch. They all got sprayed with hot oil, and until it's repaired, we can't jack over the EPM'S to the main diesels."

"Effect repairs on the double."

"Aye, aye, Skipper."

"What's that?" Burkhart started.

"What?"

"That odor, Jake! Heavy acrid smell." Burkhart dove for the station-to-station mike. "Now hear this, this is the captain. We've got a fire somewhere on this

350

boat. Find it, dammit! Find it now!" Panic nibbled at his voice for the first time. Fire would be their certain death.

"Russotto, check the batteries on four deck for chlorine gas. Maybe an internal feedline or a sump pump let go in the bilges. There could be salt water in the cells mixing with sulfuric acid."

Russotto raced through the control room, heading below for the battery deck just above the keel, where the massive acid-lead storage batteries powering the electric motors were stored.

Niven swallowed. Every possible nightmare was coming alive. Chlorine gas, the greenish-yellow poison that burned and stripped the body's respiratory organs of their ability to hold oxygen, forcing death by choking and suffocation. The thought of not being able to draw that deep breath of air forced Jake's body to go limp and his throat to tighten into a hard fist.

The control room grew deathly quiet, except for the pinging of Spike Mead's sonar dish and the light, steady, clicking of the fathometer, waiting on Russotto's report.

"Captain," Russotto's voice blared over the intercom.

"Go ahead, Chief!"

"No battery fire. Repeat, the battery compartment is dry. The problem's on two deck, where a saltwater feedline parted and caused a short circuit in the main panel. I'll have it repaired, pronto, and full power restored."

Burkhart shook his head in relief. But he knew it was only momentary. Another run that close would kill *Skate*.

"Sir," Russotto's metallic voice called again. "We're gonna make it."

"You bet your ass we are," Burkhart said, then let go of the mike's speak button.

"I ought to wait until that can is over our heads, then breach *Skate* like a goddamn mine, right under their keel, and break their damn backs," he mumbled half aloud.

"What'd you say?"

Burkhart stared at Niven. "Ah, I said I'd breach her."

"Not that. Something about a mine?"

"So?"

"What about something like a mine that we could release with some kind of triggering device on it?"

Burkhart's eyes grew large. "Nice idea, Jake boy. But—"

"Sir." Russotto was back, out of breath. "All compartments are holding their own. We'll have our girl squared away in no time. Trouble with number-one chemical air scrubber, but it's under control. Mr. Levy's lending a fine hand with our problems."

"Chief," Niven asked quietly, "what about a mine of some sort that we could release through one of the escape trunks?"

"The action basket's empty," Burkhart interrupted. "The operational orders and your Admiral Brandon Langor saw to that. We don't have any live fish aboard to build a mine." He took a breath to push out the tension building in his throat and stomach.

"Not true, sir."

"What's not true?"

"About nothin' to build a mine with."

Burkhart and Niven stood frozen staring at Chief of the Boat Jerry Russotto.

"I'm listening," Burkhart said as a deep, churning rumble pierced the submarine.

"*Shakal*'s turning flank speed, range two hundred yards," Mead called out nervously.

Burkhart grabbed the ship mike. "All hands rig for depth charge! Rig for shock! That can is coming in to chew on our girl's ass, again!"

"Left full rudder. Steady up on one three one!" Burkhart barked out.

"Sir, the rudder is hard over" the pilot screamed back as *Shakal* rumbled overhead.

Valentin Markin huddled under his hooded blue parka against the steel bulwarks of the starboard wing of the bridge, easily leaning into the deep roll of the gray seas as *Shakal* completed a one hundred-eighty-degree turn, heading back toward the trapped submarine.

The bridge wing had always been a special place for Markin. A place of peace and solitude. A place to think through important decisions. Now, that comfort was contaminated. Even the intermittent fog couldn't blunt his raw edge of self-disgust, as *Shakal*'s engines vibrated the plates beneath his sea boots. He just couldn't bring himself to disobey Colonel Lykov's orders. His career had come close to ruin once before, and as luck would have it, he was butting heads again with Military Intelligence. He hated his own self-serving weakness. Whatever crimes had really been committed aboard that submarine didn't matter. He was caught again, just like in the Gulf of Riga.

"You have done well, Captain Markin." A large hand slapped the back of his parka. Markin turned to Misha Lykov towering over him, his raw, bitten face a vile imitation of humanity.

"No, you have done well, *Palko'vneek.*" Markin appraised Lykov with a sullen glare. "You have exploited my weakness. I have allowed myself to become your personal weapon."

"Don't be so hard on yourself." Lykov smiled. "When this business is completed we just might see that you are returned from exile to a sea command in the Baltic or Black Sea."

Markin squinted. "I've waited years to hear those words, but the fucking price you charge is too high. Killing Russians."

'It will be over soon."

"When the second series of hedgehogs splashed into the sea in that forty-five-meter ellipse, I tried to imagine the panic on that submarine."

"But the hedgehogs missed by a decent margin."

"There is no decent margin, you idiot!" Markin turned his back to Lykov. "With hydrostatic charges, those pressure waves can hammer them to death turning the inside of the boat to pulp."

"I have taken full responsibility."

"As captain of this vessel I am responsible for whatever happens. The why of it is always unimportant."

"Then do as you were ordered," Lykov snapped.

"I always carry out my orders, but first let me tell you something, *Palko'vneek*. I've been burned before, remember? I've dealt with your kind. You are beyond insult, stuffed with an overinflated ego, just waiting for the chance to kill or bully. Even your stinking breath bristles with self-importance."

Markin stiffened his back. "I am not at war against anyone, especially against Russians. Killing is killing. It's not some sport practiced for the exclusive amusement of the Party, the Admirality, or those Kremlin fat men hiding comfortably behind Borovitsky Gate. I'll drop depth charges on those poor devils inside that steel coffin, but first, you get off my bridge! Your fucking presence offends me!"

Lykov started for Mark's throat but caught himself at the last second and translated his movements and energy into a cruel smile.

"You have thrown away your last ticket out of this ocean exile. Your type belongs in the provinces. Just don't fuck me, and do as ordered, or you won't even have this." Lykov swept his arm about the old rust-stained steel superstructure.

Markin reached over and pushed the intercom button. "Ring up maximum turns and make ready the stern depth charge rails. *Palko'vneek* Lykov is laying aft to observe the run."

Lykov grunted and turned to step out of the cold. "You might win after all, Captain."

"I lose no matter what the outcome." Markin turned his back to watch *Shakal*'s bow dig into a moderate sea, pushed along by her pounding engines, straining to put out maximum power.

49

"The reactor tunnel is a cluttered mess, but the lead shielding and core vessel are still holding. There's no radiation leakage." Chief Russotto, his face grimy and filled with uncertainty, looked up pleadingly at Burkhart on the stand.

"She can't take no more! It's that simple. That last series came too damn close. The next series will peel her skin."

Burkhart shoved a fresh cigar into his mouth, tasting the cheap, dry tobacco on the back of his tongue. He stared darkly past Russotto and Jake Niven.

"All right, do it! It's a long shot, but go for it. Just do it fast! We're out of time!" Charley Burkhart swept his eyes down across their faces, his sweat-stained khaki shirt offset against the gold dolphins pinned above his left pocket.

"It'll work. They're not expecting it, and for some reason, when *Shakal* makes her run on us, she proceeds at least a thousand yards before turning back on us. She's done it twice. I can fit into that seam."

Burkhart leaned over the stand, gripped Jake's shoulder and spoke in a whisper. "You have to know that if this fails, I'm committed to—'' His voice trailed away as he drew on the glow of the cigar.

"I won't surrender my boat or crew, and I have nothing left to fight with. I won't go home in disgrace, with *Skate* a Russian monument. That's the straight shit, Jake. Chrissakes, we won't even be a SUBMISS, because we don't even exist. Remember, we've been cut out of the loop. I'm afraid even the gulls won't get a chance to pick our bones white. We'll just be a little waterbug that goes pop in the deep ocean."

From the glare in Burkhart's eyes and the set of his jaw, Jake knew he had carefully thought it through, and would take *Skate* down a last time.

"I'll put Mead's plotting of *Shakal* on the intercom, so your work party can gauge your time against their next approach." He puffed again on the cigar, but it had died.

Silently, Jake turned and examined the bulging white canvas bag sitting benignly in a crowded corner of the control room, lashed securely with thick nylon line to deck cleets.

"I'm wasting time!" Niven snapped.

Burkhart relit the cold cigar, careful to keep the flame from the zippo away from the ash tip.

"How long will it take—'' The distant strains of a bagpipe interrupted him. "What the hell—?"

"It's Winebelly," Russotto mumbled, "playing 'Scotland The Brave,' over and over."

"For Chrissakes, Chief! We're a Fleet Attack Boat at battle stations!" Then Burkhart thought it over, softening.

"That last series made a shambles of his galley and scullery. The coffee urns fell over and spilled. Everything's broken up. The enlisted mess looks like a junkyard. Broken dishes everywhere. Even the dining tables were torn from their mounts. When I came through on my way from the engine room, Winebelly was blowin' that Scot tune on his bagpipes like a crazy man, marching back and forth in the mess, looking like a certified crazy with his baker's apron and hat on. He was threatening everyone who came through that he's going to serve the Russian to the crew for chow unless we get *Skate* away from the Soviet can.''

''Winebelly always did have spirit, but he's gonna have to wait on this one. We need that Russian's body intact if we have a chance of getting out of here alive.'' Burkhart drew on the cigar again. It was as close as he would come to feeling an inner hope.

''I knew the world went to hell when they stopped saying mass in Latin,'' he said as an afterthought.

Niven again touched the clotted gash on the side of his head and winced. ''Levy's coming forward to help out.''

''How long will it take?''

''Don't know, Charley. The *Bear Pit* boys, in torpedo, have already rigged and set a hatch tackle purchase for hoisting.''

Burkhart groaned.

''Don't worry, we won't blow *Skate* apart.''

''It really doesn't matter if this doesn't work. Let me know when you need the lifting bags and the Russian.'' Burkhart looked at his watch. ''Do it fast or it won't matter one tinker's damn!'' He gripped Niven's wrist tightly. ''If you don't think it'll work, get on the horn to me and I'll prepare the crew. Each man has a right to a few minutes to make his peace, before we head down.''

Niven stooped his head through the hatch into the forward torpedo room. Three *Bear Pit* crewmen were laboring over a chest-high, eleven-and-a-half-foot olive-green torpedo resting on a steel skid with the bright yellow stenciling, MARK 37 MOD O. The entire affair was supported by thick steel winch chains. A torpedoman had pulled the working hatch on the afterbody of the torpedo.

"She's ready to start on, Chief." The short, beefy *Bear Pit* chief smiled at him with tobacco-stained teeth, then handed Russotto a small carton. "I was just checkin' it out to see if we might jury-rig some sort of system to launch this baby at that son of a bitch."

Russotto nodded and peered into the opening. "It's hopeless. We scavenged the Otto motor, starting gear, and every damn part that we could use to repair other torpedoes during the past year. Thank God I forgot to ship this warshot back to ordinance. The captain chewed my ass royally on that one."

"Well, we got plenty of exploders in the locker," the chief offered, pointing to the box he had handed to Russotto.

Niven squeezed past the men and looked about the compartment butted with six large round stainless steel torpedo tube breech doors surrounded with brass and bronze fittings in two columns of three. The compartment was cluttered with sleeping racks above the torpedo skids.

"Mr. Niven?"

"Yeah, Chief."

"I'd like to rearm the warhead before we disassemble it from the afterbody and tail section."

He nodded. "Chief, I've never worked with Torpex. Do you think the warhead is powerful enough without having forward velocity."

"Christ, Mr. Niven, we're talkin' about three hundred thirty pounds of high explosive TNT mixed with metallic flakes. He turned to meet Jake's eyes. "If you can get this baby close enough to *Shakal* with the proximity exploder, it'll bust her guts apart, once inside her magnetic field."

"Yeah, if."

Akivor Levy entered the compartment, wearing his greasy overalls. All that was missing was his UZI. 'You're really going through with it?'' An astonished expression swept his face.

"Seems so, Akivor. There's nothing else."

"You crazy bastard, you're as good as dead."

Jake rubbed his face, which was burning with exhaustion. "It beats the alternative."

Levy grunted. "Let's get to it."

Carefully, Russotto loosened four stainless steel screws inside a tiny compartment, holding down a metal cover plate just above the nose of the warhead. "I've done this a thousand times before I became a chief, so why the hell are my hands shaking?"

Slowly his hands found the four bolts holding the sonar exploder in place. After a series of twisting contortions, he slid in a three-eighths-inch socket wrench and removed each bolt with the ominous clicking sound of the wrench.

When certain the exploder was free of its mount and each of three electric connections severed, he delicately removed the device from the warhead.

Levy leaned over Russotto's shoulder and peered into the cavity of the long, thin torpedo. "How the hell is he going to arm the exploder? If you can't do it, the warhead will never explode. It looks damn complex. Damn impossible."

"They said the same thing about those Russian diesels until you put them back together."

Levy moved his mouth into something imitating a smile. "So? How are we going to part the Red Sea?"

"After the propeller vane has been set, based on range and speed, it spins the programmed number of turns and stops, triggering a spring-loaded striker plug. It's really a primitive but effective arming device."

"How strong is that spring?"

"If you can apply ten pounds of pressure, the spring will snap, triggering the exploder." Russotto wiped his dirty face.

"When the warhead is within ten feet of a magnetic field large enough to surround a ship hull, a current is automatically produced that fires the detonator."

Niven looked into Russotto's eyes visualizing what he would have to do as another electronic echo from *Shakal* slammed into *Skate*.

"Prepare for shocks," the speaker announced. Dimly at first, then with high definition, the pounding engines of *Shakal* drew over their heads, ready to swallow them.

"Rig for shock. Rig for large angles. Rig for depth charges." Burkhart's emotions were squashed by the small metallic box, but not enough to disguise what he was feeling. He was trying to coax something from them that had been eaten away by the two previous attacks.

"Get the hell away from our boat!" Niven closed his eyes.

"Not much chance of that happening" came a dark whisper.

Jake turned as Burkhart stepped through the small hatch into the torpedo room. "I wanted to see what was going on. The suspense was killing me." Burkhart wasn't smiling.

The intercom squawked again. "*Shakal*'s starting her run. Two heavy splashes. She's just released two depth charges."

Niven felt his body tense as he dug his fingers into the steel frame of the torpedo skid, waiting for the first depth charge to reach *Skate*.

"Rig that torpedo tight, dammit!" Burkhart hissed.

"I don't want that thirteen-hundred-pound bastard falling on us."

"It's covered, Skipper," Russotto called softly. "The fish is lashed tight as a drum to the skid—"

A horrid scrapping steel sound clawed through the hull like a steel ball bouncing slowly off *Skate*'s skin.

"My God. The depth charge is right on us, just forward of the sail!" Russotto choked. "Listen. It's scraping the hull."

Misha Lykov slammed the bridge hatch as *Shakal* dipped into a sea, rose with a shudder bringing her screws out of the water, then dropped back as her keel settled, waiting to attack the next sea.

Slowly he turned, taking in the flat, wide bridge, until he found Kapitan Markin leaning over the gyrocompass.

"A perfect run. Perfect." Although tired of fighting the pain in his body and throbbing head, Misha Lykov was pleased as he approached Valentin Markin. "Your crew is well trained in antisubmarine warfare drills, despite the antiques *Shakal* has to fight with."

"What measure of moral man are you, *Palko'vneek?*" His voice and eyes clouded with fear.

'There is no place in this ocean for morality," Lykov snapped. "Its time has long since passed."

"I sure as hell can't argue that. But those are Russian seamen down there. What you have ordered me to do is inhuman."

"Those Russian seamen, as you call them, have kidnapped Captain Belous of *Minsk*. They are not Soviet citizens, they are outlaws."

Markin raised a hand. "Spare me the bullshit."

"I will do my job."

"Torture?"

"Mental torture, if you will allow it. That will accomplish my goal of raising that submarine intact."

"One of those depth charges actually scraped the hull of three three one, *Palko'vneek*. Do you understand the pressure cooker of fear, waiting for one of those charges to explode, squashing them two hundred ninety meters beneath the surface?"

"Of course I do." Lykov evened his voice. It was so matter-of-fact, Markin couldn't help shivering inside. "I never had any intention of setting the depth fuses. Fear is the most powerful siege weapon ever invented. Once you learn to roll the fear between your fingers and shape it like dough, it is easy. Now it's time to use your underwater telephone."

Markin shook his head in disgust, but somewhere inside he admired Lykov's animal cunning.

"What is the range of the phone?"

"We're within range," he said sarcastically. *"Shakal* is sitting right on top of those poor bastards." Markin picked up the engine-room phone. "Engineering, Bridge. Reduce revs to one-quarter ahead on both starboard and port engines." He looked over at the coxswain balancing the ship's chrome wheel in his hands.

"Helm, hold the course."

"Aye, sir," replied the young seaman. "The course is steady on one eighth two and the rudder is amidships."

Lykov stood impatiently in the companionway. "If I fail to make effective contact, then it will be your job to kill them on the next run, Captain Markin."

50

After a number of adjustments, the lifting tackle worked smoothly, and suddenly the blunt-shaped torpedo warhead was airborne and secured to the top of the overhead at the escape hatch. Enough room had been left for Niven to squeeze past on the escape ladder.

Niven watched carefully as the live warshot strained against its holding lines, swaying to the motion of *Skate*. Thick, waterproof grease filled the cavity at the tip of the bomb, where the little propeller had been removed.

"Will it hold?" Russotto wouldn't take his eyes from the warhead.

"Who the hell knows?" Burkhart shrugged.

"The sheave blocks and tripod are ready when you need them, sir."

"Very well, Chief."

A calloused silence overtook *Skate*'s men. Burkhart has never seen anything like it. Their fear had hardened into a primordial anger, set against the muted strains of Winebelly's bagpipes echoing throughout the boat. Suddenly they were no longer frightened. *Shakal* hadn't broken them.

"The bastard's good. Real good," Burkhart muttered, chewing on a cigar butt in the torpedo room.

"Who's that?"

"That Russian frigate captain, Jake boy. He could have blown us apart on three separate runs. But Sweet Jesus! To dump three ash cans and have one of them scrape our hull. That's damn good shooting in any league. I thought it was impossible."

Burkhart wrinkled his forehead and looked up at the explosive warhead hanging precariously beneath the hatch. "Christ, how the hell are you gonna arm that monster in six-foot seas?"

Niven solumnly held up a large screwdriver. "A very sophisticated weapons system. The warhead will be lashed underneath the three large flotation bags. When I'm in position I'll reach under and plunge the screwdriver into the nose of the warhead with enough force to arm it."

"How will you get that rig out away from *Skate?*"

"I'll use one of the rubber rafts and tow it out with a paddle."

"In those cold seas, trying to maneuver your raft? Pull your thumb out!"

"The warhead will act as a keel for the flotation bags," Niven countered.

"You still need help."

"You're right, Captain," offered Akivor Levy. "I volunteer to paddle and look after this crazy bastard."

For a long minute Niven looked at Levy, thinking about it."

"You want it to work?" Burkhart rubbed his mouth.

"All right, Levy, it's your funeral."

"I want to see home. To touch Moshav." He smiled. "Farm soil. Now, what about that Russian seaman's body. Has he been dressed yet?"

"Yeah," Niven said.

"What about Belous's clothing and the canvas ring switch bag?"

"Belous's uniform is stuffed full of rags and towels, and the ring switch has already been removed from the control room."

"The perfect package," Burkhart quipped. "All we have to do now is get *Shakal* to cooperate and—"

"Forward torpedo, control."

Jake twisted and stared at the metal speaker.

Burkhart reached over and flipped down the lever. "This is Burkhart. What's up, Irish?"

"You and Niven better get your tails back here right away. You've got a long distance call."

Misha Lykov gripped the underwater telephone closer to his mouth. He could taste the triumph.

"You don't have any choice, Niven. It's over! Do you hear me, you prick, it's over!" Lykov calmed his shouting as he stared about the empty radio compartment. Why was he still resisting? Even through the washing static of a thousand feet of ocean, he could tell Niven was scared. Scared and outfoxed. Yet Niven couldn't handle the failure of his beloved HAWK-SCREECH.

"Jacob." Lykov warmed his voice and only hoped it would carry down to *Skate*. "You know what I must have. I don't want to sink *Skate* and kill all those innocent men." Lykov paused. "What happened aboard *Minsk* is finished. Once we're back in Moscow, we'll strike an arrangement."

"Some arrangement. Just like you made arrangements for Lionel Crabb?"

"Our many years of friendship haven't been wasted," Lykov went on. "We'll help each other. I can't come in without you and that damn ring switch.

366

You know the rules of the game. *Quid pro quo*. Langley and Moscow Ring Road are the same. What happened with you and my father is past. Do you hear me!''

There was a long pause of gurgling, hissing static, then Niven came back on the line.

"How can I trust a fucking scumbag like you? I can't risk *Skate* or her crew."

"Bastard! You don't have any choice. It's tap city." The throbbing inside Lykov's skull was growing unbearable. "All right, all right, Jake." Desperation was growing in his voice.

"I can't accept a thousand yards off. Here's my last offer. If you refuse, we both die. *Shakal* will stand off five hundred yards from *Skate* after you surface. That's close enough to visually observe the raft holding you, Belous, and the ring switch. Then your *Skate* can dive out of danger. That's it, Jake. Your life and Belous's, and the ring switch for the lives of *Skate* and her crew."

51

"I told you to kill him, Jake. A pig's a pig." Levy balled his thick hands into fists.

'I thought you killed the bastard?'' Burkhart threw the wet tattered cigar butt across the radio compartment. It hit the light-green steel bulkhead with a splat of dripping brown tobacco juice. "At least that explains why the hell we were bushwacked."

"He was bleeding to death when we left the weapons hangar bay on *Minsk*. I swear I felt his skull give and shatter in my hands."

"Well, I guess the bastard climbed off his deathbed to crap all over us." Burkhart eyed Niven with a cold stare, started to let his fury build, then checked himself.

Sorrell and I had been together for so long. I just couldn't—"

"No matter." Burkhart rubbed the back of his bright pink neck, calming himself. Venting on Niven wouldn't get his boat to a safe harbor.

"It works out." Jake stood up. "I'll give him just what he wants," he said coldly. He turned and swept his eyes over the group. "Three hundred pounds worth. His ego's going to kill him like it did his father. It was their greatest weakness. My plan hasn't changed."

* * *

Easy now, easy, watch your angle," called out the diving officer to the helm. "Periscope depth, Captain. Two hundred feet," he shouted over the sound of gushing air tanks.

"Up scope!" barked Chief of the Watch, Russotto.

Burkhart, on his knees, grabbed and flopped down the steel training handles just as the small attack periscope barrel cleared its well. A tiny trickle of saltwater leaking from a packing gland rolled down the barrel in front of Burkhart's face. Slowly he spun around and rose as the greased barrel extended fully and then locked into position. Irish Brennen stood behind him, checking the bearing markers as Burkhart swiveled the scope. Viktor Belous, invited into the control room, quietly watched the ritual.

"There she is," Burkhart mumbled. Single stack, raked bow, no ASROC Deck. Two bow turrets. Confirm it's a Riga Class, all right." He flipped up the right handle to increase magnification.

"Range, seven zero zero yards and closing. Bering, mark!"

"One eight two degrees," Brennen called out.

"Seas five to six feet, intermittent fog and low clouds." Burkhart swept the scope around, making another full bearing sweep and search. "Surface is clear except for *Shakal*. Down scope!

Burkhart picked up the ship mike and depressed the speak button. "Now hear this, this is Burkhart. We'll be on the surface momentarily. You've all done a hella'va job. I'm gonna keep *Skate* on electric propulsion, so there won't be much propeller wash across the rudder or steerage in the currents. It'll get pretty rough until we dive again. Nothing to worry about. The deck party is making ready in the forward torpedo room. Everyone just hang tough."

369

The surging currents and waves took hold of *Skate* as she neared the surface.

"The sail has broken the surface, Captain," called the diving officer. A moment later, "Decks are awash. The bubble is neutral."

"Very well, give me five feet of freeboard. Let's make it as easy as we can on the deck party hauling out that three-hundred-pound firecracker."

Every eye in the control room locked on Burkhart.

"Aye, sir. Pump her up slowly. Two feet. Three feet. Four feet. Five feet and holding. Captain, you have five feet of freeboard."

A deep sea sent *Skate* rolling on her beam, forcing everyone to hang on for dear life.

"Irish, go forward and do what you can to help out Niven's deck party. The thought of that warshot swinging from the overhead of the torpedo room makes me shudder. I'll take the Conn up in the cockpit." Burkhart turned and picked his blue Soviet parka off the chrome railing.

"Just one more time," he mumbled. He looked up. "Russotto, crack the hatch. Officer of the Dive, stand by to pull the plug and blow down. Rig for deep submergence. Helm, swing your bows to zero zero five degrees and hold that heading. I want to shield the forward escape hatch from *Shakal*'s bridge until Niven's in the water and underway."

Jake Niven took a deep breath, clipped his safety harness to the deck track, and inspected the boat. Surfaced, *Skate* showed her scars. Forward, he could see a large crease in main ballast tank number one. The hedgehog attacks had ripped away huge chunks of paint from the lethal slapping of water pressure against the hull. Large, irregularly shaped patches of gray primer paint lay exposed.

"Jesus," he muttered. Carefully, Niven turned his

attention to the waves rolling under *Skate*. The gray seas swelled almost up to her deck, so launching the flotation rig and survival raft would be possible.

"The old girl really held together," Brennen remarked grimly as he turned back to supervise the raising and assembly of the tripod lifting tackle, consisting of three large blocks. It would be used to winch up the warshot from inside *Skate*. A quick thinking member of the *Bear Pit* crew brought up a large tarp that he and another crewman held to shield the equipment as it came up. The bizarre scene was reminiscent of a Manhattan sewer crew in midday rush. Three orange flotation bags, each with a lift capacity of three hundred pounds, were brought up and quickly inflated.

"Five minutes, dammit! Now move your lazy deck-abe asses," Brennen yelled as the flotation bags were lashed together.

Jake worked quickly, securing the body of Petr Deriabin in a small valley created at the base where the bags were joined. Next, David Lathrick was secured to the bags. Gently, Jake touched his forehead. It was cold, lifeless stone.

Carefully, the torpedo room crew manhandled the warshot and shackled it to the underside of the flotation bags with a webbing of cable and thick hemp.

"Okay, Mr. Niven, you're up one more time."

"Thanks, Chief." Niven made his way to the base of the sail and peered cautiously toward the stern of *Skate*. Off in the mist, *Shakal* was holding position at five hundred yards.

"Let's go," he yelled to the deck party.

With the help of guide ropes, the survival raft slid down *Skate*'s canted steel hull into the churning water, then Niven and Akivor Levy jumped in. The flotation rig slid over the side, pulling the warhead with it. Instantly they were bobbing like small corks as Niven secured a tow line from the ark to his raft.

Levy's powerful strokes pulled them away from *Skate*. A deep trough pulled them down and he lost sight of the submarine completely. A moment later, the raft and flotation ark slid up the back of the next comber and Niven caught a glimpse of Burkhart studying them through binoculars.

"How much farther, Levy?"

"We're out about forty yards. Let's give it another ten yards for insurance. Let's not blow up *Skate*. That should do it, Jake."

Niven shifted his weight in the raft and pulled the ark toward him.

"Try to be casual, *Shakal*'s watching."

Ignoring the comment, Niven waited until the dead ark bumped their raft. He stared for a moment at the dead actors sitting atop the flotation bags in silent comedy. Carefully, Niven found the all important guide line and pulled with all his strength until the warhead was maneuvered close to him. He pulled his hands from the water and they were already beginning to turn blue from the icy water. Crouching over the top of his raft, Niven gripped the screw driver.

"Hurry up, dammit! *Shakal*'s making smoke!"

Niven popped his head up. Damn Lykov! *Shakal* was beginning to move towards them.

"I can't pop the screwdriver in with enough force to trigger it! I've got to go in!"

"That water's twenty-five degrees! You won't last more than a minute!"

"No time. No time left. I've got to make it work!" Then he was gone over the side of the raft, making certain his left hand was secured under the guide line surrounding their rubber boat. The foaming seawater was a thousand knives stabbing at his body as the little train skied

372

up the back of another wave. He opened his mouth, sucked in a breath of air, and dunked his head under.

Levy dropped his paddle and swung the UZI off his back, moving to the rear of the raft, waiting for Jake to raise his head. Out of the corner of his eye he saw *Shakal* looming larger on the horizon.

Just as Levy pulled himself half over the side, Jake's head bobbed to the surface. It was bluish-purple and his eyes cast a dim, vacant stare. With a grasping hand, Levy seized ahold of Jake by the back of his wet suit and muscled him into the raft. He hadn't been in the water more than fifty seconds yet he was powerless to move because of the intense cold. Levy found the screwdriver balled tightly in his right fist.

"Did you arm it?"

Niven didn't answer.

"Jake!" Levy raised a hand and slapped the side of his face with a sharp crack. "Did you arm it?" he repeated.

Jake weakly nodded his head. "Cut the rig loose," he whispered painfully.

Levy untied the knot holding the tow line and gently pushed it away. Then he looked into the water. The warhead was impossible to detect from the surface. It was acting as a perfect keel in the rough seas.

Levy resumed his kneeling position, paddling from side to side back toward *Skate*, watching as *Shakal* approached to within two hundred fifty yards. Levy, paddling like a man possessed, finally turned back. Jake was lying motionless, his skin a deep-tinted blue. He was losing what little body heat he had left. Yard by yard, *Skate* grew larger, and when Levy felt he couldn't paddle another foot, they were alongside the bow. Seeing their dilemma, Irish Brennen tossed Levy a line while the deck party prepared to bring the raft back aboard.

"Don't fuck with the raft, just get them on deck. We're out of time." One burly torpedoman careened headlong down the side of the canted ballast tank, lost his balance, and almost capsized the small raft as he landed on Levy. He righted himself, stood precariously in the raft, and lifted Jake in both arms. Timing his move perfectly, he waited for the sea to swell, pushing them almost up to deck level where another crewman firmly grabbed the torpedoman and pulled him to the deck. Levy jumped from the raft to *Skate*, turned, slid the UZI machine pistol to his belly, flipped off the safety and opened fire, spraying the raft until it was an airless, yellow rag.

"What the hell was that?" yelled Brennen.

Levy turned and his stomach dropped. Water spouts of white were moving cross the sea in an even track approaching *Skate*.

"Gunfire!" Levy jumped.

Brennen turned and waved the deck party below, looked up at Burkhart, who had already hit the diving alarm, fiercely waving Brennen down the forward escape trunk. At the same time he pointed to the approaching *Shakal*.

AH-OO-GAH AH-OO-GAH. AH-OO-GAH AH-OO-GAH.

The klaxon shrieked through the boat as Brennen pushed Levy down through the forward hatch. For an instant Brennen hesitated and turned his face to the sound of a thumping staccato of cannon fire walking across the steel deck that sent ricocheting fragments in every direction. Levy looked up through the hatch just in time to see a twenty-five milimeter cannon shell explode at the base of Irish Brennen's neck with a sickening pop. One moment he was shepherding his deck party to safety, the next moment he was a headless torso, spraying brain tissues and bone fragments about the deck.

52

"It's time, Markin. My bargain with the submarine commander is that when the raft hits the water, we move. Proceed ahead DEAD SLOW," Lykov ordered, letting the binoculars drop to his chest. Even the pressure of the glasses dangling from his neck caused his head to throb unbearably. He had never known such pain. But it would all be over soon and he could rest.

Markin continued to examine the submarine rolling on the gray horizon through the rectangular bridge windows, all the while ignoring Lykov's demand. His eyes slowly followed the long wiper blades as they cleared their arc.

"Captain?"

Markin pushed out a breath and lowered his glasses.

"I see someone sitting atop those lifting bags, dressed in Captain Belous's uniform. Is it really him?" Markin bit his lower lip, turning the doubts over in his mind. His gut instinct was pushing at him, but the feeling was vague and indefinable.

"Fuck your face, Markin! Who the hell do you think it is?"

Markin shrugged. "Who's the other officer atop the raft?"

"The sub's Number One. It's part of my bargain." He turned again and decided it was time to feed Markin another small crumb. "We always win. That officer is another form of insurance that they, in fact, will return to Vladivostok."

Markin shot him a dark look. "I believe it. We all believe it. Every damn Russian *muzhik* believes it."

"Don't be so negative, Markin. I already said that you will be transferred to a new command for the assistance you have rendered. A recommendation for The Order of Lenin can't hurt your cause to escape this life."

Markin looked into his eyes and examined Lykov's ugliness. God, he wanted to believe him. Maybe this human leech, this eater of men's dignity, offering up state decorations and hope, might be his savior after all. He needed desperately to believe it. That's why he hesitated to mention how strange the F class submarine appeared. Her snorkel mast didn't look right. Possibly it had something to do with the nuclear powerplant that had been experimentally installed. He had participated with F-Boats, in antisubmarine warfare exercises for years in the Pacific and Baltic, and he had never seen one as squat or beamy. Even her overall length—

"Did you hear me, Markin?"

"What?"

"Yes, I know you were thinking about your recall." The pressure in Lykov's head wouldn't allow him to smile. Everything hurt. Every move now forced a strange new economy on him.

"I want you to remain at action stations to make the proper impression on the crew of that sub."

Markin turned and narrowed his eyes. "I don't see what—"

"You will," Lykov muttered, opening the door to the starboard bridge wing, allowing a blast of cold, moist air to swallow *Shakal*'s inner sanctum as he stepped out and leaned over the rusted bulwarks.

A moment later he returned, and for the first time, Markin could see an angry smudge of bright red pushing its way through Misha Lykov's head bandage.

"Chief engineer, bridge. Make revolutions for DEAD SLOW AHEAD. Prepare to answer bells ASTERN."

Markin pushed another button on his intercom system and spoke into the phone. 'Now hear this. Boat Crew B, stand by your boat station. Prepare to launch and retrieve a raft and men in the water from that submarine."

Lykov placed a large hand on his shoulder. "First bring the raft alongside for examination before you make any attempt to recover it. If they are playing games, I want to be ready to go after the sub again without having to worry about bringing a launch back aboard."

"Belay that order, Boat Crew B. Starboard Deck party, prepare to bring the raft alongside with boat hooks."

"What about that *Degtyarev* single mount, in the gun tub below the starboard bridge?"

"What the hell do you want with that twenty-five millimeter cannon?"

Lykov ignored the question. "Ammunition?"

"It's manned and ready. Remember, we're still at action stations."

Lykov pointed a finger at Markin. "You just bring that raft alongside. I'll do the rest." Then he disappeared through the starboard hatch door.

Lykov moved unsteadily down the steep bucking ladder through the steel bridge works, making his way to the gun tub just beneath and forward of the bridge. The light, single-mounted twenty-five millimeter cannon was a throwback to the unsophisticated needs of the 1950's.

To the surprise of the two-man crew, Lykov climbed into the gun tub and motioned the battle-helmeted gunner out. Bracing his shoulders into the padded, curbed steel grips and strapping his waist into the harness, he painfully raised the cannon with his body until its long barrel was depressed below the horizon. It had been years since he's fired a Degtyarev, but it was something one didn't forget.

Carefully he checked the two large revolving magazines that fed shells alternatively to a swinging tray. Both drums were fully loaded.

Lykov pressed his face into the reflector sight and swung the gun on its ball joint to his left, near *Shakal*'s starboard bow. He reached down for the trigger handle grip with his right hand and found *Skate* growing in his gunsight. He blinked and everything went fuzzy. Misha Lykov squashed his eyes shut and opened them again, to find his vision restored. Quickly he flipped on the electric gun switch and squeezed the trigger bar.

THUMP THUMP THUMP THUMP.

The Degtyarev's recoil and vibration dug savagely into Lykov's wounded body with the torque of a slow motion jackhammer, as he walked the exploding cannon shells, mixed with occasional red tracers, across two hundred yards of ocean onto *Skate*'s deck, forward of her sail. He laughed to relieve the awful pressure in his head and watched the small figures scrambling desperately for cover as the shells fragmented against *Skate*'s steel hull. Ever so slightly he elevated the gun and watched a round explode in a man's face as he continued to squeeze the trigger. That would slow the bastards down. Fuck Burkhart, he screamed inside his head. That would keep them from springing one of Niven's clever traps. For an instant he raised the gun-sight to the figure riding atop the sail cockpit. He knew it had to be Burkhart. Then he was gone. Dammit! He'd waited too long. What the hell was wrong with him? His reflexes seemed to slow as he watched *Skate* begin to flood down, no more than one hundred fifty yards from his gun.

Suddenly his head felt as heavy as a wrecking ball as he slumped forward. He dimly felt a pair of hands sit him up. His vision blurred, then cleared again as he cast his eyes down to the water. *Shakal* had thrust her screws into reverse to stop her forward momentum, in preparation for bringing the raft alongside. Something disturbed Lykov as he watched *Skate* disappear beneath the waves. He glanced over at the young loader inside his gun tub and shook his head.

Again he looked dimly from the mount to the water as the raft drew closer. He cocked his head and his eyes again lost their focus. Cursing, he squeezed them shut, reopened them into a clear field of vision. The raft was sliding on the backs of waves to them and was very close to the bow. Markin's plan was to let the raft slide down the hull in *Shakal*'s wash, where a deck party would halt its progress at the quarterback.

For a moment he took inventory and studied the men sitting atop the flotation rig. The white canvas bag was there, and so was Jake. Jake! He screamed to himself. The echo reverberated against the inside of his damaged skull. Petr Deriabin! His eyes flashed to the other figure dressed in Viktor Belous's uniform. It was even more lifeless than Deriabin. Helplessly Misha Lykov could feel his stomach sink. He rose in half step from the gun tub, his mind in a white hot frenzy. He didn't want to believe it. It couldn't be! He'd never felt such panic.

"Bastards!" he screamed in English, then raised his eyes to the bridge to scream for Markin, but it was too late. A bright orange flash caught his eye and snapped his head as he turned toward it. The young loader gasped in disbelief, and all Misha Lykov could think about in that moment was his father, screaming in pain across the Gulf of Finland.

Two sharp echoing blasts quickly followed, but strangely, Lykov never heard a sound as he felt a hot concussion wave seize hold of his body and thrust him into space from the gun tub. He didn't feel any warmth, or the chill of the summer arctic air. The last thing he was conscious of was tasting saltwater and a sting over his entire body, but his head was at last free of that awful pressure.

For the remaining few minutes of his life, bobbing in the five-foot seas, where the first explosion had carelessly tossed him as a piece of useless wreckage, Misha Lykov watched *Shakal* break in two, swallowing herself in sheets of orange flame, black smoke, and exploding ordnance. It was such an unbelievable dream that it left no room within him for anger or hate, or even Jake Niven, who had killed him, just as he had killed his father.

Conscious, but now fully paralyzed from the effects of hypothermia, Misha Lykov rode atop the crest of a wave and watched curiously as *Skate* once again broke the surface, fifty yards from him. She appeared as ghostlike as a piece of sky and wind. A moment later, the Soviet battle ensign was struck and a broom was lashed to the sail staff as the ancient submarine symbol of a successful mission. Misha Lykov's eyes lost their focus and the light for the last time, as the faint sounds of bagpipes reached his ears.

53

Ellie Mallori shivered as she stared out at the alien greenish blue light bathing Alcan Harbor and the Bering Sea. For a long time, she watched the murky horizon, then turned to the approaching footsteps of a lone figure. Aside from those two people, and the debris littering the small harbor, they were very much alone.

"Welcome to summer in the Aleutians, Ms. Mallori. I've waited a long time to meet you." The short man's smile was as dazzling and cold as the northern light.

"I suppose I should thank you for bringing me here. At least I know my life hasn't been a crazy fantasy for the past six months." Ellie rubbed her bare hands together and took in the intense blueness of Admiral Brandon Langor's eyes as she surveyed his magnetic face. Jake was right. Langor's presence couldn't be ignored.

"You want to tell me why, Admiral? Shemya Island isn't exactly where I expected to meet you."

Langor laughed. "Good, you're tough. Lord knows you'll have to be if you want to survive Niven."

Suddenly her eyes came alive. "I was told you had

information about Jake. At least my escort told me that, to get me on that airplane to come over here." Ellie let out an audible sigh and forced herself to stare Langor down. "Is he alive? That's all I want to know."

"Yes, Ellie, he's alive."

"Oh, thank God!" Relief flooded through her veins and she felt herself go weak. "I hate your damn ass, Admiral," she whispered through her tears. "I hate what you are and what you make Jake do. *Damn you.*"

Silently Langor gazed out to sea, the purple flush of his marble head eventually returning to a cold baby pink. Finally he turned to face her anger. "I can understand your feelings, Ellie. Jake's been through a great deal these past few weeks. You must know that he has provided a great service to his country—"

"How long does he have to serve? How much does he have to give? When does it stop for him and start for me? She could feel her voice rising in the meager summer air.

"It's up to Niven," he said flatly. "It always has been. I don't make him do anything he doesn't want to do."

"Oh, for Chrissakes, Admiral, you own him! I don't know why, but you do." Ellie looked away. "I want you to give him time . . . give us time to build our lives."

Langor grunted and turned his eyes back to face the harbor.

"He's on his way," Langor finally said. "I received word about fifteen minutes ago that the copter carrying Jake and Commander Burkhart should arrive momentarily." He turned and squared himself before her beautifully dark face. "Very seldom in life are there real heros. Niven is now a real hero for what he has accomplished. I'd never tell him to his face, but I'm telling you. If he could, the President would shake his hand for what he's done and I—"

His voice was cut down by the sharp slapping of a large helicopter approaching low on the horizon and then suddenly the Sikorsky Sea Stallion bumped down fifty feet from where they were standing.

Langor grabbed Ellie's coat sleeve as the rotar blades slowed to a stop. "I think I like you, Ellie."

She turned and saw Jake and Charley Burkhart descending the short ramp and found herself running toward them.

"God, you're alive!" she sobbed, squeezing him with her entire body. His special scent—the timbre of his voice. He was real. Their love was real and alive. "I was with you all the way," she whispered, searching his tired, unshaved face.

Slowly, Jake's fatigued smile gave way to a wide childlike grin. Carefully he moved his hands over her stomach, feeling for the special, life-giving rhythm. "Why didn't you tell me about our baby?"

She held him tightly, her body finally giving in to a massive shudder of relief. "I—I don't have any great, glib answer. I just wanted it to be right." Gently, she reached up and kissed him, running her lips over the deep rough angles of his tired face. "Now it's right."

"Let's go home, Ellie."